THE KING

THE JESTER KING FANTASY SERIES: BOOK 4

K. C. Herbel

Epic Books Press
RICHMOND, VIRGINIA

Epic Books Press
P.O. Box 358
Quinton, Virginia 23141
www.EpicBooksPress.com

Publisher's Note: This is a work of fiction. Names, characters, places, and incidents are a
product of the author's imagination. Locales and public names are sometimes used for
atmospheric purposes. Any resemblance to actual people, living or dead, or to businesses,
companies, events, institutions, or locales is completely coincidental.

Cover Artist: SelfPubBookCovers.com/Viergacht

Ordering Information:
Quantity sales. Special discounts are available on quantity purchases by corporations, as-
sociations, and others. For details, contact the "Special Sales Department" at the address
above.

Library of Congress Control Number: 2017940784

The King / K. C. Herbel. -- 1st ed.
ISBN 978-1-944314-20-0

To my dearest, Mary Anne,
whose patience I have stretched beyond human limits.

Book Four

THE KING

"Uneasy lies the head that wears a crown."

— WILLIAM SHAKESPEARE

CHAPTER TWENTY-ONE

The Dead of Night

Fire burned in the fountain of Dyven's town square. The blackened, granite fish, which once bubbled water from its mouth, rose up above the flames to gasp at the starry sky. Two Gwythian soldiers ambled across the cobblestones, accompanied by random chimes from pottery shards strewn beneath their feet. Their long shadows made haste from the flickering light and charged ahead of them up the street.

Hugh retreated into the welcoming darkness of an alley. He hugged the wall with his back and held his breath. It stretched his belly wound to stand so erect, but he held his tongue as blood seeped through the bandages.

This was the first time he'd dared to leave his hole in the wall. He had wandered the streets of Dyven since his youth, but now they were as strange to him as hell to an angel. If he had not stumbled across the fountain, he would still be lost amid the gloomy labyrinth of gutted buildings, broken walls, and rubble-clogged streets.

He scolded himself for leaving without Aeth as the Gwythies strolled into the alley. The first soldier stopped and halted his companion. He stared directly at Hugh, whose entire body clenched.

The second soldier looked about. "What?"

The first soldier handed his spear to the second and shuffled into the shadows, fiddling with his drawers.

"Oh, not again!" the spear-carrier groaned.

"What?"

"Didn't ya go back a'the tavern?"

"Well, the decurion forced me to drink all them ales."

"Oh yeahr. I caught a wink at his knife in yer back."

The man relieving himself in the shadows guffawed. "Ha-ha!"

"Wha's ole Rusty Bottom so worried 'bout anyways?"

"The execrution—execution detail."

"What, that?"

"It's less than a day off."

"So why don't Hereweald just kill the kelpie-woman and let's be done about it?"

"There are procedures, my friend. Pro-ced-ures."

"Twaddle." The second soldier rested one spear in the crook of his arm and put both hands around the other to demonstrate his proposal. "The prince walks in, grabs her scrawny neck, and wrings it like a goose. End o'procedures."

"Ya can't do no noble lady like that!"

"Why not?"

"Lady Cyndyn must be made an example of. 'Sides, I don't think Hereweald is done wif her yet." The man laughed and punctuated his words by thrusting his hips back and forth, in crude mockery of lovemaking.

"Example of? You think after what we done to 'em, these wretches are gonna care 'bout her?"

"Look, you an' me will spit on the trollop's grave when this is done, but to them people she was their—"

The first soldier looked down at the knife protruding from his chest. His drunken eyes had not seen the quick hand that had taken it from his belt, nor the man in the shadows who wielded it. He stared at it and said, "Knife."

His companion turned to him. "She was their knife? What does that mean?"

Hugh's voice replied from the darkness. "It means I put the knife in the right spot."

At that moment, his dark form leapt from the shadows. Though the second Gwythian had two spears at his disposal, neither was of any service. In his surprise, he dropped one and tripped on the other. He fell back against the wall of the alley with the man from the darkness upon him.

The Gwythian hit the wall with a crack. His eyes popped open as the blade went in, but his attacker corked his scream behind a firm hand. He struggled in vain to pry at his assailant's steel grip. With each hanging moment, the soldier's blood spilled out on the cobblestones.

The man from the shadows released his prey and fell to one knee, holding his middle. The soldier slid to the ground, just inches from his face. He stared up at his killer and whispered, "Who are you?"

Hugh looked him in the eye. "Someone who loves Lady Cyndyn."

Hugh stood as the Gwythian sighed his last breath. He then staggered around the corner, entered the market square, and scanned the buildings to get his bearings. It was difficult. The houses and shops here were in unrecognizable ruin. They had received special attention from the vengeful Gwythies. However, the Turret of the Guard, which had loomed over the skyline of this neighborhood for years, still stood. Upon sighting the tower, Hugh started across the square.

He reached the far side before he realized his hand was shaking. The firelight that followed him up the street revealed a red stain running from blade to wrist. He stared at the unfamiliar fist at the end of his arm and recalled the two men he had delivered to Death in the alley. *Am I a murderer, then? Do I serve Death?*

The rumble of cartwheels on cobblestone echoed from the street Hugh had chosen. He crept back to the square and waited in the ruins of the corner shop. When the carts grew nearer, Hugh heard the crunch of boots and the tinkle of chains dragging across stone.

"Psst."

Hugh spun and tackled the small man who had snuck up in the darkness behind him. He clamped his hand over the man's mouth and raised his newly acquired knife. The man clutched Hugh's wrist, and they tumbled. As they rolled to the moonlit floor, a very singular eye stared up at him. The eye shifted between Hugh and the trembling blade, just inches away.

"Aeth?" Hugh withdrew his weapon. "What are you doing here?"

The boy pushed Hugh's hand aside. "Keepin' an eye on you. And it weren't easy. You took the crookedest ..."

Hugh covered Aeth's mouth again. "Shh!"

He got off Aeth's chest and returned to his dark corner. He peered around the opening where a door once stood, being careful to remain in the shadows. His companion kissed his locket, picked up his walking stick, and took up a position on the opposite side.

The sound of the wagons grew louder, and so Hugh risked a whisper, "Did I hurt you?"

"No harm done."

"Are you well enough to travel, then?"

"Guess so. Why?"

"I may have need of your services tonight."

A moment later, Gwythian soldiers prodded a group of ragged men into the square. The men had chains around their bare ankles, and their guards forced them to pull a pair of heavy carts, piled high with corpses. The smothering reek of death descended on the square. Both Hugh and Aeth turned away, struggling to keep the meager contents of their stomachs.

The wheels of the front cart lodged on some debris, and it came to a sudden stop. The prisoners groaned, and many of them collapsed where they were. The second cart, still half in the alley, was forced to stop. The prisoners pulling this cart did as those in front.

"Look alive there!"

"Get up!"

"Come on, you dogs!"

Hugh pulled the neck of his tunic over his nose and looked back to the square. Just a few feet away, the guards yelled at their prisoners, kicking them and jabbing them with the butts of their spears. Some of the poor wretches got to their feet and tugged at the carts, but without all the men, it was pointless.

"You! Brute!" the decurion in charge yelled. "Get on your feet and push the front cart."

The prisoner he addressed didn't budge.

The decurion kicked the man. "Get up! I say, get up!"

Still the man didn't move.

The decurion tore off his helmet and bashed the prisoner on his head.

The man rose and kept rising. Once on his feet, Hugh could see that he was as large as two men and a good two feet taller than the decurion. The giant frowned at the little man before him, and then crossed his arms. At that moment, Hugh recognized him as Camion, the only other survivor of the *Gyldan Mene*.

Three guards came to back up their leader. They glared at the giant, and then—one by one—drew their swords.

"Please, just a moment, sirs." Another prisoner stepped in-between the antagonists. "Surely, we could all stand a wee break from this morbid drudgery."

Hugh could not see this man through the crowd, but found his voice familiar. *And that accent. ... He's from Caithness Shire.*

The man continued in his highlander brogue, "I'm sure my large friend here would be pleased to push your cart again, once he's had the opportunity to catch his breath. I'll even juggle for ye while ye wait."

Hugh heard the pitter-patter of juggling and watched in awe as the Gwythies backed away and sheathed their swords. The smooth talking entertainer was none other than Malcolm the Magnificent. Hugh smiled to see his friend still alive. The decurion, on the other hand, frowned. When he realized he was standing alone against the dour giant, he snorted.

"Fine. Your friends shall have a rest, for as long as you can juggle these."

The decurion opened up a large leather pouch and presented three nasty-looking caltrops. Cruel, sharpened spikes, designed to cripple a horse, jutted from the iron balls.

Malcolm made his juggling balls disappear and eyed his tormentor's treacherous toys. He then picked up the caltrops and felt their weight.

"Well? What ya waiting for?"

"Why, for my audience to sit down, of course. They aren't a rest yet."

"Si'down, si'down," the little tyrant ordered.

The prisoners sat, as did several guards. Camion ambled to the building next to the second cart.

The decurion called after him. "You! Brute! Where ya think you're goin'?"

Camion turned and sat upon the steps with his back to the corner. "To sit comfortable. Malcolm juggles long time."

"We'll see 'bout that!"

"One, two, three." Malcolm began to juggle the caltrops. He moved carefully at first, his already sweaty brow wrinkled in concentration. One wrong move could wreck his hands. More than once, he made a misstep and then recovered with only a minor scratch. His audience applauded.

Hugh leaned forward and whispered into Camion's ear. "Don't speak and don't turn around."

The giant flinched and turned his head, but covered by scratching his chin. He stared into the shadows behind his shoulder, attempting to see who was talking.

"It's Hugh. Sir Hugh. Give me your hand."

Camion shifted his weight into the doorway and turned his face back to Malcolm. He then put his hand behind his back and slipped it inside.

"Squeeze my finger once for yes and twice for no. Do you understand?"

The giant squeezed Hugh's finger.

"Not so tight!"

Camion gave a lighter squeeze.

"Do you know where they're keeping Lady Cyndyn?"

One squeeze.

"Is she still in Cyndyn Hall?"

One squeeze.

"Are you taking those bodies anywhere near Cyndyn Hall?"

Two squeezes.

"Are you taking them out of the city?"

Two squeezes.

"Are they to be burned?"

Two squeezes.

"Buried then?"

One squeeze.

"Where could they bury ... are you taking them to the abbey?"

One squeeze.

"The old orchard graveyard?"

One squeeze.

"That's perfect. Look, I need your help to rescue Lady Cyndyn. Will you help me?"

At that moment, Malcolm yelped as one of the caltrops cut him. The decurion cackled, and Camion leaned forward. Despite the damage to his hand, Malcolm soldiered on and kept the caltrops flying.

Hugh repeated the question. "Will you help me?"

Camion still hesitated.

Malcolm slipped up again, and his sadistic juggling balls wounded him. He was tired already, and each wound made it even harder to concentrate. However, he was determined to keep the caltrops up. The guards cheered him while the decurion crowed.

Camion leaned back and gave Hugh's finger a single, firm squeeze.

"Good. Here's what you need to do ..."

*

Camion stood and bellowed, "Enough!"

The Gwythian soldiers and those they had pressed into service jumped with a start. Two of the caltrops Malcolm had been juggling clanked on the cobblestones while the last landed with a thud on the decurion's foot.

The decurion yelped and pulled the spike out. He got up and hobbled over to Malcolm.

"You fool!" The decurion wagged his caltrop at the highlander. "Look what ya done to me foot!"

The men snickered, and the decurion threw the caltrop at Malcolm's feet. The highlander skipped away, and the weapon skittered harmlessly across the stones. The decurion reddened.

"Shudup! Shudup! It's not funny!"

The louder the decurion shouted, the more humorous the situation became to his prisoners, and his men. Their stifled giggles grew harder to contain until the decurion, consumed by anger, stomped his punctured foot on the ground with all his might. The decurion's face took on the appearance of rotting apples, and the men's laughter exploded.

Prisoners and guards gathered around the decurion to gape, laugh, or offer help to their commander. Two guards knelt before the decurion and tended to his foot while several prisoners tore strips from their ragged clothes to bandage the hands of Malcolm, their newfound hero. Both groups chewed the fat amongst themselves, each appearing unaware of the other.

The decurion kicked the soldier bandaging his foot and stood. He then shoved his men back with a growl.

"Where's the oaf what started this mess? Where's that blasted giant?"

The prisoners glanced about, and their guards fanned out to herd them together. There was no sign of Camion.

"Where's the giant?" The decurion frothed at the lips.

The brutal guards jabbed the prisoners and threatened them with further violence if they refused to tell where the giant had gone. The prisoners were frightened and confused.

At that moment, Camion strolled out of the alley from behind the rear cart. He straightened his belt and coughed.

The Gwythies jumped again and turned to face him. They circled around him, shouting and shaking their spears.

"What ya doin' back there?" One of them smacked the giant across the back with his spear.

"I had to go." Camion indicated his privates.

Another guard thumped him on the arm. "No one goes lest he's got permission, see?"

"I see. I see."

"Quiet! Quiet!" The decurion remained red faced.

As the men hushed, the clatter of horse hooves echoed from the alley. The footfalls were plodding and irregular as if the animal were tired or strained.

"It's him! Get to ya posts," the decurion hissed.

The guards beat their charges into position around the carts and prepared to start off again. At that moment, a man on a black cob squeezed by the rear cart and entered the square.

"What's all this about, Decurion?"

The decurion sat upon a pile of rubble fumbling with his boot, which was too small to fit over his bandaged foot. He scowled at the corpulent rider and returned to his footwear.

The horseman stopped his overburdened mount at the decurion's feet. He adjusted his unkempt cloak and leaned over to look down upon him.

"I said, what's all this about, Decurion?"

Without looking up, he answered, "Injured me foot, Derian. What does it look like? 'Sides, prisoners needed a break."

Derian sat back in his saddle and stared with contempt at the prisoners. Until the Gwythians put him in charge of pressgangs, he had been the town's thief-catcher, and these men, the common citizenry of Dyven, had been his masters. Such was the lot of a shiftless but wily burglar literally caught by his budding belly in the abbot's window. His slothful nature, love of wine, and weakness for stolen pastries had both launched and wrecked his chosen career, but he had blamed "heartless Dyven" for all his misfortunes.

"These wretched dogs?" Derian clenched his fist. "They've not but rested their whole lives! If the salt of their sweat is not to their likin' then let 'em taste the whip!"

With that, Derian grabbed the bullwhip looped over his saddle. He allowed the business end to uncoil and flop to the street.

One of the Gwythian guards stepped forward. "Tha's not necessary, gov'na. We got 'em reined in."

"Not necessary?" Derian growled through his teeth.

"Silence," the decurion yelled at his man, but it was too late—Derian was incensed.

The bloated bully flung back his arm to crack his whip. In so doing, he unintentionally smacked his horse on the nose and rear in rapid succession. The poor confused animal flinched and bucked. The kicking, spinning beast knocked two of the guards to the ground before they could scatter. Derian tried to regain control of his mount by yanking on the reins. The horse reared up and Derian tumbled to the ground with a grunt.

The horse spun, kicked him, and again hoisted its weight high in the air. When it returned to earth, the beast plunked its hooves down upon its fallen master and leapt away. A few heartbeats later, the animal stopped its wild gyrations, and the square became still.

The cob twitched and flicked away the last of its flare-up with a lash of its tail. Then, grunting and pawing at the cobblestones, the animal skewed its head to stare at the man lying on the ground. Derian's duteous mount ambled forward and sniffed at him like a dog. It nudged him with its nose and snorted.

One of the Gwythies made a grab for the horse's reins. It lurched away and bolted across the square into the dark of an abandoned street. As the clatter of its hooves faded, the men in the square edged forward in a circle around Derian.

One of the soldiers knelt and put his ear near Derian's mouth. No one dared to speak, nor did they budge.

"He still breathes."

Suddenly, the solemn wake birthed a clamor that rivaled the days when this dim ruin of a square was a lively market. Every man spoke and gesticulated at once, growing louder and more frenetic as they attempted to relate their astonishment and the greater measure of it to the others.

The decurion beat the cobblestones with his boot. "Silence!"

The hubbub fizzled to an uneasy murmur. The men drew nearer.

The soldier, still kneeling beside Derian, lifted his palm from the cobbles and saw that it was red with blood. He rolled the thief-catcher onto his side and discovered one of the decurion's caltrops buried in the man's back. The soldier crossed himself and muttered a prayer.

The decurion turned him by the shoulder. "What are ya doin' that for, man? This devil would steal yer soul, then lie an' say 'twas his own."

"Aye, but he's not long for this world."

"Say a prayer for a dying thief?"

"Aye."

"So, he is dyin', then?"

"Your caltrop made sure of that."

"Gimme that! Tha's the last thing I need, is for the prince to think I done him in."

The decurion's men collected all the caltrops and handed them to their leader. He began to clean them and asked, "How long 'as he got?"

The kneeling soldier shook his head. "The Angel o' Death is close on his heels and will shortly be here to collect 'im."

"Are ya sure?

"Certain."

Without a further thought, the decurion spit on the dying man. Some of his troops looked at him in shock. He leaned over Derian. "Thought you could 'ave me, didn't ya? Ya miserable bastard! Tried to get behind me back to the prince, didn't ya? Now ya see what ya gets in hell, traitor! Sneak!"

Derian squirmed at the pronouncement of his damnation and muttered. His face wrinkled sourly, and then—through clenched teeth—he growled, "Damn you."

"What's this?" The decurion jumped back. "You said he was dead!"

"I said he was dyin'."

"And now he's cursin' me from his bloody grave!"

"I don't think he were speakin' to you, Decurion."

"You think I want a dead man's curse hangin' o'er me head? When I'm on campaign?"

"He weren't talkin' to you."

"What's that?"

"Look, sir. He's still not conscious."

The decurion leaned over once more to examine the subject of his fear and loathing. He eyed him most judiciously, trying to decipher his troubled movements and vague expressions.

"If he weren't speakin' to me," the decurion said at last, "then who?"

"Angel o' Death, maybe." The soldier shrugged. Then he whispered, "He's so close now. Maybe I'll say a prayer for me own sake."

At that moment, the rear cart of bodies squeaked and joggled. Something stirred in the alley behind. All eyes shifted towards the rear as a shrouded figure shuffled out from the shadows.

"Saints preserve us!", "God, forgi'me!", and profuse oaths, prayers, and hasty promises were offered up to Heaven, by means of shouts and quaking mutters.

The figure advanced again, and the men struggled for their breath as if each shambling step of the apparition tore wind from their breasts. The creature drew near and stopped. It then adjusted itself on its crutch and stared about with its singular cold eye at the pale and frozen men gathered around the body of Derian.

"Evenin', gents." Aeth's amiable voice burst from the stillness like a thunderclap.

The men flinched, as each one, taut and trembling, prepared to bolt away.

Camion stepped forward. "What you want, boy?"

"Couldn't help but overhear your predicament," Aeth said.

The decurion snapped out of his shock. "Boy?"

Camion looked back at the decurion and gestured with his thumb to Aeth. "Boy."

Malcolm scratched his head. "Boy?"

"Yeah, boy!"

"Boy?" the chorus of soldiers and prisoners exclaimed.

"Yeah!" Aeth held out his arms. "I'm a boy. What's the matter with you fellas?"

The decurion laughed. "A boy!"

All the other men in the square joined him. They slapped their knees and each other on the back, regardless of whether the recipient was from Gwythia or Lyonesse.

"Ya sure had us goin', boy," the decurion said between guffaws. "For a dash there, we took ya for a spirit!"

"A spirit?"

"Aye, … we thought ya was the bloody Angel o' Death hisself!"

With this, the laughter multiplied until many a man held his side or wiped away tears. When their great amusement died to stifled sniggers, Aeth spoke again, "Decurion, let me take this man off yer hands. I'll take care of him, and see that he gets to a doctor."

"He don't need a doctor, boy. He needs an undertaker."

"Then when his breath is gone, I shall get him to the churchyard."

The decurion scratched his chin. Now very wily and leaving behind any hint of mirth, he asked, "An' why should ya do this thing? Did ya know him?"

"Once, sir. An' I owe the man."

"An' why should I trust you?"

"I seen what happened, sir. I know'd ya were blameless in this bloke's death. An' if anyone should ask …"

"If anyone should ask, *what?*"

"I should tell them, sir."

"Tell them what?"

"Why, that you was blameless, sir."

"Ya talk real pleasant like for a little gutter snipe, but why shouldn't I just toss him on board one of my wagons here and be gone?"

"Why, he's not dead, sir. It wouldn't be decent … sir."

"Decent? You think that fraud of a thief deserves decent?"

"Please, sir. Please."

"Oh, quit yer whinin'. Yer worse than a sick pup! I'll leave him in yer hands, but if I come by here on the morrow and find his miserable corpse stinkin' up the square, it'll be you they'll be buryin' next! Have ya got me, boy?"

"Yes, Decurion. Thank you."

The decurion turned and made an apathetic gesture to his men, who herded their prisoners into position around the wagons.

"Let's go, men. The sooner we're to the churchyard, the sooner we can to bed."

The prisoners grunted in unison, and the wheels of the wagons began to roll over the debris-strewn cobblestones. Aeth followed them with his eye—the only one aware of the pair of eyes staring back at him amid the heaped up corpses. In a minute, the grim caravan had turned the corner and disappeared from sight.

Aeth kissed his locket and squatted next to Derian.

"Just you an' me, old man. Alone at last."

He grabbed Derian's face by the cheeks and turned his head to face him. Then he patted his face.

"Wake up. You an' me got business."

When this failed to revive the old thief catcher, Aeth shook him and repeated his demand. He shook the man with increasing violence, raising his voice with each request.

Then he spun around and sat upon Derian's chest. He struck his captive with a quick slap.

"Wake up, ya cheat! Ya crooked old turncoat!"

Aeth grabbed Derian's tunic and shook him again. "Ya think ya can do to me what ya done, then sleep through the better part of pain and dyin'? Ya robbed me, you thief. Ya robbed me, and ya shan't rob me o' this! Wake up! I'll have ya 'member who I am an' who it is that sits by yer death bed and shoves ya into yer grave. Now, wake up!"

Aeth smacked Derian with the back of his hand. Derian gasped, then coughed. His eyes fluttered open, and he stared at the boy riding his chest.

"Hurt?" Aeth asked.

Derian grimaced and nodded.

"Good. Yer dyin', you ole goat. You shrew!"

Derian coughed. "Then ... you'll be wantin' ... me confession."

"Not I, old devil. Not I. I'd see yer crimes drag ya down to the deps o' Hell."

Derian squinted to see the lad more clearly. "Yer no priest."

"Hardly. My station here is more executioner."

"And judge, it would seem."

"I have much to judge ya by, old thief. Though that nag o' yers done half me job."

"Who are ya?"

Aeth held up his crooked, mangled hands. "When last we met, ya give me these."

Derian stared at the twisted, bandaged fingers, then back to Aeth's face. "I don' recall any one-eyed boy."

"I had two good eyes then, to match me quick hands an' quicker feet."

"I don' wanna play this game."

"It's no game, villain."

"I don' know ya."

"I think ya do. They used to call me Stitch, 'fore ya brung me to the tower and did yer worst upon me!"

At these words, Aeth caught a glimmer of recognition in the dying man's eyes.

"I don' know ya," he said more strenuously. "Na let me go!" He raised a hand to move the boy aside, but Aeth pushed it away with his crutch.

"Na who's playin' a game? Liar. Traitor."

"What want ye of me?"

Aeth leaned close. "I wants ya to feel the pain and fear of dyin'. I wants ya to know that ya not see another sunrise and that there be one right beside ya what could bring ya comfort or healin', but will no. I wan' ya to feel what I felt when ya ha' me in yer dungeon, ya devil!"

Aeth shook Derian with all his might. Derian coughed, and a bit of blood appeared on his lips. His eyes drifted, and Aeth shook him again.

"Don' you dare fall asleep on me!"

Aeth let Derian drop to the paving stones. A trinket, strung on a thin chain around Derian's neck, slipped out of his tunic and came to rest in the valley of his throat.

"Do ya feel the fear, old man? Do ya ..."

Aeth's eyes glanced a second time upon the item around Derian's neck, and he froze. He reached down and picked the item up to get a better look at it. Derian grasped at his hands to protect the trinket, but he was too weak to stop even the hands he had crippled.

"Thief. You gutter snipes even steal from a dyin' man."

Aeth ignored him and pulled the object closer. He opened his hand to examine it. It was a small, well-worn copper locket in the shape of a heart, with faint lacey engraving on its surface. He turned it over to reveal the image of a woman's face. The face he knew, though his memory of it was nearly as faded as the tiny portrait.

Aeth tore the locket and chain from Derian's neck. Then he picked him up by his vestments again and shook him with rage.

"Where did you get this?"

Derian looked at Aeth for a moment. "It's mine."

"It is not yers!" Aeth punctuated this with a slap.

"It's mine, I tell ya. I got it from me sweetheart."

Aeth was about to poke the devil in the eye for lying, but stopped as a terrible thought formed in his mind.

"Who is she?"

"Is this a part o' yer game, boy?"

"Who is she, this sweetheart of yers? Some cheap trollop? One of yer wharf floozies'?"

"What matters it to you?"

"Who is she? Damn you!"

"She was my wife." Derian seemed to focus far off. "Not by a priest, mind ya, but ... we were as two married."

"An' where did she get it?"

"Well, it were me that give it her, an' when we parted, she give me this half."

Aeth's stomach went hard. His hands shook. He swallowed hard—the muscles of his face flexing to brace it like a crumbling bridge.

"What was her name?"

Derian's expression was distant. His eyes wandered as if gazing at the stars.

"What? Have ya forgotten it, villain?"

"Nay, never. ... Myra." He spoke as if addressing a person before him, and then he whispered it again, "Myra."

Aeth closed his eye and reached inside his own ragged clothing to pull out his mother's locket. He placed the two pieces side by side in his palm and opened his eye. The pieces were a perfect match. He nudged them together and found that they yet fit. He turned the unified locket over and stared at the two portraits within the two halves. The woman's portrait, he had never seen before this day, and still he recognized it as his mother. The image of the man in his mother's half was suddenly unfamiliar, though he had possessed it for many years. It took on a new appearance when he recognized the features of a younger Derian staring back at him.

His eyes moved to the face of the dying man beneath him. He considered every unforgiving line and cheery wrinkle—his hopes divided into two warring camps.

At last, Derian spoke, "Will ya give it back to me, Stitch? At least, until I'm dead."

"My name's not Stitch. It's Aeth."

With that, Aeth turned his hand around and showed Derian the two pieces of locket now joined into one. Derian stared at it and frowned.

"Your name is Aeth?"

Aeth nodded. "An' yer name is Douls."

"Never liked tha' name."

"Douls or Aeth?"

"Neither. Myra ..." Derian paused to reevaluate the boy. "Your mother insisted on Aeth."

"F-father?" The word stumbled across Aeth's lips. He looked up into the night sky as tears tumbled down his cheeks. "Oh God, my father?"

"Aeth—my Aeth."

Aeth glared at Derian. "Oh, how I hated you!"

"I know."

"Still hate you!"

The old thief dropped his gaze in shame. "I know."

"Father, I ..."

"Bit of a disappointment, aint I? Tha's why I never went back."

"We gotta get ya to a healer!"

"It's too late for that."

"No! Adwythane can fix this!" Aeth scrambled to his feet. "I just need to get ya to Cromllech Dunom."

"Nay. I'd be dead before we made the West Road."

"That's no matter. Adwythane can bring ya back ... "

"No!" Derian said with surprising volume. He began again, when the echo of his voice had died. "I am tired of this world, son. It's given me naught but pain. I know I deserve nothin' from ya, but do me one kindness."

"What?"

"Bury me bones next to yer mother."

"Mother?"

"When I was with her. ... That's the only time I remember being truly happy."

Aeth turned and scanned the square. "Ya can't die now. Not when I just found ya."

"I am a miserable, mean man, and a cruel drunk most of me wakin' hours. Count yourself lucky, ya knew me as little as ya did. Aeth. Aeth! Come here, son. Heed me last words."

Aeth knelt next to Derian and pressed the locket into his palm. "I'm here."

Derian stared into Aeth's face and tried to smile, though the tears welled in his eyes. "I'm sorry. There's naught I can do to make up to ya for what I done; too much wickedness for three lifetimes. But lookie here, after I came into it, a seer told me this locket would bring good fortune for my son. I tried me own hand but squandered the loot. It's yours now."

Derian pressed the locket back into Aeth's hands. Then he raised a shaky finger to his lips. "Shh. All these years, it were the secret I kept even from myself. Right under God's feet. Couldn't find me way back with half a heart. But now you know. Your heart is complete."

Derian grinned. Aeth looked at the locket in his hand.

"Father ..."

"It's your turn, son."

"Father ..."

"Your turn ... follow the heart. ... Follow ... God's feet ... "

The spark of life left Derian's eyes, and his head rolled to the side. Aeth grabbed his shirtfront and shook him.

"Father!" He repeated the word, again and again, clubbing at the man's chest and sinking further into an embrace of his father's bosom until he could hardly breathe and his broken words bubbled out in sobs.

A nudge from behind brought Aeth back to his senses. He turned and found Derian's cob waiting to take its master on one last ride.

CHAPTER TWENTY-TWO

Shadow of the Deep

Billy drifted off for a short time. When he awoke, he found the crew in the rigging and a favorable wind behind them. The sky still hid behind a cloak of grey clouds.

Sylvys snored disagreeably a few feet away, no doubt the demise of Billy's sleep. Shaldra rested atop the stern castle. The forest elf sat with his bow in his lap, one eye trained ahead and the other on Drif. As for the mysterious female warrior, she sat among her dark armaments, polishing as if nothing had happened. Billy decided that all was passably well with the world, nudged Sylvys onto his quieter side, and nestled into his own corner of the deck to sleep.

"Billy! Billy! Your Majesty!" Shaldra shook him.

Billy glanced up as the excited elf leapt past him toward the ship's bow. They were still far from Lyonesse, so Billy doubted he could have sighted land already.

"What is it?" Billy stretched. "A ship?"

"No, look!"

Billy stood and followed Shaldra's finger to starboard. Aside from the evening sun bouncing golden light off the million mirrors of the ocean's surface, he could see nothing.

Sylvys and Drif appeared next to Billy and stood on either side of him. They stared out at the water, and then Drif put on her helmet. She measured the dim sky watchfully before buckling the strap and drawing her sword.

Billy rushed forward. "What's goin' on?"

Shaldra continued to scan the sea. "I don't know, Your Majesty, but I've got a bad feelin' about this."

Once again, Billy strained to see through the autumn glare of the sun. Something unexpected caught his eye in the distance, moving towards them. It looked like a pale green wave that stretched across the horizon. Billy glanced back as Sylvys grabbed his spear and helmet. Billy was shocked to see the same pale line on the opposite horizon, also rushing towards them.

"It's surrounding us!"

Shaldra looked back and gasped. The next thing Billy heard was Shaldra's sword clearing its sheath.

"Find cover, Your Majesty."

Billy assessed the ramshackle ship. "Where?"

Shaldra scanned about. "I see what you mean."

"Up there." Drif pointed to the captain.

Billy ran up the stairs of the stern castle. From the high ground, he had a better view of the pallid loop of water as it closed in on them, drawing tighter like a noose.

Beyond the shrinking loop, all the way to the horizon, the sea grew paler while the water near the ship turned gloomy as if all shadow had left the ocean depths to gather beneath them. Darker and darker it became, as the pale waters rushed in.

Billy and the others braced for impact. The pallid waters surged towards the ship. The rushing waves then dwindled to lap harmlessly against her sides.

Billy watched as Sylvys peeked with one eye from under his tarnished helmet. The satyr then straightened to his usual relaxed stance and walked

THE KING | 23

to the side. The thud of his hooves on the wooden deck hovered on the air.

It was quiet. Even the ocean's relentless roar was tamed. The waves were but ripples, the wind a mere breath.

Billy caught the shifting eyes of Shaldra and Drif. The elves stood with their swords drawn, ready to strike. It was so still, Billy could hear their breathing.

He stepped forward and stared over the railing at the charred and splintered deck below. From this angle, he could see all the way through the broken hull to the water beneath the ship. It was black as ink, like peering into a bottomless pit.

A dense black geyser jetted up through the hull and raced for the sky. On contact with the atmosphere, the tarry fountain coagulated, and the viscous stygian oil became the leathery skin of a giant tentacle. The air thickened with the reek of death.

The extremity flopped down and wrapped itself around the ship just as another was ejected from the pit. Before the second could entwine itself in the rigging, Shaldra leapt to the deck next to Drif and attacked.

The two elves hacked at the monstrous blubbery tentacles with their swords. Each time they struck, jets of wine-like blood sprayed forth from the beast, accompanied by a piercing screech and an increase in stench.

In response, scores of whip-like tentacles streamed onto the deck along with the next great limb. These smaller offshoots wriggled and writhed, snaking over everything, blindly searching and grasping while the third massive appendage curled itself into a fist.

Shaldra brought down his sword with all his might, severing the largest limb that gripped the hull, and leaving his sword stuck in the planks. While he tried to free his weapon, the whip-like tentacles snapped around his ankle. He glanced down just as the large, rolled up tentacle swept over his position. The blow caught the elf and knocked him across the deck into the far railing.

Shaldra squinted and rubbed his neck. A moment later, the small tentacles were grasping at his boots. He pulled in his feet, then ducked and rolled away as the hammer-like tentacle demolished the railing behind him.

Once on his feet, Shaldra looked up and saw Deordrif floating above the deck as she had during the lightning storm. Beneath her, countless squirming feeler-tentacles flailed about, searching in vain while she rained down blow after blow on the heftier tentacles.

"I must learn how to do that."

Billy grabbed Shaldra's bow and quiver and ran to the side of the stern castle where the elf had landed. "Here!" He handed down the bow.

The lesser tentacles surged towards Shaldra and a dark, corpulent mass boiled out of the hole and onto the deck. The ship let out an agonized groan and listed under its weight. Shaldra grabbed the end of the bow and Billy hauled him up to the stern as the main deck was overrun.

Shaldra climbed up onto the higher deck. "Many thanks, Highness."

They both glanced over the edge at the squirming tentacles and bubbling mass below. The central core of the creature was now on deck … growing, peeling off, and spitting out more appendages. It left three more colossal branches coiling back into the darkness below.

Above, the clouds opened and the heavens wept at the sight of the abomination, releasing a heavy drizzle.

The ship twisted and shuddered. Billy realized that spell or no spell, the vessel couldn't take much more. The monster was just too powerful.

"Captain, we need the help of your crew!"

The crew continued to sail the *Gyldan Mene*, oblivious to the behemoth ravaging her. Shaldra shot two arrows into the beast, which it tore out. It screeched and blindly flung its appendages about, shattering boards and tangling itself in the rigging and wreckage. Billy turned to face the captain.

"Captain, you must help us or the ship will go down!"

Billy paused, staring at the blank eye socket of the captain. He couldn't tell if it focused on him or on the sea. *You want the ship to go down, don't you?*

"Very well. Order the crew to fight this monster now, and I will release you when we reach Lyonesse."

Shaldra glanced back from the steady stream of arrows he was showering on the monster. "But how will we get back home?"

Billy continued to stare at the captain and answered, "If we don't get to Lyonesse, there won't be a reason to get back!"

"Look out!"

At that moment, one of the giant tentacles scraped over Billy's head and narrowly passed by the captain.

"Captain!"

The captain's skull tilted on his scrawny neck and bowed. Billy imagined the old sea dog giving him a wry smile and a wink.

The captain drew his rusty sword and held it aloft. This signaled the skeletal crew to drop from the rigging with a heavy net. They hemmed in the main bulk of the beast, lashing it to the deck with pins and cleats, and then stabbed it feverishly with their knives.

The creature shook and screamed in outrage. It thrust up against its restraints—tearing ropes, breaking pins and bending cleats, but still the net held. The monster bellowed and a mass of flat, hooked tentacles shot through the net to wrap around the sailors and draw them in like kelp. Though it snapped and pulled their bones apart, the crew continued to stab and slash at the black monstrosity.

Just then, a fist-shaped protrusion thrust up and tore through the middle of the net. A great, blood-red eye appeared near the new summit of the beast. It focused on Drif and two of the largest tentacles encircled her legs. She cleaved off one of them, but as she raised her sword to smite the other, a third enveloped her arm and bent it back behind her. Drif yelped. Her weapon dropped to the deck like a dart.

Shaldra shot an arrow into the tentacle around Drif's arm. It jerked in response, causing her to grunt and drop the dagger she had been drawing with her free hand. The two limbs around her then lifted and spread apart. Drif cried out as the tremendous strength of the behemoth stretched her body. Shaldra shot another arrow into the monster's extremity.

Billy appeared next to him and pointed. "No! Shoot the eye! The eye!"

Shaldra fixed his eyes on the new target and shot true; straight through the scarlet orb.

The creature shrieked and released Drif's arm. The massive limb then swooped down on the stern castle. Shaldra pushed Billy back but was himself seized along with hunks of splintered decking from beneath his feet.

Billy watched in horror as the monster hauled Shaldra and Drif high above the deck and rolled its many tentacles around them. The elves gasped and cried out under the crushing pain.

"No! Stop it!"

Billy scanned the broken stern deck for something to attack the beast with—something to kill it. Lura Zahn rattled at Billy's side. He started for its hilt but changed his mind when he saw Shaldra's weapons lying in the debris.

Billy pushed aside the splintered wood and snatched up the bow and quiver. In so doing, the last arrow in the quiver slid out and fell towards the hole in the deck. Billy dove for the edge and caught the arrow's sharp point in his palm. Though it stung, he held tight.

He stood with the arrow nocked and drew back the bow. His heart pounded at the walls of his chest.

"Show me your heart, if you've got one!"

Billy felt burning in his ring finger and saw a flash of light at the arrow's tip. He breathed in, as Onian had taught him, and held it as he released the arrow.

The arrow sang off the string and pierced deep into the core of the horror, completely disappearing. A small plume of ichor spurted from the entrance wound before it resealed. The entire creature seemed to freeze, then it jerked and flopped and sputtered as if suffering a coughing fit.

A moment later, the large, sanguine eye reopened and slid down the black, gnarled surface to stare at Billy. Shaldra's arrow still protruded from its center. The eye elongated and divided into two smaller eyes, leaving the arrow to fall away. The eyes continued to shrink until they were human sized. Then they fell into place on a smooth black face—the face of a young woman. A well-formed human head and torso emerged as the tarry mass melted away. Billy's arrow jutted from its chest, pointing directly back at him.

Something about this new form presented by the monster was familiar. Though smothered in black ooze, Billy recognized the features as those of Lady Maeven's younger sister—a shy girl he'd met amid the intrigue at Castle Orgulous.

"Caenne?"

The red eyes smiled. "You think I am the daughter of Feolaghe?" the thing rasped. "You are as weak as he who sent me. I will destroy—"

"Who are you?"

The creature clutched at the arrow in its chest and snarled. "You think you can know me, little man? You think you can dissect one replete with wisdom, with your puny magic, your crude tools?" She pulled at the arrow, but only caused more anguish.

"Perhaps not so weak. But no mortal has ever bested me! I am a breaker of circles, a digger of northern graves ..."

The nature of the fiend became clear. Billy had read about such foul creatures in the Witan's library: the beings dubbed, "replete with wisdom." The important thing, as he remembered, was to get their "true" name.

He strengthened his resolve. "Who are you?"

"Very well," the sinister entity hissed. "You wish to know the name of your destroyer? I am master of the hidden places, lord of secrets, creator of storms, conqueror of the deep—"

"Your name!"

The monster gnashed her teeth. "I am Dheumon."

"Hi. I'm Billy."

Dheumon grabbed the arrow and jerked it from her chest.

"Dheumon!" Billy called. "Put down my friends."

The fiend looked up at the two elves, still held high in its tentacles. "Certainly." Then, in a swift movement, it bashed Shaldra and Drif together like dolls in the hands of an angry child. Both elves went limp and dropped to the deck.

Billy swallowed hard and widened his stance. "Dheumon ... go away!"

The demon stared at him. Then its lips twisted into a wicked grin. "Fool. Did you really think it would be that easy?"

Lura Zahn leapt into Billy's hand. A moment later, the demon cranked open its jaw and spat a long tentacle at him. Billy held the sword out in front of him and split the tentacle in two. Dheumon quickly retracted the massive tongue and ejected it again. The two halves rushed Billy. He made a wild swing with both hands and split the tentacles down their length once again.

The demon roared and whisked its spurting, quivering tongue high into the air. The long wounds inflicted by Lura Zahn turned bony yellow. This discoloration spread in rapid succession over the four ends, encrusting them in jagged, barnacled armor. The creature limbered its new appendages, flexing them like fingers.

The newly formed talons swooped down at Billy. He swung and missed. At once, the claw grasped his middle, knocking him back into the captain. Billy's hands and Lura Zahn became absurdly tangled in the skeleton's ribcage. The demon's tongue ripped Billy from the stern castle, leaving the sword behind.

As Billy slammed down on the main deck, he saw the mouth of the demon had grown to replace the form of Caenne. The giant, clawed tongue dragged him in towards rows of sharp, curved teeth. Billy beat and kicked at the extremity, but to little effect.

In desperation, he gripped his assailant and concentrated on his mother's ring. Putrid smoke peeled off the tongue. The demon bellowed and thrust Billy back against the wall of the stern castle. It battered him repeatedly against the boards until they broke. He collapsed, and the grotesque tongue drew his slumped body from the wreckage. He felt helpless as the monster towed him back to its waiting maw.

All of a sudden, a heavy bronze spear pinned the muscular organ to the deck. The flesh surrounding the weapon quivered and smoked.

"Not so fast."

The demon's eyes grew large with fear and anger upon seeing Sylvys. It stretched open its humungous mouth, yelling and tugging on its trapped tongue.

"You? Who is this puny boy to you?"

"My king."

At that moment, the captain of the *Gyldan Mene* appeared next to Sylvys with Lura Zahn in his bony hand. The satyr nodded to the captain and he lopped off the demon's tongue with a clean stroke. The monster bellowed and shook, rocking the entire ship with its might.

Sylvys yanked his ancient spear free and stood his ground between the demon and Billy. A voice boomed from behind him.

"Dheumon!"

Both Sylvys and the captain turned. Billy sat cross-legged on the deck, scribing a circle deep into the planks with one of Shaldra's arrows. A large black book sat open in his lap.

Sylvys shrank away when he spied Billy's downcast face. His eyes showed white while the rest of his face hid deep in hollow shadows. Billy held out his hand to reveal Eleanor's ring spinning like a top in the center of his palm. The ring shone with a pale blue light.

Billy opened his mouth, and in a booming voice said, "Dheumon. Baal. Leviathan."

The ring spun faster. It quickened until it became a glowing, whistling globe. Billy blew, and it jumped from his hand and danced across the deck between the captain and Sylvys' feet.

Dheumon pulled back from the advancing light. Without warning, the ring dropped through the hole in the deck and out of sight.

"Ho-ho-ho-ho." Dheumon oozed its putrid mass forward once again.

"Oh hell," Sylvys muttered before stepping back. "I hope you've got more than that up your sleeve, Highness. Highness?"

Sylvys glanced back and found Billy slumped over on the deck. "Highness!"

Dheumon raised its mass to rush forward, but before the demon could lay a tentacle on them, it was dragged backward. It screamed and jerked, scrambling to stay on the deck, using all its extremities to hold on.

The entire ship creaked, and Sylvys felt off balance. He looked to the side and saw that the ship was spinning. The narrow horizon, where the shrinking sun set, whipped by his view faster and faster.

A waterspout erupted through the deck between Dheumon and Sylvys. It spun violently, pulling in the demon's tentacles—sucking in its tarry flesh. Sylvys' hair, however, was only tussled by a gentle breeze.

The satyr leaned forward and stared into the gaping hole in the deck. A great maelstrom raged beneath the ship. Crushing forces of rock and water tore Dheumon to ribbons.

The demon's bulk sank back into the hole. One by one, the grinding vortex wrenched its tentacles from the ship and sucked them down.

"No-o-o!" Then, whoosh, it was gone.

The now black cyclone became ropey and danced off the deck before shooting into the sky. Below, the maelstrom subsided in a big, belching bubble, leaving the ship spinning slowly on a calm sea.

Sylvys knelt beside Billy and felt for his heart. "My king ... Billy ... Wake up!"

Billy's eyes fluttered open. Sylvys stared down at him. A dim golden light illuminated the satyr's concerned features.

"What is it?" Billy flinched. "Ouch, my head."

"Lay still, my king."

"What has happened?" He rubbed his head. Then he sat up. "Where's Shaldra? Where's Deordrif?"

The forest elf sat up from across the deck. "What? Who?" He spotted Billy and Sylvys near the remains of the stern castle. "What happened to you? Where are we? Are you hurt?"

Before they could answer, there was a clatter of armor and a brief battle cry from the stern. They all turned to see Drif crouched on one knee with her fists raised up to strike. She was breathing through her nose like an angry bull until she spotted the others reclining on the lower deck. She took a deep breath and cracked her neck with a jerk.

"Are you well?" Billy asked her.

The proud warrior continued to loosen the kinks from her body.

"Deordrif! I said, are you well?"

Deordrif glanced over. She seemed surprised that Billy directed his question at her. Her eyes shifted from side to side, and then she gave him a curt nod.

Shaldra rolled his eyes. "Oh, I'm just splendid, Your Highness. Thank you ever so much for asking."

Billy grinned and shook his head. He then grabbed Sylvys' hand, enlisting his help to stand.

"Are you sure you should, Your Highness?"

"I'm fine, Sylvys."

Sylvys steadied Billy once he was on his feet. "Where's the book?"

"What book?"

Sylvys searched the deck near Billy's feet. "I could have sworn ... I thought you cast your spell from a book."

Billy knew what Sylvys was talking about, but he felt ashamed and afraid to talk about the black tome. He held up empty hands. "I don't have a book."

The captain, who had been standing in their midst throughout the conversation, stepped forward and presented Lura Zahn to Billy. He examined the blade briefly and sheathed it.

Billy scanned the ship from bow to stern. "Where's the crew?"

"What?"

"The crew." Billy gestured to the air around him. "The godforsaken bony crew that sail this ship."

Sylvys leaned on his spear. "All gone, except for him."

Billy turned to the captain. "Can you still get us to Lyonesse?"

The captain shrugged and marched to his post at the stern.

Billy rubbed his aching head and let his hand slide down his tired face.

"My king, where is your ring?"

Sylvys smiled at Shaldra and patted Billy's shoulder. "He threw it overboard."

Billy looked down at his hand. His mother's ring was gone! Gone! The word hung hollow and alone in his mind. The word did not relate to the ring, nor could it ever. It was an unthinkable thought to him. Gone.

Billy gripped Sylvys' arm. "I did what?"

Sylvys looked Billy in the eye, then gave him an encouraging grin. "You threw it overboard."

Billy blinked and stared off into the vast ocean in shock. "Did I at least have a good reason?"

"Oh yes, Your Highness. Very good."

Billy looked at the laconic satyr. "Well?"

"You know I'm not good at stories, Your Highness."

"Go ahead."

"Well, you—you used it to destroy a powerful demon."

Billy blinked, and then blinked again. He saw the ring spinning from his hand into the sea. "Oh yes. I did, didn't I?"

"Are you well, Highness?" Shaldra asked.

Sylvys smiled. "I think His Highness cracked the royal head, didn't he?"

Billy rubbed the back of his head and nodded.

Just then, there was a thumping and pounding sound as random objects rained down on the ship. Billy and the others covered their heads as the items pelted them. Then all was quiet.

Billy and Shaldra bent down together to examine what the strange rain had brought. There were dead fish, pieces of wood, clothing, rope, bits of bone, and even human skulls amongst the debris. Shaldra picked up a large bone attached to a piece of wood and stood up.

Billy heard a soft but insistent ringing in his ears. He pushed over a seashell by his feet and revealed a small golden object spinning on the deck. He snatched it, and the ringing stopped. He didn't have to look in his fist to know what it held. Its smooth, warm touch was one he remembered well.

Billy stood and faced Shaldra. "What'd you get?" he asked playfully.

Sylvys held up a fish. "Dinner."

Shaldra raised the femur. "I got a bone with a … stick on it. What about you?"

Billy wanted to keep Shaldra in suspense for as long as he could. He loved the feeling of keeping a cheery secret. However, the sheer joy he held in his hand could not be tamed, and he exploded.

"I got my mother's ring back!" He held out his hand.

The elf and Billy gaped at the mystifying ring. Billy laughed, and then Shaldra and Sylvys joined him.

Moments later, all the bones rattled on the deck and began to pull together. The three friends stood back to back and looked on in awe. Within seconds, several skeletons stood around them.

Billy drew Lura Zahn, Sylvys gripped his spear, and Shaldra reached for his empty scabbard.

"Curses." The elf raised the femur bone above his head like a club.

One of the uncanny figures hobbled towards Shaldra, holding out its hand. The elf tensed to strike, but Billy's hand on his shoulder stopped him.

"Wait, Shaldra. I think that belongs to him."

Shaldra froze, but eyed the creature before him and the makeshift weapon in his hand. He relaxed and sheepishly handed the bone over. The apparition reinserted it into his pelvis, then turned and shambled away.

All the skeletons took to the rigging, and Sylvys turned to his companions. "Looks like we got the crew back."

"Yeah. Looks like."

Billy elbowed the elf. "What are you complaining about?"

"Nothing, my prince. Absolutely nothing! Now, where's my sword?"

Billy started aft and met Drif at the base of the stairs. They each turned to allow the other passage and waited. At last, Drif slipped by Billy. She strode across to her sword, which remained fixed in the deck where it had fallen. She shot a sideways glance at him through the corner of her eye and yanked the long black blade from the planks. Then she sheathed it with a flourish and marched to the bow with her head held high.

"Captain." Billy climbed up the rickety stairs to the stern castle. "I believe we were headed for Lyonesse."

The captain leaned into the rudder, and the *Gyldan Mene* obligingly turned to the south.

CHAPTER TWENTY-THREE

Guilt and Love

Ergyfel leaned against the balustrade of his balcony, staring over the high walls of Castle Orgulous at the hills and woods that surrounded Loch Nyraval. The setting sun surrendered the land to lengthening shadows. The world slid out of focus as he became lost to a thought: *How can I rid myself of this guilt?*

"My lord?"

Maeven's voice brought him back to his senses. Until recently, her voice had brought pleasure, but now it stung like a lash. He tried to ignore her, but she whipped him again. His body became rigid as he fought to resist her call. He closed his eyes, attempting to meditate her away.

All at once, her hand was on his arm. His defenses came crashing down, and her implacable voice entered his mind like a battering ram.

"My king," she whispered. "At last, I have found you."

Her arm encircled his as she brought her body up against him. He breathed in her perfume and felt the warmth of her hand on his. He wanted to melt away from her touch and merge with the cold stone balustrade beneath his fingers: anything not to look at her, not to look into her face and see Caenne. In the end, her warmth won out.

He turned his face towards her. "You were looking for me?"

For an instant, he saw Caenne standing next to him with her lifeless hand on his. A chill ran up his spine.

"Yes, my love."

Maeven's words jerked Ergyfel back from the unholy fabrication of his mind. He inhaled sharply.

"What's wrong, my love?"

He pulled his hand away and rubbed his forehead.

"It's nothing. I'm only tired."

"My lord. Since you used your powers to search for Caenne, you have not been yourself."

"I'm tired."

"No, my good lord. It is more."

Ergyfel looked at her, his eyes searching for any sign that she knew of his crime. "What more?"

"My lord, you are brooding too much of late. You eat little, and you seem ..."

"Preoccupied?"

"Melancholy."

"What of it? I have a lot on my mind."

"As always, my lord. But now, you seem to be avoiding me. You no longer show any desire for my affections."

Though she dared much in speaking this way to her king, she knew not to make eye contact. Nevertheless, Ergyfel turned away again.

After a pause, she spoke, "I believe I know what has happened. You are no longer in love with me."

Ergyfel spun round to protest her remark. "I ..." He raised his finger, pursed his lips, then closed his eyes and retracted his finger, making a fist.

"Is there someone else?"

Ergyfel's eyes snapped open. Someone *had* come between them.

Caenne has come between us.

He reached for Maeven, then strode from the room without a word, leaving her alone with her tears.

*

As Maeven sobbed, she leaned over the balustrade, and her tears fell to the ward far below. She pulled herself back from the edge with a sniff. At that moment, on the stones below, Ergyfel walked through the inner ward. He pulled his cloak around him and brushed off all servants and guards that approached.

"Where is he going?" she muttered. "Looks like he's going into town."

She left the room and scurried through the passages of Orgulous, then crossed the inner ward at a quick pace and ran to the main gatehouse. She cared nothing for what onlookers might think. When she reached the gilded gates of the outer bailey, she caught a glimpse of Ergyfel disappearing around a corner. The sky had turned deep purple, and the night watch was lighting the torches of Nyraval.

Still focused on her prey, Maeven ran to where she had seen Ergyfel. She peered around the corner and saw him treading up the street alone. She observed him a moment before following. Though she kept a discreet distance between them, she could see by his gait that he was deep in thought. She followed him through several streets, thankful that his pace allowed her to catch her breath.

At last, he came to a narrow backstreet without lights and entered. Maeven approached and looked into the darkness. He had vanished. She stepped forward to enter, but a door opened and bright light spilled out into the alley. Maeven pulled back into the shadows and held her breath as a man with white whiskers greeted the king and closed the door behind him.

She waited in the darkness at the alley's mouth for as long as she could bear it. Two night-watch patrols passed by her position before she could bring herself to creep deeper into the alley. As her eyes became accustomed to the dark, she made out the dim outline of a window with heavy shutters next to the shadow of the doorway.

As she neared the window, she paused to listen. She could hear the muffled voices of two men coming from inside. Several pungent smells mingled with the stench of waste from the gutter. She scanned around her in the darkness, then stepped up to the window and pressed her ear against the shutters.

"Well, Your Majesty," a dry, raspy voice said. "I believe it's nearly done."

"How much longer?"

"Not long. Not long. Just a moment more."

"Good. The sooner I can forget her, the better."

"And so you shall."

Maeven shifted her position, trying to see through the tiny cracks around the shutters.

"Ah! That change in color means it's ready."

She pushed her ear up against the shutters again.

"Here, Your Majesty. Now speak the words and drink while it's still warm."

"By my will, … I will remember her no more."

Maeven pulled with all her might on the window shutters, and they flung open. In the dim light of the small shop, she saw the white-whiskered man wearing a stained apron, and Ergyfel standing next to him, downing the contents of a small stoneware cup.

"No!" Maeven shouted while she stretched into the room as far as she could throw her body through the window.

Ergyfel dropped into the chair behind him, staring at Maeven as the apothecary rushed forward to catch her. But rather than helping her through the window as she expected, the apothecary forced her back into the alley and closed the shutters. A moment later, the door opened with a rattle, and the old man scurried out.

"What have you done?"

"Sh-sh-sh." The apothecary kept himself between Maeven and the doorway. "I have only done as the king commanded. Now, quick, tell me, did he see you?"

Maeven looked past the old man to see Ergyfel still sitting in the chair, staring with empty eyes. "What's wrong with him?"

The apothecary glanced over his shoulder at his royal customer before answering. "Nothin'. Now, did he see you?"

"Then why is he just sitting there like that?"

"It might take a few winks for some effects of the potion to wear off."

"What potion did you give him, old man?"

The apothecary closed the door, plunging them back into darkness. He sighed before he spoke again.

"I know who you are, milady. And because o' that, I will tell you what the king entrusted only to me. The king has taken a potion of forgetting."

"Why did he wish to forget me?"

"Now, now, lass. The king did no' wish to forget you. 'Twas your sister he wished to forget. I only hope ya did no' botch it."

"I don't understand."

"If he saw you just before he drank from the cup, then it could be you that he's forgettin'."

"Then you've got to stop it!"

"No. 'Twill only do him harm at this point, lass. But do ye really think he saw you before drinkin'?"

"Well, he had the cup to his lips and he ... he had already tipped his head back before he looked at me."

The apothecary sighed. "Then all is well."

"So you say, but why did he come to you for this potion?"

"Ya see, lass—now, the king had to explain this part to me—but when he sent out his mind to search for your sister, he did no' find her, an' because o' that there's still some part of his mind a-lookin'. Until it returns, I doubt he could make a potion of such complexity on his own. His mind is too divided. And that is why he come to me."

"What I meant was: Why forget my sister? Why forget Caenne?"

"I tried to talk him out of it, but he said it was the only way—the *only* way—he could look at you and no' feel terrible sad."

"Sad? For looking at me?"

"Aye. I think it's on account of you lookin' so much like her."

"But, why sad?"

"Lass, I do no' want to be the one to tell you."

"Tell me what?"

There was no answer.

"Please, sir, tell me."

The apothecary frowned. "He said that when he could no' find your sister, it could only mean one thing."

Maeven stood in silence with the apothecary's words cleaving to her ears.

At last, she spoke. "He thinks Caenne is dead."

"I'm sorry."

Maeven turned away, biting at the back of her thumb to stifle her tears.

"I could make you a little somethin' too, … to help you forget."

"No, no." Maeven sobbed. At last, in control of herself, she asked, "So, will he remember me?"

"Most assuredly, milady. He may not remember the last few days with much clarity; heavens, he might not even remember that he just drank a potion, which is why I insisted on payment up front, but *you* he will surely remember."

"Will he remember that he loved me?"

"If he loved you last week, then he'll love you the same today—or tomorrow!"

"You seem so uncertain."

"These things can be a little unpredictable."

Maeven contemplated this for a moment, and then turned to leave. She stopped and turned back to him.

"Thank you." She reached into her purse and held out two coins to the apothecary.

"I told you, milady; the king has already paid."

"This is a reward from me to you, for risking to tell me."

The apothecary took the coins. "Thank you, milady."

"I don't think he should know I was here."

"Quite so. The fewer questions about tonight, the more likely the potion will work properly."

Maeven then turned and disappeared into the dark of the alley.

***

Ergyfel burst into Sir Feolaghe's chambers with one question on his lips: "Will you give me the hand of your daughter, sir?"

A long pause followed as the gaunt lord and lady stared across the table at one another and then back to their king.

"In marriage," Ergyfel added.

Sir Feolaghe put down his fork and knife and forced himself to swallow the chunk of meat in his mouth as he stood to greet his strangely buoyant liege. "Your Majesty," he managed at last, as he bowed before the king.

"Your Majesty," his spouse said from beside the table.

"Where's Maeven? I want to share the news with her."

"Your Majesty." The lord gestured to a side chamber.

"Is she in there? Maeven, come out here!"

"I'm afraid she isn't here, my liege."

"Where is she? Where's Maeven?"

"I'm not entirely sure, Your Majesty."

"You, servant!" Ergyfel snapped his fingers at the serving girl frozen behind the dining table. "Find Lady Maeven at once, and bring her here!"

"At once, sire." The girl gave a curt bow before escaping the room.

Sir Feolaghe now stood in the doorway to the side chamber and invited the king to enter. Ergyfel glanced about, then ducked into the room. Feolaghe shrugged to his wife's silent question, then closed the door behind him.

"Your Majesty, please sit down. Can I get you a drink? Some food?"

"What is it, Feolaghe?" Ergyfel's demeanor crossed from the high road to the low. What game is this? What is it you are after? What infringement on my joy? Do you want money? Power?"

Feolaghe, not wishing to see the king's good humor turn further south, held out his open hands. "No, no. Nothing like that, sire."

"What then? Quickly, man! Before I lose all good charity."

"This is all just a bit sudden for us, Your Majesty. My wife is not yet over the loss of our youngest."

"Loss?"

"Why yes, Your Majesty."

"I don't understand. Do you have news?"

"No, Sire, but we can hold out our hope no longer. The weight of it threatens to crush Barane completely. She is not well. The physician has even now just left her. He gave her a strong medicine to calm her. This is the first time I have convinced her to eat much of anything since Caenne disappeared."

The name of Caenne clanged like a sword-struck helm on Ergyfel's head. The disappearance of Feolaghe's youngest daughter came rushing back to his conscious mind. He saw the great hall of Orgulous filled with courtiers and soldiers, and remembered issuing a command to search for the missing girl, but that was all.

"Forgive me, sir." Ergyfel took a seat. "I've been ill, and your tragedy had somehow slipped my mind."

"No need to apologize, Your Majesty. Maeven has told us how sick you were with fever."

"Yes. Fever."

At that moment, Maeven broke into the room. She froze when she saw her father and Ergyfel across the room from one another. They each looked at her and smiled.

"Oh, daughter of my youth. Come in. Come in."

Maeven bowed to her king, and then crossed the floor to give her father a kiss on the cheek. Her eyes never left Ergyfel.

Feolaghe embraced his eldest around the shoulder with one arm and motioned to the king. "His Majesty has just asked me for your hand in marriage, my dear!"

Maeven blinked, then broke free of her father's grip and ran to her lover. She threw herself to the floor before him and placed her hands on his knees. She stared up into his dark eyes. "Oh, my lord, is it true?"

Ergyfel smiled. "Would that please you, my love?"

Maeven rested her cheek against his knee. "More than anything."

Ergyfel looked to Sir Feolaghe. "Then it's settled."

"Yes, Your Majesty."

"Good."

Ergyfel stood and walked to the door. Maeven was close on his heels.

"Stay here, beloved." He took her hand and kissed it. "I'm sure you and your parents have much to discuss, and much more to plan. We wed on the full moon. As for me, I go to set this castle spinning."

"The full moon, beloved! That's not a week away!"

"My liege! That's not enough time for the lords of the kingdom to gather!"

"We are at war, sir. We'll just have to forgo some ritual. Besides, the king must have his queen—and heirs—if he's to rule in peace. The lords will empathize."

"Yes, Your Majesty. Good night, Your Majesty."

"Good night, Sir Feolaghe. Good night, beloved." Ergyfel paused in the doorway, then turned back. "Come to me on the morrow. The father of the queen must wear more than a knight's spurs. We will work out the treaties, formalities, and trivialities of all this and your new titles after breakfast."

CHAPTER TWENTY-FOUR

Grave Business

"Nothin' down here." Camion thumbed behind him.

"Only thin' that way's the abbey." Malcolm waved his torch.

Hugh scratched his head. "The abbey?"

"Yeah, I could hear 'em chantin' up there."

"Anything else?"

"There was a trap door, an' when I popped 'er open, Jesus was starin' down at me from the cross. Needless to say, I got out o'there!"

Hugh sighed. "I tried a number of tunnels this way, and almost didn't find my way back. They all look the same.

"What now, Hugh?"

"How should I know? I didn't expect to get down here without my guide."

"The boy?" Camion asked.

Hugh nodded and doused his torch in a pile of rubble. Camion followed his example.

"He's been down here before?"

Again, Hugh nodded. "Apparently he's the only one, besides Billy, who has ever successfully navigated the catacombs from Cyndyn Hall to here."

"If we cannot find a way through the catacombs ..." Malcolm looked down the tunnels that surrounded them. "Then we'll have to go back through the orchard and get there over land."

Camion grasped Malcolm's shoulder. "Someone will see us."

Hugh's large companion was right. Too much open ground lay between the abbey and Cyndyn Hall, and far too many Gwythie soldiers were about. Also, without the cover of the catacombs, they would need to get away quickly, and Hugh didn't know if he could put his hands on the necessary horses.

"There's got to be a way. Blast it, Aeth, where the devil are you?"

"Right here."

Hugh spun around, ready to punch, and saw Aeth silhouetted against the pale moonlight filtering in through the hole in the ceiling.

"Aeth. Thank the Lord. You've got to quit sneaking up on me like that!"

"I thought it was fittin' considerin' the orchard's crawlin' with Gwythies."

"Point taken."

"So, this is our guide."

"Aye."

"Guide?" Aeth asked.

"Malcolm, meet my good friend, Aeth. Aeth, this is Malcolm ..."

"The Magnificent?"

"At your service." Malcolm gave Aeth a curt bow. "And this scrawny runt is Camion."

The giant laughed. "He's right. I am the smallest of my brothers."

Aeth nodded to Camion, and then turned to Hugh. "What's this 'bout me bein' your guide?"

"That's why you're here. That's why I needed you to come."

"I don't get ya."

"You're the only one besides Billy that's traversed the catacombs between here and Cyndyn Hall."

"No, I'm not."

"So, you're not the only one. What matters is—"

"I'm not anyone of 'em."

"What are you saying?

"I'm saying I don't know the way across the Cyndyn Catacombs."

"But you told me, back in the hole in the wall, that you had stole into the old orchard graveyard, navigated the catacombs to Cyndyn Hall, and come back."

"No, I didn't."

"But you said—"

"I said the single best burglar in Dyven did that."

"And you said he was more a boy than a man, and in better condition when he did it."

"All true."

"I assumed that was you. But that's not you, is it?"

"No. Do you remember what they used to call me?"

"Stitch."

"That's because I cut purses, not rooftops. I'm no burglar."

Hugh's voice became biting. "Then who is this burglar that should be standing next to me instead of you?"

"It doesn't matter now."

"Who is he? I need to find him. Now!"

Aeth raised his voice in anger. "It doesn't matter because he died tonight!"

His voice reverberated in the ancient hallways of the catacomb. The last echoes betrayed his bitterness.

The four men waited in the intersection, holding their breath and praying that Aeth's outburst hadn't alerted any Gwythies. When he was sure it was safe, Hugh spoke. "Please, tell me you're not talking about Derian."

"I am."

Aeth produced his locket and showed it to Hugh. "His real name was Douls, ya know?"

Hugh recognized the locket. "It's complete. ... Then you found ... Derian was your father?"

"Aye. ... That no good, two-faced scoundrel ..."

Aeth began to cry. His crippled hand wavered before him, cradling the newly complete locket in his palm. Malcolm turned to the side to whisper in Hugh's ear.

"We need to act soon, Hugh. Time is running out."

"I know, I know. We need a plan."

"I say we have to ..."

Hugh looked up at Malcolm. The highlander appeared mesmerized, his eyes staring at the locket in Aeth's hand.

"What is it, Malcolm?"

"That locket ... I've seen it before."

Aeth opened his eye and examined Malcolm and the locket.

"I saw it tonight," Malcolm said.

Hugh looked in Aeth's palm. "It's a heart."

"No. It's more than just a heart. It has an unusual design on it, and I saw that exact pattern over there."

Malcolm turned and marched down the tunnel he had been searching in previously. The others grabbed their torches and followed. Before long, the highlander turned a corner and entered a squat corridor that was very different from the rest. The walls and the ceiling were made of smooth, dark, tight-fitted stones. The floor was also of stone but set in a basket weave pattern unlike the rest of the catacomb. A couple of casks stood lined up against one wall, and a small shelf hung above, stocked with candles.

Malcolm halted and held his finger to his lips. The others stopped. They heard the faint sound of chanting coming from the ceiling.

"The good brothers are still at it." Malcolm lit Hugh's torch with his own.

At the end of this hallway, a short ladder led up to a small trapdoor. As they approached the ladder, Malcolm raised his torch to illuminate the hatch. It was a dark oak panel with an iron ring for a handle and bound by an elaborate iron hinge that spread out across its face in the shape of a heart. Aeth examined his locket and saw that the patterns on the two hearts were identical.

"What does it mean?" Camion asked.

Hugh looked at Aeth. "What do *you* think it means?"

Aeth shrugged. "What's up there, Malcolm?"

"Why don't you have a look?"

Aeth climbed the ladder and nudged the trapdoor open a bit at a time. The chanting became louder. He stood on the ladder for a minute, and then closed the door and came down. The others stared at him, waiting for his report.

"Well?" Hugh asked.

"I'm not sure. Never been in a church before."

"Not even on Christmas or Easter?" Malcolm asked.

Aeth shook his head.

Camion knelt down and eyed the trapdoor. "What you see?"

"I seen a man. He looked very sad, and he was in so much pain. He was beat-up somethin' terrible and had thorns mashed into his head. His hands and feet ... he was ..."

"Nailed to a cross?"

Aeth looked up at Hugh and nodded. "I guess so. It did look like the cross I seen 'round the Abbot's neck."

"Jesus," Malcolm whispered.

Aeth looked at the highlander's face and saw that he wasn't swearing. "That's Jesus?"

"Aye, Jesus the Christ," Hugh said. "Our Savior, God in the flesh."

"Looked like a statue to me."

Malcolm smiled. "Aye. 'Tis that; a statue of the son of God—God in the flesh."

"But ... they beat him."

"Aye. And more."

Aeth examined his broken, bandaged body. "Sorta like me."

Hugh knelt down beside Aeth and made eye contact. "Aye. What you suffered was for Billy. What Jesus suffered was for all of us."

Aeth searched Hugh's eyes. All at once, he dropped his eye and stared at the floor. Hugh put a comforting hand on the boy's shoulder. It was plain he was working something out in his head.

Aeth looked up. "I wanna hear more 'bout him, but first, I think we better rescue Lady Myrredith." He stared at the locket and took a step away from his companions. "Wait a minute! Wait a minute."

He tapped the locket against his forehead as he paced in his shambling manner up and down in the passageway. Then he stopped abruptly and faced Hugh.

"Under the feet of God. This is under the feet of God. We're under the feet of God!"

The others stared at him.

"It's something Derian was trying to tell me before he died. He said now that my heart was complete, I should follow it. This heart is now complete. He also said it held the secret he kept even from himself ... right under the feet of God."

Hugh examined the trapdoor above his head. "So, what's the secret?"

Aeth stared at the locket. "I don't know, but I'd bet Bezants to beeswax this locket somehow holds the answer to our troubles."

"Is it the way through the catacombs?" Malcolm asked.

"Could be."

Hugh and Malcolm gathered around Aeth, and Camion came up behind them. The giant held his torch high as he looked over their shoulders at the simple copper locket. Aeth opened it up, revealing the tiny portraits of his parents. He turned it over and flipped it around. He closed it, opened it, rubbed it, shook it, pressed it, squeezed it, and pulled on it, all at the direction of Hugh and Malcolm in their attempt to figure out its long-held secret. At last, Aeth opened it up and stared at the two pictures inside.

"What under pictures?"

Aeth looked up at the giant in surprise. "What?"

"What?" Hugh and Malcolm looked back at Camion.

"Friend o' mine—sailor on the *Gyldan Mene*—had a pretty, like that one, with pictures inside. Had a different picture for each port."

"Each port?" Hugh asked.

Malcolm nudged him with his elbow. "Different port, different girl."

"How you know?"

"Lucky guess."

Aeth slipped a thin blade into one hand and used it to pry at the tiny groove around the picture of his father. The small portrait popped out of the locket and into his palm. He eyed the vacant, tarnished back and spotted two tiny crosses etched on opposite sides and a number of short lines haphazardly scattered in the space between.

He took the blade and pried at the locket until the picture of his mother came free. Under her picture, he found an arrangement of etched lines that formed a complex geometric pattern that spiraled in towards the center.

"A map?" Aeth asked.

"A labyrinth, laddie."

Hugh nodded. "Aye. To keep the dead in, but the map's not complete. Look, there are gaps all over."

"To keep the dead in?" Aeth's eye grew large.

"Fear not." Hugh chuckled. "It's just a legend."

"Yeah, a legend that's managed to stay keen for more than six hundred years."

Hugh stared at the highlander in surprise. "You know about that?"

Malcolm scoffed. "Who hasn't heard of Caesar's Lost Legion, or the ghoul king that took them?"

"You believe every story you hear?"

"Only the ones I retell for my patrons."

"Hey, what's that?" Aeth handed the locket to Hugh. "Under that lip, I think it's letters, but they're too small for me to make 'em out."

Hugh knew that Aeth couldn't read, but took the locket without a word. Under the lip, he could make out some faint loops of writing scratched into the copper. He took the edge of his sleeve and rubbed the copper until it shone around the letters.

"It says ... It says, 'Search with an open heart' ..."

Hugh took the locket and searched around the lip on the other half. A quick buffing brought out more letters.

"And this side says, 'but keep one eye on your plans.' Keep one eye on your plans."

Hugh absently closed the locket, handed it to Aeth and continued to ponder the inscription.

Malcolm ran his index finger over his lips and chin. "Search with an open heart."

Hugh nodded. "But keep one eye on your plans."

"Sound advice," Camion said.

"Aye." Hugh sat on one of the casks. "But hardly helpful right now."

While the others talked, Aeth examined the locket's exterior and interior again. He detected nothing new. He closed it and then opened it quickly, hoping for a different result. The locket was unchanged. He snapped it closed, shook it, then brought it up to his eye and cracked it open slowly. As he stared at the yellow-brown metal emerging from shadow, he saw a miraculous thing. When the locket was about halfway open, he could see the side closest to him reflected in the side opposite. Without warning, all the tiny random lines on the one side lined up with the reflected pattern of the other and completed the map. The two tiny crosses were on opposite ends of the maze. Aeth traced from one cross to the other and found that there was one meandering path running through the middle of the labyrinth that connected them.

"I've got it!"

The others stared at Aeth and once again fell into a very uncomfortable silence. Their eyes moved to the ceiling and the trapdoor. The chanting had ceased. A few seconds passed, and then it began again. The group sighed in relief.

Aeth signaled for the others to follow him and he led them away from the tight hallway. Once they were back in the catacombs, he spoke. "Look." He was bursting with enthusiasm. "If you hold it like this, you can see the entire catacomb layout and the way through to Cyndyn Hall!" He then demonstrated the proper way to hold the locket.

Hugh took the locket and tried it. "It's hard to line up."

"You gotta use just one eye."

Hugh closed one eye and looked again. "I'll be ..." He then handed the locket to the others and allowed them to see the tiny miracle it held.

Camion took a last squinty look, then handed it back to Aeth. "Here. Your one eye sees more than our six."

Aeth smiled, then Malcolm and Camion patted him on the shoulder and back. Hugh came beside him, put his arm around the boy's shoulders, and waited for him to make eye contact.

"I told you. You are my guide."

The two men from the hole in the wall smiled at each other and started up the tunnel in front of them.

"So, which way from here?"

"This way." Aeth pointed to the tunnel on his right.

Malcolm and Camion fell in behind Aeth and Hugh as they turned the corner. The four disappeared into the blackness of the catacombs with torches and spirits held high.

***

"I need to rest." Aeth hobbled over to the side of the square chamber they had just entered. "We're halfway there. I just need to rest for a minute."

The fatigue in the boy's limbs was obvious to all. They had been pushing to get across the catacombs and the pace was hard for Aeth with his broken body. Even Hugh's abdomen was yowling from the exertion.

"Aye. We've made good time. Just tell me which way we're going from here before you sit down."

"That one." Aeth pointed to the doorway across the room. "We're in the middle of the maze. This room is the center."

Hugh walked to the doorway, picked up a piece of chalky rubble, and scratched an "X" on the arch. "There. Don't want to get lost at this point."

As he reached up to strengthen the mark, his wound snarled, and he yanked his hand down. With one hand on his stomach and one on the arch, he took a deep breath and let it out.

"You up to this?" Malcolm asked.

Hugh straightened and looked down at the bloodied bandages around his belly. "I'll be fine. This is old."

Malcolm and the giant exchanged glances, then split up and sat on opposite sides of the doorway they had entered. Hugh and Aeth took up positions opposite them. In these dismal surroundings, no one had the heart to talk. The heightened spirits they had felt upon commencing their trek across the ancient tomb had fled from them; bled away by the never-ending darkness held ephemerally at bay by their torchlight.

For this reason and many others, Hugh remained silent. His mind churned with doubts about the coming rescue attempt. He couldn't fool himself into thinking it was anything more than a desperate half-baked attempt. How would he find Myrredith? How many guards would they run into? Would they have to do battle? If they did, how would he fare? Would Myrredith be happy to see him, or would she cast him off at the first opportunity? Could they get her out of Cyndyn Hall without raising the alarm? Where would the prince be during all this?

Hugh had started with a simple plan: enter Cyndyn Hall by way of the catacombs, free Myrredith, and escape back through the catacombs. Maybe it was too simple. Most of his life, he had kept his plans simple, and that had served him well. He had chosen the path straight ahead, the path of the arrow. The closer he examined his current plan, the less it looked like an arrow and the more it looked like an angry viper.

A faint sound interrupted Hugh's thoughts. He sat up and turned his head, attempting to find the sound again.

"What?" Camion asked.

"Shhh. I think someone's coming."

The four companions listened to see if they could detect which of the four doorways the sound had come from. A moment later, Malcolm motioned to the others that the sound came from behind him, from the way that they had come.

They hid in the side tunnels and doused their torches. Like heavy velvet, the ancient darkness wrapped itself around them. Sweat rolled a cold finger down Hugh's back. He clenched his fists to crush a tremor. The oppressive dark took on substance, mingling with the cold, musty air, and raking his senses on edge. Something stirred behind him—shambling steps, the whisper of Latin not spoken in four hundred years …

At that moment, Hugh felt a hand on his arm and he flinched before Aeth could whisper, "It's just me."

Though he could see nothing, Hugh frowned at the little thief. "I told you to stop doing that. Wish I had a blade."

"Where's your knife?"

"Lost on the corpse wagon."

Without another word, Aeth took Hugh's hand and placed something in it. He felt the item with his fingers and found the sharp end of a blade. Then he turned back to face the square chamber, the weapon poised in his fist.

The moments passed slowly, and then pale amber light peeked around a distant corner of the passage they had come from. With cautious advance, the light grew brighter, expanding and encroaching further into the central chamber.

Hugh strained to hear what he could of the men following them. They did not tromp around in noisy war-sandals or boots the way Gwythic soldiers did. In fact, they made no noise with their feet at all. Instead, what Hugh heard was the same sound that had first alerted him—the sound of someone adjusting a heavy load on his back. Within moments, they were at the doorway to the central chamber. The amber light filled the archway, spilling light into the side passages. Hugh leaned back into the shadows to avoid detection.

Without warning, the newcomers stopped their advance. Hugh held his breath and tightened his grip on the crude knife.

A soft whisper split the silence, "Wait, Your Highness. I sense a trap."

Your Highness? Prince Hereweald? Down here? This could be our chance to turn things to our favor.

He risked a peek around the corner and saw a short, slight man wearing a cloak, his face hidden in the shadows of its hood. A small orb of light, with the color and intensity of a torch, floated in the air near him. The little man slipped his sword from its sheath, and the orb moved away to circle the room.

Hugh inhaled and readied himself to attack.

Just then, another cloaked man stepped out of the shadow beyond the archway. Like the first man, he was short and kept his face hidden within the recesses of his hood. He had a long cloth-covered package strapped over one shoulder, and in one hand he wielded a short curved sword of a design Hugh had never seen before. He extended his other hand, and a bluish orb of light appeared, floating above his palm. It shot to the arched ceiling of the chamber, where it intensified.

I have to act while I've still got surprise on my side. And quick as a bolt before they can cast a spell on me. His muscles tightened to spring.

"Sir Hugh?" the second man said.

Hugh froze.

The little man raised his hand, and the bluish orb became as bright as daylight, causing Hugh to squint. The second man then opened his sword-hand, and his weapon disappeared.

"Sir Hugh?" The second man probed the darkness beyond with his voice. "Is that you?"

The voice was so familiar to Hugh, and yet he could not place it. It seemed like a voice that crossed oceans of time to reach his ear.

Is this some trick of magic? A demon's spell to catch me off guard?

At that moment, the second man pushed back his hood and revealed his face.

Billy! It cannot be!

Malcolm stepped into the room from the opposite archway. "Billy!" He showed his empty hands to the first little man and advanced.

The man stepped in front of Malcolm, barring his way.

"It's all right, Shaldra. He's a friend."

Shaldra pushed back his hood, lowered his sword, and stepped aside. For a moment, his pointed ears and almond shaped eyes struck Malcolm dumb, but then he remembered Billy.

"Billy!" The highlander threw his arms open.

Billy rushed forward into his embrace.

"I thought I'd never see you again, my boy."

"And I, you!"

At this, Camion ambled out of the dark. His size caught Shaldra and Billy off guard. Shaldra raised his sword, and Lura Zahn appeared in Billy's fist.

Malcolm, still holding onto Billy, put his hand on his arm. "He's no trouble. He's with me."

"I remember you," Billy said to the giant. "You were on the *Gyldan Mene.*"

Camion nodded. "Glad to see little people still alive." He eyed Shaldra and the point of his sword. "All little people."

Shaldra smiled and lowered his weapon.

"'Member me, Billy?"

Aeth leaned against the archway. Billy stared at his crooked, bandaged body and frowned. Finally, he made his way up to the boy's face and his one eye. "Stitch?"

"Aye."

"What happened to you?"

"'Tis a long story. Maybe I'll tell ya sometime, but now we need to be rescuin' Lady Cyndyn."

"Right." Billy walked to Aeth and put his hand on his shoulder. "It's good to see you."

Hugh remained slumped half in the shadows, on the floor behind the doorway. He was staring at Billy with tears rolling down his cheeks. He still held Aeth's crude knife in his hand.

Billy stepped to Hugh and removed the long package slung over his back. The blue orb of light dimmed and moved to the archway. Billy sat cross-legged in the pool of light, in front of Hugh, with the package across his lap.

"Yeah, … it's good to see you too."

Hugh remained mute.

Billy opened his shirt and showed Hugh the scars the dragon had left across his chest. "We meet again, old friend."

The crude blade in Hugh's hand fell to the stone floor with a *tink,* and he rolled to his knees. He grabbed Billy and plucked him off the floor, wrapping his arms around him, like a man drowning in a river grabs hold of a fallen tree.

"Hugh," Billy gasped. "You're crushing me."

Hugh loosened his grip but kept hold of him. He closed his eyes, but the tears continued to roll down his cheeks and catch on his smiling lips. His breath drew in slowly but escaped in bursts as if his lungs could not hold it.

"I saw you die."

"I know. I know. But, in fact, it was you that saved me."

"What?"

"That little coffin you brought aboard the *Gyldan Mene* saved my life."

Hugh relaxed his embrace of Billy and sat back onto his haunches to examine him. Unable to let go completely, Hugh held onto his newly restored friend at arm's length.

"The coffin?"

"Aye." Billy picked up the long package that lay on the floor between them and held it out to Hugh. "This belongs to you."

Hugh released Billy and put his hands around the long cloth-wrapped package. When Billy let go, its well-balanced weight fell into his hands and told him exactly what it was.

"Is this a dream?"

Billy smiled. "Shall I pinch ya to make sure?"

Hugh stared at him and the item resting in his hands.

"Go ahead. I kep' it oiled for you, just like you taught me."

Hugh loosed the tie strings and flipped back the open top of the sack. The bluish light sparkled off tiny silver leaves and bone as the silky cloth spilled away from Hugh's ancestral sword. The blue gemstone in the pommel winked at him in greeting.

"I never dared to dream. I am forever in your debt."

"No. True friends have no debts between them, only gestures of kindness."

Hugh put his hand behind Billy's neck and leaned in until they were touching foreheads. "Right. Right."

As they drew apart, Hugh said, "Say, how did you know it was me?"

"When?"

"Just now. Before we came out of hiding, you called my name like you knew it was me."

"Well, who else would be down here with four men preparing to storm a fortress guarded by a legion of well-trained elite forces in order to rescue one lady from under the nose of her war-seasoned royal captor?"

Hugh laughed, and Billy joined him. Their infectious laughter spread to the others, but it didn't last long. There was still some work to be done.

Billy and Hugh stood up, and Hugh strapped on his sword.

"I suppose that's a long story too." Billy pointed at Hugh's wound.

"Not really. I got drunk, insulted some very patriotic Gwythies, and when they grew bored of beating me, their sergeant used me for sword practice."

Billy reached out and touched the site of Hugh's wound. He closed his eyes and concentrated. After a moment, he straightened. "Shaldra, bring me Elzgig's balm."

Shaldra slipped off his backpack and brought it to Billy. He then opened it and handed over a small clay jar.

Billy nodded at the backpack. "Might as well give him those."

Shaldra reached into the pack and pulled out a helmet and a pair of gauntlets. He handed them to Hugh while Billy doctored his wound.

Hugh and Shaldra just stood and stared at one another.

"Oh, pardon me," Billy said. "Shaldra, this is Sir Hugh, the King's Champion. Sir Hugh, this is Shaldra, my friend."

Shaldra straightened with pride.

"I'm not the King's Champion anymore. I'm not even a sir any longer."

Billy looked up from his bandaging.

Hugh caught his eye. "Ergyfel."

Billy nodded. "And that fine fellow behind me is Stitch."

"Not Stitch anymore. Name's Aeth."

Billy looked over his shoulder to the giant. "I never learned your name, but perhaps that's to my advantage. No doubt, it too has changed recently. Whatever it is, I owe you my thanks for the *Gyldan Mene.*"

Camion grinned and bowed at the waist.

"And you, Malcolm, what do they call you now? Are you still the famous Malcolm the Magnificent?"

"Aye." The master juggler smiled. "Though I've not felt very famous or magnificent lately. My friend's name is Camion."

Hugh blurted out at Shaldra, "You're a faerie, aren't you?"

"I am of the Faerie Court, though of all the names men call us, I think I prefer 'elf.'"

"The Faerie Court?"

"Aye. The court of my prince."

"That's enough." Billy stood up and handed Shaldra the jar of balm. "We don't need any more of that."

"Yes, Your Highness," Shaldra whispered.

Then Billy turned to the others. "Come. It's time we rescued Lady Myrredith."

CHAPTER TWENTY-FIVE

Ghost of a Chance

The new rescue party continued into the dark of the catacombs. Though he could sense his way to Cyndyn Hall with his ring, Billy allowed Aeth and his locket to lead. Shaldra took up a position at the ex-pickpocket's side with orders from Billy to, "protect him as if he were me." Billy and Hugh came next, with Malcolm and Camion guarding the rear. Billy split up his faerie light into a half-dozen orbs and spread them around so that no one had need for a torch.

After turning two corners, Hugh spoke to Billy in hushed tones. "You seem to know a great deal about what we face."

"Unlike you, I can't afford just to make it up as I go."

"Funny. And yet you brought only the two of you."

"You only brought four!"

"Yes, but I brought a very talented sneak, two skilled warriors, and a giant."

"We brought weapons."

"Good point."

"But seriously, my plan depends on stealth and a speedy escape."

Hugh raised an eyebrow. "Speedy escape?"

"Aye. Two members of my company are waiting with horses at the old stable, south of Cyndyn Hall."

"The old ruin under the hill?"

"Aye."

"How many horses?"

"I figured on one spare mount per rider, so ten."

"There will be nine of us with Myrredith."

"Then we'll just have to do without spares."

"Good plan."

"I know."

"How do you intend to get Lady Myrredith out of Cyndyn Hall and to the old stable?"

"There's a secret passage that Lady Myrredith made me swear never to reveal to anyone. It goes under the walls of Cyndyn Hall to the south."

"I know that passage, but there's a great deal of open ground between the exit and the hill."

"If we move quickly, we can make it before sunrise. Shaldra?"

"Aye."

"Can we pick up the pace a bit?"

Shaldra glanced to Aeth, who nodded.

"Yes, Your Highness."

"Let's move."

The party quickened their steps. Hugh continued to march with the group, but his eyes were on Billy more than the path ahead.

Billy noticed his stare. "What is it, Sir Hugh?"

"Please, just Hugh."

"Sorry, Hugh."

"Hearing Shaldra call you 'Highness' brought back to my feeble mind the truth of your identity and the meaning of your return. I was so overwhelmed and happy to see you alive, that it completely slipped my mind. In fact, I think it's slipped all our minds, save Shaldra."

"The meaning of my return?"

"Recently, a seer told me that I might save Lyonesse. With Ergyfel on the throne, I couldn't see how that was possible, but now that you've returned, my direction is clear."

"Hugh, why do you think I've returned?"

"To reclaim the throne, of course."

"I came back to save Lady Myrredith."

"I've been thinking about that. Once we get to the crypt under Cyndyn Hall, you will wait there for us to return with Lady Myrredith. This rescue is far too risky for our future king. You must stay safe for the good of Lyonesse!"

"You're not listening." Billy put his hand on his friend's forearm. "I didn't come back for Lyonesse."

Hugh fixed his eyes on him. "You are the heir. You have a responsibil-ity—"

"I have other responsibilities."

"Not to a whole kingdom!"

"Yes, to a whole kingdom."

Hugh halted and grabbed Billy's arm. "What are you talking about?"

Billy looked around as the others of their party gathered. He sighed. "I was hoping to avoid this 'til later, but ... My mother, Queen Eleanor, was also queen of her own land. That is where I have been."

"Where's that?" Aeth asked.

"Tirn Aill."

"Tirn Aill?" Malcolm and Hugh exclaimed.

Hugh shook his head. "There is no such place! It's a child's bedtime story, a faerie—" Hugh gazed at Shaldra. "—tale."

Shaldra smiled and shook his head. "That's the difference between men and faeries. Men believe the tales about us aren't true, but wish they were. Faeries believe the tales about men are true, and wish they weren't."

"So." Hugh rubbed his forehead. "You're the heir to *two* kingdoms?"

"Aye. I'm her sole heir, so Tirn Aill needs me more than Lyonesse."

"How can you say that? Have you looked around you?"

"If I don't succeed in my mission, Tirn Aill will ... suffer. Even more than Dyven."

"If you don't help us, Lyonesse will die."

"Lyonesse may have an enemy on her shores, but she has her army, and knights, and warlords, and a king to defend her."

"That usurper doesn't know how to win a war!"

"I can't say that I would do any better."

"But they will all fail. The army, the knights, the warlords will all fail because the man on the throne does not belong there."

"Maybe. But even if the war is lost, Lyonesse will live on."

"What, as a nation of slaves?" Hugh shook his head. "It would cease to be Lyonesse."

"Lyonesse will live on for as long as we hold her in our hearts. I thought that you, more than anyone else, understood that Lyonesse is more than an army or a castle ... or a king."

Hugh sighed and contemplated Billy's words. "When did you become so wise?"

Billy shrugged. "It was sort of thrust upon me."

"Well, now that you are so wise, do you mind telling me why Tirn Aill deserves your help more than Lyonesse?"

Billy looked at Shaldra and frowned. He had hoped to keep secret from all the inhabitants of Tirn Aill, and especially his questing comrades, the burden he felt was his alone to endure. He didn't dare tell them, for fear they might lose all courage or fall into despair. But here it was, the moment of truth. Billy thought about sending Shaldra away to "scout up ahead" but then decided that the elf had even more right to hear the truth than the others.

"Because, I have seen the cost of my failure. If I fail ... every flower, every tree, every animal, every bee, every bird ... every person on Tirn Aill will die."

The corridor became a quiet tomb.

"Come. Lady Myrredith is waiting."

***

The rescue party found itself in yet another dark, anonymous corridor, indistinguishable from all the unremarkable corridors before. Shaldra suddenly smacked Aeth across the chest and knocked him onto his back.

"What is it?" Billy asked, with Lura Zahn in his hand.

Aeth sat up and rubbed his chest. "Yeah. What is it?"

Shaldra stared at the floor in front of him and sent his amber faerie light for a closer inspection. Without warning, it disappeared below the floor. Shaldra concentrated and made it brighter until it revealed a large gaping chasm yawning before him. The other members of the party came up behind him as he withdrew his light and sent it to the ceiling.

Billy brought his own faerie lights into the area and surrounded the hole.

Hugh grunted. "It's got to be fifteen feet across."

"It's bigger," Billy muttered.

"No." Malcolm came up beside him. "I think Hugh got it. Fifteen feet. Maybe a bit more."

"What I meant, was that it's bigger than it was when I was here last."

"You were here before?" Camion asked.

"Yes, and we need to get past this place quickly!"

"Why?"

Billy made eye contact with Hugh. "This is where I last saw *him*."

"Him?"

Billy paused, looked around, then whispered, "Rory."

Hugh tensed. His face paled.

At that moment, Aeth tossed a piece of rubble into the hole.

Billy and Hugh looked at him in horror.

"What are you doing?"

Aeth shrugged. "Just thought we should know how deep it is."

There was a tick, then a skitter, then a clack, and then another tick. The sound of the rock tumbling down the cavernous hole continued to reverberate up to them until, at last, there was a splash.

Hugh put his hand to his forehead. "Well, that counts out climbing down and back up."

Malcolm nodded. "How sure are you this is the right way, Aeth?"

The boy examined his locket again. "I'm certain."

"He's right," Billy said. "This is the shortest way to Cyndyn Hall."

"The shortest?"

"Aye, Hugh. There is another way around this—I took it the last time I was here, but that way will take far too long now."

"So, we go across."

The others stared at the giant, sizing up him and his statement. At last, Malcolm stepped aside of the others and eyed the chasm.

"I think I can jump it."

"I also think I can jump it," Shaldra said.

Billy looked at them and nodded, then his eyes came across Aeth and he stopped. "What about Aeth?"

Again, Camion piped up. "On my back."

"What?"

"I jump with him on my back."

"And you'll make it?"

"Does fish swim in sea?"

"Just leaves you and me, Hugh. With what Malcolm taught me, I think I can make it."

Hugh smiled. "I'll be fine."

"What of your wound?"

"It'll be fine. It feels better since you doctored it."

Billy looked at Malcolm and Shaldra. "Well?"

Malcolm and Shaldra took a few steps back to get a running start on the leap over the pit. Malcolm turned to Shaldra. "Shall I go first?"

Shaldra turned, sprinted to the hole, and sprang into the air. Billy inhaled and held it. A long moment later, the elf touched down on the opposite side.

The entire party exhaled.

Malcolm went next, performing a flip in the middle. When he landed, he turned around to face Billy and bowed. "Billy, remember what I taught ya 'bout using your weight in a flip to gain distance?"

"Aye. I remember."

"Now would be a good time to show me how well ya learned it."

Billy stepped back a few paces until his back came against a wall. He breathed several deep breaths and looked at the hole in the floor.

Look at your target, he told himself, remembering Malcolm's training. *Not what you've got to cover. Look at your target.*

Billy raised his eyes and focused on the floor on the other side of the hole. He took a last deep breath and pushed off the wall. He sprinted to the edge of the hole and leapt with all his might into the air. He tucked tight into a ball, and closed his eyes before the fall beneath him could steal his nerve and draw him down into its depths. He allowed his body to move by memory in the way it had learned after an hour of practice with Malcolm.

Billy opened his eyes and found himself on target. He put his feet down, and his momentum carried him into the arms of Malcolm and Shaldra.

He straightened himself, and then bowed to Malcolm. "Ta-da."

"Ta-da, indeed," the highlander grumbled. "You better stick to juggling. Your tumbling master robbed ya blind."

"But I didn't pay him anything."

"There 'tis. Ya get what ya pay for."

Billy and Malcolm laughed, then turned to face the others across the pit.

Aeth climbed onto Camion's back with Hugh's help, and the giant stepped back. He took only a few steps before he made his leap. Aeth squeezed Camion around his neck and did his best to hold on with his crooked legs. Though he didn't move with grace, the giant's strength propelled him over the gap, and the two oddly paired companions arrived safely on the other side.

*

Camion let Aeth down off his back, and then he and the others turned to Hugh. They stood back from the hole, coaxing and encouraging him to come across with their hands.

Billy gave him a smile. "You can do it."

Hugh took off his sword and threw it across to him. Then he threw over his helmet and gauntlets.

"Well … here I come."

Hugh stepped back as the others had done, took a deep breath, and ran up the corridor. He got up to a good speed, placed his foot at the edge of the pit, and pushed off. At that moment, the bit of masonry under his foot gave way, forcing him to dive for the distant ledge.

Hugh stretched out with all his might to reach the other side. He grasped at the stonework on the ledge as his weight carried him into the chasm. Before he could get a hold on anything, he slammed into the face and bounced off.

He fell. He scrambled to hold onto something. His eyes searched below him. Then his descent stopped as something gripped his wrist. The wound in his gut opened, and he cried out.

When his head cleared, Hugh looked up at his extended arm and found Camion holding his wrist with one hand and the rock face with the other.

"Hugh."

"Aye, Camion."

"Hold my leg. I can't hold us with one hand."

Hugh threw his arms around Camion's leg, and the giant reached up to hold the rocks.

Malcolm appeared at the edge and shouted down, "Hugh, can you find somethin' to hold on to?"

Hugh looked around him, but it was quite dark.

"Billy, send down a couple of lights."

Shortly, several glowing orbs of light descended into the cavern and surrounded Hugh. He could now see the wall in front of him. It was a slippery hodgepodge of dark stones and black soil with nothing solid to hold. As he scanned for footholds, something further down caught his eye. It was pale and smooth and stood out from the dark stone and earth.

"Billy. Can you make the lights brighter?"

As the light increased, Hugh could make out rough shapes. There was an arm and a leg, and a head. The light revealed a human skeleton, resting on a ledge below him.

"Camion, swing me forward."

The giant swung his body forward and then back, forward then back. The next time he swung forward, Hugh let go of his leg and fell.

"Hugh!" the giant exclaimed.

Billy, Malcolm, and Aeth rushed forward. "Hugh!"

"I'm well. I'm on a ledge down here."

Billy leaned out over the chasm. "What are you doing?"

"Look, just get Camion up, and then lower me down a rope and some kind of sack."

"If we had a rope," Malcolm yelled, "we'd have it around your waist now, you maniac!"

"I have a rope."

Malcolm, Billy, and Aeth stared at Shaldra until he shrugged. "Nobody asked."

They then set to work to bring Camion up from the pit. Without Hugh to weigh him down, Camion was soon up with the others. Shaldra then emptied his pack and lowered it to Hugh with his rope.

Before long, Camion had hauled Hugh out of the pit. Once on his feet, Hugh removed Shaldra's pack from his back and set it on the floor.

The others gawked at the small, intact skeleton that occupied the pack in a cramped sitting position. Dust and cobwebs had all but replaced the fine clothes that once adorned the remains.

"What the devil?" Malcolm made the sign of the cross.

"Not the devil," Hugh said. "A little boy."

Billy crossed his arms. "Lady Myrredith's brother."

Shaldra stared at the skeleton in his backpack. "Why'd you bring it up?"

"I m laying him to rest with his family."

Billy nodded. "It's time he found rest."

Shaldra motioned to the bones. "This is the one you told me about? The Ghost?"

"Ghost?" Aeth jumped back.

Billy grinned. "Nothing to worry about. He's harmless. I don't think he'll bother us."

"You don't *think?*"

"We're taking him home. With any luck, he's already at peace."

"Luck. Ha." Shaldra continued to stare at his backpack. "If I've learned anything on this quest, it's that dealing with corpses is anything but lucky."

***

When Shaldra returned from his scout, he squatted low and invited the others to join him as he scratched out a map on the floor. "Just like you said, there's a room only a few turns away. It's large and round, with several resting statues on large slabs of stone here and here."

"That's the crypt," Billy said.

Hugh stood. "Good."

"Wait." Shaldra touched his leg. When Hugh hunkered down again, Shaldra continued. "There are four guards sitting around a plain slab here, playing some kind of gambling game ..."

Hugh stood again and drew his sword.

"Wait!"

Hugh looked down at the elf. "The element of surprise. I'll catch them off guard."

Shaldra stayed put and stared at Hugh until he squatted. "There are two others eating over here to the right, one sleeping on the floor here behind this statue, and one watching the passages to the left. There are also three standing watch in the shadows of this passage with steps going up."

Hugh scratched his chin and pointed to Shaldra's floor map with his sword. "Three in this passage?"

"Aye." Shaldra nodded.

"How are they all armed?"

Shaldra thought for a moment. "No shields or spears. Light armor. Daggers and short swords only."

"What about this passage? How many on this one?"

"None."

Billy pointed at the map. "Unless you count the two eating in front of it."

Hugh looked up. "That one leads to the room you stayed in, just down the hall from Lady Myrredith."

Billy nodded. "I came down into the crypt from my room, but I couldn't have told you which passage it was."

"It was that one. This passage, right here, with the three in the shadows, is the one that leads directly to Lady Myrredith's room. That's our goal."

"That's if she's still in her room," Malcolm said. "The prince has likely moved her elsewhere."

Hugh thought a moment. "Then why put guards on this passage? And why are they all concentrated in this quadrant? No. They're guarding this passage."

"What about the one guarding these passages?"

"He's just pacing. They aren't serious about defending the room from these passages. They aren't armed heavily enough to fend off a strong attack."

"Aye." Malcolm nodded. "But there are enough of them to make it nigh impossible for us. What if one of them escapes and sounds the alarm?"

"Well, Camion will rush in and tackle those four before they can act, you'll take this one, and I'll take—"

Hugh stopped explaining his plan and turned to stare at the gaunt, ashen boy now kneeling beside him. The others likewise stared at their unannounced guest and his deep-set melancholy eyes.

"Hello, Rory," Hugh said.

The boy smiled at him, then pointed at the map and laughed.

"Shhh." Hugh put his finger to his lips.

The boy became quiet and focused on Hugh.

"Rory, do you remember me?"

The boy nodded.

"Myrredith is in great danger. We need you to be quiet so we can rescue her. Will you help us?"

Just like that, Rory faded into thin air.

Hugh reached out to touch him but found nothing.

Aeth exhaled. "That were him, huh?"

Billy nodded.

"Didn't seem like such a bad sort ... for a ghost."

Hugh made uneasy eye contact with the others, and then continued to spell out his plan of attack, which left Billy out of the fighting. With one dissenting vote, the party agreed they had little choice but to follow Hugh's plan and hope for the best.

The rescue party crept down the corridors toward the Cyndyn family crypt. The voices of the Gwythie soldiers echoed off the walls as they neared their destination. When they came to the last corner, soft lamplight painted the ceiling around the turn. Billy and Shaldra extinguished their faerie lights and drew their swords while Hugh peeked around the corner.

Each member of their party stood ready, squeezing their fists and weapons to relieve the tension of that moment. They breathed through their nostrils, fighting to maintain a quiet, calm pace against the racing of their hearts. At any second, Hugh would give the signal that would set them flying with all speed and cruelty into the midst of their foes.

The sound of a boy's taunting laughs suddenly burst from the next room. Billy stuck his head around the corner as the spirit of Rory Cyndyn leapt onto the slab-turned-game table. The four soldiers around it looked up in surprise as he kicked, and their coins splashed in all directions. One fell back to the floor while two others grabbed for him and banged heads.

"Get him!" the fourth player shouted.

All the men in the chamber scrambled to their feet as Rory lithely leapt from slab to slab, just out of their reach. One by one, they circled around him, closing in, backing him into the left end of the chamber where the lone guard stood barring the way to several doorways.

Rory leapt to the slab in front of the last man and landed on tiptoes on the statue of a knight. The clamoring soldiers behind him were now pushing and elbowing each other to get to him. Rory feigned left, then right, and finally leapt over the last guard's head and rolled into the dark corridor behind him.

Rory stuck out his tongue, then laughed and ran up the corridor, with the guards giving chase. The rescue party listened as the ruckus of the guard detail faded into the distance.

Billy and Hugh looked at each other, amazed and amused. Before they could laugh, Shaldra's face came between them, and he placed his fingers to their lips.

They pulled back behind the corner, and Shaldra whispered, "There's still one on the steps, in the shadows. He's a sly one. Maybe the leader."

Hugh motioned for Malcolm. The highlander came and knelt beside them.

"There's one left," Hugh whispered. "In the stairwell."

Malcolm took his dagger and turned it around so that he held it by the blade. He then looked at Shaldra. "Where, exactly?"

"Straight back in the shadows, behind the column on the right."

Malcolm stood and peeked around the corner. He scanned the shadows of the alcove until he caught a glimpse of movement. He turned, made eye contact with Shaldra, and nodded.

While Malcolm limbered up, Billy whispered to Shaldra, "You're the fastest. If he misses, you'll have to stop him."

At that moment, Malcolm side-stepped into the center of the corridor, raised his arm, and threw. Shaldra sprinted around the corner with his sword drawn. Malcolm's dagger chopped through the air, hit with a thud, then clattered on the stone steps of the dark passage.

The party ran through the crypt to the passageway, with Billy's blue faerie light leading the way. When they arrived, Shaldra stood and handed Malcolm his dagger.

"Nice throw!"

Malcolm sheathed his dagger and rolled his eyes at Billy. "If he misses ..." he scoffed.

Billy smiled and looked down at the Gwythie guard lying at the foot of the steps. A goose-egg-sized bump was rising on his forehead.

Billy shot his old juggling master an expression of surprise. "I thought you ..."

Malcolm frowned and shook his head. "Naw. Didn't need to."

Just then, the Gwythie guard came to. He scrambled to his knees, pushed Malcolm back, and reached up to grab a rope, which had its lower end tied to an iron sconce. Lura Zahn flew from Billy's outstretched hand, sliced the rope above the guard's grip, and returned. A moment later, Malcolm and Shaldra were on top of the guard. Hugh stepped forward into the tangle and knocked the guard unconscious with a mighty blow.

While Shaldra and Malcolm tied and gagged the unconscious guard, Hugh stashed the backpack bearing Rory's remains in one of the corridors. When he returned, he gave orders for Malcolm, Aeth, and Shaldra to guard their escape while he, Camion, and Billy went up to collect Lady Myrredith.

"And if things get too chancy, take and hold that passage over there." Hugh indicated the passage he had stowed Rory's remains in. "That's our way out."

Billy patted Shaldra on the shoulder. "I'll be fine. We need your sharp eyes and ears here." He then turned and followed Hugh up the steep winding stairs.

At last, Hugh, Camion, and Billy stood at the secret door leading to the bedchamber of the master of Cyndyn Hall. Hugh reached up and grabbed the lever to open the door.

Abruptly, Hugh glanced back at Billy with an expression of apprehension. "Is she in there?"

Billy closed his eyes and concentrated. A moment later, he smiled, but then deep furrows creased his brow.

"What is it? What do you sense?"

"She's in there, but there's something wrong."

"Wrong?"

"Something strange—a stranger."

"She's with someone?"

"Not exactly."

Hugh became frustrated. "How can you not exactly be alone?"

"She is alone, but. ...You'll understand once we're with her."

Hugh pulled on the lever and the catch opened. He pushed on the wall, and light spilled in through the doorway that appeared.

Hugh stuck his head into Lady Cyndyn's bedchamber. The dying fire in the hearth bathed the room in dim red light. The subject of their mission lay alone in the large bed on the far side of the room. The first hint of morning's light peeked through the small southern window.

"Blast, it's late. We've taken too long!"

The rescuers crept into the room. Camion squeezed out of the secret passage and crossed the room to secure the door while the others approached Lady Myrredith's bedside.

Hugh paused for a moment to take in her beauty as she rested beneath her furs and blankets. He reached down to wake her, and Billy grabbed his wrist.

"Be careful. She may try to scream at first."

Hugh gave Billy a curious expression, and then sat on the edge of the bed and put his hand over Lady Myrredith's mouth.

The lady's eyes popped open; she looked at Hugh and attempted to scream. Hugh applied more pressure with his hand as the struggle began. Lady Myrredith flailed about as Hugh and Billy attempted to hold down her arms and legs.

"Camion."

Camion left the door and came to lend Billy a hand with the determined Lady of Cyndyn Hall. The giant's strength and menacing size put an end to her thrashing.

"Myrredith, it's me! It's Hugh!"

She looked at him and made another feeble attempt to break free.

Billy then gave it a try. "Milady. Milady, it's me, William."

"It's like she doesn't know us."

"That's because she doesn't."

"What sorcery is this?"

"It's not sorcery. She's taken a blow to the head."

"Milady. Milady. We mean you no harm."

"We're here to rescue you."

The lady stopped struggling, and then looked at Hugh and mumbled something under his hand.

"You promise not to scream?" he asked.

She nodded, and Hugh removed his hand from her mouth.

"Rescue me?"

"Aye."

Myrredith looked around. "From what?"

"He didn't tell you. The prince didn't tell you."

"Tell me what?"

"The prince is going to execute you."

"You're lying."

She took in a deep breath, but before she could scream, Hugh clamped his hand back over her mouth.

"'Tis true, milady," Camion said. "The town crier—he said Prince Hereweald will execute you in the town square, tomorrow." Camion glanced at the growing light in the window. "Make that today."

Lady Myrredith thrashed about again, and the men fought back. Billy grabbed her face and forced her to look at him.

"Look at me, milady. We are great friends, you and I. We met at my father's inn in the Valley of the Yew. You asked Princess Kathryn to make me your brother. Try to remember!"

The lady shook her head from side to side.

Billy sighed and sank down in his frame. He looked at Hugh and Camion. "Gag her and tie her up. We'll take her with us."

"Wait. Isn't there some kind of magic to make her remember?"

"We're out of time." Billy backed away from the bed. "I'll have to try later."

"But ..."

"Someone's coming."

The latch of the door rattled. Hugh and Camion crouched on instinct, hushing one another and glancing about as if some miraculous means of escape would present itself.

A woman spoke from behind the door. "Milady?"

Silence.

Again, the handle of the door rattled ineffectively, and then the woman banged on the door.

"Milady, are you well? Why is the door locked?"

Billy signaled for Hugh and Camion to hold Lady Myrredith still. He took a deep breath and began to mutter and make circles in the air with his fingers. In a matter of seconds, the lady's bedclothes twisted themselves into ropes. They then entwined her body, wrapping around her arms and legs and bringing them together.

Once again, the door latch rattled.

"Milady, don't do anything ... impulsive!"

Lady Myrredith screamed with all her might from behind Hugh's hand. Though he held on tight, the feral part of it escaped his grasp.

"Milady!" the woman outside cried. "Guard! Guard! Open this door."

With Lady Myrredith's hands and feet bound, Camion went to the door and bent the key in the lock. The latch rattled, and then the door shook as a man on the other side grunted. Camion braced himself against the door as Billy gave one more flourish with his hands and directed a silken sash to slither round Myrredith's head. It then constricted and became a gag.

A ruckus ensued outside as the guard raised his voice and called for help. A moment later, a chorus of voices rose outside the door, along with a great deal of banging.

Hugh tried to pick up Myrredith but found his wound wouldn't let him. Billy came to his side and, together, they grabbed up the lady and lugged her towards the fireplace.

"Grab that lamp stand!" a new voice shouted from beyond the door. "Good. Now, one … two … three!"

Boom went the door, and rafter dust fell onto Camion's head.

"And again!"

Boom!

"We gotta get out of here *now*," Billy said.

He and Hugh dragged their captive into the secret passage without much thought for her comfort. Billy then went back into the room and focused on the door. He closed his eyes and pressed his hands together.

Boom!

The door cracked and bowed, though the giant held his weight against it. Camion looked at Billy and frowned. He couldn't hold them back forever.

Billy concentrated and the door swelled against the floor and surrounding doorframe. It creaked, and then the hinges and latch smoked. All the iron turned red. The door emitted a groan that became a deep creaking, akin to a chuckle.

Boom!

This time, the door held fast. Billy stood next to the secret passage and waved for Camion to come. "Quick! I don't know how long that will hold 'em."

The giant wriggled through the secret passage as fast as his massive body would let him. While Billy was pushing Camion through the narrow opening, he spied an iron poker resting against the hearth. As soon as Camion was through, Billy ran over and picked up the poker.

Crash!

The door cracked in half, and chunks of wood and splinters flew into the room ahead of a handful of guards carrying a large lamp stand. Before the men could spot him, Billy ducked into the secret passage and pulled the door closed behind him.

"Camion, take this poker and jam it into the hole with that lever."

The giant did as Billy bid him.

"Now, bend the poker up there and lock it in place."

Camion grunted, and the iron poker yielded to his strength. He then jammed its end into a niche below the lever.

"Great, Camion! That should slow them down."

At that moment, the lever jumped. Then it jumped again, but it could not move far enough to unlatch.

Hugh handed Myrredith to Camion. "Let's go."

They descended the turning steps with all haste, their charge thrown over the giant's shoulder. Billy squeezed ahead of them and lit the way with his faerie lights.

Billy spotted Malcolm and Aeth near the bottom. "Quickly. Where's Shaldra?"

"Here." The elf appeared from around the corner.

"Good. We haven't any time to waste."

"I take it things went poorly?" Aeth said.

"Take it how you like; we gotta get out of here!"

Billy crossed to the passage in which Hugh had stored the backpack. "Come. This way."

Malcolm stopped in front of the new passage. "Where's Lady Myrredith?"

"Right here."

Camion entered the crypt with his bundle still on his shoulder. Aeth stepped out of his way, and then Camion and Hugh laid Lady Cyndyn on one of the slabs. While they leaned on the slab, panting, Aeth approached the lady and examined her condition.

"Why is she tied up like that?"

"She didn't want to come," Hugh said between breaths.

Shaldra turned to Billy. "We came all this way and risked our lives, to rescue someone who doesn't want to be rescued?"

"No. She wants to be rescued; she just doesn't know it."

Aeth grinned. "Good thing you're the king."

"Why's that? And I'm not the king ... not officially!"

"Well, when you make it official, you can officially pardon us for kidnappin' a noble."

"We haven't got time for this. Soon they're gonna figure out where we've taken her, and then we'll have a devil of a time getting away."

Billy turned to Camion and gave orders. "Camion, take the lady—gently, gently. Hugh, you know the way. Take Shaldra and lead us out of here. Camion, you're next. Malcolm, give Aeth a hand, and I'll watch the rear."

The party passed through two narrow corridors and came to another crypt. Most of the burial niches were empty, and there were fewer sarcophagi on the floor.

"Wait." Hugh stopped and took off the pack with the bones in it.

The party halted. He then motioned for Camion to set the lady down in a niche, opposite a small stone sarcophagus that rested in the center of the room.

"Help me with this." Hugh indicated the sarcophagus.

"Have we got time for this?"

"It'll only take a moment, Shaldra."

Camion and Hugh heaved on the stone cover of the sarcophagus and slid it back. Hugh then took Rory's remains and placed them inside. Then he and Camion closed it back up.

Just as the lid dropped into its home, a light appeared and coalesced into the spirit of Rory Cyndyn. He stood in front of the stone coffin, staring at Lady Myrredith. His face looked healthier than before, with no hint of sadness. A faint glow surrounded his body. He smiled at his sister and stepped forward to touch her cheek.

Billy snapped his fingers, and her gag fell away. She remained silent, mesmerized by the visage before her.

The spirit turned and laughed as he strode back to his coffin.

"Rory?" Myrredith said, her voice hesitant.

The boy turned and walked back to her.

"Rory, I—I'm sorry. It was my fault."

Rory broadened his smile and shook his head. He then leaned over and kissed his sister on the cheek, where tears now flowed. Then, just as suddenly as he had appeared, he vanished.

Billy knelt before the lady, and Hugh stepped in behind him. Myrredith looked up from the floor, first to Billy, then to Hugh.

"William? Hugh? I just saw Rory."

"Yes."

"Am I dead?"

Hugh smiled. "Quite the opposite, milady."

Myrredith went to reach for them and found that she was bound. She looked down at her restraints. Immediately, Billy and Hugh loosed her bindings. As soon as she was free, she reached out and grabbed Billy and Hugh by the arm. Then, letting out a deep sigh, she bowed her head. "Thank you." She looked up with a smile and addressed her would-be rescuers. "The Lord has answered my prayers."

Billy stepped forward and threw his arms around Lady Myrredith. She squeezed him tight, rocking and kissing his hair. "Oh, William. William. My William."

Myrredith looked up at Hugh, who stood off to the side. "I suppose you think that if you tell me you brought back my William, I'll forgive you."

"Well ... it's actually ..."

"And you would be right."

Billy pulled back from Lady Myrredith. "I wouldn't be here if it weren't for Hugh."

Lady Myrredith glanced at Billy before returning her eyes to Hugh. "I was hoping Sir Hugh would answer for himself."

Billy turned and smiled at Hugh.

Lady Myrredith raised one eyebrow. "Well?"

Hugh cleared his throat. "Who am I to argue with my king?"

Myrredith took her hands off Billy. "Oh my! Then it's true! I heard before—after the Gwythies came—but I thought it was a rumor or a dream. Apologies, Your Majesty."

"Now, hold it right there! I'm not your king, and you and I were practically brother and sister before I found out who my real mother and father were, so I don't want any of you getting *peculiar* about the whole king thing. I'm still me, Billy."

Myrredith grinned. "Well, it certainly explains why you felt so familiar when we first met."

At that moment, Shaldra leaned in out of the shadows. "Your Majesty. We should leave with haste."

Billy turned to him. "Are they coming?"

"Aye."

"Quick. We'll lose them at the secret passage."

Myrredith took in her surroundings. "What are we doing here? Was that a faerie I just saw?"

"He prefers 'elf'."

Billy held out his hand. "That's a long story, milady. One best saved for another time and place."

**

Prince Hereweald paced on the highest turret of Cyndyn Hall with one arm wrapped across his chest and the opposite hand pulling at his lower lip. Occasionally, he looked up from his tramping feet to spy the pleasant fields and hedgerows of the surrounding countryside, or frown at the still smoldering ruins of Dyven and shake his head, or scowl at the courtyard below, where his men frantically upturned baskets and haystacks in search of their missing prisoner.

"Your Highness." A soldier came up the stairs.

"What is it, Fyrdan? Have you found her?"

"We found nothin'." The man fought to catch his breath.

"Nothing?"

"She managed to escape ... through the secret passage ... just as you said, Your Highness ... then, somehow, she got past your guards in the catacombs."

"Somehow. Somehow. Tell me, Fyrdan, do you think she might have had help?"

"I don't know, Your Highness."

"You don't know? So ... what you're saying is that a lone woman *somehow* out-fought and out-maneuvered ten trained soldiers and their decurion?"

"No, Your Highness. She must have had help."

"Are you implying we have a traitor among us, Fyrdan?"

The man gaped at his prince in shock. "I—I assume it was from outside our ranks, Highness."

The prince stroked his chin as his eyes shifted from side to side. "So do I, Fyrdan."

"So, what now, Highness?"

"Send more men after her, you dolt!"

"I already have, Your Highness—another twenty, but it's a labyrinth down there."

"I don't care if they've got their own Minotaur down there! You do whatever it takes, and you bring her back to me unharmed. Anyone you catch with her, I want for questioning. *Now*, Fyrdan."

"Yes, Your Highness." Fyrdan ran for the stairs.

The prince spun and marched to the ramparts of the high tower. As he came to a stop, his eyes caught movement to the south. There, on a lightly wooded, grassy knoll, seven figures appeared from the brush and made a run for a break in the hill. He scrutinized the party, and in a flash recognized the long red hair of Lady Myrredith.

"Wait!" the prince shouted.

The lady stopped and turned to look back. Her pale face tilted up until she was staring at the top of the south tower. There she stood, gazing at the prince with a taut expression. A moment later, the shortest of the men tugged on her arm, and she turned to follow him.

"Yes, Your Highness?" Fyrdan came back up the stairs. "I'm coming."

Prince Hereweald watched as the Lady of Cyndyn Hall, still dressed in her nightgown, fled with the ragtag band of men through the gap in the hill and disappeared. He continued to scrutinize the rise, wondering when they might reappear.

Fyrdan approached the prince's back. "I am here, Your Highness?"

"Stop there!" Prince Hereweald pointed a finger behind him.

Fyrdan froze several paces away and stood at attention.

Hereweald waited. He held his breath. Then a cluster of horses with riders burst out into the open from the far side of the hill and headed into the woods to the west. Halfway to the trees, Lady Myrredith slowed to look back.

"Your orders, Highness?"

Hereweald thrust his palm at the man behind him but continued to stare to the southwest. He stepped up into the crenel on the wall and watched as the last trace of red hair disappeared between the dark trunks of the trees.

"What is it, Your Highness? Do you see something?"

Hereweald still maintained his vigil on the distant wood. Though he knew she was racing deep into the heart of the forest, something held him in place, hoping for one more glimpse of the fiery Lady of Cyndyn.

"No, Fyrdan. It's nothing."

In that instant, the prince became aware that he was grinning. Hereweald slipped into his face of stone and stepped down from the wall. He strode past Fyrdan, leaving him flat-footed and confused.

CHAPTER TWENTY-SIX

The Wedding Gift

"**D**o you swear upon the Sword of Lyonesse to keep sacred your vows?"

"We swear," Ergyfel and Maeven answered in unison.

The oak-priest continued. "Then seal your promise with a kiss."

Ergyfel faced his bride and gave her a tender kiss on her lips.

"As your hands are bound together, so now shall your lives and spirits be joined in union of love. May your way be blessed."

The royal couple turned to face the throng of lords, ladies, knights, guards, and commoners who packed Orgulous Chapel, by command of their king. The chandeliers, drawn up high to the arched ceiling and brimming with an overabundance of candles, shone like tiny suns over their heads.

Sir Feolaghe, as the king's new champion, remained at his post, facing the crowd from the first step of the dais, bearing his broadsword across his thighs. Each wedding guest held a flickering candle, the light of which sparkled on Feolaghe's polished armor, transforming him into a constellation. Even his furrowed brow glistened with candlelight. The effort of wearing the heavy armor required for wartime champions at such ceremonies showed.

The bride's weeping mother sat in the first pew alone, save Hengest, who kept his distance from her, measured in spear lengths. Despite the festive occasion, the king's brother reclined in the only shadows with his arms folded. He frowned at his candle, which lay unlit on the stone floor.

"Lords of Lyonesse," the priest announced. "I present to you their Majesties, Ergyfel and Maeven, husband and wife, sun and moon, king and queen. Long may they rule!"

Feolaghe thrust his sword at the ceiling.

"Long may they rule!" the assembled guests cried.

The priest raised his hand. "Let us now withdraw, holding peace and love in our hearts until we meet again."

Ergyfel and Maeven stepped through the wicker arbor erected on the dais where a stone cross once stood. They descended the steps to the flower-petal-strewn floor and paused before the Stone of Bally-Dun.

The common people called the engraved chunk of marble the "Rock of Fate," and held that it would denounce any false claimant to the throne who dared set foot upon it. Ergyfel had managed to avoid this observance previously, by holding his unorthodox coronation in the great hall, but Maeven's mother had insisted on a "church wedding" and her father on Orgulous Chapel "for security," and so here he was, staring at the inescapable step. The new grout surrounding the rock attested to the success of Hengest's secret assignment, and should have allayed his fears. Ergyfel's head told him it was a lifeless stone, and yet he held his breath as he and Maeven stepped onto its broad white surface. Ergyfel exhaled with a grin as the stone silently sanctioned their marriage and dominion.

The king's new father-in-law handed him a silver longsword. "To defend the home and the homeland."

His new mother-in-law then approached and handed her daughter a light, broad basket of wheat. "To feed the home and the homeland."

Ergyfel hooked the sword on his belt, and then continued down the aisle with his bride. When they reached the center of the sanctuary, the two knights, whose duty it was to keep the main doors sealed during the ceremony, pulled the locking pins from the heavy oaken bars.

At that moment, there came a loud bang on the doors and muffled shouts from outside. The guards posted to either side of the enormous carved doors looked at each other and their king. Ergyfel and Maeven stopped. The shouts became more distressed. The guards drew their swords, and Ergyfel stepped in front of his bride. Another bang knocked dust from the doorframe. The king signaled for his warriors to open the doors.

The men lifted the heavy wooden bars and stood back.

The giant doors blew open, and a breath-like zephyr snuffed out the candles of the sanctuary with a snarl. Light from the newly risen full moon flooded into the chapel with extraordinary brilliance.

The guardsmen stationed outside maintained their positions with their backs to the chapel. They held their pole arms locked behind their sergeant, supporting him as he shouted at someone and struggled to push the person back from the doors.

"I'm tellin' you, you can't come in here with that ..."

All at once, the sergeant and his men fell back onto the floor of the chapel with a clatter of arms. All eyes trained on the silhouetted man, who crouched, panting in the doorway, carrying a long and unwieldy bundle draped over his arms. The sergeant's helmet spun to a stop on the floor, leaving only the sound of the man's labored, raspy breathing.

The stocky, ragged figure shambled through the door and stumbled over the feet of the fallen guards. The warriors on either side of him raised their weapons and stepped forward. He collapsed to his knees, shifting his load to his lap, and cradling it close with one arm. He cringed from the oncoming swords and raised one trembling hand above his head in surrender.

"Stop!" Ergyfel shouted, though his instincts said not to.

The king's warriors halted their attack. They lowered their weapons to a guarded attitude and looked to Ergyfel for direction.

"I want no stain of blood on my wedding day." Ergyfel studied the man.

He glanced to the side and saw that Hengest was almost to the rear of the crowded chapel. He caught his brother's eye and those of the two armed knights near the door and signaled them to remain ready to attack.

"Let him come forward."

The cowed man opened his lopsided eyes and relaxed his pose. He flashed a grin at Ergyfel, and eyeing the armed men around him, slipped his free arm back under his bundle and heaved up to his feet with a grunt.

The bright moonlight from behind the man reflected off a large puddle of water at his bare, big-toed feet, and it became clear that he and his bundle were dripping wet. He was a short, broad-shouldered man with dwindling straggled hair smeared feverishly about his head. His clothing was little more than dirty rags—the tattered ends of which trailed behind in his watery footsteps. As Ergyfel took in this wretch, he noticed the wet trail left in the man's wake.

Purposefully, the ragged man limped his way towards the king, grumbling in rhyme as if singing to his weary bones was habit. The crowd recoiled as he advanced. Then gasps and disdainful oaths rippled through the guests as they became acquainted with the stench of dead fish that preceded him. The foul odor impacted Ergyfel's senses and stiffened his neck while the man was still fifteen feet away.

The uninvited guest staggered to within ten feet of the king, and then dropped to the floor, exhausted. With labored breath, he laid his bundle gently on the floor between himself and the king and straightened it. At first, it looked like a large bundle of sailcloth, but then the stranger flung open the wrapping and exposed the pale body of a young girl. The body of Caenne.

Screams and fainting followed the unveiling, and Maeven dashed to the floor in front of her sister's body. She grabbed the girl and pulled her to her chest. "Caenne! Caenne! No! Caenne."

Ergyfel stared, shaken by the unpardonable wounds on her body. *What sort of monster could do such a thing?*

"I'm sorry, milady," the cruel deliveryman said. "I foun' 'er in the loch while I was fishin' this evenin'."

Caenne's mother and father appeared next to Maeven and huddled over their baby, sobbing and clutching her, rocking back and forth on their knees.

"Oh God! Take it back! Take it back!" her mother shrieked. Her cries quieted as fast as they erupted, becoming thin wavering sobs. "Oh God, no. Not my baby. Take it back."

Despite the growing stench the guests crowded in, attempting to get a look at the body and feeding some ancient appetite. Tighter and tighter, they packed in around the little drama, unable to restrain their morbid curiosity even when movement and breathing became difficult, even when the air grew heavy with the reek of death.

Again, the crude fisherman spoke. "I heard the bells of the chapel, all the way down on Loch Nyraval, callin' everyone to service ..."

The crowd hung on every word of the fisherman. He stole a gap-toothed smile and continued to draw them in with his tale.

"And then, pop! There she was. Come right off the bottom of me favorite fishin' hole."

Ergyfel sensed the air grow close. "Quiet, you!"

"Had a bit o' trouble draggin' her into me boat."

"I said, quiet!"

"Lass was so waterlogged she dragged me in with her."

"I said, shut up!"

With this, a tiny eel came out of the wound on the corpse's neck and slithered onto the wet, slimy floor.

The throng erupted in panicked screams as the guests nearest the body struggled to escape the human trap they had built for themselves, and those in the rear continued to push forward like cattle driven into the slaughter pens. Men and women fell and were trampled on by their spouses and friends as they tried to get away.

Ergyfel's ears rang and his chest tightened. His heart beat irregularly, in opposition to his resolute will. The more he fought to remain calm, the harder it became. At that moment, he noticed that a thin layer of water covered the floor of the chapel. The air was thick with decay. ... Decay laced with magic. He focused on the fisherman, whose lips curled on the verge of laughing.

"Stop it!" Ergyfel struck at the beastly man.

The fisherman caught the king's fist and turned his skewed eyes up to look at him. He put his free hand into his clothing and drew out a black iron knife. Ergyfel tried to pull away, but the fisherman's grip was adamant.

He held the blade out. "I found this on the shore near her body."

Hengest appeared and swung his heavy Saxon blade at the fisherman. The blade sliced through the air, then stopped abruptly. The room fell silent, and the light dimmed.

"That's enough from you, fierce one." The fisherman's voice took on a different timbre. He then flicked the edge of Hengest's weapon, which hummed like a tuning fork.

Ergyfel glanced about at the mob. All were frozen, like fish caught in ice, their mouths and eyes flung open in untamed terror. Water droplets, splashed up by their frantic feet, floated motionless in the putrid air.

"You're welcome, Ergyfel."

The king looked down at the fisherman and found him staring back. His eyes were now bulging red orbs, and a black stain that originated from his lips bled into his face in tiny sprawling tendrils.

"I knew you would want to thank me for bringing your wife this unsurpassable wedding gift." The fisherman showed his ice-like teeth and the inky inside of his mouth.

"Dheumon?" Ergyfel stared, wide-eyed.

The demon grinned. "Good. I'm gratified that you still remember me."

The demon tossed the iron dagger to the feet of Sir Feolaghe. It struck the floor with a curt chime, and then froze with the blade lodged under the knight's boot.

Ergyfel's mind reeled. He didn't know how he knew Dheumon. His diligent research on the ancient altar in Loch Nyraval had only recently yielded that particular name. Though he had meant to, he had not yet drawn upon its power.

"I don't understand. I did not summon you."

"I come and go as I please, Earth-bound."

Ergyfel's eyes went to his wrist where the fisherman's fingers had become squid-like tentacles, which bit into his flesh with sharp-edged suckers. They squeezed and twisted, and Ergyfel went to his knees.

"Oh." The demon gave a euphoric grin. "Your pain is exquisite."

The king pulled his wits together and spoke. "Is that why you've come, demon? To torture me?"

"Ergyfel…" Dheumon mocked dejection. "I come bearing gifts."

"How can you be here?"

Dheumon glanced about the chapel in a casual manner. "You and your brother desecrated this temple long before I did."

"What do you want?"

"Look here, mortal." Dheumon pulled Ergyfel near. "I am under no compulsion to answer your questions, but since this is your wedding day, I am inclined to consent."

Ergyfel looked into the demon's callous eyes. "My wedding day means nothing to you."

Dheumon smirked. "Right you are. And why should we have lies between us—such good friends."

"Why do you say we are friends?"

"Because it pleases me. I learned a great deal about human pleasantries from our last meeting, and how much I appreciate them."

"Our last meeting?"

"Yes. But one thing I do not appreciate is lies."

"Lies?"

"Yes, Ergyfel. Lies."

"What are you talking about?"

"I have no patience for lies."

"What lies?"

"Lies the mortal tongue should never speak."

"What lies?"

"Lies between one such as you and one such as me."

"I have not lied to you."

"I think it is time you received your gift. This is my wedding gift to *you*, Ergyfel. I give you ... the truth!"

At that, Ergyfel felt a jolt arc up his arm and sear his brain. A blinding light shone as if a curtain had been torn from a sunlit window, and then memories flooded into his mind. Memories of a hunting trip, of tapping the power of the altar rock, of a midnight ride through the woods, of Caenne staring up at him from the stone, and a cold iron knife in his hand...

Ergyfel flung open his eyes with a scream. His heart raced. He gasped for breath. He wanted to scream again, but all that came out was a kind of sob. He gulped down another breath of air as Dheumon continued to speak.

"You pledged to me the daughter of Feolaghe, and yet there she is beside you, newly bound to you as your bride!"

Ergyfel looked to his side, where Maeven kneeled next to her sister's body, her face buried in her mother's shoulder. Dheumon then pointed to Caenne.

"That is a poor substitute, a cheap trick, a forgery, a swindle! You think you can appease me with a clever mincing of words when I can read what is in your mind and smell what is on your heart?"

Ergyfel once again examined Caenne. The knowledge that he had inflicted her wounds magnified the horror. Now, feeling awakened, he realized he had been living a dream. He struggled to stabilize his mind as it caught up to his restored reality. It was jarring, and yet fascinating to Ergyfel how easily a few memories could rearrange his self-image. He remembered, now, the alchemist and his elixir of forgetting. Then, a terrible thought crossed his mind.

"Have you come to take Maeven?"

"You may keep her." Dheumon waved his hand in a dismissive gesture. The demon then turned to leave. "My interest in our little game is over."

Dheumon moved with surprising ease through the twisted mass of frozen wedding guests. He oozed between them with a squishing sound, changing shape as needed to fit through the tiny gaps, yet overall maintaining the unpleasant appearance of the fisherman. Ergyfel rose to his feet.

"Is Billy dead then?"

"Recovered your wits already?" Dheumon continued for the door. "I admire your resilience, your quick acclimation to your true identity, Murderer of Innocents."

"Is he dead?"

Dheumon reached the rear of the chapel and caught himself on the doorframe. On the threshold, he turned to face the king. His face was submerged in shadow, but it was obvious that he smiled from ear to nasty ear.

"That one?" Dheumon chuckled. "He is the reason I am leaving you alive."

The demon ducked through the doorway, and the chapel plunged back into chaos. Hengest's sea-axe came down on the stone floor with a clang, and the mob surged in around Ergyfel. It surrounded him and tossed him side to side to side. Even his bodyguards had become part of the feral, undulating throng.

Still more guests fell under the feet of the rabble. Sir Feolaghe threw himself over his family. The pushing and pulling continued and swelled until it heaved like a tempestuous wave rushing blindly into the confines of a narrow harbor.

Ergyfel had to do something quick, or all the guests and his beloved Maeven would perish. He focused all his will on a spell, and then thrust his hand into the air above his head with a shout. A deafening boom sounded as a blast of air knocked everyone off their feet.

When the crowd came to their senses, the oak-priest hobbled over to Ergyfel and offered his hand. Ergyfel, crippled by the pain in his arm, gratefully accepted the help, and then staggered over to help Maeven and her family.

"A powerful demon, my king."

Ergyfel turned about to face the priest.

"I did not see your battle, my liege, but I sensed it. Will the demon return?"

Ergyfel stared at the robed man, measuring the likelihood of Dheumon keeping his word. In the end, he answered from his heart and not his head. "I ... No. It will not return."

Long after the priest had walked away to give aid to the wounded and last rites to the dying, his question haunted the king. And, worst of all, the king knew that it always would.

***

The funeral procession dragged around Guthfana Tor and passed between the stone giants that lined the entrance to Tawel Nef. It was a lonely, forgotten warren of overgrown barrows marked by the occasional cairn. The sight of it further dampened Ergyfel's mood and caused him to tug his cloak closer against the monotonous cold drizzle.

The common folk of Nyraval had long since ceased to bury their dead in this dreary place. They much preferred the graveyard on the Loch Road, just outside the city's north gate. Many of the victims from the wedding calamity would be interred there. But none would be buried on this day. On this day, all else was put aside to mourn the tragic death of the queen's younger sister. To that end, most of Nyraval had turned out to watch or follow the black pageant as it wound its way to the resting place of kings. The crowd was not as large as the one that attended King William's funeral, but it had the added presence of a living king.

Caenne's body rested on a catafalque, like a thick bed of flowers, in a cart draped with black sashes. She lay with her head at the front and propped up on a small pillow. She looked, to those who followed the cart, as if she might be sleeping. A gauzy black veil draped over her body and allowed the viewer to detect the gold thread that adorned her favorite pale-blue dress. The horse pulling the cart had been chosen for its ebon color, as was his handler's elaborate garb.

As the head of the deceased girl's clan, Ergyfel's position was on the right side of the cart. His new bride walked just to his right, with her grieving parents falling in behind them.

A narrow, meandering road led the way through Tawel Nef and ended in the center of the sprawling necropolis, at the Royal Mounds—a row of three large but lazy hillocks, with the largest resting in the middle. Wide slate steps led halfway up the central tumulus to an angular dolmen of black stones.

On the approach to the base of the central mound, the cart hit a rut and lurched to the right. Caenne's left hand flopped out from under the veil, just inches from Ergyfel. He stared at the appendage and examined the lacy cloth and ribbons that wrapped around her wrist. He shuddered. He knew exactly what the wounds looked like underneath the absurdly feminine bandages.

He gnashed his teeth to drive away his weakness before glancing behind, but no one else had noticed. The mourners bowed their heads; all eyes fixed on the ground. He stared at Caenne's hand for a moment more, then abruptly reached over to place it back on the cart.

The girl's hand grasped his. Ergyfel's head snapped up to look at Caenne's face and found dull, grey, fishlike eyes staring back. She grinned at him and terror tore through his heart.

"Why did you kill me, brother?"

Ergyfel tried to pull away. Caenne's hand continued to cling to his. Its cold robbed him of heat, even through his glove. He scanned around him, but the mourners remained in position with their heads bowed.

Just then, his wife slipped her hand into his. He fixed his eyes on her, but she stared at the muddy road and continued to put one foot in front of the other, one tear behind the last.

"What can she do for you that I cannot?"

Caenne's dead eyes glared at him. Her grip held him firm. The arcane wound on his hand squealed, and he felt his bandages growing wet with blood.

"What do you want?" he whispered.

"I want the man that did this to pay," Maeven said.

Ergyfel flinched. He didn't think his bride had heard him. He stared for a moment at the road up ahead.

Then the corpse spoke again, "I want what she wants."

Ergyfel glared at her. Confusion, pain, and anger crossed over his taut features.

"I want everything she wants. I want you to hold me, Ergyfel, the way you hold her, the way you did that night, just before you gave my hand to Dheumon. There was a moment when you held me the way you hold her."

Ergyfel shook his head and attempted, again, to pull away, but the dead girl's grip on him was tight. The tender, inflamed skin under his bandage tore and he inhaled sharply.

"You must secretly want me, too. I know why you cannot bring yourself to be intimate with my sister. It's because of me. I know you sometimes see me when you look at her. It's nothing to be ashamed of. We two share a special bond. I feel it too. I love you, Ergyfel. I want us to be together forever."

"Stop it!" Ergyfel yanked away from Caenne.

The entire procession came to a halt and stared at their king. Ergyfel was stuck in an awkward pose in the middle of the road, bent over at the waist, and holding his left arm between his legs. The pain threatened to drop him to his knees.

Maeven leaned over. "What is it, my love?"

A drop of blood escaped his gloved hand, and Maeven crouched before him and offered her help.

Ergyfel straightened and stepped to the side of the road, cradling his arm. He glanced over his shoulder and saw that Caenne was resting peacefully on her bed of flowers, her hands resting just where her family had placed them. He turned his back on her as Maeven approached, and shuffled toward a stone bench between two nearby tombs.

"It's nothing."

"My lord."

Ergyfel sat. "I'll be all right. Please, continue. Let's get this over with."

Maeven placed a soothing hand on his back. "Yes, my love." She then turned and waved for the procession to continue. "Will you follow, my love?"

Ergyfel nodded. "Yes, my love. Soon."

The procession found its way to the tomb without the king. The bearers picked Caenne up by her flowery bed and carried it up the slate steps with her family in tow. As the body disappeared into the dolmen, many of the mourners turned back and began their trek home.

Ergyfel scrutinized the army of mourners as it disbanded. The long black train fractured into haphazard groups, which then broke into smaller clumps and traveled like leaves in a stream to Nyraval. His bodyguards, a handful of nobles, and a smattering of curious commoners milled about on the road, huddling together and gossiping in hushed tones. Only his bodyguards made direct eye contact with him. The king studied those who left and those who stayed, wondering if any had seen the dead girl take his hand. How many were avoiding his eyes because they had heard her damning words?

Did Maeven hear? No. She wouldn't love me if she knew. Her parents? Feolaghe would have tried to hack me to pieces by now—guards or no guards.

That woman with the blue necklace. ... She's staring at me! Who is she? Maybe
she saw. Maybe ... maybe it was an illusion—Dheumon still stirring around in
my head. Maybe ...

"Just in my head."

"What's in your head?"

He spun around. Hengest leaned against a cairn of boulders. He picked
at the damp rocks with his index finger and stared past Ergyfel at the
dolmen high on the hill.

"Is your conscience bothering you, brother?"

"Why, Hengest? Is yours?"

"Honestly? Yes. I'm beginning to see things—"

Ergyfel stood. "You saw her, didn't you?"

"Saw who?"

"The girl! Caenne!"

"Of course, I saw her. Everybody saw her."

"What? ... Why didn't somebody do something?"

"Do something? That's the point of a funeral, isn't it? Give everyone a
peek at the corpse before they hide it away. Before the unbearable truth
of it humbles us under its heel?"

"No! I'm not talking about ..." Ergyfel bit his lip. "You said you were
beginning to see things. Things like ... Caenne's corpse grabbing my
hand?"

Hengest stared at his brother through a long uncomfortable silence.
Ergyfel held his breath, waiting to hear his answer.

Still staring at his brother, Hengest answered, "I was going to say, I'm
beginning to see things *differently* now. Clearer."

Ergyfel turned from his brother. "I see. Since when did the specter of
death have power over you, the mighty warrior?"

"Since I came face to face with it."

"One little graze with death and you're a philosopher."

Hengest rubbed the red scar on his neck. "No. You're right. It wasn't
at the wedding. I've been wounded badly before, though not with my own

weapon. And I've seen fields running deep with blood while the crows feasted on my friends. No. What's chewing on me is witnessing the senseless murder of a girl child."

"It may appear senseless to you." Ergyfel pointed a finger at his brother. "But I assure you, it served a need."

"Whose need?"

"Keep your voice down."

"Whose need did it serve, Ergyfel?" Hengest asked through clenched teeth. "Whose need?"

Ergyfel took a step towards his brother. "Leave the philosophy to me, brother. Stick to your sword. It's the only thing you were ever good at."

Hengest turned away, and the king grabbed him by the forearm, bringing them nose-to-nose. The brothers jostled about, pushing and pulling. Ergyfel grabbed Hengest's throat, and Hengest drew back his fist. The king's bodyguards shouted and drew their weapons to charge. Ergyfel held up his hand to stay them, and Hengest lowered his fist.

"You're still saving me from beatings."

When the guards had returned to their position across the road, Hengest whispered, "I saw your eyes. That night, when you came out of the water. ... Doing what you did served a need in *you*."

"No."

"I saw it in your eyes, brother."

"I only gave the demon what it wanted."

"That's not what I read in your eyes."

Ergyfel thought back to the night of the sacrifice. He remembered stumbling out of the cold water, invincible and terrified. He could only guess what emotion his brother had glimpsed in his eyes.

"You are wrong, little brother. I did not want to kill the girl. I had to."

Hengest studied his brother's eyes. "It doesn't really matter, does it? What matters now is the blame."

"No one can lay the blame on me—on us."

"Someone already has."

"What are you talking about?"

"The body, the knife—they were laid at your feet."

"By a demon!"

"A demon you summoned."

"No one knows that."

"That won't stop them from gossiping."

"Let them gossip."

"Have you forgotten what a few wagging tongues did to our mother?"

"Have you forgotten the girl's blood is on your hands as well?"

"How could I forget?"

Ergyfel noticed blood trickling from the wound on Hengest's neck. "Oh dear. I seem to have undone my handiwork."

Hengest touched his fingers to the weeping wound and examined them.

Ergyfel put his hand over his brother's neck. "Hold still." He closed his eyes and concentrated on a weak wound-knitting spell, attempting to draw on the merest amount of power to seal the wound. His left arm stung, but not enough to break his concentration. A few heartbeats later, he was done.

"There. That should hold it."

Ergyfel put his hand behind Hengest's neck and leaned in until their foreheads touched. "Look, little brother, I'm counting on you. Try not to worry so much. Go ... comfort Cairmac's widow or, better yet, his daughter. Really give them something to gossip about."

Hengest turned and walked away, leaving Ergyfel to wrestle with his doubts alone. The king watched him leave.

He walks like a man who is about to stumble.

***

The builders erected the dark looming dolmen to hide the entrance to the royal tomb from rain and the light of day. As Ergyfel entered its shadow, he was grateful it hid him from the eyes on the road.

Steps descended from the back of the dolmen straight into the mound and to a long narrow gallery lined with tall, dark slabs of stone, which tilted in at the top and formed a stepped ceiling. Oil lamps hanging on long chains from the peak of the ceiling lit the way. A tight, complex band of carved knotwork wove its way along either side of the gallery, still gilt from the days of heroes long forgotten. At the end of the gallery, a squatty door with a broad stone lintel over the top broke up the uniformity of the wall.

Beyond this passage lay the grand chamber—an immense, lithic structure with a high, conical ceiling, decorated with gilt signs of the sky. The polished, circular floor sloped down towards the middle, sliced by an inlay of a spiraling white snake. Steep steps formed into a rough basin fifteen feet across at the heart of the chamber, and a deep censer of glowing coals jutted up from the focal point of the bowl, spraying mystical patterns of light through the images cut out from its body.

When he entered the chamber, Ergyfel's eyes were drawn to the censer, and then to the snake swimming through the reflection of the heavens. Only a few mourners remained in the grand chamber, but their every step and whisper resounded in the king's ears, sounding like a mob. He tarried there a moment, hoping to catch a treasonous tongue, but before he could distinguish individual voices, they fell silent. These courtiers, most of whom were friends of Maeven's family, bowed to their king, their solemn faces too brittle to smile.

Seven squatty exits led from the ornate grand chamber, with narrow, ambling passages constructed in the same fashion as the entrance gallery. Each one led to a cist where the chieftains and kings of Lyonesse had been interred since before the Waning of Giants.

The mourners parted before the rightmost passage, and Ergyfel entered. Here, the golden ribbon of knotwork on the walls was less dense and had a pattern that rolled with the rhythm of a gentle sea. A bold Christian cross had been carved into the lintel of the last doorway, the only sign of the new religion in the ancient tomb.

Ergyfel stepped through the final portal and entered the cist where Caenne would find her rest. It was an oval-shaped limestone cave with a high, smoke-stained ceiling that receded into an abyssal seam. Around the circumference of the chamber, niches were carved out of the rock to form beds for the dead. In the center of the room sat a low granite pedestal carved in the likeness of a small ship. The well-preserved remains of King William lay on the deck, adorned in battle armor and clutching a great sword to his chest. His head rested on a cushioned block that elevated his face to look at the door.

Ergyfel froze at the doorway. In the dim light, it appeared that his dead uncle was glaring at him. He had not seen the late king since his death, and having no interest in his final resting place, found his sudden appearance here alarming. Once he'd regained his breath, he crossed to a niche on the far side of the cist, where Caenne's family grieved over her body. As he passed by the dead king, he looked down on his face.

"He's hardly decayed." *Must be the poison I used.*

"Gives a nice color to my cheek, don't you think?" King William said.

Ergyfel jumped back from the corpse. Petrified, he stared at the body until he was sure that it wasn't moving. After a deep breath, he scanned the room and was relieved that no one had noticed him.

It's in my head. It's all in my head. What has that demon left behind in my mind?

He arrived beside his bride just as Caenne's mother kissed her little girl goodbye and was drawn away by her markedly aged husband. The noble couple bowed their heads to their king and walked away.

"Go ahead, Mother." Maeven touched her mother's arm. She made eye contact with her father. "I wish to stay just a moment longer."

Sir Feolaghe nodded then walked away, supporting his unsteady wife.

Caenne lay atop the cool limestone shelf, still surrounded by her bed of flowers. She looked still—peaceful.

Maeven took her husband's hand and continued to stare at her sister's lifeless body. Tears flowed down her cheeks. She was far beyond trying to stop them. She turned and planted her face in Ergyfel's shoulder. He wrapped his arms around her and held her as she sobbed.

Ergyfel embraced Maeven, just living in the moment, wishing he could take away her pain. He marveled at the hurt she must be feeling, and then his conscience reengaged, and he felt ashamed. Intrusive.

Since Dheumon had dispelled the apothecary's potion and returned his memories, his mind ran along two distinct trails, merging occasionally but more frequently clashing. Ergyfel knew who he was and what he was, but the taste he had once savored was now bitter.

He wondered how long he would have to stand there and hold her. He felt caged in their embrace—the monster trapped in broad daylight with his victim. As his self-loathing grew, he tried to come up with the right words to break the moment. Words that would make her want to leave. And, if she wouldn't leave, then the excuse that would release him.

"It'll be all right. I promise."

Much to his surprise, Maeven's face came up, and she did her best to sniff away her tears.

"You *will* make it right, won't you?"

Ergyfel leaned back. "Of course, my love."

Maeven produced the iron knife Dheumon had left on the chapel floor. Before he realized what it was, she had its blade very near his face.

Ergyfel snatched at her hand. "What are you doing with that?"

"It is the weapon that killed my sister."

"We don't know that!"

"I do."

Ergyfel stared at her and the knife and pondered just how she had come into such certainty. *How does she know? Is this more of Dheumon's scheming? Does she know it is mine?*

Maeven interrupted his thoughts. "I want you to find its owner ... and kill him."

"I ..."

"Use whatever means you must. The blackest magic, if you have to. I will pay the cost."

Her words echoed in his mind, bringing back the promise he had made in haste to Dheumon—the same pact that had brought about this tragedy.

"No!" Ergyfel released her hand and spun away from her.

Maeven stood and gaped at her husband. She bowed her head and walked to his side. When she was next to him, she looked up into his face. "So, you won't do it?" Hurt dimmed her eyes.

"No. I mean ... I will do it, but you will not have to pay any cost."

"What will it cost, husband?"

"It will cost you nothing. There is no *extraordinary* cost for what I will do."

Maeven gave him half a smile, then placed the knife in his hand. He took it and crossed his arms over his chest.

"Come along, husband." Maeven held out her hand at arm's length. "I'm sure my parents are waiting."

Ergyfel stared at her hand for a moment, remembering that just a few moments ago, he wanted nothing more than to walk out of the tomb with her. However, that feeling had left him and had been replaced by a desire to stay or, at least, be removed from her company.

"What is it, my love?"

Ergyfel didn't budge. Then he dipped his head and uncrossed his arms, putting the iron knife in front of his face. It wavered there, before he reached up with his other hand and took the blade between his fingers. He continued to focus on the knife and pretended to examine it.

"I, um ..." Ergyfel tapped his fingers with the flat of the blade. "I want to think about this." He punctuated his words by showing her the knife. They made eye contact over the point of the blade, and his mind came to a sudden halt.

"Think about it?"

"Yes. I want to think about how I'm going to find ... the owner ... of this knife."

"Are you well, husband?"

"Yes, I'm fine. I just need to be alone."

"Very well." She bowed her head, and then exited the cist.

With a deep sigh, Ergyfel leaned back and found the limestone ledge behind him with his seat. Now in deep contemplation, he stared at the knife in his hand. Before he had used it at the loch, it had been among his ceremonial tools for years. In fact, he remembered it was the first magical tool his mother had given him.

"No, wait!" he whispered, conjuring up old memories. "You *stole* it from her, didn't you?" He chuckled. "Yes, but only after the ole hag stole it from *Hengest*."

The impish smile fled from his face. He stared at the knife and tilted his head as if a different angle of light might reveal to his eye something of what his mind had glimpsed.

He tugged on the thin leather strap that wrapped the handle. It was no use. The strap was too tight. He shook his left hand and reached into his purse to pull out a small crystal. He then placed the crystal on the knife and rocked and chanted in whispered tones. Then he drew his hand back as if from boiling water and held it clenched and shaking by his cheek while he scrutinized the knife's handle.

"Ah!" His eyes penetrated the leather bindings. A moment later, he perceived a set of crude, shallow runes forged into the iron handle. "Yes. Still there." He released the crystal and his breath.

Ergyfel rested and allowed his muscles to relax, drained from the pain and exertion that scrying magic caused him. A comforting hand touched his shoulder and massaged its way to his neck. He allowed his head to roll to the side and relax toward his chest as the hand, though cold, pushed the tension out of his frame.

"That's nice."

"I told you I could do for you."

The voice was Caenne's. Ergyfel sprung from the niche and tripped backward over the foot of King William's granite pedestal. He scrambled to his feet and continued to back away. Caenne was motionless and posed as her family had left her.

He closed his eyes. "It's in your mind, Ergyfel. It's all in your mind. Now focus!"

When he opened his eyes, he saw that Caenne was stock-still. He then noticed the iron knife and crystal on the floor and retrieved them. With one last glance at Caenne, he turned and walked to the exit.

"Ergyfel."

The king spun and faced the niche where Caenne's body rested. The corpse was reclining on one elbow and grinning at him.

"See you tonight, lover." Caenne winked.

Ergyfel ran up the passage and through the grand chamber, pushing his way past anyone in his path. He did not stop until he was breathing the outside air, which he inhaled in great gasps as if he'd escaped from ten fathoms of water.

***

Ergyfel's wife and in-laws waited for him at the bottom of the hill. Maeven stood by her father, looking up the road towards Orgulous. As Ergyfel came down the last few steps, Lady Barane walked towards him.

Ergyfel nodded and began to address her. "Lady Barane. Shall we—"

Before he could finish, the Lady of Feolaghe Tor grabbed a rock from the road and chucked it at the king. Ergyfel broke from his shock just in time to duck. While he was still recovering on the slippery slate steps, the lady scooped up mud with both hands and rushed him.

"Murderer!"

She hurled the muck with all her might and fell face-first into a rut. Daubs of mud and pea gravel peppered Ergyfel.

"Are you crazy?" He bounded from the steps to the hillside.

Lady Barane pushed up from the sticky road and renewed her verbal assault of the king. "Liar, murderer, thief, brigand."

"What's wrong with you?"

Now up on one hand and one knee, she continued to fling mud and insults at the king. "Animal, butcher, devil!"

"Stop it, Mother!"

"Barane!" Feolaghe shouted.

"Stop her!" Ergyfel hopped away from her sloppy projectiles.

The king's guards sprung somewhat clumsily into action. They banged heads and shoulders as they scrambled to gather their spears and shields. Three lost their helmets, and two went down in the mud before they comprehended the nature of the danger.

Lady Barane flailed in the filthy road, flinging whatever she could at Ergyfel and yelling curses.

"God strike you, filth! Murderer! Fish guts!"

Her daughter and husband attempted to take her by the arms, but she would have none of it. She slipped away from them and rolled in the sticky mess of the road. As they tried to catch her, Sir Feolaghe fell to his knees, and Maeven had to catch herself on his shoulder to remain standing.

Ergyfel was confounded. What could he do? If he responded with violence or magic, he could lose Maeven. If he didn't shut the woman up, she would continue to proclaim to the world that he was a murderer.

"Dung!" Barane slung another handful of mud at him.

"Barane, stop it!" her husband cried. "Stop it!"

"Mother, please!"

The lady's family was now down on the road with her. Her husband held her around the waist while Maeven gripped one arm and attempted to gather the other. Lady Barane smeared them, wherever she could reach, with gritty muck.

"Liar! Toad! Spittle! Whittle! Vomit! Eye!"

"Hush now, Barane."

"Mother. Mother. Mother! Look at me, mother."

Ergyfel finished moving across the road and stopped to stare in awe at the berserk woman. She put mud in her mouth and spat it out at him.

"Kittle! Pluck! Cabbage!"

"Mother!"

Feolaghe took one hand and forced his wife's face towards his chest.

Still staring out the corner of her wide eye at Ergyfel, Barane continued to rant and kick her legs. "House! Maggot! Rain. Salt. Rabbit. Boot. Flour. Chalk."

At that moment, the king's guards arrived and jumped in to help. As the queen and her family disappeared behind the thicket of men's legs, Ergyfel could hear Sir Feolaghe ordering the guards to "be easy." Lady Barane continued muttering a string of unconnected words that deteriorated into unintelligible gibberish and blubbering.

Ergyfel turned and walked away.

Up the road, what was left of the fractured band of mourners had reformed ranks, unifying to gossip and gawk at the spectacle. It looked to Ergyfel as if their number had swollen beyond its original size.

He was furious. What would this scene with his mother-in-law cost him? What would it cost Maeven? Sure, the rumormongers whispered, nodded, and nudged courteously now, but that would not be the way of it later—when a belly full of free ale coaxed the fifth or sixth retelling. The gossiping rabble would dole out the story all the way home, if they bothered to go home, and their disloyalty would spread like a disease. Before morning, the entire city would be able to recite the tale as if they'd been present.

The leather of Ergyfel's gloves creaked when he made fists of both hands. Tighter and tighter he made his fists and arms until the pain in his left hand was squeezed out. Thus trembling with pent-up rage, he spat on the road and gave voice to a terrible curse.

"What you've seen you should not tell,
for if you do, your tongue will swell;
your gossip only leads to trouble,
when your tongue begins to bubble;
blisters in-between the boils
are payment for your tattling toils;

the pain and blood will just increase,

    until your wagging tongue you cease;

if you persist in loathsome quips,

    you'll find it's spread onto your lips;

your throat the burning sores make tight,

    your fingers rot if you should write;

so here your story I will quell,

    this curse will spread to all you tell."

There was a brief moment of quiet as the magical energy left Ergyfel's body. An instant later, the pain exploded in his left arm, all the way to his shoulder. His hand flew away from his side and flung him into the wheel of the funeral cart beside him. As he slid to the road, he plunged his hand into the mud, attempting to douse the fire-like pain. He forced his eyes open to examine the extremity, sure that flames engulfed it.

Ergyfel, though angry, had not chosen to use "rhymer's magic" without thought; it used less energy than casting other kinds of magic and required no materials. By Ergyfel's reckoning, it was the consummate way to weave a curse. He had even used this same curse before, although not on such a large number of targets.

There's so many. Shouldn't have tried to curse so many at once!

At that moment, a scream arose from the road. Then someone in the crowd of mourners was coughing and another moaning in pain. The sounds of distress increased and grew into a clamor.

Ergyfel eyed the mob. Many bent over, holding their mouths or throats, some spat, while others vomited on the road. The pain in his arm receded as the flow of energy subsided, and his sadistic pleasure grew.

The king pulled himself up by the wheel and sat on the end of the cart with his feet dangling off the back. He called for the groom leading the horse and ordered him to take him home. The young man turned the cart around and led the horse towards Orgulous.

Ergyfel held his arm and watched the ground pass under his feet. He felt exhausted, so he laid back on the cart and closed his eyes.

"Your Majesty!"

Ergyfel sat up and looked back to see his new champion, muddied from head to toe, trudging after the cart. He watched him, wondering how many steps before the old man gave up.

"Your Majesty!" The weary knight huffed. "I must apologize."

"Stop the cart."

Sir Feolaghe finished his quick-march and knelt before his king, who sat enthroned on the burial cart of his daughter. He bowed his head, panting.

"Speak."

"I must apologize for my wife, Your Majesty. She is not herself! Caenne's death has completely undone her. She's very confused. She didn't know what she was saying. She ... didn't know what she was doing. I don't think she knows where she is. I—I don't think she even knows who I am or who she is. Please, forgive her, Your Majesty. I'm sure, in her right mind, she would never have attacked her king."

Ergyfel studied the man before him. Having just lost a cherished daughter and faced with the real possibility of losing his wife, he was hanging by a thread. One little push and he could be made to do almost anything. Ergyfel wondered to what ends he himself might go to save his love, Maeven.

The king put his hand on his noble servant's head. "All is well, Feolaghe. Have my bodyguards carry Lady Barane to Orgulous. When she is safely in your chambers, call for my physician. Everything will be done, that can be, to make her comfortable."

"Thank you, Your Majesty. You are most gracious, Your Majesty."

"Now, go without consideration for anything, save your wife's well-being."

"Thank you, Your Majesty."

Sir Feolaghe rose and turned to walk away.

"Wait."

Ergyfel waited until the knight had returned to his former kneeling position. "There is one more thing."

"How may I serve my lord?"

Ergyfel held out the iron knife before Feolaghe's eyes. All the king's champion could do was stare at the hateful weapon in his master's hand.

"Take it."

His dutiful servant picked up the knife and held it.

"Now put it away."

Feolaghe slipped the knife into his belt.

Ergyfel leaned forward and whispered, "My powers have revealed to me that the owner of that knife is near."

Feolaghe stiffened. "Who is he, my liege?"

Ergyfel shook his head. "I do not know his name, but he lives among us in Orgulous. I don't know how to explain, but if you burn the leather off the handle, it will reveal the man's name. Do you know how to read the old runes, Feolaghe?"

"My grandfather taught me."

"Good. You will have need of them. When you have read the murderer's name, I trust you will know what to do."

"Yes, Your Majesty."

"But be warned, my trusted servant. My powers also revealed that this man is crafty. He lives by trickery, and fools all those around him. You must be careful. He is also a skilled warrior. You must approach him with stealth and deal swiftly with him before he can trick you, and before he can kill again."

"Again?"

"Even now, he seeks his next victim."

"It shall be done, my lord."

"Home," Ergyfel ordered over his shoulder, and the cart started up the road to Orgulous.

The king watched with great interest as he passed through the quiet mob of mourners. They had begun to break up again. The groups were smaller, less chatty, and more introspective. Thus satisfied, the King of Lyonesse smiled and reclined on the funeral cart for a nap.

CHAPTER TWENTY-SEVEN

Flight

"Hugh, stop!"

Hugh slowed his mount. "What is it?"

The giant rode the two horses up to Hugh at a trot. "We slow you down."

Hugh examined the winded giant. The lathered horses beneath him were lashed together with a beam and rope. He then fixed his eyes onto the smaller half of "we," and noticing Aeth's pained face, came to a complete stop. The others turned their horses and circled around the giant and ex-cutpurse.

"Sorry, Hugh. It's my leg. Can't take it no more."

Camion grinned. "His leg, my bum."

Sylvys dismounted and clomped, in his boots, over to the two horses under the giant. One of them neighed and nosed his shoulder.

"They've tried, Sir Hugh. They can give no more. Not at this pace."

Hugh surveyed the road. It was a portion of the King's Road scarcely traveled by merchant or noble. Any movement was certain to attract the attention of the invading army.

Hugh caught Billy's eye and nodded at Shaldra. Billy turned to the elf and tipped his head in the direction they had been traveling. The elf nudged his mount and charged up the road to have a scout.

The party of nine had been on the run for three days now. Each day had seen Camion and Aeth further behind than the day before. There was no argument from the rest of the party. All knew what a fix they were in and that they could have covered much more ground without their two stragglers.

Billy came closer. "We've got to keep moving. We're not even past the enemy lines."

"We know," the stragglers said.

"We probably shouldn't even be on this road."

"Hugh's right."

Malcolm rubbed his chin. "Agreed, milady."

Hugh sighed. "What do you intend?"

Camion tilted his head back. "Dyven is back there."

"Camion and me been talkin', and we both miss our sweethearts back in Dyven."

Malcolm leaned forward to see around the giant. "Sweethearts is it?"

"Aye." Camion grinned. "And warm food."

Hugh and Billy exchanged some quick glances. They knew very well that Aeth didn't have a girl back in Dyven, but neither of them cared to call him out. He was leaving them for their sake as well as his own.

"Well ..." Myrredith shifted in the uncomfortable Gwythian war saddle. "I can't thank you enough for rescuing me. Perhaps, when this is all behind us ..."

"Yes." Camion grinned. "Behind us."

"Perhaps, next time, we'll 'member to rescue some of your clothes, milady." Aeth laughed at his own joke, and the others joined him.

Lady Myrredith straightened the collar of her nightgown. "I don't know. It beats the dress my executioner had picked for me."

"And you." Billy turned to Aeth.

"What?"

"When all this business with the Gwythies is done—"

"Don't forget Ergyfel."

"Yes. Perhaps, but when this is all done, somehow, I'll make it up to you."

"Make up what, my king?"

Billy chortled. "You just won't give up on that tune, will ya?"

Aeth grinned and Billy reached over to take his arm. "Remember that day you first found me in the city?"

Aeth nodded. "Aye."

"You said, 'we're practically brothers, you an' me.' Do you remember that?"

"Aye. I do."

"It still goes."

Aeth grinned with all his teeth.

At the same time that Billy was saying his goodbyes to Aeth, Hugh was wishing Camion a safe journey.

"Thanks, but it is *you* going into danger, my friend."

"It's all in the way you look at it. Right now, you couldn't drag me back to Dyven."

"You haven't seen my woman."

"That's true."

Camion suddenly leaned in to Hugh and whispered, "But I see your woman." He gave a slight nod towards Lady Myrredith. "Take good care of her."

Hugh glanced back over his shoulder. "I shall."

Malcolm's mount had grown restless. It pitched back, but Sylvys grabbed its bridle and steadied it. "We've tarried long enough."

"Aye." Hugh gathered his reins. "Let's be off."

The six turned their horses up the road and galloped away. The giant and his newest buddy watched them go around the bend, and then turned their mounts in the direction of Dyven.

***

The six riders trotted west up the King's Road at a spirited pace. They had left Camion and Aeth about an hour before. They turned a sharp bend and, at once, saw a rider headed for them at a gallop. Shaldra.

"Run!"

"What?" Billy pulled up on his reins.

The rest of the party slowed. Shaldra continued riding at top speed.

"They're right behind me!"

"Who?" Hugh asked.

"It's an ambush! Run!"

The elf rode between them, splitting their ranks and turning the corner.

"Who is it?"

"The whole Gwythie army!"

The group exchanged glances in rapid succession. Their mounts turned in uneasy circles beneath them.

Billy was the first to break the relative silence. "Surely he didn't mean the whole—"

Billy stopped in mid-sentence. Drif had sidled up next to him and placed her armored hand on his elbow.

"Listen."

Billy remembered how Onian had taught him *spirit-listening*. He closed his eyes and took a deep breath.

A sound like a waterfall began to fill his ears. A breath later and it was like a heavy downpour on the roof of his father's inn. Then the raindrops became the clank of armor and thunderous hooves pounding the earth. Billy tried to focus in on the source, but it was too chaotic—there were too many. There were hundreds.

Billy opened his eyes. "Go!"

Billy and Drif turned their horses to follow Shaldra and bolted up the road with the others moments behind them.

Hugh spurred his horse to catch Billy. "What's happened?"

Billy looked over his shoulder. "There's an army on our tail! At least fifty!"

Drif glanced at him. "Eighty."

"How close?"

"They're almost to that sharp bend behind us."

"Our best bet is to get off the road."

"Aye, milady." Billy surged ahead. "Shaldra!"

The elf, still lengths ahead of Billy, slowed just enough to get close to his prince. "What is it, Your Highness?"

"We need a good place off the road to hide."

Shaldra was still looking back when Billy saw a score of knights wearing the colors of Gwythia coming up the road ahead of them. One of them looked very much like Prince Gaelyn. Shaldra saw Billy's eyes and mouth widen and turned around.

"Turn!" Billy shouted to his companions. Both he and Shaldra yanked their reins to the right and their mounts collided.

The road became a squall of dust and kicking horses. Sylvys gave a shrill whistle and the beasts leapt through the narrow gaps in the cramped forest that confined the road. Their riders had no choice but to hold on and pray.

They turned left and right, first by one tree, then between two, under low branches, over a log, skipping past a boulder, and then scraping by another tree and through a bramble. The ancient and forsaken forest offered no quarter and, in fact, grew denser. It closed in on them, forcing them to a course, like water in a streambed.

No stopping. No turning back. The Gwythians crashed through the woods behind them, shouting and blowing horns. Billy got a chill when he glimpsed Drif just off his flank. Being chased with the shadowy elf so close behind reminded Billy of the day he escaped the clutches of the Night Queen.

As they rushed through the tangled forest, a steep, rocky hill came up to meet them on their left and forced them back towards the west. They followed the contour of the hill, with the Gwythian horns growing louder. Then, without warning, the forest unraveled and they found themselves at the edge of a large meadow that rolled away from the hillock.

"Which way?" Billy was frantic.

Shaldra pointed back to their right, to a corner of the meadow where the deep tree shadows made a cave. At that moment, Gwythie warriors burst out of the darkness and flowed into the tall grass.

"So much for choices!" Malcolm slapped his mount on the rump and headed across the meadow after Billy and Shaldra.

They continued southwest beside the stone hill, but far enough into the meadow to avoid the rocky ground at its base. Drif threw up her shield and stopped an arrow that struck with a loud pop. A moment later, the air filled with arrows, falling around them like rain.

Shaldra looked up. "We've got to get Billy to those trees."

Sylvys reached back and pulled on the mane of Billy's mount. "Come on, you nag! Hurry up!"

Just then, something slammed into Billy's right shoulder blade and knocked him from his horse. He tumbled to the ground, stunned. By the time he stopped rolling and pulled himself up to his seat, the arrow in his back was screaming.

Billy cried out and reached back with his left hand to grab the arrow, but the offending missile was out of his reach. A moment later, a sharp pain in his ankle vied for his attention, and other injured parts started reporting in.

The rest of Billy's party, moving too fast, passed him by. Fortunately, they took the hail of arrows with them. First Shaldra, and then the others, turned around and headed back.

Billy waved them away. "No! Get to the trees!"

He tried to stand up, but the instant he put weight on his ankle it gave out and he fell back to the ground.

"Go back! Leave me!"

They would not heed him. Billy took a deep breath, closed his eyes, and tried his best to concentrate past the pain. He wished he could cast a spell from the black tome that would turn the arrows back against the cursed Gwythies.

Pain is not death, but life. Soon, it will pass. Look past the pain, past the pain, past the pain.

The peace Billy had hoped for came, and he remembered a simple spell taught to him by the Witan.

"A bird flies on two wings,
    the arrow, it has none.
When wind blows with mighty strength,
    they both shall be undone."

The next volley of arrows raced towards his companions. A sudden gust of wind came up from behind him. The arrows tumbled in the air and fell to the ground as if spilled from a quiver.

*

A moment later, Billy's friends arrived. Hugh, Shaldra, and Malcolm all jumped from their mounts and ran to Billy's side. Lady Myrredith dismounted and followed them as a gust of conjured wind defeated another swarm of arrows. Following Hugh's commands, the companions helped Billy up and Sylvys brought over his horse.

"Up on three. One, two, three."

The men heaved Billy up as Myrredith held the stirrup, but at that moment, a dense flight of arrows rained down on their position, and the zealous gust that came to their defense spooked the mount. It bucked and pulled away from Sylvys. However, the satyr held fast to the beast's mane and pulled its head down to whisper in its ear. After a half-hearted buck, the beast quieted, and Sylvys nudged the beast back towards them to try again.

"On three," Myrredith said.

Hugh nodded and started the count. "One, two ..."

Thud!

An arrow appeared in the saddle where they meant to place Billy, followed by a dozen more that stabbed into the ground around them. Malcolm grabbed the arrow and tore it from the leather.

"My spell shouldn't have stopped working … "

The meadow resounded with the howl from a Gwythian horn.

"On three."

Malcolm began the count. "One, two …"

"Wait!" Hugh looked to the sky for the next anticipated volley of arrows. "Wait 'til after the next volley."

They each held their breath. A moment went by and then another. Then they realized the arrows had stopped raining.

Hugh looked over his shoulder and saw twenty Gwythian knights descending on them from the rear. The banner of a prince and a battle signal-flag snapped over their heads.

"On three," Malcolm shouted, determined to get Billy back on his mount. "One …"

Hugh released Billy. "There's no time! They're on us!"

"Hugh! I can get him on myself."

With that, the Highlander began to lift Billy, but Myrredith caught his arm. She trained her eyes on Prince Hereweald. "It's too late, Malcolm. He's here."

Hugh drew his sword and stepped forward between Billy, Myrredith, and the closing knights. An arrow from Shaldra's bow whooshed over his shoulder and struck the knight carrying the prince's banner. The man grabbed his throat and tumbled off the back of his horse.

The Gwythian prince shouted, "Shields up!" and his knights raised their shields.

Hugh gritted his teeth, knowing that the next order would be "lances down."

Shaldra nocked another arrow and sized up his targets for a weak spot. Drif drew her sword; her hand bathed in an eerie, crackling blue light.

Malcolm pushed his horse forward to blunt the coming attack and filled his hands with daggers as he joined Hugh.

The Gwythians spread their formation into a line as they bore down on the companions. The prince raised his hand and commanded them to "Halt!"

The knights pulled back on their reins and brought their mounts to an unusually quick and orderly stop. Their leader leapt gracefully from the saddle, borrowing the speed of his horse to carry him just ahead of their dust-cloud and into the open ground between them. Hugh raised his sword and ran forward. The prince came to a stop and stood at an equal distance from his men and Hugh—no more than a lance-length either way.

Hugh continued his charge into the dust-cloud and swung at the prince with all his might. The prince pulled back, and Hugh's blade scratched his breastplate. Before the prince could react, Hugh spun his sword round and struck at his head. Once more, the prince tried to duck his attack, but Hugh's sword cut the strap on his helmet, and it went flying. The prince stumbled back.

Half the knights behind the prince rose up over their shields, with crossbows aimed at Hugh. At that moment, he heard the creak of Shaldra drawing back on his bow and the crackle of Drif's spell as she prepared to hurl it. He also heard Malcolm mutter, "One, two, three, follow me," as he raised his arm to throw.

The prince stood up and raised his hands. It was only at this point, with the dust settling, that Hugh realized they were empty; the royal sword remained in its scabbard. The prince held his hands out towards his knights and Hugh's companions.

"Wait, wait."

Hugh's enemy stood defenseless before him—less than a sword length away. One quick stroke and the prince would die. Hugh's grip tightened around his sword. At that moment, an owl hooted from the woods over his shoulder, and he gritted his teeth.

"You'll not rule me today," he muttered. Hugh dropped his sword arm. "Hold your fire!"

Drif concentrated and forced back the energy of her spell until it was a faint spark, which she released to the air. At last, when both sides had relaxed their stance, the prince and Hugh faced each other again.

"I did not come all this way to fight ya, Sir Hugh. Though, someday I might welcome the challenge."

"How do you know me?" Hugh looked down at his somewhat ragged attire. "I wear no colors. No marks of rank."

"Who else in Lyonesse would stand before twenty charging knights with no armor or shield and only a sword? Such valor is not common, in any kingdom. I also saw what you did at the battle for Cyndyn Hall, and have heard tales of your ferocity on the beach at Sceula Tor."

"No doubt from your father, Prince Hereweald."

"Ah! So we're acquainted to each other."

"If ya haven't come to fight, then why have you come?" Malcolm asked.

"He's come to kill me, haven't you, Your Highness?"

"No, Myrredith!" The prince attempted to see her face, but she was well behind her guardians and friends.

"You were going to execute me!"

Hereweald shuffled back and forth, trying to catch her eye. "No, well ..." He closed his eyes and scrunched up his face. "Yes, but thankfully you've outlived the date of your death warrant, and I have no mind to sign another."

Myrredith peeked around Malcolm's shoulder. "That's it then?"

"Aye. That's it." The prince smiled.

"Then, you must have come to kill me." Billy stepped between Hugh and Malcolm so the prince could see him. The prince tore his eyes from Myrredith to stare at Billy.

"And why should I want to kill you, little man?"

"I am Billy, son of Queen Eleanor and King William, and I am the reason you've come to these shores."

The prince's smiling eyes narrowed and seethed as he stared at Billy. "You killed my brother!" Hereweald drew his sword and stepped forward.

Hugh and Malcolm closed ranks in front of Billy, and Shaldra aimed his bow at the prince. The Gwythian knights again raised their crossbows.

"Whoa, whoa, whoa!" Lady Myrredith waved her arms and came out from behind her friends. She took a step towards Hereweald. "William is innocent of that crime, just as I am."

"You know I've come to believe in your innocence, despite what I've been told. Don't use that against me."

"He didn't do it."

"How do you know that? How can you really know that? You weren't there."

"I know William."

At that moment, the eighty mounted Gwythie archers arrived from the far side of the meadow, with Aeth and Camion in tow. They fanned out and formed a semicircle with the prince's knights surrounding Billy and his companions.

Aeth looked up from his heavy shackles. "Sorry, Hugh, milady. We didn't get far."

"The prince caught us."

Hugh nodded, grim-faced.

The commander of the archers dismounted and approached Hereweald. "Your Highness." He gave a crisp bow.

The prince nodded to the commander, then motioned for him to return to his men. "As you were, Centurion."

The prince then returned his attention to the lady. "I wish I could believe you, Lady Myrredith."

"You can."

"After you ran away from me?"

"Did you want me to stay and be executed?"

"No." Hereweald looked away.

"Then what?"

Billy put his hand to his head. "I don't feel so good."

The prince turned back around. "Just hand him over to me."

"And then what?"

"And then I will spare your lives."

"Never!" came the unanimous chorus.

"Never!" Sylvys thrust his spear in the air and knocked off his helmet.

He tried to cover his horns and reach down to scoop up his helmet. As he did this, there was a loud ripping sound, and his tail popped out the back of his pants. The satyr shot upright, tried to spin around to hide his tail, and tripped on his spear. Thus spinning off balance, he stepped out of his troublesome boots and stumbled in an arc until he regained his stability a short distance from his friends.

The Gwythies muttered and whispered. Sylvys froze where he was.

Prince Hereweald gawked at Sylvys, then strolled past Myrredith without blinking. His sword dangled in his hand. A few paces away, the prince bowed. Sylvys tentatively returned his bow with a nod.

"You are a satyr."

Sylvys looked at the human members of his party, who were likewise staring at him in amazement. He then looked to Billy. "I guess the bud has blossomed on our little secret, Your Highness."

Billy fell back on his elbow, blinking and shaking his head. "I ... guess ... so."

A heartbeat later, he was out cold.

CHAPTER TWENTY-EIGHT

Conspiracy

Billy awoke slowly. He didn't want to wake up. His bed felt comfortable. However, a sharp pain in his back prodded him into consciousness. He tried to roll away from the pain, but it just became more insistent. Finally, he woke enough to reach for the pointed object that was ruining his sleep.

"Don't touch that." The voice drifted through his daze.

His head and stomach ached, though not as sharp as the pain in his back. There was also a persistent tangy taste on his tongue. He cracked open his eyes and tried to sit. Immediately, he felt nauseous and rolled over to vomit next to his cot, where he found a pail and a bloody pan.

"That's to be expected."

When he was feeling better, he rolled back on the bed and saw the silhouette of a woman sitting next to him. In the dim light, his sleepy eyes could not make out her face. Above her head, ripples rolled across a large tent as they stirred in a gentle breeze.

"William, are you feeling any better?"

"Lady Myrredith. What happened? Where's Sir Hugh? Did we get away from the prince?"

"Not quite," Hereweald said.

Billy blinked and looked past Myrredith to the man sitting in a chair at the far corner of the tent. He sat next to a small table set with cups and plates for two, and a pair of stubby candles. The meal opposite the prince hadn't been touched. The flickering candlelight painted half his face, leaving the rest to swim in shadow. Even so, his resemblance to Prince Gaelyn left little doubt of his identity.

Billy woke fully.

"Summon the bowman."

The prince got up and crossed the fur rugs covering the floor to stand beside Lady Myrredith. Even in the dim light, Billy saw her tense. He also observed the prince reach to touch her, but then draw back.

"Lady Myrredith, would you leave us alone? We two princes have business to discuss."

Myrredith bowed her head. She then rose and turned to leave.

Billy noticed her fine dress—something that had been missing since their escape from Cyndyn Hall. "You look very nice, Lady Myrredith."

She looked down at her garments and smiled. "Thank you, Prince William. Prince Hereweald was kind enough to bring some of my things." She then bowed to Billy and left through a large flap in the tent.

The Prince of Gwythia picked up an object from the floor near Billy's bed. He wiped it off with a bloody rag and sat in the chair Myrredith had vacated.

A moment later, a voice came from outside. "Your Highness: Carius, the bowman."

The prince turned his face. "Come in, Carius."

The man entered, bowed to the prince, then stood very erect and still.

"This is the man who shot you."

"How do you know that?"

"There were quite a few who shot their bows in the meadow, but he was the only one to use a black arrow." The prince held up the broken arrow he had been fiddling with in his lap.

"Black arrow?"

"Poisoned."

"What?"

"My physician removed the arrow easily enough, but the poison is another matter. Carius, do you have any antidote for the poison?"

"I beg Your Highness—"

"Do you have any antidote?"

"No, sire. I haven't a dram." The man bowed his head but otherwise remained at attention.

"I see. I don't know whether to promote you or execute you. What say you, Highness?"

The archer shot Billy a fearful look.

Billy studied him. "If those are my choices, then I say promote him."

Both Gwythies flinched in surprise, and Carius smiled.

Hereweald leaned forward. "Why?"

"Killing him wouldn't change anything."

"But I have standing orders to use the black arrows *only* when commanded."

"A soldier's honest mistake."

"Tha's right, Your Highness. It were a—"

The Gwythian prince cut Carius short with an icy stare. He held it until the man dropped his eyes. "Well ... get out before I change my mind."

Carius wasted no time in vanishing from the prince's sight.

"So, as a dying man, do you wish to clear your conscience?"

Billy looked into a dark corner of the tent. "About what?"

"How about your part in my brother's murder?"

Billy looked Hereweald straight in the eye. "I loved your brother."

"People kill for love, do they not? Even the ones they love, on occasion."

"Not me."

"I wish there was some way I could believe you."

"I've never killed anyone!"

"No one?"

Hereweald's words cut across Billy's thoughts, to the deaths of Sir Banarel and Dhwen, King William's physician. They seemed an age ago, and yet the sting was still there.

"Well ..."

"Who was it? Did you kill my brother?"

"No. But there are two deaths I feel responsible for."

"So, you admit you *are* a murderer."

"No. But they died because of me." Billy sighed. "Oh, wait ... how could I forget?"

"What?"

"Don Miguel. Him, I killed."

"And who was he?"

"The man who killed your brother."

The prince sat back in his chair. He rested his face against his fist. "Is that the way you wish to die—as a liar?"

"Look." Billy sat up with unexpected strength. "If you're so sure I did it, then why are you asking me?"

"Why indeed? Well, it looks like the antidote is working. See, you're already regaining your vigor."

"Antidote?" Billy examined his raised fist.

"I ordered my physician to administer it after he removed this." The prince waved the broken arrow.

"Then, you saved me?"

"So it would seem."

"Why?"

The prince rubbed the stubble under his chin. "I don't know. Maybe it's because I'm superstitious. Maybe I don't wish to kill a prince without first hearing his side. Maybe it's because you travel with a satyr."

"With Sylvys?"

"Aye. Were you aware they cannot tell a lie?"

"No. I never heard that."

"It's true. My people have revered them for centuries."

Hereweald paused to pull a large, bronze medallion from his tunic. He held it before Billy's eyes. It had the image of a woman on one side and a satyr on the opposite. As the disk spun in the dim light, the two images came together in an embrace. Billy couldn't help but smile at this simple illusion.

The prince leaned back in his chair and spoke over his shoulder. "Bring me the satyr."

"Yes, Your Highness," came the disembodied voice from outside.

"Carefully!"

"Yes, my prince."

Hereweald sat up straight. "My mother's clansmen were priests in the old days. And though most of the nation have turned to the Christian god, the old ways live on."

"And you?"

"I was bred for one purpose: war. My father needed a son to fight his battles. Even when my older brother sits on the throne, I will be fighting his wars."

"What's that got to do with—?"

"I have no time for this Christ. What matters right now is my belief in the purity of satyrs."

"Purity?" Billy chuckled.

"Aye. Not by your Christian standards, but by virtue of their very nature."

"Why do you say I'm a Christian?"

"You have their weakness for forgiveness." With this, Hereweald held up the broken arrow once again.

"As I said, it would change nothing to execute Carius."

"It is weakness. He is your enemy. He invaded your country, killed your people, and burned your towns. You must hate him. We are at war! It is weakness not to diminish us, even by one man."

Billy sighed. "I saw what you did to Dyven. I felt all of those things and more. I assure you, it took more strength to give life than death."

"Spoken like a Christian."

Billy smiled. "I really don't know much about it. My father thought us Christian because our king was, but the valley I grew up in had no church, nor priest."

"They didn't need one. They had you, preachin' forgiveness and peace—weakness."

"Maybe I just know the truth when I hear it."

"Ah, the truth!" Hereweald sat back in his chair again. "I nearly forgot where all this was going."

The prince very deliberately put his fingers together, forming a bridge between his hands. He stared at Billy over his fingers. "You have an uncanny knack for conversation, young prince."

"Thank you."

"I admire an opponent with cunning."

The voice from outside announced, "Sire, the satyr is here."

"Send him in."

The prince stood as Sylvys entered the tent. He wore not a scrap of clothing or armor, and other than his graying hair and downtrodden face, he looked just as Billy remembered him on their first meeting.

"King Billy, are you well?"

"I'm feeling better, my friend. The prince has supplied me with an antidote for the poison."

"My thanks to Your Highness."

Prince Hereweald bowed to him. "Sylvys, is it?"

"Aye."

"You called him 'king' instead of 'prince.' Why is that?"

"I only speak of what is to be. Or so is my hope."

"So, you hope Billy will become king?"

"He is already my king."

"Is it true satyrs cannot lie?"

"Lies always seem like such a waste of time, don't they?"

"So you *don't* lie?"

"Not that I recall, though on our current quest, I did attempt to deceive, not with my tongue, but by disguising myself. However, as you can see, it was ultimately a waste of time! My brothers didn't understand why I did it."

"I do."

"You do?"

"I would have done the same in your position." Hereweald turned to Billy. "You see, the very concept of lying is foreign to them."

Sylvys shook his head. "Oh, I know of lyin'."

"I'm sure you do, just not in your own kind."

"Quite true. Although, if you consider *Greater Faerie* my kind, then I can tell ya, Malkry is the mother of lies. That elf hates the truth. And don't get me started on Goblins ..."

"Truth." Hereweald circled the satyr. "That's what I want from you, Sylvys: the truth."

"If it's the truth you seek, then you shall have it."

"Good. Then tell me, did Prince Billy kill my brother, Prince Gaelyn of Gwythia?"

"And Lyonesse."

Hereweald glanced at Billy. "... And Lyonesse."

Sylvys cleared his throat and stood up straight and tall. "I don't know."

"What do you mean, you don't know?"

"I wasn't there when the fair prince was slain."

Hereweald frowned and crossed his arms with a grunt.

"I can tell ya that I believe Billy did not slay your brother."

"On what basis do you believe that?"

"He told me."

"He told you, and you believed him."

"I still believe him. I believe him because I believe in him."

"I was told that satyrs, when you could get them to talk, were creatures of few words. But not you."

Sylvys looked down. "As of late, things haven't been great for me. I'm not myself."

The prince grunted again. "You may leave."

Sylvys bowed to Billy, and curtly to Prince Hereweald, then turned to go. Without warning, the prince grabbed Sylvys by the tail and plucked out a hair.

"*Ouch!* It was bad enough when they started turning grey. Now I've got humans pulling them out!"

"My apologies." Hereweald examined his prize.

Billy squinted at the hair. "Why did ya do that?"

"Because I am in need of a truth compass."

"A truth compass?"

"Aye." Sylvys sighed. "Though I'd hoped men had forgot that trick by now."

"We've not all forgotten the old ways."

"Your Highness is a wizard, then? I did not sense it in you."

"No, Sylvys. But my mother comes from a line of oak-priests and bards."

"So, what is this truth compass?" Billy asked.

The prince lifted his index finger and indicated that he should be patient. "I'll show you." He went to his table, picked up a large metal bowl, and dumped its contents on the floor. He then poured some wine into the bowl. With the bowl in hand, he turned around and searched the floor of the tent. "Ah! Perfect." He bent down and picked up a sizeable rowan leaf that had blown in. He placed the leaf so that it floated on the wine, and then he placed the hair plucked from Sylvys' tail on the leaf. He put his hand over the bowl and stood. "*In vino veritas.*"

Sylvys smiled. "I always liked that line."

Hereweald came back to Billy's bed and sat in the chair, holding the bowl with both hands. "Truth compass. Point to me."

The leaf turned slowly, to point with its tip towards Hereweald.

"Truth compass, point to Prince Billy."

Again, the leaf turned and pointed to Billy.

"Wow!" Billy's eyes widened. "It's magic."

"Ptach!" Sylvys frowned. "A cheap trick."

Hereweald ignored Sylvys and continued with his calibration of the truth compass. "Truth compass, point to your maker."

After a slow turn, the leaf pointed to Hereweald.

"Now, truth compass, when the truth is spoken, you will point to your maker's right hand. When a lie is spoken, you will point to your maker's left hand. "I am Prince Hereweald."

The leaf pointed to his right hand.

"I am the third Prince of Gwythia."

The leaf pointed to his left hand.

"Good. I believe it's ready."

"Bah," Sylvys said.

Prince Hereweald turned towards the satyr. "Please, leave us."

Sylvys again made his bows and left.

Hereweald returned his focus to his captive. "Prince Billy, tell me, did you kill my brother?"

"No."

They both watched as the leaf moved to point at Hereweald's right hand. The prince stared at the compass for a while, and then he looked up.

"It seems you were telling the truth."

"Yes."

"Tell me a lie. Something I know is untrue."

Billy thought for a moment. "Your brother, Gaelyn, hated you."

The leaf turned to point at the prince's left hand, and he closed his eyes. A pained expression crossed his face and then vanished. When the prince opened his eyes, Billy thought he detected a glint of friendship.

"I loved him too," Billy said.

The leaf moved more quickly to point at its maker's right hand.

Again, the stony face of the second Prince of Gwythia seemed to crack. A brief grin landed on his lips, but then threatened to flutter away. "He was easy to love, was he not?"

"Aye. I especially loved his laugh."

Hereweald's half grin expanded into a smile, and he snickered. He closed his eyes, which bled a tear. Again, pain clouded his expression. He caught the eye of the young man across from him, and an enduring moment passed between them.

The prince's face lit up. "Do you know who killed my brother?"

"Yes."

The leaf continued to point true.

"Who was it?"

"Don Miguel was the assassin, but he didn't act alone."

Hereweald fixed his eyes on the truth compass. "And this Don Miguel is dead?"

"Yes."

"What of his conspirators?"

"Ergyfel, the usurper, now King of Lyonesse."

"Who else? Were there any others?"

"Sygeon, Ergyfel's half-brother, and ..." Billy hesitated.

"Yes. Who else?"

"I don't know, but I suspect there was another."

"Why?"

"Someone had to plant that second dagger in my room. It couldn't have been Ergyfel, and I know Sygeon was away from Orgulous."

"My spies tell me Sygeon died choking on his own blood."

"He's dead?"

"Aye. Rumor has it that King William cheated me of the pleasure."

"Oh."

"That still leaves me Ergyfel."

"And the other."

"Yes." Hereweald's eyes shifted. "The other ... Truth compass, I command you to point now to truth if the answer is yes and to lie if the answer is no."

"What are you doing?"

"The truth compass will only function for a short time. I must use what time I have left to find out what I can."

Hereweald closed his eyes and breathed deeply. Billy swallowed hard in anticipation.

"Truth compass, is the mystery conspirator living?"

The compass held on truth.

"Is he still in Orgulous?"

The leaf turned to indicate no.

"Is he still in the employ of Ergyfel?"

No.

"Is the conspirator far from Orgulous?

Yes.

"How far?" The prince grimaced. "You can't answer that. You probably couldn't tell me if the conspirator was in my own camp!" The prince growled and looked to the side, brooding.

Billy pointed at the compass. "Look! It's moving."

Hereweald looked as the leaf turned in the bowl. "It's probably broken now."

The leaf continued to rotate until it pointed at the prince's left hand.

"It's still working."

The compass began to point to true.

"That means it moved ... because something I said ... was false."

The compass stopped on true.

Hereweald looked at Billy. "What did I say?"

"Well ... You asked it how far from Orgulous the second conspirator was."

"Yes, but it can't answer that kind of question!"

"No," Billy muttered to himself. "Ah! But then you said ..."

"Yes ... ?"

"Let me think. You said ... it couldn't tell you if the conspirator was in your own camp."

"That's it!" the prince exclaimed. However, his excitement quickly turned into brooding. At last, he leaned over the bowl and whispered. "Is one of the conspirators in my camp?"

The compass remained on "yes."

Hereweald thought for a moment before asking, "Is the conspirator in this tent?"

No.

"Do I know the second conspirator?"

Yes.

Prince Hereweald stood up and addressed his truth compass. "Truth compass, point in the direction of this conspirator."

The compass wavered for a moment and then pointed toward the tent exit. The prince turned around, and the compass held its position on the tent flap.

Billy grunted as he rolled to the side of the bed and put his feet on the floor. He shrugged his aching shoulder and gripped it with his left hand. Surprisingly, his ankle hurt little.

"Where do you think you're going?" his captor asked.

"I'm coming with you."

"Remain in your bed. This is no concern of yours."

Billy looked the prince in the eye. "Oh, really?"

The prince narrowed his eyes, but when Billy didn't budge, he smirked. "Very well. Come if you must."

"I must." Billy stood to follow the prince.

The prince grinned once again and turned to exit the tent, still carrying the truth compass with both hands.

"Allow me." Billy pushed aside the flap.

The prince nodded and exited the tent.

They stood outside and surveyed the camp. The night remained cool, and the ground wet from a recent shower. It was a much larger camp than Billy had expected. The tents for five thousand men—a rippling sea of canvas—floated over the bottom of a broad valley. The moon shone from its seat high up in the sky and turned the white fabric of the tents pale blue, except where the amber glow of firelight forced its retreat.

The sentries on either side of the tent entrance snapped to with their spears pointing to the sky.

The prince turned to one of them. "Stay here. I'll watch the prisoner."

"Yes, Highness."

Hereweald and Billy followed the compass towards the middle of the camp. As they cleared the innermost circle of tents, Billy spotted all the members of the rescue party, including the giant Camion, Aeth, and their damsel in distress, Lady Myrredith. They huddled around a campfire, surrounded by guards on all sides. The only one not fitted with chains was Myrredith.

When they approached closer, the compass led them straight for the prisoners. Lady Myrredith rose and turned around to face them. The prince froze and stared at her. Billy got on his tiptoes and saw that the compass pointed directly at her.

"You lied to me!" The prince was fuming.

"Oh William, what are you doing up?"

"Never mind him. You were the one who conspired to kill Gaelyn."

"No." Myrredith backed up half a step.

The prince advanced to maintain his distance. "I tried to show you my heart, but all you wanted to do was tear it out."

"No." Myrredith stepped to her right. "I …"

"Stop!" Billy exclaimed.

"You weren't satisfied with bringing down the fairest Prince of Gwythia. You had to finish your foul purpose with me." His eyes boiled with murderous intent.

Myrredith looked terrified. Again, she stepped to the side, and again the prince followed in kind. Billy reached out to stop him.

"Your Highness, that's not possible."

"Quiet! She obviously fooled you as well."

"But she wasn't there."

The prince stopped. He then looked down at the truth compass and saw that it pointed away from Myrredith and towards a tent just behind the prisoners.

At that moment, the compass jiggled, then moved. The prince turned and stepped towards the tent. He froze, and the compass continued to move. Billy strained to see what direction the leaf pointed.

Myrredith stood behind them with her hands on her hips. "What's going on?"

Both princes shushed her, and she stepped back.

A moment later, the flap of the tent opened, and out popped Lord Snegaddrick, half dressed and stumbling. The former ambassador blinked and rubbed his eyes.

"What's going on out here? I was trying to sleep—" He shut his mouth when he saw his prince a few paces away. "Your Highness. What can I do for you?"

"You can take a few paces that way." The prince nodded to his right.

Puzzlement writ on his face, Snegaddrick pointed to his left. "What, over there?"

"Aye."

Snegaddrick looked down, shrugged, and walked to his left.

"Stop. Now walk in the other direction."

Snegaddrick pointed. "That way?"

"Aye!" The prince had a bit of fire in his voice.

Billy watched as Hereweald followed Snegaddrick with his truth compass.

"Now walk around me in a circle."

His advisor adjusted his garments and walked in a circle.

"What is that you are holding, Your Highness?"

"Keep walking."

All the guards and prisoners were watching with great interest as Hereweald ordered his advisor this way and that, and each time, his voice grew more forceful.

"What is it, Your Highness?" Snegaddrick made another turn. "Have I been lax? I'm no soldier, you know. All these orders. Is it something I said? Something I did?"

"Halt, you miscreant."

Snegaddrick turned and faced Hereweald. "What?"

The prince took two quick strides and kicked Snegaddrick. "Traitor!"

Snegaddrick fell back to one knee. "Your Highness—"

"Villain!" The prince gave another kick, which sent Snegaddrick onto his back.

"There's obviously been a mistake!"

"Yes, Snegaddrick, and you have made it."

The prince snapped his fingers. Guards, who had been watching the event, grabbed Snegaddrick by his arms. They picked him up from his rear, and then shoved him onto his hands and knees before the prince.

"What is it you think I have done, Highness?"

"You conspired to kill my brother … "

"No."

"The third Prince of Gwythia … "

"No."

"… and heir, with his wife Princess Katherine, to the throne of Lyonesse."

"No, Your Highness. That's not true."

"My truth compass says it is."

"Your truth compass?" Snegaddrick stared at Hereweald's hands. "Why, that's just a myth, Your Highness. They don't really work."

"This one does."

"But you would need hair from the tail of a—"

"Satyr?" Sylvys appeared behind the prince's shoulder.

The prince turned and nodded appreciatively.

"I ..." Snegaddrick fidgeted. "I—I—I ... I can't believe this!"

"Speak, you swine-hearted, treacherous, lying dog!"

The prince's anger exploded, and he kicked his former advisor in the face. While he was still down, Hereweald spat on him and kicked him in the ribs. He then bent over him and continued to batter him with insults. "You spineless snake! You worthless toad! You worm! You're cow dung! You're nothing! Nothing!"

Snegaddrick shuddered with each insult as if struck by a heavy fist. At last, Hereweald took a step back, and his victim pulled himself out of the mud to a kneeling position.

"I didn't mean for it to end that way, Highness. You must believe me."

Hereweald turned to a messenger, who stood watching from nearby. "Bring me a scribe." The man ran away with speed and purpose, and then Hereweald turned back to Snegaddrick. "Go on, Lord Snegaddrick. I'm dying to hear how you'll try to worm your way out of this one."

"I would not waste my prince's time with such games, or press his patience."

The prince turned to Billy and handed him the truth compass. "Truth compass, treat Billy as your maker and tell us when Lord Snegaddrick is lying. Billy, watch him closely."

When Billy took the bowl, he felt a small amount of magic pass from his mother's ring into the bowl. The leaf, which had been drifting a bit, snapped into position.

At that moment, the scribe arrived breathlessly with the tools of his craft. He rolled them out on the ground and sat next to the prince. Hereweald acknowledged the scribe, then turned back to Snegaddrick, wiped his hands, and crossed his arms.

Snegaddrick sat back on his knees. "You see, Your Highness, from the beginning, I was against the marriage. Sure, I sent my glowing reports of

Princess Katherine. All true, I might add. But I was not ready for peace with Lyonesse and especially not with the king who'd killed my son."

"You had a son?"

"Yes, Your Highness, long ago. He was killed at the battle of Sceula Tor."

Hugh stepped forward. "Your son was there?"

Snegaddrick glared at Hugh. "Aye, Butcher of Sceula Tor!" He spat at the ground as if to punctuate. "It brought me great pleasure seeing you named a conspirator in the murders. Too bad I won't live to see you hanged."

Hereweald snapped his fingers to get Snegaddrick's attention. "You were saying ... "

"I honestly don't know how it occurred. ... I think it was over a few pints of ale, but Ergyfel's brother Sygeon and I got to talking. He wasn't from Lyonesse, you know. Turned out, neither of us wanted the marriage to go forward. He arranged a meeting with Ergyfel, and the three of us planned the assassination of Princess Kathryn. But I had only a small part in it."

Billy watched, as the leaf spun to point to his left hand. "He's lying."

Snegaddrick shot an incensed glare at Billy. Hereweald stepped forward and slapped the ex-ambassador across the face.

The guards grabbed him up and once again threw him facedown before their prince. Snegaddrick righted himself to his knees and stared at the ground.

"What do you want, Highness?"

"I want to hear your part in it. *All* your part in it!"

"Why? It won't bring back Gaelyn. It won't bring back our bonny prince."

Hereweald stepped forward and struck him again. "You will not say his name again. To hear you speak his name with your treacherous tongue disgusts me."

After a moment to collect himself, Snegaddrick restarted his tale. "It was I who recruited Don Miguel. Humph. They were going to use one of Sygeon's clumsy operatives. They didn't know a trained assassin was right under their haughty noses, but I did. You see, I had used him before. But that is another story."

"Yes. One story at a time."

"Well, there really isn't much more to tell, Your Highness. Don Miguel was successful in his mission, but before he could make good on his escape, your brother and Billy caught him. If it weren't for that encounter, your brother would be alive, at home in fair Gwythia."

"What happened next?"

"Ergyfel was hosting a feast that evening, a kind of diversion, and I was in attendance, partly to secure my alibi should I come under suspicion. Shortly after the feast began, I saw the Spaniard whispering in Ergyfel's ear. By the way he held his hand, I could tell Don Miguel was injured, and I could see that whatever he had said to Ergyfel had upset him. So, after a short while, I approached Ergyfel. He pulled me aside and told me to collect a particular dagger from Don Miguel and hide it in Billy's room. I found the Spaniard telling one of his degenerate tales to some eager gluttons. When I sat next to him, he slipped me the dagger, and I naively did as I was told. I think Ergyfel had planned to betray *me*, but he made Billy his scapegoat instead. So, I slipped back into the feast and continued as if nothing had happened until the alarm sounded. The rest, I think you know."

"And what was the reward for your part?"

"What do you mean, Your Highness?"

"Surely you would have bargained for something more to help Ergyfel; something to sweeten the pot."

"But I've already told his Highness. My reward was revenge for my son and continued war with a country and king I hate."

Billy cleared his throat. "There's something more."

Hereweald glanced at Billy, and then back to Snegaddrick. "A shrewd man like Ergyfel would never have trusted those motives alone. He would have wanted to know you had a tangible price. And I'm sure, knowing you, it was steep."

Snegaddrick grunted. "I have sorely underestimated his highness's resourcefulness." He bowed his head, admitting his defeat. "My apologies."

"So, what was it?"

"All right." Snegaddrick held up his hands. "Ergyfel promised to pay me a healthy sum in gold and jewels for my part. But that's it."

"That is all?"

"Yes, Your Highness."

Hereweald turned to Billy. "Well?"

Billy watched the compass. "He's holding something back. There's still something more."

"That thing can't be working!" Snegaddrick shouted. "My prince, surely you cannot believe that—that—that fairytale over my word!"

"It's working fine." Hereweald looked over Billy's shoulder. "In fact, I believe it is working better now than a moment ago."

Hereweald then stepped closer and leaned forward so that his face was very near to Snegaddrick's. "What are you hiding?"

The prince's one-time advisor turned away, but Hereweald grabbed him by the jaw and forced his face forward. Snegaddrick clenched his eyes closed, and then pulled away from the prince's grip. They repeated this a few times before the former ambassador relented. He stared into the prince's eyes; his own filled with anger and pain.

Snegaddrick held his gaze and whispered, "I cannot tell, Your Highness."

Hereweald stared at him. "Your life is already forfeit, man. What profit is there for you in holding back?"

"I'm not concerned for my life, Highness."

The prince narrowed his eyes as he examined Snegaddrick's face. "Whom are you protecting?"

Again, Snegaddrick whispered. "I still have a wife and a daughter." Then he leaned back from the prince and announced, "I throw myself upon the mercy of the king."

Hereweald looked surprised, but then stood up and walked in a circle around Snegaddrick, while scratching the stubble on his chin. At last, he stopped. "As a Lord of Gwythia, it is your right to request judgment by the king, and so you shall have it."

The prince turned to the guards. "Take him to my tent and make sure he doesn't leave."

The men picked up their charge and hurried him away. Hereweald made eye contact with Billy and held it.

"How are you feeling?"

Billy scrunched his injured shoulder and flexed his ankle. "I'm actually feeling better, thank you."

"Then come with me."

Hereweald and Billy followed the soldiers who carried Snegaddrick, and the scribe got up to accompany them. The prince turned to the scribe and held up his hand.

"Go back to your tent, and perfect what you have transcribed while it is fresh in your mind. Then make the usual copies. I will call for you later."

The scribe bowed and left.

As the two princes approached Hereweald's tent, the Prince of Gwythia turned to his young companion. "Billy, on your princely right as heir to the throne, do you promise never to reveal to a living soul what you are about to hear?"

The prince's demand of an oath took Billy by surprise, but he nodded. "I do."

The prince looked up from the truth compass in Billy's hands. "Good."

Hereweald held open the tent flap for Billy, and then entered behind him. He ordered the guards on either side of Snegaddrick and those outside the tent to leave.

When the prince was satisfied, he turned to Snegaddrick. "There are no royal scribes, nor warriors to hear. It is only you and me, Snegaddrick, and this Prince of Lyonesse, whom I have sworn to a solemn oath on his birthright never to reveal what passes between us."

Snegaddrick looked up at Billy with tear stained cheeks and then to Hereweald. "Very well, my prince. What will you have of me?"

The prince grabbed a chair for Billy, then one for himself, and they sat in a close semicircle, with Snegaddrick on the floor before them.

"As before, I want to know everything about this plot. As cunning as you are, I know you wouldn't plan a nap without some kind of permission from above. Who in my father's court conspired with you, and what was your price? I want the truth, now."

"You don't know what you are asking for, my prince."

"Let me be the judge of that. You just tell me what you know, and Billy will see to it that you don't wander from what's true."

Snegaddrick bowed his head.

One spell from the black tome and he'd beg to tell us the truth, Billy thought before forcing down his desire for revenge.

Hereweald crossed his arms and leaned back. "Tell me, Snegaddrick. You hinted that your wife and daughter might be placed in danger if you should tell me what I wish to know. Let's start with that."

"I assure Your Highness that if what I know were to leave this tent, they would be dead shortly."

"How is that possible? How can you be so sure they would die?"

"Because I know well the man who would have it accomplished."

"How could this man act with such impunity?"

"Because their deaths wouldn't be seen as a crime."

"What? How?"

"Public execution, Highness."

"Public execution?"

"By strangulation."

The prince shot up and paced around his tent. After a few laps, he stopped behind his chair and examined the man on the floor.

Billy felt uncomfortable in the silence. "He's been telling the truth ... so far."

Hereweald addressed Snegaddrick. "I know now why you have been so circumspect, *Lord* Snegaddrick. And why I have felt that you were keeping something back from me on this campaign. Yes, a great many pieces to a complex machine I unwittingly brought with me from Gwythia are coming together."

Snegaddrick nodded. "Of that I'm sure."

"When I received news of Gaelyn's murder, I was offshore of Albion, awaiting final orders to invade. The whole Albion campaign—building ships, training, hiring mercenaries—it was all a ruse, wasn't it?"

Snegaddrick bit his lip. "Aye."

"How long have you coveted your current title, *Lord* Snegaddrick?"

The former ambassador smiled. "You might as well ask me how long I have wanted to breathe."

"My father knew you wanted it, didn't he?"

"I suspect he did."

"Yes. Father seems to know each man's price before the man himself."

"He has a singular talent, Highness."

"Tell me, in the *master's* plan, was Gaelyn weighed on the scales?"

Snegaddrick looked at Billy and the truth compass, then back to Hereweald. "I had hoped you wouldn't ask that."

"That's not an answer."

Snegaddrick closed his eyes. "The possibility did come into the conversation."

"Who brought it up?"

"Your father."

"And what was his verdict?"

"It was ... an acceptable risk."

Billy cleared his throat. The leaf of the truth compass oscillated between true and false.

"He was more than an acceptable risk, wasn't he?"

Snegaddrick didn't answer.

"What was your deal with Don Miguel?"

"Triple his fee if he *happened* to get the prince. I was surprised how little a prince's life is worth."

Hereweald turned and went to the tent flap. "Guards!" Then he returned to the tent. "I've heard enough." He grabbed the truth compass from Billy and flung it across the tent.

"I am sorry, my prince." Snegaddrick stood. "I *did* wish to spare you that burden."

"You have nothing to be sorry about. You are a faithful servant of your king. There should be no shame in such patriotism and loyalty."

"I thank Your Highness."

"Unfortunately, a royal scribe has taken your testimony. You will be tried by my father and likely strangled."

"I suspect so, Highness."

"But you can still spare your family's life."

"Yes, Your Highness." Snegaddrick looked to Billy.

Hereweald put a hand on Billy's shoulder. "The lives of a woman and her daughters now rest in your hands, Prince."

"They have nothing to fear from me."

"Good. Good. … What's wrong?"

"Why is the tent spinning?" At that moment, Billy stumbled to the cot and vomited into the pail again. A moment later, he collapsed to the floor.

*

One of Prince Hereweald's bodyguards entered the tent. "You called, Sire."

The prince turned from Billy to address his soldier. "Take Lord Snegaddrick to his tent. He is under full arrest. Place guards and see to it he doesn't wander off."

The guard saluted, then grabbed Snegaddrick to take him away. As he rose, the prince addressed him again.

"Send for my physician right away, and Lady Myrredith. Prince Billy has suffered a relapse."

"Right away, Highness."

Hereweald went to Billy's side. He scooped him up off the floor and laid him back on his cot. He peeked under Billy's bandages and frowned.

"Stanch little man. Might make a good king someday. But will you side with me or against me?"

***

Billy woke up shivering.

"William?"

"Myrredith."

"At last! How do you feel?"

"Cold. So cold."

"You have a fever, William. You should never have left bed."

"I had to."

Billy saw the shadow of a man standing behind Myrredith. "Who's that with you?"

"It's me, Hugh."

"Where is the prince?"

"He's in bed with a fever," Shaldra said. The elf appeared from the shadows—smile first.

Billy forced a tiny smile. "Good to see you, my friend."

Hugh knelt beside the bed. "Hereweald is meeting with his commanders. Judging by the commotion, he's getting ready to move his army."

Billy tried to sit up, but Myrredith pushed him back and plumped his pillow.

"What has happened?" he asked.

"We were hoping you could tell us."

"What do you mean?"

Myrredith took Billy's hand. "Since your meeting with him and Snegaddrick, the prince has changed."

Hugh nodded. "After making his physician staunch your bleeding, Hereweald ordered our chains removed, and quartered all of us in his officers' tents."

"And he's allowed us to move about freely."

"Freely?" Hugh laughed. "You obviously haven't noticed the two bookends I'm dragging around."

"Oh, Hugh. They're just escorts."

"Heavily armed escorts, which I've noticed you haven't been shackled with, milady."

Shaldra leaned in behind Hugh. "Don't worry. They're slow. We can slip away from them easy enough."

"Perhaps, but to where, and to what purpose? Until we know what Hereweald is up to, our best course is to stay attached."

Myrredith tucked in Billy's covers. "Besides, William isn't well enough for an escape."

Billy felt like his skin would cook on his bones. He kicked off the furs covering him, but again Myrredith stopped him from getting comfortable.

She shushed him. "Lie still. You must rest."

"What's wrong with me?"

Myrredith looked to Hugh. She then turned back to Billy.

"Is it the poison?"

"No, Billy. No. The physician is certain it's not poison."

Shaldra leaned in. "I also checked. It's not poison."

"Then what?"

"I don't know. The Witan didn't teach me what to do next. You're lucky I remembered how to fix your ankle."

Hugh stood up and gripped the hair on top of his head. "We don't know. The arrow was a clean removal, and your wound is clean and stitched up nicely. There's no infection. It wasn't that deep. But in the past few days, it should have healed more."

"Days? How long was I out?"

"Three days, William." Myrredith brushed a lock of his hair aside. "We've been so worried."

"Your Highness," Shaldra said. "I spoke with Sylvys and Drif. We all agree that your mother's ring has the power to heal you. Now that you're awake, use it, and let's get out of here."

"Mother's ring." Billy felt lightheaded. "And Drif agreed?"

"Aye."

"How is she handling captivity?"

"Not happily, Your Highness, though she's got her *bookends* falling over themselves to impress her."

Billy smiled.

"Now, Your Highness. It's time you used the ring."

"Yes." Myrredith touched his shoulder. "Please."

Billy nodded and closed his eyes. At first, it was difficult to concentrate—the heat and aches of his body kept interrupting his composure. At last, his mind reached out and touched the ring to tap its magic for healing, as he had done before, but something was different. The way the ring interacted with his mind was all wrong. It had always felt warm and accommodating, but now it was frigid and unwelcoming. The edges of the ring grew sharp, and then it pushed him away.

Billy's eyes snapped open just as Prince Hereweald entered the tent.

"Ah! The young prince awakes."

Hereweald passed by his guests and knelt beside Billy's cot. He nodded to Myrredith, then placed his hand on Billy's arm. "The preparations are complete. Two legions have already set out, and we march for Nyraval on the morrow. Beyond that: Orgulous. Soon, you and I will rid the world of this villain, Ergyfel!"

"Ergyfel," Myrredith muttered.

"Aye. I swear on my brother's blood, I shall not leave Lyonesse until the tyrant of Orgulous is dead!"

CHAPTER TWENTY-NINE

Desperate Call

The tyrant of Orgulous sat upon his stolen throne, meditating on the tattered leather scroll that rested across his lap. His eyes drifted to the pile of books and scrolls next to the throne, but gravitated back to the crumbly, fur-trimmed parchment before him with its curled edges and bold red symbols. He focused on the most complex glyph, which stood alone at the bottom. The intricate lines stirred within their parchment prison. Its power was tangible.

Ergyfel closed his eyes and gripped the bone horn, which had been lashed to the scroll by a silver necklace with a large, vacant gem setting. A small twitch flickered in his neck, followed by another. He inhaled sharply and opened his eyes. He nodded, then stared at the scroll, taking in its entirety.

"A warding pact."

The quiet but hurried footsteps of a servant approaching roused King Ergyfel from his trance. He watched the intruder through the corner of his eye as the man fidgeted. Ergyfel counted by moving his fingers. He got up to three before the man cleared his throat, and Ergyfel restarted the count. The servant's limit for patience soon proved to be four, a sure sign that something was amiss.

With his amusement fading, Ergyfel turned to the man. "Speak."

"Ambassador Snegaddrick has just arrived, sire."

"What insolence!" Ergyfel erupted from the throne. He descended from the dais and, grabbing the messenger by the collar, backed him into a corner against the steps. "Is he here to gloat? Is he here to bargain for our surrender?"

"I—I—I don't know, Your Majesty. I was only told to inform you of his approach."

"Where is the snake now?"

"The outer ward, I should think."

"The outer ward? You let him into Orgulous?"

"I—I—I didn't ..."

"How many in his entourage?"

"I believe he's alone, sire."

The king released his grip on the man and turned away. "What is he up to?" He scratched his beard. "Could he be here to kill me?"

"Your Highness?" The timid servant stepped back.

Ergyfel spun around and, again, pinned the servant to the steps of the dais. "How many warriors are with him? How many bodyguards?"

"A—a—as I said, sire, he is alone."

"Alone." Ergyfel turned and ambled back to the throne.

He plopped down in the seat and rested his mouth against his fist. He tugged on his lips, then turned to the servant. "Go. Fetch my brother. Have the seneschal greet Snegaddrick when he arrives at the donjon. That Gwythie blackguard is to wait out there for one hour. Then *you* shall let him in. But ..." Ergyfel held up a finger. "No fanfare; not one dram of deference. Don't even announce him. Am I understood?"

"Perfectly, sire."

***

The main entrance doors to the great hall of Orgulous, through which all dignitaries entered and exited, were a pair of richly carved, copper-clad oaken giants designed to humble even the haughtiest prince. Built into the massive southernmost door was a narrow, cupboard-like entry, used by servants and messengers. This seldom-used access at the rear of the great hall creaked open, and Lord Snegaddrick stumbled in.

Ergyfel and Hengest watched from the dais as the former Gwythian ambassador peered into the dark recesses of the great hall and scuttled past them, shuffling over the spacious stone floor to the dais. His usual meticulously cultivated bearing was less aloof than on previous visits to this court. Despite the hour-long opportunity given him to rest and pre-pare, he still appeared disheveled, sweaty, and breathless.

Snegaddrick reached a respectable distance from the king and halted. He glanced from side to side and then bowed. As his head reached its low-est point, a long span of chain fell from the folds of his cloak to the floor. He snatched it up as if no one had seen and resumed an erect, composed stance.

Ergyfel and Hengest exchanged glances and stifled grins.

"Ambassador Snegaddrick. I am at a loss. Why have you come before us?"

"I have come because I have an offer for his majesty."

"Offer? What can my enemy offer me, except to die?"

Hengest unsheathed his sword and leaned forward.

Snegaddrick retreated a step and bowed his head. "I am not Your Majesty's enemy!" he announced in a bold voice.

"No, Snegaddrick? Then what could you possibly have to offer me?"

The Gwythian scanned the nooks, crannies, and balcony overlooking the hall. He then leaned forward. "Are we alone, Your Majesty? Are we free to speak of our former relationship?"

Ergyfel grabbed Hengest by the bicep. "This is my brother, Hengest, from whom I have no secrets."

"Then he knows of our former arrangement?"

"Yes."

"With the Spaniard?"

Ergyfel sighed. "Yes, he knows, as I've told you."

"Shall I kill him now, brother?" Hengest stepped forward and raised his naked blade.

Snegaddrick recoiled and dropped his chains once again. This time, his shackled condition was unmistakable.

Hengest stopped at the steps of the dais and laughed.

Ergyfel laughed too. "I instructed my servant to be inhospitable, but I didn't expect him to put you in chains. I shall have to commend him for his zeal."

"It was not your servant, Your Majesty. It was my prince."

"Prince Hereweald put you in irons?" Ergyfel cackled.

"Sadly, yes."

"Ah, Snegaddrick. There were times I would have paid to see you like this."

"In a way, that is why I am here in this state before you."

"How is that?"

"Because you paid for a certain deed to be done."

"My patience is wearing thin, Snegaddrick! Speak plainly, or I will have Hengest flay you where you stand."

Hengest grinned.

"I am in chains because Prince Hereweald knows of our conspiracy to assassinate Princess Kathryn and Prince Gaelyn."

"I had no part in planning your prince's death. That was an accident! Your assassin got careless!"

"The prince does not know that."

"Oh, really? So if he knows about our conspiracy, how is it he does not know I am innocent of his brother's blood?"

"It never came up."

"Never ... !" Ergyfel pounded the arm of his throne. "And how is it he knows about the conspiracy at all? Did *you* tell him?"

Snegaddrick dropped his eyes.

"You fool!"

"The prince throws a mean beating." Snegaddrick returned his eyes to Ergyfel. "Between that and a magic truth compass, I had no choice."

"Magic?"

"Aye."

"Is the prince a sorcerer?"

"No, Your Majesty, but he is familiar with the old ways."

"Folk magic?"

"Some call it that."

"You let him beat you with folk magic?"

"That and his boots."

"So you've said."

"But it wasn't just folk magic. His truth compass really worked!"

"Truth compass.... Wait. I think I know this one ... but he would need to find a real, live satyr." Ergyfel laughed with his brother.

"He travels with a satyr, Your Majesty."

Ergyfel fell silent.

"And an elf and an elf-witch—"

"What? You've lost your wits, man!"

"That's not all, Your Majesty."

Ergyfel studied his former conspirator, who was now mum. He sat back in his throne and folded his hands just below his chin. Then, still staring at Snegaddrick, he put his index fingers to his lips.

Not an echo stirred in the hall.

At last, Ergyfel lowered his fingers. "How much is this going to cost me, Snegaddrick?"

"Very little, Your Majesty."

"Remember my patience, Snegaddrick. How much?"

"Foremost, I want Your Majesty's protection and your word that no one will harm me."

"And ... ?"

"My former quarters here in Orgulous."

"And ... ?"

"Well ... a small stipend to cover expenses, say one gold Lion a day? And another thousand when I leave."

"A thousand?" Ergyfel exclaimed.

"I have valuable, timely information about Prince Hereweald, his army, and his plans."

"Very well. But if I find you have deceived me in anything, you'll wish I had let Hengest flay you."

Snegaddrick bowed.

"So, tell me about these *creatures* traveling with him."

"Well, Your Highness, in all truthfulness, they are traveling with Billy, the son of William and Eleanor."

Ergyfel shot up from his seat with a shout. "What?"

"It's true, Your Majesty! In fact, he and Hereweald have formed an alliance of sorts."

Ergyfel contemplated this and returned to his throne. "Yes. I believe you because I have seen it in my dreams. Tell me, quickly, does Billy still bear a simple ring upon his hand, with a small iridescent stone?"

"Well. ... Aye. I did notice a small ring on his hand when he was helping the prince interrogate me. He was the one holding the truth compass."

"Yes, of course. I might get my hands on it yet."

"On what, Your Majesty?"

Ergyfel looked up. "What about troop strength and location? What are his plans?"

"He has three full legions—"

"Three legions?"

"Yes, Your Majesty, plus two more that have taken heavy casualties. But I don't think they will trouble Your Majesty, as they're licking their wounds and marching far behind the others."

"Three full legions? And he came here with five?"

"Caesar's second and successful invasion of the Britons took five legions. The king—your opponent—is a great admirer of Caesar and would emulate his success."

Ergyfel frowned and rubbed his temple. At last, he turned back to Snegaddrick. "How many mounted?"

"Each legion includes three-hundred cavalry."

"And knights?"

"Hereweald has twenty in his personal guard, but there are easily sixty more still able to ride and do battle. Oh yes, and Sir Hugh."

The king sat straighter. "Hugh has joined Hereweald?"

"Well, technically, Hugh and the others are still prisoners of the prince. They're not in irons." Snegaddrick shook his chains. "But they're not free to carry arms either—at least, not yet."

"But, ... you suspect that will change."

"Despite my efforts, Hereweald is quite taken with the Lady of Cyndyn, who is also his prisoner, and he has become oddly fond of Prince William."

"Of Billy?"

"Yes. I've seen him doting on Billy like a little brother."

"How cozy. So, where are they?"

"By now, they will be a day or two from Hillshire, Your Majesty."

"Hillshire? Already?"

"Yes, the prince is of one mind now. Since he learned of our little arrangement, he's skirted around any major town or stronghold. He's set his eye on Orgulous."

"Hillshire's no more than three days from here."

Hengest produced a stone and began sharpening his sword. "An army that size will take at least five."

"Four," Snegaddrick said, with an apologetic bow. "Our legions are mostly hardened troops, trained for forced marches. The mercenaries, he's paying extra to keep up. If they continue with no resistance, they will easily be here within the week."

"Well done, Snegaddrick. You have proven your worth to me, but I'm curious: why risk coming here when you could have easily disappeared altogether?"

"Where else could my information be of such value, Your Majesty?"

"I know you love money, Snegaddrick, but as jaded as you are, you're still a patriot."

"I am a pragmatist."

Ergyfel cocked an eyebrow, and Snegaddrick continued. "To 'disappear,' as you put it, from the royal family when you've provoked their wrath is no mean trick. It will take a heap of gold. I calculate about one piece a day to keep out of reach."

Hengest examined the edge of his weapon. "So you're giving yourself a thousand days."

"If I haven't sailed off the map, fallen through a crack, and vanished in a puff of smoke by then, I'm as good as dead."

Ergyfel smirked. "Quite. Leave us now and go to your quarters. I will summon you when I have more questions. Until then, rest easy. You are safe here in Orgulous."

Snegaddrick bowed and turned to leave.

"Oh, yes ..." Ergyfel waited for the Gwythian to face him again. "Go to the smith and have him remove those ridiculous chains. And send the seneschal in as you leave."

"Yes, Your Majesty." Snegaddrick bowed again.

Hengest sheathed his sword and returned to his brother's side as Snegaddrick coerced his feet to the ignominious portal of his entry. The king followed the Gwythian's every step.

Hengest glanced at his brother. "Do you believe him?"

"Mostly."

"Do you trust him?"

"Only as far as you can throw him."

"I'll throw him from the top of Orgulous if you like."

"Patience." Ergyfel smiled.

"I don't like it. You can never trust a traitor."

"We can trust him ... until he gets his gold."

Hengest nodded. "As you wish."

The seneschal of Orgulous entered the great hall. Ergyfel leaned towards Hengest. "By the way, I am pleased to see you have done away with that unbecoming piety and returned to your former sensibilities."

Hengest's jaw tensed as he glanced at his brother, then back to the approaching servant. "Blood is the strongest morality."

The king looked to his brother and saw him staring back. "Aye. That was mother's favorite adage."

"I know my path lays with you, brother."

Ergyfel smiled with his eyes.

When he had finished giving instructions to his seneschal regarding the care, feeding, and surveillance of Snegaddrick and was again alone with his brother, he turned to Hengest. "So, what news from your friend Leif?"

"He camps near Lys Scosek, in Cornwall, as we speak."

"How many men was he able to gather?"

"Some five thousand and longboats enough."

Ergyfel gave a resentful grunt. "We shall need every one." He picked up the tattered scroll. "And something more."

The king grabbed up quill and parchment and scribbled.

"What's that?" Hengest asked.

Ergyfel answered while he wrote. "Orders for Feolaghe. He will be commanding my army. He must gather all my armies to ... Rowmeadow. Yes, that's the perfect spot."

"You can easily hold Orgulous and Nyraval with the army you have now."

"And have Hereweald starve us into submission? No."

"I suppose you're right. In a siege, your army would make short work of the food."

"Precisely." Ergyfel scribed on his orders once again. "And thanks to King William's generosity, we haven't got much. How soon can you have Leif and his men here?"

"Four or five days, with favorable winds."

"You have three."

"That's impossible."

"Not if I help you."

"The way you helped me return here after Amaranth Heath?"

"Yes."

Hengest shivered. "I'd rather you didn't."

"Look, brother." Ergyfel put down his quill. "Hereweald's legions could be battering the Gleaming Gate in six days. I mean to stop him before he gets to Nyraval."

"Very well."

"I will gladly send someone in your place. Actually, I'd rather you stay here to help me plan."

"Leif will not deal with just anyone. Besides, I'm the only one who knows the location of their secret camp."

"Then go and prepare everything. Collect the gold you will need from the vault and meet me here in the great hall." With that, Ergyfel sealed his orders for Feolaghe, using his signet ring, and stood up.

Hengest also got to his feet. "I only need to gather a few items, brother. If you wait but a short while, I'll be right back."

"Take your time, brother. Have something to eat. I must leave Orgulous for a few hours, but will send you to Leif upon my return."

"Do you need me to accompany you?"

Ergyfel picked up the tattered scroll and paused. "No. It would be best if I go alone. I'll take a troghoul for protection." He turned to Hengest. "There is one small task you can do for me before you leave."

"What is it, brother?"

"Our new friend Snegaddrick has implicated me for what was probably his involvement in Prince Gaelyn's murder. See to it that Hereweald knows exactly where the old fox has run."

"My man shall leave at once. But, brother, where are you going at this late hour?"

"To treat with a very old ally, who may even our chances against Hereweald."

***

Guthfana Tor, a desolate rocky butte, rose from the plane of Gadrian with its back against the Hag's Teeth—a vertical stone ridge that petered out to the north, but to the south, joined the Draig Mountains that protected Nyraval on three sides. Ergyfel remembered Caenne's funeral as he left the road to Tawel Nef and headed up the steep track to the summit.

The last time I summoned a spirit to my cause, things did not work out so well. Could this be a mistake?

He looked up from his saddlebow and saw Caenne standing beside his path.

"Hello, lover." She gave him a crooked smile. "Mind if I tag along?"

Ergyfel ground his teeth. At that moment, Reiver, the troghoul loping just ahead of his horse, passed through her image, and she dissipated like steam. He closed his eyes, took a deep breath, and exhaled. Despite two more appearances by Caenne, Ergyfel remained calm to the top of the butte.

The top of Guthfana Tor was as stark and flat as Loch Nyraval, which Ergyfel observed glittering under the moon in the distance. An ancient watchtower slept in ruin next to a large firepit at the center of the mountaintop. The lonely site's long abandonment was journaled on wood and stone alike by remarkable colonies of lichens.

As the king approached, he could see that the blackened stones circling the firepit were stolen from the old tower. In their center, a tangled pile of half-petrified sticks and logs still waited to signal warriors who had long been in the ground.

Ergyfel called Reiver to his side. The loathsome creature ambled over to its master, sniffing at the ground and air.

"Anything?" Ergyfel eyed the cavernous shadows of the ruined tower.

The creature shook its head and Ergyfel dismounted. He then pulled out the leather scroll and presented it to Reiver. After a quick sniff, the beast circled round the firepit and entered the ruin while Ergyfel stayed his ground. Shortly, the creature emerged from the shadows and made its way around the broken structure. When this short patrol was finished, Reiver came back to the firepit, squatted, and shrugged.

Ergyfel tied his horse to a low-lying shrub and stepped to the rim of the pit. *I suppose we could use a fire.*

He picked up a pinch of dead grass, clapped his hands, and rubbed them together while creating a tiny cave with the grass in the middle. As he stepped closer to the firepit, he whispered into the gap between his hands and blew. A faint light appeared between his palms and he blew some more, coaxing the tiny spark into a flame. Then, in a quick movement, he threw his palms towards the dormant pyre and shouted, *"Ignis viva!"* A fountain of embers shot forth from his hands, igniting the twigs and logs.

The pain and energy drawn by this simple task—this simplest of spells—was far more than Ergyfel had counted on. He dropped to his knees before the growing blaze, gripping his arm and baring his teeth.

"How could that take so much?"

Eventually, the pain subsided, and Ergyfel pulled out the old scroll and horn. While he examined it under the firelight, he noticed that an anonymous author had cut three mundane runes into the surface of the bone horn—three runes from the old ways. When he tipped it into the light, he could see them plainly. The first and last were both simple, but the middle symbol was a dark, byzantine sign.

Ergyfel translated them. "Our ... calamitous—no—*dire* ally."

An ominous prophecy, but for whom? "Surely it's for our enemies." *Of which I have many!*

The thought of all his enemies encamped together against him tightened Ergyfel's gut. He put the horn to his lips and blew. The sound that issued forth was a shrill, warbling, mournful call. As his wind and the sound tapered off, it echoed in his head and stirred up an achy feeling of vulnerability and helplessness at his core. Desperate to end the feeling, he blew the horn again. While the sound of the horn was strong, he was calm. As the sound died, the aching returned stronger than before and his desperation climbed, trying to tear free of his flesh. He inhaled and blew the horn with all his might as if to exhale the alarming emotions trapped in the bottom of his lungs.

The mountaintop was still.

Ergyfel collapsed next to the fire and rested. An hour went by, and still nothing stirred. Then another. Even Reiver, who had remained vigilant through the first hour, had curled up across from his master for a nap. The fire had consumed nearly all the wood and become a bed of glowing coals and darting salamander flames.

Ergyfel sat up and dusted off in preparation to leave. Without warning, a shadow leapt from the darkness of the ruined tower and descended on the troghoul. Ergyfel scooted back as his horse reared up with a whinny and then bolted for home. Reiver squealed in pain as the monster crushed his bones and sank its teeth into the flesh of his neck. A second later, a sickening snap sounded, and Reiver lay dead. Ergyfel froze.

The king watched in shock and horror as the thing hunkered protectively over the troghoul and devoured it. A tattered scarlet shroud hid the greater part of the fiend's body while a black bearskin cape crested high over its shoulders and tapered to a well-worn point that dragged on the ground behind it. Its bony hands and feet, the only members visible, appeared human, though the flesh was dark grey and the long, filthy nails on each digit were thick and curved like talons. These gory appendages cracked bone, shredded flesh, and plunged into the troghoul's carcass to pull out bits of organs and shove them into what, presumably, was its mouth, hidden in the shadowy recesses behind the pale horned skull of a dragon, which it wore like a masked helmet.

All at once, the nightmare stood, holding up the troghoul's heart to the sky. It stared at the moon as it ate the heart, oblivious of the man trembling a few feet away.

The demon's form was like a man with gnarled joints. The same sickly grey flesh covered all its extremities while bronze scale mail adorned the chest. A broad, black girdle drew in its red shroud at the waist with an old, worn gladius affixed to one side and a variety of artifacts dangling from the girdle on cords.

It snapped its head around to look down at Ergyfel, then crouched and picked up a large club that laid on the ground next to Reiver. The club was a bundle of long bones lashed together into a cudgel, with the blackened skull of an infant on top. Once the club was in hand, the demon strode towards the king. Ergyfel scrambled back until he pressed against a rock.

The monster came upon him. The air surrounding it was oppressive, like the stench of a tomb. The demon grabbed the king up by his tunic and raised the club high above its head. The stench threatened to overwhelm Ergyfel's senses. He remembered the old leather scroll in his hand and thrust it at his assailant. The demon halted. The black pits that served as eyes seemed to examine the scroll. It dropped its weapon and held up its bloody palm to the parchment. It sniffed the scroll and ran its claws over the surface. Ergyfel felt a tingle of magic from the scroll. The pungent smell of death and decay still filled his nose.

The scroll drained power from Ergyfel's body. Pain shot through his arm, and he wanted to drop the scroll, but the demon locked its bony grip around his wrist and hand and forced him to hold on.

As the pain grew, Ergyfel heard a strange, indistinct whispering, and felt the demon trying to force its way into his mind. Like Dheumon, it wanted to sink its darkest hooks into him, using pain as a conduit. But this creature, as powerful as it was physically, was no Dheumon.

Ergyfel pushed back, and as their thoughts collided and twisted together, the king saw images of warriors lying dead on a beach. They wore furs and carried flint weapons. The image shifted, and he saw an army with bronze weapons and armor lying dead in a meadow. The images continued to shift, each time showing another battlefield and another army dead, and each time, he saw the ecstatic demon running into the field to feast on their bones. The images acted like footholds, allowing the demon deeper and deeper into his mind. At last, despite the distraction of the whispering and gory images, Ergyfel found what he was after.

"Deimog, Deimog-ghul!"

At once, the demon retreated backward, bowing its head. It was then that Ergyfel recognized the artifacts hanging from its belt; items that before had been meaningless trinkets. Among them was a bronze spear tip from an ancient Albion tribe, pieces of Viking hack-silver, an iron dagger bearing an Irish slogan, and a golden eagle that had topped the standard of a Roman legion.

The demon turned away and went back to its grisly feast. Ergyfel got to his knees. The pain from the arcane wound throbbed all the way up to his shoulder. He could still hear the demon whispering in his head, and saw something alien—a tiny worm with teeth, wriggling as if in his body—and he knew that, like Dheumon, this foul spirit had left something of itself behind. He pondered if the ghoul had also taken some part of him.

Without looking up, the fiend spoke in a raspy, wind-like voice, "Your sacrifice is acceptable." It hissed between swallows. "The pact will be honored."

"Then why all the ..."

"Games?" The demon seemed to grin.

"Yes. You could have honored the pact without that! Deimog-ghul. I demand you tell me why."

The demon shifted its position, as if uncomfortable, and sniffed. "You still smell of the one replete with wisdom that came before me."

"So."

Deimog cocked its head and looked at Ergyfel with its empty eye pits. The whisper in the king's head made a disparaging sound, and he felt like a scolded child.

"Where there is room for one, there is room for many," the demon said.

Ergyfel caught another glimpse of the demon's presence within him as it slithered through his mind. He gritted his teeth and attempted to bear down on it and expel it, but it was too fast, too slippery.

"So. Now that we know one another, what is thy bidding, King of Lyonesse?"

"My enemy—"

"I know your enemy." The demon raised its face towards the sky and inhaled. "I smell them even now."

"Yes, they are growing near."

"But I am curious, great king, … why does your enemy smell so much like you?"

Ergyfel looked aside. "There is one among them who shares in the royal bloodline."

"I see. And you would have me show this one special care."

"Above all others, he must die! I know how fond you are of trophies, so you will understand I want the ring he bears. You will bring it back to me."

"I am no house servant, to come and go by your leave. One of your predecessors made that mistake. And though I was still bound under the pact, he paid dearly. I give you this warning: I have appetites that will be fed."

In Ergyfel's mind, he saw Orgulous: strewn with bodies, not a soul left alive, a giant reeking tomb, a feasting hall for Deimog. Even his beloved Maeven sat dead upon her throne.

Ergyfel shook the vision from his head and took a moment to calm his heart. "Then you shall send the ring back with Sir Feolaghe, the commander of my army."

"As you say, but surely there is more."

"Indeed. Feolaghe has orders in hand to wait for you on the field of battle, at a place called Rowmeadow, beyond the high pass. The very sight of you will likely send the enemy running home, especially if you first thin their ranks. However, should there be an opportunity to treat with them, allow Feolaghe to negotiate, with one exception: our first demand is that the prince of my bloodline be handed over. In return, their lives shall be spared. If they refuse, kill the prince. Do this much, send me his ring, and I shall consider your part of the bargain complete."

"What of the others?" The demon stretched out its hand.

"Kill them all, save the Prince of Gwythia. He shall fetch a considerable ransom. Send him back alive with my other trophy."

"As you say."

"The battle will be in—"

"Worry not, dark king. I never miss a feast. I shall know when it is time. Until then, I shall gather my power."

Deimog bowed his head. "All as you say." He then shrugged, making the fur of his bearskin stand on end. Black feathers protruded through the fur. A strange breeze picked up from behind him, causing his thin shroud to flutter. The breeze grew to a strong gust. A clap resounded, and Deimog transformed into a jumbled, cawing murder of crows that flew past Ergyfel and disappeared into the night.

Ergyfel looked across the cold, dead fire and saw that scattered bones were all that remained of Reiver. He fell back to the ground, exhausted. The energy of dealing with the demon had been more than he'd expected.

**

"My king, my king!" Maeven dropped from her horse and ran to her husband's side. Tears streamed from her eyes as she examined his body. "My love! My Love!"

Ergyfel lay unmoving on the stony ground.

Now kneeling beside her love, Queen Maeven put her ear to his chest. A moment later, royal guardsmen surrounded the queen and king. Each man eyed the other and the eerie surroundings, with their hands on their weapons.

At last, the queen sat up. "Thank the gods, he still lives!"

At that moment, she noticed the sleeve of Ergyfel's left arm was soaked in blood and a yellowish fluid. "Bring a light."

One of the six royal guards grabbed a lamp from his mount and brought it to her. He placed it on the stones, and then turned to the others. "Fan out. Set a perimeter. Protect the king and queen."

While the guards did as ordered, Maeven tore open the king's sleeve. She gasped and bit the back of her hand when she saw that the strange wound, once only affecting his hand, now enveloped his entire arm. Tears ran down her trembling cheeks as she reached down to touch the flesh, which now had the bizarre appearance of charred wood. At first, it felt quite firm to her, but then she went to touch another spot farther up the arm and the entire outer shell crumbled like ash to the ground.

The queen stared in shock and horror at the arm beneath. She opened her mouth to scream, and then fainted over her husband's body.

***

The king awoke, and seeing his wife asleep on his belly, reached up to brush away a lock of hair from her face. But it was a dark, ugly hand with long, black claws that reached towards her face. He stopped and stared at the hideous troghoul hand frozen before him. Of course, he had seen troghoul hands before, dozens of them. He tried to seize it, but it moved as he moved, and he saw that the monstrous hand was his own. He reached up toward the sky and saw that his entire arm had transformed.

Ergyfel shot up to his elbow and examined his other hand, then the rest of his body. He fell back to the ground, reached up with his trembling right hand, and touched his face. He let out a sigh when it felt normal, and then he let his hand into his tunic and felt the smooth skin of his chest. He kept moving left until he came to the wound that circled his shoulder. Beyond the wound's boundary, coarse, hairy, leathery hide supplanted the smooth skin.

Ergyfel sat up fully, raised his new beastly fist, and shouted at the sky, "A curse on you, faeries!"

"Your Majesty!"

The king looked to his right to see the leader of the royal guard coming towards him. Quickly, he hid his left arm and scanned the area to see the other men standing guard in a large circle around them.

"Stay back! Return to your posts."

The first guard came to a stop. "Your Majesty?"

"Stay back. The queen has fainted."

"Then, perhaps, I should—"

"No. I shall attend her."

"Are you not injured, Your Majesty?"

"No, I'm—I fell from my mount, but I am well. Toss me ..." He scanned the area and saw that they had recovered his horse. "Toss me that large sack and the wineskin from the back of my mount, then return to the line."

The guard followed his orders. Ergyfel put his left arm inside the sack and tied the drawstrings up to sling around his neck. He took a sip of wine, and then placed the wineskin to Maeven's lips. He allowed just a few drops to fall into her mouth.

"Wake up, beloved."

He patted her face. When this had no result, he bent over and kissed her on the forehead, then the nose, and then the lips. At last, she responded, and he sat up.

Maeven's eyes fluttered open and she looked up at her king. "I had the most horrible dream."

"I know, my love, but it's over."

She sat up, and Ergyfel shifted to hide his left arm from her in the shadows of his robes. He then sat behind her and supported her back.

"It seemed so real." She smiled, then giggled. "I'm such a silly girl."

"So, tell me, my silly girl: Why is it you have come all the way up here to find me?"

She spun around onto her knees and faced her husband, then grabbed him by the shoulders and stared into his face. "I thought someone might have killed you."

"Killed me? What made you think that?"

"Because ..." The queen hesitated and retracted her hands to her lap.

"What is it, beloved? Tell me."

She dropped her eyes to her hands.

He put a finger under her chin and lifted her face. He kissed her on the lips. "Tell me."

She swallowed, then turned her teary face away. "Your brother has been killed!"

Ergyfel thought for a moment. "Did you say, 'my brother has been killed'?"

Maeven managed to nod.

"That can't be! I still need him!"

"I know, husband."

"How? When?"

Maeven sniffed. "He was found in his quarters."

"How was he killed?"

"I. I—I cannot tell you." Maeven threw herself into her husband's bosom and sobbed.

Ergyfel caught the eye of the leader of his royal guardsman. "Come here."

The man approached and bowed at the king's feet.

"Tell me, has my brother truly been slain?"

"Regrettably, sire, yes."

"How could this be?"

"The assassin is being sought as we speak, Your Majesty. We do know that Lord Snegaddrick is innocent, as he was under our watch the whole time."

"He's anything but innocent. But come, tell me, how was my brother slain?"

The guardsman cleared his throat. "By a knife, sire. The assassin left it in his back." The guard shifted his weight and glanced about. Then he leaned closer to whisper. "The hilt bore his name, in the old runes."

"What?"

"The knife bore his—"

"Yes, I heard you the first time!" the king roared. "And where is Sir Feolaghe?"

"He has done as your orders bid him, sire. He has left Orgulous to marshal the warlords and the army."

Ergyfel fashioned a fist from his right hand. The guard eyed it in anticipation of the strike. A moment passed, and then, very deliberately, the king rapped his shaking fist on the man's shoulder three times. The strikes were more pushes than punches.

"So he has. So he has. Prompt as ever to his duty; my champion."

The king looked down at his sobbing wife. "Is this why you thought someone had come to kill me?"

Maeven nodded.

"Because my brother's name was on the knife that killed him?"

Again, she nodded and continued to sob. "When I heard what happened to Hengest, and heard about the knife, I ran looking for you. The seneschal said you had left Orgulous and were late returning. While I was still speaking with him, your mount returned to the Gleaming Gate. The royal guard immediately began searching. I gathered these men you gave me and searched for you myself."

"You should have stayed in Orgulous."

"I could not stay there, dying by grains of sand."

"How did you find me up here?"

The guard nearest the king bowed. "There was a report earlier of a fire in this direction, sire."

Maeven pawed at Ergyfel's chest. "That's right, my love. The closer we got—I just knew you had to be alive. I simply would not have it otherwise.

My heart dragged me to you until I thought it would wrench itself from my chest. And here you are."

"And here you are."

"But what happened, my king?"

"I came up here for solitude. To be alone and plan our strategy in the coming battle. It was I who lit the fire, and when I went to leave, my horse was spooked by a wolf, and I fell where you found me."

"A wolf!"

"Fear not, my love. It has long left the area. Just like the assassin."

"Your brother's assassin, Your Majesty?"

Ergyfel looked at the guard. "Aye. My brother's killer has left Orgulous and will never return."

"How can we be sure, Majesty?"

"Because *I* am sure. Because I *know* he has gone. But come, we are wasting time. Send a man ahead. Tell the castle we are well and on our way. Ready baths and a light meal. Recall all search parties. Summon my tailor, my scribes, the royal messengers and heralds, the ten most senior members of the night watch, and a priest, to the great hall. I want every male in Nyraval old enough to shoot a bow or hold a sword, in the outer ward by mid-day tomorrow."

CHAPTER THIRTY

One Man's Demon

Billy swam in a fevered nightmare, floating between the world of men and the world unseen, between life and death. When he lost consciousness, his mind drew lines on the grey blankness that surrounded him. Each was written from a spell that stretched out into a dark, wavy line. He wrote these lines, never finishing one, never completing a spell. Each line begat more lines, crisscrossing one another at various angles and forming patterns. Then objects formed out of this patchwork: bricks and stones that became part of a giant, curved wall.

Then he would wake up. Before his closed eyes, it was the same awake or asleep: lines and more lines. At last, he would gather the energy to open his eyes and see the world of men that had become the inside of a tent, alternating with the inside of a wagon. Quite often, Myrredith was there with a kind word and an offer of cool water or food. The mere mention of food made him wretch, and so his menu promptly reduced to water.

One or two swallows of water and some medicine made from herbs and tree bark, and he would lose consciousness again. Once recaptured by his subconscious, he would return to writing the lines, over and over again. There was no rhyme or reason, only a feeling of desperation. He had to finish the wall before time ran out.

A black cloud surrounded his wall of scrawling words—seeking a way in—and Billy knew why he was building the wall. Soon, the cloud found the opening Billy was desperately trying to close and poured in, filling the void around him. As if it knew no other purpose, Billy's mind began drawing the arcane web of lines in white against the blackness, but they were different words, different spells, and he realized he was no longer the one writing them. Again, the lines multiplied of their own accord, but now they formed only right angles and only in particular regions. Before long, the pattern of a large rectangle emerged. The lines looked like moonlight reflected off ripples in an inky pond. The rectangle rose out of the pool, which was now like tar. The tar bled off the surface of the rectangle and revealed the black tome Billy had taken from the Witan's home.

He took hold of the book warily and pulled with all his might until he wrenched it from the tarry surface. The black curtain surrounding him evaporated, leaving Billy standing under a star-littered sky, in a tiny clearing surrounded by dense forest. He felt a sharp pain in his hand and dropped the book.

The iron bindings of the big volume split and fell away from the cover, smoking and glowing red with heat. The faint smell of sulfur burned his nose. Drops of blood stained several of the tiny claws that topped the points on the wavy cover.

Billy absently put the new wound in his mouth as he studied the book. The taste of blood was real enough. *Is this a dream?*

Then, the book floated up and hovered a few feet above the ground. The tiny claws unhooked from the leathery skin and thrummed the surface like the crawling legs of a centipede. The separate leathery waves then slipped around the book at alarming speeds in opposite directions, rubbing against each other with a dry hissing sound. The leather grew loose, and then snapped open into huge, bat-like wings that widened and curled around Billy in a semispherical shape.

The rest of the book exploded, filling the clearing and bordering trees with loose parchment pages covered with written spells. At first these pages flew chaotically, but then unified until they were swarming like a school of fish. They became aggressive and flew around Billy, forming into a whirlwind that shot across to the dark center of the wings. There, the pages transformed into the bones and flesh of a male humanoid creature with muscular arms and chest, a long face, and six horns circling its brow like a tall crown. Though formed up top, its legs descended into wispy, insubstantial shapes that were difficult to make out, as if distorted by powerful waves of heat. Indeed, all the air around it wrinkled and shimmered, driven by invisible flames.

Finally, the last layers came to rest, finishing the creature in dark, smooth skin and gold jewelry. Its lower half wore loose silk pantaloons. The face, though vaguely goat-like, was pleasing to look at, and sported a short, well-groomed beard of black that circled its mouth. The letters and symbols that formed magic spells on the pages now appeared like tattoos, which migrated across the surface or faded as if submerging beneath the skin to be replaced by new symbols welling up from within.

Then the creature opened his eyes. They were black, with a twinkle that bespoke of timeless wisdom. A thin, sooty smoke seeped from his eyes and mouth as he smiled, showing a mouth full of fine sharp teeth. The delicate smoke then rose from its body and swirled lazily around it in the hazy shimmering cloud.

"Greetings, Prince." The creature bowed its head.

Billy spit out the blood from his wounded hand. "Who are you?"

"Your humble servant," it answered, giving Billy another sample of its exotic accent.

"How are you my servant?"

"You rescued me, and now I am yours."

Billy saw the moment he took the black tome from its shadowy hole in the Witan's tree. "What are you?"

"You might call me ... a spirit."

Billy examined the creature before him. It was, in some ways, like the wild irregular and brooding creatures the elves of Tir na Aill called "forest spirits." A striking and threatening, alluring yet abhorrent creature. But the way it moved, the way it spoke, its physiognomy all felt like a very polite lie. Billy hoped he was wrong, but his gut said this handsome devil, this self-proclaimed spirit, was actually a monster playing at being a civilized man.

Billy crossed his arms. "Spirit ... or *demon*?"

"One man's demon is another man's spirit."

"But a wise man knows he can never be another man."

"Oh, you are a cunning one, my prince! Very cunning. Far too cunning for a spirit like me. That is why I have presented myself in my true form."

"As opposed to what?"

"Well ... I usually appear to my masters as something less *jarring*, like this." He waved his hand and transformed into a handsome black-eyed man in the robes of a prince.

"Or this." Again, it waved its hand. This time, it transformed itself into a duplicate of Billy, except for the eyes, which remained wells of black ink.

It returned to its original horned form. "Harmless spirit games, really."

Billy shook off the creepy feeling at seeing himself. "For the sake of argument, what kind of *spirit* are you?"

"A guide, teacher, helper, rescuer, builder, king maker, siege breaker, guardian, hunter, storm rider, home finder, dream catcher, wish granter ..."

"Dream catcher?"

"Have you a dream—a wish? I can help you catch it. All is within my reach. I make everything you ever wanted easier to get, most especially magic."

"What if I don't want you to make it easier for me?"

The spirit threw back his head and laughed. "Don't be absurd. If you didn't want me to make your life easier, you never would have drawn me from my confinement."

"That's not why I did it."

"Of course it is." The spirit smiled broader than ever. "I whispered to you before you ever saw me. My offer is the same as it ever was; take me, learn from me, and I shall give you your desires. I shall make you what you want to be.

"You want to be rich—powerful? Allow me to help you, and it shall happen. You want to learn magic? Want to get there fast? I can make you a wizard faster and easier than a swift horse coming home. And power! You will have no equal!"

"But that's not why I drew you out!"

"I know, Prince. I know. You wanted to save your friend, save your kingdom. It's very noble. But you never would have looked for me. You would never have found me, if you hadn't first accepted my precept and my offer."

The spirit held out his hand. Billy stared at it.

"Just because I needed something fast—something easy—doesn't mean I accepted any offer."

"No? ... Remember when you were on the beach in Tirn Aill? When your quest appeared defeated by that treacherous goblin captain? Who was it that came to you when you filled with frustration, anger, and hopelessness? Who offered to help, when you couldn't see anything but blind rage?"

Billy allowed his mind to drift with the spirit's words and saw himself on that perfect beach, on that clear day—without a ship. All of a sudden, the spirit was whispering in Billy's ear.

"It was I, of course."

Billy turned his head, but the spirit had already returned to his place in front of him.

"I offered you a way out, a way to solve your dilemma ..." The spirit vanished, and then reappeared, whispering in his other ear. "And you took it."

Again, Billy turned; but as before, the spirit was gone. It moved behind him and walked around him in a circle with its arms out wide.

"I put more power in your grasp than decades of study and practice could ever give you—all the easy way, and why not?"

The spirit's head appeared over Billy's shoulder, nearly cheek to cheek with him. "Wasn't your need great? Your cause just?"

"Yes." Billy spun around. "But I dragged those sailors up from their eternal rest to serve *me*."

"And you let them go as soon as we arrived in Lyonesse."

"Aye, but to where? To be slaves for Finvarra?"

The spirit muttered as he walked past Billy. "That is where they came from. You gave them a reprieve, however short."

Billy turned to find the spirit lounging on the bough of a tree on the edge of the clearing.

"Oh, and while we are speaking of Finvarra … " The spirit waited for Billy to walk to him. "Let's not forget what we did together in the Hall of Lost Souls! That was beautiful! The way you called up the fire elemental, and then opened a portal to the world of men. … Ha! Finvarra was furious."

Billy couldn't resist a smirk. "He was at that." But then Finvarra's words came back to him. "People died as a result of that *prank*."

"Nobody you knew." The spirit moved past Billy.

He spun around and followed after. "That doesn't matter!"

"You're the one that cast the spell."

"So, now you're saying it's all *my* fault?"

The spirit turned to face Billy. "It always has been. That is the way I work. I only supply the way; *you* supply the will. That and some power borrowed from your ring."

"You knew people would die all along, didn't you?"

The spirit paced around Billy. "Truly, Your Highness, I'm not such a bad fellow. You wanted out. You wanted some revenge on Finvarra and to get his attention. I merely provided you with the knowledge—an easy map, if you will. I don't confuse myself by judging the means. I focus on the ends, and you would be happier if you did the same.

"I can't. If I may have caused someone's death—"

"You don't know for certain that you did, do you? Besides, how else could you have gotten Finvarra's attention? What *great magical power* did you learn from the Witan that would do the same?"

"I—I don't know. I just should have waited. Eventually, Finvarra would have returned."

The spirit eased in behind Billy and, again, spoke to him from over his shoulder. "Aye, but you could still be waiting for him, and your friend Myrredith would be dead." The spirit paused for a moment and watched Billy as his words sank in.

"So," it began again, "you may, *possibly*, have harmed some faceless turf cutter in Erin, but for that tiny risk, you *saved* your dearest friend in the whole world, didn't you? And *that* is something you know for sure."

"I suppose that it was necessary ... to save Myrredith."

"Of course, it was."

The spirit smoothed his beard as he sauntered back in front of Billy. "So, where was I? Oh yes, that demon from the depths of the ocean. Now, that was a surprise! His blows weakened you so much that I was forced to do most of the work myself, but again, it was you who reached for me. You see? Together, we beat it."

"You saved yourself, *and* you lost my mother's ring."

"You got it back." The spirit turned his back on Billy. Then stared at the starry sky.

"Only by chance."

"I knew it would come back. You sound like you're complaining for having your life saved."

"I'm grateful to be alive, but be honest, you only did it to save yourself."

The spirit spun around, opening his immense, leathery wings to encircle Billy once again. He then stepped forward, enfolding him further in his wings, pulling him closer.

"I saved *us*, Billy. Don't you see? There is no more you and me, only us. I am now more a part of you than your mother."

He felt a sudden itch on his back, looked over his shoulder, and gasped when he saw the spirit's wings merging with the flesh around his shoulder-blades. He could see tendons and blood vessels that they shared between them. Blood pumped from his body while thick black ichor pumped in.

Billy pulled and spun away from the vampire-like wings and found himself standing across from the spirit in the center of the clearing. He looked and grabbed over his shoulders, but, aside from the bandages for the arrow wound, there was nothing out of the ordinary. He turned back to his visitor, who stood still, examining his fingernails.

"My mother?" Billy scowled. "You know nothing of my mother!"

"Not so." The spirit appeared hurt. "She gave you a magic ring that sometimes doesn't want to work, cast a spell upon you, which you had to break, and sent you on a pointless, endless quest that would get you killed, if not for my help. Not exactly the model of motherhood."

"My mother died protecting me, and her quest—*my* quest, is not pointless! You know as well as I do, I must learn the secret of spellbinding in order to save Tirn Aill!"

The spirit straightened and crossed his arms, cocking one slender eyebrow. Then he smirked. "I could teach you the secret of spellbinding."

"Really?"

"But of course. It is child's play for one replete with wisdom." The spirit bowed.

"Replete with wisdom," Billy repeated this under his breath.

"What's wrong now?"

"Replete with wisdom. Demons can never resist crowning themselves with that title ... can you?"

The demon looked down and smiled. "Look. Billy. It's still the same me, and the same you. I'm still offering the same deal, which I *can* deliver. What difference does it make who or *what* I am?"

"The difference is, you're another man's demon."

"I prefer the name djinn, and the man who imprisoned me is long dead. But you are the master; call me what you will."

"Djinn or demon, you're all tricksters and deceivers."

"You make it sound like a bad thing. I am your servant. That means my powers of deception are at your command."

"The only one you serve is yourself. Moreover, you have been deceiving me from the beginning. Any deal you think you struck with me, you didn't." Billy turned away. "I wish I never laid eyes on that accursed book!"

"I'm sorry you feel that way. You're one of the more interesting people I've worked with. And you cannot deny, I did help you."

"Stay away from me!"

"The first man to command me—the man who imprisoned me in the book—was a great man, a king and the son of a king, and he ruled most wisely. He was wise enough to defeat and bind me. He raised great cities and fortresses with my power. You could be as great, maybe greater.

"Give yourself over to my teaching, and I will make you the greatest wizard-king of all time. I will make you more powerful than all your foes put together. I will destroy your strongest enemies and put them under your feet."

Billy had a vision of casting a powerful dark spell against Ergyfel. He stood atop the ruins of Orgulous, with Ergyfel and all his minions dead or dying at his feet. Prince Hereweald lay crushed under a nearby tower. Ergyfel reached up to him and said, "How could you do this to me?" then died. Billy turned away from him and looked closer at the ruins. The innocent people of Nyraval and Orgulous also lay dead under the rubble. He turned again and saw Myrredith and Hugh underneath the tower with Hereweald.

"No!" Billy was back in the little clearing. He stared with contempt at the demon. "You have nothing I want."

"Fine."

The demon rushed Billy and grabbed him by the wrists. The demon's hands were hot. Billy struggled with him, but the demon was much too strong. The more Billy struggled, the hotter the demon's hands became.

"To think, … I was going to teach you the secrets of spellbinding, and the casting of spells without word or gesture. We could have done great things together, but if you are unwilling, then I have no choice. I will take your place, and you shall take mine."

The heat in the demon's hands exploded, splattering sparks all around. Billy cried out and fell to his knees.

"You will be bound in the book, and I will rule Lyonesse as its king … forever!"

"No!"

Billy looked down and saw the iron bands, which had bound the black tome, shackled around his wrists. They cooled quickly, and the burns under them began to heal. He felt tingling in his ring-finger and realized that his mother's ring was working again.

The demon circled Billy. "While you and that ring of yours have been trying to form your pathetic spell walls—and failing miserably—I have been growing strong."

Billy rose to his feet, but when he tried to get away, an invisible force hindered him. He looked down and found a circle in a fine silvery dust on the ground that marked the boundaries of his confinement. He realized the demon had been creating the circle while they talked. Billy tried to break the circle with his foot, but could not. He crouched down to break the circle with his hand, but could not budge it, not even when he concentrated, using his mother's ring. At the same time, the demon was busy laying down the lines of two intersecting triangles surrounding the circle and Billy.

"What are you doing? Let me go. Help!"

The demon looked up from his task and smiled. "Doing? Why, I'm binding you into a book. The same as was done to me." He held out his hand and showed Billy a few silver coins. "By the way, thanks for the loan."

The demon then ground the coins together in his fist. A moment later, he opened his hand, and Billy saw that he had turned the coins to powder. The demon then stooped low and used the silver dust to draw the last line of the second triangle.

When the demon had finished, he stood up and, again, transformed into the likeness of Billy. Billy flinched, but then scowled at the demon.

"Oh yes," the black-eyed counterfeit said. He blinked his eyes, and they became blue. He rubbed his hands together, and the twin to Billy's ring appeared on his finger. "I had nearly forgotten. Thank you."

"You won't get away with this!"

The demon turned to walk away. "There's no one to stop me."

"My friends will know you're not me!"

"Yes." The demon faced Billy from several paces away. He drew a large circle around himself. "But not at first, which is precisely why I shall eliminate them promptly."

"No!"

"Yes. But don't blame me; they're your nosey friends."

Billy threw himself against the cylindrical barrier, but only got a sharp reminder of his wounded shoulder-blade. "Help!" he shouted towards the sky. "Help! Somebody help me!"

The demon stretched and cracked his knuckles. "I fought it too. There's nothing you can do to get yourself out, so you might as well relax. And don't worry, my friend, the first hundred years are the worst."

The demon then chanted in a deep, guttural language Billy didn't recognize. His hands and body made simple gestures and movements.

Billy's chest felt tight. His extremities stretched out away from his core, and his limbs seemed to swell. Soon, he felt as if he would burst. He drew on the power of the ring, and the pressures decreased. "Help me! Won't somebody help me?"

The demon continued with his incantation while Billy struggled against the forces threatening to pull him apart. The battle cut back and forth, draining the combatants with each passing moment. First, the demon would gain ground, and then Billy. Sweat poured off Billy's brow, and he felt his energy and that of the ring waning.

He looked at the ring. At that moment, strange magical symbols and spells appeared on his skin like tattoos. They rose and faded, migrating up and down his arms, and even around his fingers. He continued to grow weaker and closed his eyes so the symbols in his skin would not disturb his concentration. The feeling that he would explode intensified.

I can't hold on much longer. I need someone's help. Someone who has beat a demon before.

"Iblis!"

Billy and the demon both stopped and looked to the edge of the clearing. The instant the demon ceased casting his spell, the magic pulling on Billy dissipated.

The bent, gnarled form of one of Tirn Aill's Witan emerged from the trees. He ambled into the clearing with the aid of a long oak staff—the top of which was as bent and gnarled as he.

"Gwylid!" the demon said.

"Gwylid! Help me! He's trying to trap me in the black tome!"

"Of course, I am. Trying to put you back where you belong."

"Where *I* belong? Where *you* belong!"

"I wish I'd never laid eyes on that accursed book. Help me, Gwylid. Help me put him back in the book."

"Be careful, Gwylid. He's a demon. Don't turn your back on him."

The shaggy Witan stopped in the center between the two magical circles and held up his hand, indicating that he wanted quiet. Billy and the demon complied.

After a moment of contemplation, the ancient faerie said, "I'm going to ask you each a question, and you are to answer one at a time." Gwylid turned to his right and addressed the Billy standing in the big circle. "Of all the people in the world, living or dead, who do you love most?"

"What kind of question is that?"

"It is the question I chose to ask you."

"But how can I answer such a question? You should ask me how I trapped the demon or how I learned the means to bind him in the book."

Gwylid smiled. "But I already know how you achieved such things; you have read and learned from the book. It's rather obvious, and a question either of you could answer. That is why I chose to ask whom it is you love most."

"How could you know the correct answer to such a question?"

"Because I know the heart of Billy, the heir of Tirn Aill, and shall recognize the answer that best fits him."

"Well then. ... My answer is ... my father, King William."

The Witan nodded his approval and turned to the Billy wearing the iron bands. "Now it's your turn. Of all the people in the world, living or dead, who do you love most?"

"Well, that would be ... a tough question!"

"You see?" the other Billy said. "I told you it was hard. He has no idea how to answer. Now do you believe me?"

The Billy in irons stood erect. "I was going to say that it's a tough question, but I know the answer."

"You're stalling."

"Hush," Gwylid said. "I will hear his answer."

"The person I love the most in this world is my father."

"That's what I said. He's just copying me."

"My father, John."

Gwylid turned and walked to the Billy in the big circle. He leaned towards him. "I will help you put the demon in the book."

The Billy in the big circle smiled.

"No!" Billy yelled.

"But," Gwylid continued, "you have forgotten something from your magic circles."

"I have?"

"It must have been omitted from the book."

"Oh."

"It's preparatory and may have been viewed as separate."

"I see."

"No matter. I shall fix it, and we shall continue."

The gnarled old faerie hunched over and drew more lines on the ground with his finger.

"Gwylid!" the Billy in irons shouted. "You can't believe him! I'm Billy! He's tricking you! Ask me another question! Any question!"

Gwylid pointed at the hysterical Billy and scolded him. "Speak, once you are spoken to."

The Billy in irons became silent. He opened his mouth, but nothing came out. In desperation, he returned to kicking and ramming the containment field that surrounded him.

Gwylid returned to his lines, first making two long ones that started on either side of the existing circles and crossed in the center. Then he went around behind the Billy in irons and closed the two lines with a third, forming a large triangle. The last line closed the two lines behind the other Billy, which turned the whole into two long triangles with their tips touching in the middle.

"Is that it?"

"Not quite. I will say an incantation to sanctify these lines, and then we will see the demon go back into the book."

"Good."

Gwylid stepped into the large silver circle and took out a thin wand. He then tapped himself on the head saying, "*Ack, ack, wyrt du thack.*"

"What was that?"

"Just a precaution. Are you ready?"

"Get on with it."

"Very well. Here we go ...

    mirrim, mirrim, durud

    gelic, trada, gelic

    durud, mirrim, mirrim

Good bye."

The Billy standing next to Gwylid snapped his head to the side and gaped at the old faerie. Before he could say a word, there came a sound like a huge bellows drawing in air, and he disappeared.

A moment later, there was a popping sound, and Billy reappeared next to Gwylid. He spun around and examined his body. Fresh scars circled his wrists, but the irons were gone. He opened his mouth to speak, but nothing came out.

The demon-Billy, who was now in irons across from them, shouted, "Villain! Cheat! Liar!"

Gwylid turned to the Billy next to him. "Your Highness."

"Gwylid," Billy replied with a sigh. "How did you ... ?"

"Cursed faerie! Backstabber!"

"Just a moment." Gwylid then pointed at the far Billy, who continued to spout insults. "Iblis, speak, once you are spoken to."

This silenced the Billy in irons. He grew furious, and his eyes became black.

The Witan turned back to Billy. "You were saying?"

"How did you switch us, Gwylid?"

"Ah! A simple spell to switch two similar objects. I would have taught you, had we more time before. I'm just glad it swapped the two of you and not the two of us."

"What?"

"Well, it was a very small chance."

Billy shook his head. "What an adventure that would have been."

"Aye." Gwylid gave an impish grin. "Are you ready?"

"Ready?"

"To put this demon where he'll do the least harm."

"Back in the book?"

"Aye."

"I don't actually know how."

"I will cast the spell. I want you to loan me your power, using the ring your mother left you. It will focus and multiply your energy. Just keep concentrating on me."

"How does it ... ? Never mind. We'll talk about that later. Anything else I should know?"

"You'll be safe if you stay in the circle."

"Safe from what?"

"You'll see."

Gwylid chanted and made gestures in much the same manner as the demon had been doing before. Billy concentrated on Gwylid and felt a surge of magical energy leave him.

At that moment, the demon transformed to his horned manifestation and began to thrash about in his magic circle. He beat against it and rammed it with his horns. He pressed his wings against the back of the containment barrier, and his hands against the front. The magical barrier containing him deformed and expanded until it exploded with a thundering boom. Billy held up his hand to shield his eyes, but when he looked again, he saw that the demon was still hovering inside the two intersecting silver triangles. Its arms and wings stretched as far from its body as was possible and its back arched. The expression on its face was both fear and anger. Billy realized that whatever forces the demon had called down on him were now at work on the fiend himself.

"Serves you right!"

At that moment, the demon's voice was loosed, and he let out a terrible howl. He flexed and attempted to draw in his extremities. Small, wispy spirits of smoke appeared around him, holding and pulling on his appendages. The harder the demon struggled, the more visible the spirits became, and with each frustrated yank or stalled flapping of his wings, more of the spirits appeared, swarming over him like hungry wolves.

One of the spirits pulled away from the demon, taking with it a page from the black tome; ripped from his body. The demon grabbed for it with a growl, but it flew away. Soon, others followed, eroding his parchment features with each pass. Holes quickly appeared in his wings as his flesh dwindled. At last, only a half-winged skeleton remained.

The demon fell to his knees and feebly reached towards Billy, as the spirits continued to pick his bones clean. He opened his mouth and croaked, "All your power has come from me. When I am gone, you will have nothing!" At that moment, the spirits broke up the bones and threw them high into the air, where they became pages.

The individual pages flew up, carried by a whirlwind of rushing spirits. Lightning flashed and struck the ground where the demon had been. When the sound of the thunder faded into the distance, Billy and Gwylid relaxed.

"Whew!" Billy wiped his brow. "I'm sure glad it's gone."

Thump!

Billy jumped when the demon-tome landed in the center of the intersecting triangles. Smoke rose from the black cover, and the iron bindings still glowed red as Billy and Gwylid approached.

Billy turned away. "Phew, that smells like hell."

"Nah, just one demon."

"Say, what was that with the questions? Couldn't you tell me from him?"

"I figured he was the demon when he called my name first, but I had to be sure."

"I'm sorry, I only called your name after he did. If he had got it wrong, I would have too."

"Don't feel bad, Your Highness. When you have been king for a while, you will easily tell the Witan apart."

"So, why the question about who I loved?"

"Demons cannot comprehend love. Like a blind spot, while wearing a helmet, they cannot see it. It's all calculations to them. He must have calculated that King William was more valued by you, through something he observed."

"I tried to defend my father the king, even though he murdered my mother. I think he saw that."

Gwylid nodded in agreement. He then bent down and picked up the black tome, which had cooled and was no longer smoking. Somehow, it looked smaller to Billy. The old faerie put the troublesome book into a fold of his garment. "So, how goes your quest, Your Highness?"

"Well, … not well."

The Witan cocked his head. "Which is it?"

Billy grinned. "Not well."

"Ah, at least you still have your sense of humor."

"As do you, my friend."

"A good sense of humor won't deflect arrows, but it comes close. So, do you want to tell me about it?"

Billy dropped his eyes and stared at the ground. "I think our cause is in jeopardy. I lost focus on my mission."

Gwylid put a hand on Billy's shoulder. "All is not lost, my friend."

"It would be if you hadn't saved me from that cursed book!"

"Didn't we tell you not to touch the book?"

"Yes."

"But you did it anyway."

"Yes, but when I saw that book, I thought it *must* have some really great spells in it, maybe even the secret of spellbinding. It was such a big, impressive book."

"That was the demon laying his trap for you."

"I realize that now, but it kept calling to me."

"Don't you know that we have your best interests at heart?"

"Honestly, I felt unsure about the Witan, and when I touched the black tome, I felt sure that it had to hold what I needed. It felt quite a bit like my mother's ring. It seemed to promise so much—the answers I needed."

"Oh yes." Gwylid nodded. "It promises the quick way—the easy life, easy magic, easy power … and then, when you have become completely dependent upon it, when you need it most, it deserts you, breaks you, kills you. But, I am curious why it tried to get rid of you so quickly."

"I think it didn't like that I was doing things my way, without using it. It wanted to be my sole source for magic—for everything."

"The better to make you dependent. But you are blessed."

"Blessed?"

"Usually, the victim is addicted by now, a slave to the book. You seem to have some natural resistance to his charms. Perhaps your ring had something to do with that."

Billy contemplated this. "Or my mother."

"Aye. But don't forget your father John."

Billy stared at Gwylid.

"John taught you right from wrong and tutored you in listening to your conscience. Not a small thing, even for a good man."

"Aye. And yet, when the book called to me, I could not resist what I knew I mustn't do—what you told me not to do."

"The book's demon can be very seductive."

"Then, you've heard it too."

"I am the only one of the Witan to hear its sweet lies. It views me as the weakest, the most susceptible to temptation."

"Did you ever succumb to the temptation?"

"No."

"Not even a little peek, a tiny taste?"

"Who could resist honey once tasted? No. I never gave in. That's one reason I could defeat it when you could not."

"Even with the help of my mother's ring, I couldn't break the spell he'd placed on me."

"Some demons take more than power or knowledge to defeat. In those cases, you need someone's help. Someone who knows how to defeat them, someone who *has* defeated them, and someone, if you'll forgive me, greater than yourself."

"You have no need for forgiveness, Gwylid. You *are* greater than me. In fact, I'll probably never be as great as you."

"It's not a competition, Your Highness." The old elf turned and made his way towards the edge of the clearing.

Billy followed his teacher, keeping pace beside him. Gwylid glanced at him, and then continued, "My current greatness only came as a result of my past sacrifice."

"And if I wish to be great ... ?"

"Greatness comes with sacrifice. But you must choose what path you will take."

"What if I choose to follow your path?"

"My path is a path of sacrifice, but I will be there to guide you."

"What should I do now?"

"You appear tired, Highness. I suggest you rest, and when you arise, continue with your quest."

Billy lay down on a patch in the clearing with tall grass. He looked up at the Witan, who leaned over him, tucking him into his grass bed.

"You're leaving, aren't you?"

"We must each go our separate ways." Gwylid stood upright.

"So soon? I wish ..." A sadness stole Billy's words.

Gwylid smiled. "Me too." He then faded and became thin as broth.

"Tell me: what will I find?" Billy sat up.

"Greatness ... and sacrifice."

Then, like a vapor before the dawn, Gwylid disappeared. Billy lay back down in the grass and stared at the starry sky.

"Sacrifice."

Questions about the Witan's last word kept Billy up for a while. Despite this, and what had transpired in the little clearing, he felt at ease under the stars. At last, exhaustion overtook him. He fell into a deep sleep and dreamed of home, with his father, in the Valley of the Yew.

***

Billy stepped out of the Valley's Finest Inn, on an errand for his father, and found himself in Tirn Aill. The ground and streams were frozen with a foot of snow frosting the evergreens. The trees no longer bore any leaves. The air was still.

Billy called out. His only answer, an echo. He searched the shores, the rivers, and the forest, looking for someone—anyone, but found no one.

Billy gasped and awoke to find Shaldra's head resting on his chest. Rays from the dawning sun streaked across the clearing's sky, sweeping the stars westward.

"I'm not dead," Billy said.

Shaldra shot up to a sitting position. "My prince!" He shook sleep from his head. "You're alive!"

Billy grinned. "I thought I had already established that."

"Yes, of course, Your Highness."

Billy noticed Shaldra's uncharacteristic grogginess. "Were you asleep just now, Shaldra?"

"I—I. When I found you last night, you were so peaceful and still that I had to check to see if you yet lived. I put my ear to your chest and heard your heart beat. Such joy it brought me that I continued to listen. Soon, your heartbeat became mine. And then ..."

"Yes ... ?"

"Then you woke me up, Your Highness. This is terrible!"

"So you fell asleep... You were probably exhausted like me."

"That's not it, Your Highness. We elves do not sleep! At least, not as mortals do."

"Well, look, you're awake now. It's not the end of the world."

"I am not so sure."

"What do you mean?"

"It's Tirn Aill I'm thinkin' of. If the other elves have also fallen asleep ..."

In Billy's mind, he was transported back to the snow-covered Tirn Aill of his dream. He closed his eyes, to see it more clearly, and saw that everywhere he had been, the kingdom was still. Everything from the trees to the wind slept.

"What is it, Your Highness?"

Billy opened his eyes. "It's Tirn Aill. We must hurry!"

He got to his feet and looked for a way out of the clearing. Endless choices beckoned, with no obvious trail in sight. "Which way is it?"

"Are we going back to Tirn Aill, then?"

Billy turned to the hopeful elf. *Perhaps I should send him home now. Once we reach Orgulous, he will be completely out of his element, and it could become very dangerous for him.*

"Do you want to go home, Shaldra?"

"Of course."

"Then, I think you should go."

"My place is with you."

"Where I must go, it will be extremely dangerous for you."

"I will follow you to whatever end, my prince."

"Then, no, we are not going to Tirn Aill. Our quest still waits in Orgulous."

Shaldra deflated. "So, we're not escaping?"

Billy considered this for a moment. *Perhaps we should leave the others behind. We might slip into Orgulous undetected, but then what? The two of us wouldn't stand a chance if we were caught.*

"Sorry, Shaldra. We shall not escape today, but ask me again tomorrow."

"Yes, Your Highness." Shaldra grinned. "In that case, captivity awaits in that direction."

"Lead on."

CHAPTER THIRTY-ONE

The Thunder of Captains

Cheers heralded Billy's return on the arm of Shaldra, from everyone, including Deordrif, who then pretended not to care. Of course, Lady Myrredith made a fuss. First relieved, then angry, then relieved. However, the most unexpected response was from Prince Hereweald, who picked Billy up and lifted him high, like a long-lost little brother.

"Ouch!" Billy grabbed for his back.

The prince immediately put him down. "Is it the arrow wound?"

"Aye. It's gotten worse."

Hereweald's physician recoiled when he lifted the bandage. "It is infected. It is not possible for it to become this bad so quickly. The last time I examined it, the wound was clean and healing. This ... this is sorcery!"

"Well ... fix it." Hereweald gave him a stern look.

Myrredith touched the physician's arm. "Yes, do."

The physician looked at all their faces. "I know I can heal this wound, but if the magic is still at work, it will only get worse."

Sylvys stepped forward and placed his hand on Billy's back. He closed his eyes, and after a moment, announced, "The foul magic has gone."

The tent sighed in relief, and then buzzed with cheery voices.

"Well done, Sylvys!"

"I did nothing, Highness. It was gone already."

Billy cleared his throat until he had his friends' attention. "I believe the physician can take it from here."

"Yes, of course." Herewald grinned. "And we shall leave him to it."

As the tent emptied, most wished Billy well and a "glad to have you back." When it came to Sylvys, Billy asked him to stay.

When the physician was finished and gone, Billy turned to the aging satyr. "I had a fight with a demon."

"I sensed as much."

He explained to Sylvys the incidents of the previous night. "While the demon is gone, I am afraid."

"Of what, young prince?"

"I'm afraid he has stolen all my magic."

Sylvys examined Billy. "How?"

"I don't know. The demon said that when he was gone, I would have nothing, and since my battle with him, even my mother's ring will not heal the arrow wound, and I continue to weaken."

"Perhaps the infection is infernal in origin. Magic cannot affect such wounds. They must heal naturally."

"That could explain much, but still, I'm afraid that without the book, I will be helpless against Ergyfel. What's more, I sense I must face him. I don't even know if I truly know what I think I know."

"What?"

"The magic that I learned in the Witan's tree—the charms, the spells I remember casting ... I don't know if it was me or the book!"

"I cannot answer to that, Prince, but have you tried to cast any other kind of magic?"

"No." Billy looked at the ground. "I've got bits and pieces of spells flying around in my head, and no certainty with any of them. I'm afraid to try."

"Afraid?"

"You probably can't grasp my fear. If I can't do it, then our quest is for naught, and Tirn Aill is doomed. I don't want to know that I can't."

"I understand, Highness, more than you know. In part, that is why I left Tirn Aill with you. I didn't want to know what I was incapable of. I'm afraid of what that world might look like. But as long as I'm with you, on this adventure, I don't have to face that."

"You *do* understand. Look, don't tell the others just yet. Give me some time to work this out."

"Of course, Your Highness."

***

In the early evening, Hereweald arrived at Rowmeadow with his three legions. His scouts had reported the enemy numbers at less than ten thousand, so he was actually pleased to see the enemy campfires lining the western end of the vast meadow as he crossed over the small stream at its eastern border. With nearly sixteen thousand hardened warriors at his command, Hereweald was optimistic.

It was for moments like this that he was bred; a fact he did not disdain. The next day would mark him, mark history, but more importantly, mark the final thrust of his vendetta. The army before him represented all that Ergyfel could scrape together to stop him. It was a crumbling shield, and Hereweald relished the thought that soon, perhaps even the next day, he would have Ergyfel at sword point.

The lack of scouts from Ergyfel's army was evidence that Hereweald's spies were telling the truth about Lord Snegaddrick's defection. Hereweald smiled, glad that he hadn't shared his entire plan with the treacherous old snake.

He looked back at his commanders. "Enter in full parade formation. Let's give them a good look at us."

So it was that the First, Fifth, and Ninth Legions of Gwythia entered Rowmeadow with banners high and music blaring. The blasting horns, beating drums, crashing cymbals, and marching feet produced the desired response in the enemy camp. The men of Lyonesse rushed to the edge of their camp and watched as three well-trained, well-armed, and well-disciplined legions marched into view; row after row, until they filled the east end of the great meadow. The cavalry rode into a line behind the well-ordered infantry so that every soldier could be seen. Once in position, the host marched in place until the last beat of the music. A moment of silence followed, and then—in one voice—the army of Gwythia roared, "Hereweald, Hereweald, Hereweald!" and were still.

The Gwythian soldiers remained frozen. Their armor and weapons glinted with the golden light of the setting sun. Each face was iron; each shield, granite; every weapon, an adamant fang in the maw of a titan.

There was no planned response from the defending side of the chosen field of battle. There had not been such a display of power and resolve on the shores of Lyonesse for hundreds of years. And so, the baffled, wilted men of that camp stared at each other, some with uncertainty, some with fear in their eyes, and yet some few with jaws set in grim determination.

After a long moment, one of their number, a highlander by his garb, stepped forward and shouted, "'Twas grand, lads! Do ya know any other tunes?"

So, the response from the Lyonesse line became a weedy laugh. However, the boost to morale was fleeting in sight of such honed malevolence. Each man turned, when his eyes had caught their fill of that sleepless night's tormentor, and returned to their tents and campfires to grumble.

The Gwythians set heavy guards, followed by their entire camp, complete with tents and campfires. Hereweald handed down orders for the men to, "Live it up, as bold Gwythians in the face of the enemy." By nightfall, Rowmeadow reverberated with the enthusiastic noise of his dutiful troops.

***

South of Rowmeadow, on a thickly wooded hill, the sound of the Gwythian troops below could just be heard above the babbling spring whose waters streamed downhill and ran along the meadow's eastern border. Four Gwythian soldiers lay dead around the tiny life-giving pool, the warmth still in their cheeks.

A dark, horned figure in a crimson shroud removed his foot from the throat of a fifth dead man and strode back up the hill to the spring. He hesitated, listening to the song wafting up from the east end of the valley below. He then stuck the end of his bloodied club into the spring and spoke in his ancient, raspy voice. "That's it, my prize. Drink up. Be merry. Quench your thirst for death in my waters."

***

Billy lay on his cot in the tent he shared with Hereweald's physician. Despite the late hour, and the fact the Gwythian soldiers had quieted down, Billy couldn't sleep. Too much rested on the outcome of the battle ahead—a battle he would give anything to avoid.

Shaldra entered the tent with his usual stealth and touched Billy on the hand. He opened his eyes and pushed up to his elbows.

"What is it, Shaldra?"

"Where's the doctor?"

"Who's injured?"

"No one."

"Some soldiers came and got him a short while ago."

"I have been in the enemy camp, Highness."

"I only wish they *were* the enemy, Shaldra. Then I might be able to sleep."

"We may not have to fight them, or at least not all of them."

Billy sat up. "Tell me."

"The camp across the meadow is full of grumbles tonight, my prince."

"Grumbles about what?"

"They grumble much about the size of this army. They are also grumbling quite a bit about not eating in several days."

Billy scratched his chin. "Interesting."

"Yes. It appears that Ergyfel sent them out without adequate provision. But there could be another problem."

"What?"

"They are also grumbling about some new leader Ergyfel has sent them."

"A new commander?"

"No. I think he's some kind of advisor. One said that he spoke for Ergyfel. What worries me is that he's a sorcerer, or something worse, by the way they were talking. They are in agreement about one thing."

"What's that?"

"That he's evil and doesn't belong among them. They're none too happy with Ergyfel for sending him. I tried to spot him, but he must be hidden in the dark mists."

"Did you hear a name?"

"Not for the sorcerer, but their commander is someone called Sir Feolaghe, if that helps."

"Feolaghe?" Billy thought back to his time in Castle Orgulous. *Lady Maeven's father ... her sister is Caenne—the face of Dheumon! What's the connection?*

"Do you know him?"

"Not exactly. Tell me, is there any good news?"

"Many of them whisper of sneaking away tonight, and many already have. I happened across some few in the woods."

"That is good."

At that moment, Hugh stuck his head into the tent. "Are you well, Highness?"

"We're fine, Hugh. What is it?"

"A cold feeling in my gut. Something terrible is coming."

"The battle tomorrow?"

"No. I don't think so, but I must go. I've got to meet a friend from Hillshire."

With that, the tent-flaps closed, and Hugh was gone.

"Should I go after him, Your Highness?"

"No. We must tell Hereweald what you found out."

***

Shaldra was still reporting the results of his spying when Hereweald's physician ran up to the prince. "We have a big problem, Your Highness!"

The prince motioned to Shaldra to wait, and then turned to the physician. "What are you talking about?"

"Some things are better understood with the eyes, Highness."

Hereweald, Billy, and Shaldra followed the physician to a part of their camp near the brook. Men and horses littered the ground, both dead and dying.

"What's happened? Were we attacked?"

The physician shook his head. "No, Highness. These men and horses have all fallen ill. Half are already dead."

"What do we do?"

"I do not yet know the cause, Your Highness. The legion physicians have reported there are many more sick throughout the camp."

"How many?"

"Hundreds, Your Highness. Many hundreds."

Hereweald turned away from the sight, and Billy saw disbelief and horror in his eyes. He turned to one of the sick men. "Do you know what made you sick, soldier?"

"No. ... We ate the same food we had yesterday."

"What of the horses?"

Another man spoke up. "With the battle tomorrow, we fed the horses from our oats supply."

Hereweald knelt next to another stricken man. He lifted the man's head and brought a ladle of water to his lips, but the man declined. "And you? ... What did you eat?"

"I was relieved of guard duty just now, Highness. I haven't eaten anything. I don't think I could."

Hereweald laid the man down, and then stared at the water in the ladle as he swirled it. He then raised the ladle to drink.

At that moment, the centurion in charge of the watch came running beside the stream towards the prince, flapping his arms. The prince stared at him over the ladle. When the centurion was still some distance away, he shouted, "Don't drink the water!"

Hereweald glanced down at the water in the ladle, then dropped it and stood up. He pursed his dry lips as his eyes drifted from the ladle to the gentle brook that ran just a few feet away. His shoulders sank, and he stared at the water quietly passing by.

Shaldra went to the water's edge and put his hand over the stream.

When the centurion arrived, Hereweald turned to him. "Report."

"Your Highness, the men set to guard the source of this stream have been murdered!"

"When?"

"Their relief discovered them just now, Highness."

Hereweald thought for a moment. "Quickly now, spread word throughout the camp that the water is poison. Under my order, no one is to drink another drop! Let them drink wine if they're thirsty."

"Aye, Your Highness." The centurion saluted.

When the centurion had gone, Hereweald turned to the physician.

"When the wine is in, sense is out, Your Highness. Some will get drunk."

"Better drunk than dead. Besides, some of them fight better drunk."

The prince and the physician attempted to smile. Shaldra came back from the brook shaking his head.

Billy put a hand on the elf's shoulder. "What is it?"

"It's not poison, Your Highnesses."

"Then, what is it?" both princes asked.

"This sickness in the water is pure sorcery."

"Sorcery?" Hereweald pulled out his bronze medallion and kissed it.

"Aye." Billy sighed and nodded. "Before he was interrupted, Shaldra was about to report that Ergyfel might have sent a sorcerer to aid his commander. I guess this confirms it."

"Sorcery." Hereweald balled his hands into fists. "Give me men with spears and shields, slogging it out in the mud and blood, down to their last breath with bare fists. Pit me against an enemy of muscle and bone and steel, and I shall be victorious, but how does one combat sorcery? How do you defeat what you cannot see?"

"I believe Sylvys may be able to help us, Your Highness."

Billy nodded to Shaldra. "Go quickly."

While Sylvys aided the physicians and their helpers with the sick troops, the two princes called their advisors to Hereweald's tent. Long into the night, they tossed about strategies to cope with their impending predicament. It was still a few hours before dawn when Sylvys and the prince's physician came to report. Hugh was just finishing. "... but the Lord of Hillshire is sympathetic to our cause, so we should receive a small mounted contingent before dawn."

"Good." Hereweald spotted the bedraggled healers and beckoned them. "Report."

"Forgive my appearance, Your Highness." The physician bowed. "We have been working since we last spoke, to save as many men as we could."

Hereweald's body stiffened as if readying for a blow. The prince glanced at the faces of each of his officers, then back to the physician.

"What are our losses?"

The physician struggled for words. He had no doubt spent the entire march to his prince's tent thinking of the best way to break the news, and yet when the moment arrived, there were no words. Billy's extended contact with the physician had revealed the man's deep commitment to healing and the relief of pain. His marked hesitation spoke volumes.

"My prince, I ..."

The physician closed his eyes. He then bowed his head before continuing with his duty. "Nearly three thousand are dead."

The physician braved to look and found Hereweald staring at him. Again, he looked away, unable to maintain eye contact with his prince as he delivered the remaining bad news.

"More than four thousand lay ill, too weak to lift a sword. The morning shall see if they survive. Some few of the remaining troops show mild symptoms." The physician looked around at the faces in the room and added, "Of the officers, Primus Bleddyn, Primus Pike, and Tribune Estival are dead. Tribune Mael may recover."

The physician then laid several small tablets on the table.

"These are the tallies, Your Highness, in more detail. Also, the report from the ostlers, who bade me bring it to you."

The prince put his knuckles on the table and leaned upon it. "Read it to me."

The physician picked up one of the tablets and studied it. "Out of some thousand horses, there are now approximately ... seven-hundred-fifty still alive, six hundred fit for service. ... They also said that your horse and your brother's horse are well. Apparently, they were in the first group watered."

"I see," the prince said, at last. He turned to a centurion near him. "I'm promoting you to Primus of the First. Go to the centurions and order details to prepare their bodies for the journey home."

"Wait." Billy held up his hand while Drif whispered in his ear.

The prince looked askance at him. "I've lost too many good men tonight for any trivialities, my friend."

Billy beckoned Hereweald down to his level, and then whispered in his ear. The prince nodded, then stared at Billy and Deordrif in disbelief.

"We can't. Besides, it would never work." Hereweald stood up and looked at Hugh. "Once we sound the advance, it's over."

"You may not need to, Your Highness."

"There is more to the plan," Billy said.

Shaldra stepped forward. "I think you should hear Prince William out."

Hereweald held up his hand. "Look, I allowed you and your advisors to attend this meeting against good advice. Don't prove me wrong."

"Trust me." Billy tugged Hereweald down and whispered some more.

After a few moments, Hereweald stood up. "It's a shadow's gambit at best, ... but you might be right. I doubt Feolaghe could predict such a move."

Hugh shook his head. "He won't."

"On the other hand ... " Prince Hereweald rubbed his stubbled chin. "I don't like the thought of my men fighting without any sleep."

"No matter what you decide, the morning light is our enemy now."

"Aye, Hugh. It will expose our weakness. Although the sun will be in their eyes."

"We must move efficiently and with stealth," Shaldra said.

The prince looked at the elf, and Billy detected the beginnings of a grin. In that instant, the prince had decided.

He turned to the new Primus of the First Legion. "Go to the centurions. Tell them to have the men dress the dead in their armor and carry them quietly to the west side of camp."

As a grumble rippled through the tent, the tribune of the First Legion's cavalry stepped forward and spoke in a demanding tone. "What is the meaning of this outrage?"

The prince spun towards the grey-haired man and raised his fist. He hesitated, and then tapped on the man's shoulder.

"I apologize, old friend." He then turned to the group. "I apologize to you all. I am the first guardian of our people's traditions. However, I value your lives above tradition. Your sons, ..." He turned to the tribune. "Your brothers ... must wait a bit longer for their well-deserved rites. Tomorrow, our dead stand with us!"

***

Billy sat in a chair with a pillow behind his back, under the rear edge of a large red and yellow canopy erected near the middle of the Rowmeadow. Before him sat a sumptuous feast of fresh apples, potatoes, warm bread, ham, and roast beef, all freshly prepared. He stared at a candle on the edge of the banquet table.

Billy reached forward and snuffed out the candle. Once he'd leaned back into his seat, he looked over his shoulder and watched the early morning light reveal three full legions arrayed in battle formation. On the opposite side of the field, Ergyfel's army scrambled to form lines.

"You prepare a table before me in the presence of my enemies."

Billy blinked and looked over at Hugh, who was eyeing the table heaped with food. His eye was caught by a strange glow coming from Hugh's waist.

"What's that?"

"My attempt to translate scripture."

"No, that!" Billy pointed to Hugh's side.

He raised his arm to reveal the hilt of his sword. The pommel stone glowed with an eerie blue light. He looked down at the glowing gem. "Oh, that. It started doing that this morning."

"This morning?"

"Aye. About the time we arrived here, though it's brighter now."

"And you don't think that's strange?"

"When I was a child, my mother told me this sword was magic. Later, I thought she was just trying to comfort me, so I wouldn't fret when my father went to war. And there were times during the years I wielded it that I wondered—at times, I felt led … but it wasn't until you restored it to me that I truly began to believe."

Shaldra grunted. Billy looked over and saw him hanging on the front edge of the canopy, leaning towards the enemy lines, from which his eyes never moved.

"What, Shaldra? I suppose you already knew it was magic."

"In Tirn Aill, my prince."

"From the moment you saw it, right?"

"You've been in the land of men too long, Highness. Remember the forest. If you listen carefully, you can hear the sword's song."

Billy closed his eyes and concentrated on what he was hearing. It was a serene morning on the meadow. A quiet breeze tiptoed on the tops of the distant trees. Birds chirped their greeting to the sun. Behind him, tribunes roared, and Hereweald's army, in unison, shouted his name then became still. He heard the cooks feverishly preparing a feast in the camp and the babbling of the brook beyond. Just below this, he thought he heard Sylvys and Drif whispering the wind chant to coax the scent of the feast across the field to the starving army that opposed them.

Across from Billy, captains thundered their orders. The armor and weapons of Ergyfel's army clanked together, as it grumbled and muttered and panicked to get into place on the field of battle. Empty stomachs growled, and horses pawed the earth and chomped the bit as leather saddles creaked and reins pulled taut in fists of steel.

Shaldra's voice broke Billy's concentration. "Are we closer to their lines?"

"I thought we were in the middle," Hugh said.

"I think we're closer to their lines than to ours."

"Perhaps, when I ordered the tent erected, I should have been more specific." Hereweald eyeballed their position. "I told the centurion to 'place it near the middle, but not close enough for their commander to see our troops clearly.'"

"They might perceive our forward position as confidence," Hugh said.

Billy sat up. "Good."

"Confidence or folly?" Hereweald made eye contact with Hugh. "A clever commander might see it as an opportunity."

"A clever or desperate commander," Shaldra said.

Hereweald and Hugh nodded in agreement, then Hugh spoke. "I know Feolaghe well, and right now he is both."

"Do a few yards really make a difference, Your Highness?" Billy asked.

"That all depends on where Feolaghe has his archers."

"Archers?" Billy stood and tried to see into the trees.

Hereweald stepped out from under the tent and eyed the enemy lines. He felt for the direction of the wind. "If his archers are as good as mine—

and I have no reason to believe otherwise—and if I were him, and desperate … killing the enemy commander would be an option."

At that moment, Hereweald's herald galloped up to the meeting tent and dismounted. As he approached his prince, it was clear he was shaken.

"What's wrong?"

The youth bowed to his prince. "Your Highness. There is one among them, who … frightens me."

"Ergyfel's sorcerer."

The herald glanced at Billy. "Something more than a sorcerer, Highness; yet less than a man."

Hereweald grabbed the boy's shoulders. "What do you mean? Speak clearly!"

"He—it reeks of death, Your Highness. It's not a man. It's—it's pure evil, but you may see soon enough."

"Are they coming, then?"

"Aye, Your Highness. They have accepted your invitation."

"They're coming now." Shaldra pointed to the trees.

The five of them trained their eyes on the enemy lines. Motion came from the center and moved towards them.

The lines of warriors parted, and four men rode out; three encased in steel armor, and the fourth, a youth, wearing dyed-blue leathers with a silver horn slung to one side and carrying a blue and white pennant. The riders trotted towards the meeting tent at a wary pace. When they neared the halfway mark, a commotion rose from the formation behind them. Something raced through the woods and abruptly broke their lines.

Billy stood on his tiptoes. "What's that?"

Hugh stepped forward. "It looks like a chariot."

Hereweald appeared next to him. "A light war chariot, to be precise."

"I've got a bad feeling about this," Shaldra said.

The leader of the four riders, seeing the charging chariot, spurred his horse into a gallop to intercept its course. The three with him did the same, following behind him.

"Is it the sorcerer?" Billy asked.

"Aye." The grim herald stepped back a pace.

"Your herald's right." Shaldra turned to Hereweald. "We're not dealing with a man, but an evil spirit."

"Is he—is it responsible for killing my men?"

"Of that, I've little doubt, Your Highness."

Hereweald held Shaldra in his gaze. "Take your prince to the rear of the tent. You can protect him better from there if need be." He then turned to his herald. "Thewyn, plant our flag over there and stand beside it. We shan't need introductions in this."

"Yes, Your Highness."

"Remember, Thewyn, whatever happens, do not signal the advance unless I order it! Even if things get rough—no false starts. Am I clear?"

"Yes, Your Highness."

The chariot bore down on the tent. The skull helmet of its driver seemed to grin. At the last second, the four riders forced it aside, and it came to an abrupt stop.

The chariot driver stepped down from his rig and planted his bare feet in the rich soil churned up by the chariot wheels. He then picked up his bone war-club and threw it over one shoulder, with no more care than a woodcutter shows his ax. At last, he turned his dragon skull countenance to face the tent and marched towards it.

Billy pointed to the leader of the riders and whispered to Shaldra. "That's Sir Feolaghe, though he looks much older than I remember. And Lord Colomdyn, I believe. And ... "

Sir Feolaghe dropped down from his mount and moved to intercept the charioteer. His fellow riders, likewise, dismounted and turned their backs to the tent to support their leader.

Hugh and Hereweald exchanged curious glances.

Sir Feolaghe held up a hand. "Wait."

The dark spirit strode toward the tent. "Stand aside."

Feolaghe held his ground. "I am commander of this army! I will handle any negotiations."

The spirit stopped a few paces from him. "Talk. Pah!" He spat on the ground. "Speak with your blade, and let their blood answer you from the earth!"

Shaldra came close to Billy and whispered, "This is bad."

"What's bad?"

"I've got to get you out of here."

"Why?"

"Because that is Deimog, the Ghoul King."

"Are you sure?"

"As sure as I am that I cannot protect you from him."

Billy turned to Shaldra, and though the elf put on a brave face, his eyes betrayed him. He put his hand on the elf's chest and felt his heart thumping. "I'm sorry, my friend. He frightens me too, but I am committed to this strategy."

Shaldra's countenance became resolute and grim. He bowed his head to Billy and returned to his position a few steps in front of his prince.

Meanwhile, the conversation between Feolaghe and Deimog was coming to an end.

The Ghoul King wagged his club at Feolaghe. "We do not serve King William, but King Ergyfel."

"A fact I cannot forget."

"Then remember also," the foul spirit wheezed, "I will speak for King Ergyfel, as I see fit. When I see fit."

"And I am his champion and Lord Marshal. I will speak for my king in all matters regarding his army's belligerence."

"As you wish."

Sir Feolaghe turned and walked toward the meeting tent, his men falling in behind his left shoulder, and Deimog falling in behind his right. As they approached, Billy noticed that the pommel stone of Hugh's sword glowed bright like the full moon, and he heard the song of its magic. Hugh also noticed the light and cupped his hand over the pommel to hide it.

The young herald in blue leather stepped in front of Feolaghe and his men. "My Lords, it is my honor to … "

Hereweald waved the boy away. "I think we all know each other well enough."

The herald bowed his head to the prince, but looked back at his master for approval to fall back. Feolaghe nodded, and the boy stepped aside.

"Hugh." Sir Feolaghe nodded to the former king's champion. "I had hoped the reports were wrong, but here you are … standing over there."

"I have no choice."

"Spoken like the son of a traitor."

Hugh stepped forward, but Hereweald stayed his hand. Hugh glared at Feolaghe, and then the prince, who gave him his stone face. Hugh relaxed, and Feolaghe continued. "And Hillshire? What deception secured *their* treachery?"

"The deceit and treachery of your king. They are here of their own accord."

"And you, sir." Feolaghe addressed Hereweald. "By what right does Gwythia tread the soil of peaceful Lyonesse with such a force of men?"

"You roar like the Lion of Lyonesse, but Prince Gaelyn's blood roars from your sacred soil louder than ten-thousand such lions!"

"Prince Gaelyn's death was not the will of Lyonesse."

"Perhaps not, but it was the will of her present king, and his blood shall stain my sword before I'll leave her."

"Lies! You seek to put yourself on our throne, as Gwythia has always desired."

"Not so, Sir Feolaghe. Truly not. I would see Prince William, the rightful heir, sit upon that throne."

"Even were that true, the boy is dead!"

"I am not!" Billy stood.

"Quiet," Hugh muttered in Billy's direction.

Feolaghe tilted his head to the side in order to peer around Hereweald's shoulder. He stared at King William's son—sizing him up. A sudden tick in his neck seemed to spring him from his pensive state, and he spoke. "So. ... He lives." He locked eyes with Hugh. "Is that why you stand against us?"

"It is."

Feolaghe shook his head. "It changes nothing. We have our king, our sacred oath, our duty."

Hereweald stepped back. "Come. Have something to eat. Drink! Come in from the sun, lest the heat make temperate men unwise and hungry men rash."

Feolaghe and his men moved into the tent, leaving Deimog standing outside, grinding his teeth and gripping his war club. None of the men moved to partake in the feast, save the young herald, who was quickly reined in by an armored gauntlet across his growling stomach.

"No?" Hereweald took a goblet of wine from the table. "Pity. It's from the royal vineyard." He then sniffed, and drank with his eyes closed. The whisper of a grin crossed his lips. "A hint of heather and clover ... touch of oak ... I can almost feel the rich soil of home beneath my feet. Sure you won't try some?"

Feolaghe stared at him in silence.

"Very well." Hereweald sounded dismayed. "Then perhaps you will accept a bit of insight, from a commander who has sent more than his share of men to the grave. I greatly outnumber you, Feolaghe. My troops are better trained, better equipped, well fed, and battle hardened. They don't care how many children of Lyonesse will grow up without their father."

"And I suppose you do."

"You cannot win. Don't throw your lives away."

"We do not hold our oaths so cheap, nor our honor, to sell them for a pocketful of your words." Feolaghe stepped closer to the Gwythian prince.

He pointed to the ground at Herewald's feet. "And that soil beneath your feet, Highness, is our home. 'Tis far more than duty that we defend!"

"Duty. Honor. The crows know not these words, yet they will feast because of them this day if you do not yield. I urge you to consider what and who it is you die for."

Feolaghe seemed to ponder the prince's words for a moment, then straightened. "If I die this day, let it be while I defend my king, my family, and my home."

"You'll be defending your own graves, man!"

"If I must—"

Deimog strode into the tent. "Enough useless talk."

Hugh and Feolaghe sidestepped in between Deimog and Hereweald and stood facing each other.

The Ghoul King sniffed the air and pointed at Hugh. "A great many of your men are already dead by my hand. I smell them even now."

"If you smell anything above the feast we prepared, it is dead horses. We lost quite a few during the night, as you can see."

"Give me the two princes," Deimog demanded. "And I shall quit the field and allow you to live."

"You shall not have them!" Hugh said.

"Are you so eager to confront Death *again*?" Deimog rasped.

Hugh searched the dark recesses of Deimog's dragon skull for his eyes. The hungry darkness he found only reinforced Deimog's threat, but Hugh was resolute.

"You shall not have the princes."

"Then, give me the young prince, the one called William."

"Never!" Shaldra, Hugh, and Hereweald shouted in unison.

Deimog shifted his weight and eyed each of them. "Then, die where you stand!"

The Ghoul King raised his war club to swing, and Hugh went for his sword. As the silvery blade cleared the scabbard, Deimog shoved Feolaghe into Hugh. The force of the blow knocked Hugh back, causing him to trip on the tent's center post and hit his head on the table. His sword flew into the air.

Without hesitation, Deimog stepped towards Hereweald and swung his abhorrent weapon. The prince raised his left arm to catch the blow on his buckler. The blow came down like thunder and struck Hereweald's arm with a flash of orange light. Hereweald cried out as he crumpled under the demon's mighty stroke.

Immediately, Shaldra was on Deimog, slashing at his leg and weapon-arm. His blade cut deep, but where blood should have flowed, only a handful of red sand spilled out before the wounds miraculously closed. Shaldra redoubled his attack. Deimog kicked back like a horse and sent the elf flying out the side of the tent.

Deimog sniffed the air and stared at Billy. "William!" he hissed out as he strode towards him—his voice like the gasp from an opened tomb.

Lura Zahn leapt from Billy's hand as he stepped back. The shimmering blade flitted around the ghoul king, striking and harassing like an angry sparrow on a crow raiding its nest.

Deimog stopped his advance and swatted at the incessant, stinging blade. As he flung out his hand, the blade slashed him repeatedly. All of a sudden, Deimog snatched the blade out of the air and growled at it in his clenched fist.

Billy willed the blade to return to him, but it did not come. The ghoul king then focused on Billy and shook his head. The many wounds inflicted by Lura Zahn stopped leaking as Deimog stepped forward once again.

Billy tripped on the chair behind him and fell back into it. Deimog fell upon him and pinned him to the heavy chair with his foot. Billy felt as if a boulder were upon his chest. He gasped for breath and pushed against the unyielding foot.

Sir Feolaghe had pushed up to his feet with the help of Hugh's sword, and at that moment, stood staring at the silvery weapon vibrating in his hand. He straightened, muttered something, and charged towards the rear of the tent.

Deimog raised his cruel club above his head with a shout and brought it down. Billy felt his heart pounding against his chest. He turned his face to the side and threw his arms up over his head.

There was a loud crunch, an orange flash, and Billy flew backward. The chair and his body struck the ground with a thud.

Hugh's blade hummed in Feolaghe's hand; its stone sang out in shrill tones. With the demon's back before him, he struck. The long blade pierced Deimog's flesh with a screech, spitting out a shower of sparks like steel against a sharpening wheel.

Deimog's terrible weapon fell from his hand as he grasped at the blade protruding from his abdomen. He growled over his shoulder at Feolaghe and attempted to pull free, but could not. Sir Feolaghe struggled with the Ghoul King to maintain his footing as he bucked back and forth.

Hugh stood beside Feolaghe and grabbed hold of his sword. The two king's champions, with both hands upon the weapon, looked each other in the eye and then yanked upwards with all their might. The blade cleaved through Deimog's chest, spitting out an arc of fire and leaving the knights with the blade raised above their heads, glowing as if pulled from a forge.

Hereweald, who was on the ground cradling his broken arm, kicked one of Deimog's feet, and the Ghoul King collapsed in a heap of ash and charred bones. The men stared at the remains as they vanished into sulfurous smoke, leaving behind an odd collection of relics. Without ado, a raven appeared, snatched up a gold ring in its black bill, and flew away before anyone could say a word.

Hereweald and Feolaghe looked to their heralds and their lines. None had moved. Both men sighed in relief.

"Good lads," Hereweald said, as Hugh helped him to his feet. "Sturdy lads!"

"Your arm?" Hugh whispered.

"Broken." Hereweald then put on a brave face for Feolaghe. "What say you, sir? Let us take cue from our young heralds and proceed with cautious good judgment."

"Aye." Feolaghe nodded, then spat on the ground where Deimog had met his end. "Good riddance! The foul creature had no business here in the world of men, much less with the army of Lyonesse."

"Aye," all the men of Lyonesse said.

Billy still lay on the ground. His ears stopped ringing, and he realized he was hardly injured. A dull ache in his head and the chair against his back was the only real pain.

Shaldra lay on top of him. Hugh and Sir Feolaghe rolled the unconscious elf aside. They then helped Billy to sit up. When Hugh was satisfied that Billy would be well, he turned his attention to the wound on Shaldra's head.

"What happened, Hugh?"

"Shaldra threw himself in front of that blow."

Feolaghe stared at the elf. "He saved your life."

"How is he?"

Hugh looked at Billy and shook his head. "I don't know. He needs a physician."

"He shall have mine."

Feolaghe looked at the prince's arm. "I believe *Your Highness* will require his services."

Hereweald glanced at his broken appendage. "I can wait until we have concluded our business."

Billy sat up straighter. "Then we should get on with it."

Sir Feolaghe, who still knelt near Billy, turned to Hugh. "I am still the king's champion."

"Then, do your duty."

Feolaghe stood and pointed to his army. "I see far too many of my countrymen here that will not see another day should we continue into this battle."

"What do you propose?" Hereweald asked.

Feolaghe turned to his two lieutenants, who now stood behind him. Both men nodded. Feolaghe nodded in return, and then faced his adversary. "I alone must fight one of you. The victor wins the day."

"So, if you win ... ?"

"If I win, Prince Hereweald, your army will quit the field and go home."

"And if we win ... ?"

"Then the army behind me has a choice to make."

"What choice is that?"

"Whether to go home or to serve Prince William."

"Then, your fight is with me."

"No. With your shield arm broken, it wouldn't be honorable. What's more, if I were to win, we could not bear the blood of another Gwythian prince crying out from Lyonesse soil for vengeance. The war would never end."

"Then, you believe this war can end."

"Your brother made me believe it could end. There is still an ember of hope in me."

"Wouldn't it be better if kings had to fight their own battles?"

Hereweald looked at Billy. "Aye. The world would be a more peaceful place."

"Aye," Hugh and Feolaghe said.

"You should be fighting me," Billy said. "It is my birthright in the balance."

The men all stared at Billy. Feolaghe smiled. "You sounded like your father just then. I can hear his voice in yours. You also have his courage ... and his eyes. But I will not fight the king's son."

"That leaves me."

"Aye, Hugh. We'll finally have that fight you wanted."

Billy shot a look at Hugh.

"I served Sir Feolaghe as a page."

"Oh. Then you fight to first blood."

"No," Feolaghe was resolute. "We must fight to the death."

"What?" Billy stared, open-mouthed. "Why?"

"A man's honor or duty might not hold him to his best, but with his life at stake, you can trust he will give the cause his all, and thwart historians who might say otherwise."

"Sir Hugh will give his all, Sir Feolaghe, whether it is to the death or first blood. We do not need—"

"I have few doubts about Hugh, Your Highness." Feolaghe bowed his head.

They were all silent for a moment, and then Feolaghe continued. "Besides, Lyonesse is worth the price of one life, wouldn't you say? Like any great nation, it has been forged at the cost of many. I would betray them all to trade it for less."

"If you die, I think it will be for your honor, not your nation."

Feolaghe lifted his eyes to look into Billy's. "I had hoped you would understand." He sounded disappointed. "The trout cannot swim through the meadow without the brook, Your Highness. And neither can I."

Billy glanced at Hugh. He knew that his friend's honor was his life's blood. He then considered Feolaghe.

Feolaghe was an enigma. How could such an undistinguished and aging knight become the king's champion? Sure, he had participated in battles, but never well enough for honors. The only reasonable explanation was a scarcity of honor in Orgulous, which Billy could fathom, given that Ergyfel sat on the throne. And yet this hanger-on, this faded ghost of the court with a complete lack of reputation, stood before him a blaring trumpet for honor. He had even stood up to Deimog. Where did this sudden spurt of courage, at the end of a vacuous career, come from? Perhaps it was the weight of the office thrust upon him, or the gravity of the situation he found himself in, that incited his honor to such a climax, or perhaps honor was all this middling knight had left. Perhaps he wasn't a trumpet after all, but a simple drum, sounding out a steady, resolute beat, which goes unnoticed until all the horns are still.

Billy took a deep breath and let it out. Then, with measured words, he said, "To the death."

***

At the appointed time, Hugh and Sir Feolaghe rode out alone from their respective lines to the center of the field of battle. The dull clomping made by their mounts was the only sound on the quiet meadow. They dismounted and tramped through the tall grass towards each other with swords bared.

Hugh took his sword and stabbed it into the soil in front of him. Feolaghe stared at the pommel.

"This sword should serve Lyonesse, from the side of her king's champion," Hugh said. "If I am wrong in my cause—if I am slain here today—you must take up this sword."

Hugh then drew the sword he had borrowed from the knights of Hillshire and stepped forward. The weapon was plain, but it was true and sharp, and indifferent to taking a man's life.

Once the two warriors were within striking range, they circled. Their movements enthralled every eye in the meadow.

"I will do as you say, Hugh, but you must promise me something."

"What?"

"If I am slain here today, you will safeguard the lives of my wife and daughter."

"I don't hold your actions against them."

"Clearly, you are the better man."

"Look, I'm not that angry boy anymore."

"Yes, but will you protect them?"

"Of course. But why ever should I need to?"

"Give me your pledge on it!"

Billy glanced at Hereweald. Despite the prince's habitual stone mask, Billy could sense that he was worried. Deep within him was turmoil. Billy felt it too. Trust had come too quickly between them.

While Billy still eyed the prince, Lady Aderyn of Hillshire appeared beside Hereweald and offered him a pewter mug. She had her cousin Myrredith's fiery hair and looked very much as Billy imagined Myrredith would look if she were younger and had freckles instead of worries.

"For the pain, Your Highness," she said with a curtsy.

The prince took the mug, never looking from the combatants. On the other hand, the lady's eyes clung to the prince, even as she walked away.

Feolaghe thrust his shield at Hugh. "Give me your pledge, man!"

Hugh continued to circle Feolaghe. "I so pledge! But why? Why should I need to defend your family?"

"Because my daughter is Ergyfel's queen."

Hugh stopped and lowered his shield, inviting an attack from Feolaghe.

Hereweald stepped forward. "What's he doing?"

Feolaghe struck, and Hugh raised his shield to block the heavy blade. The clank reverberated in the meadow.

"Sir Feolaghe had to strike the first blow," Billy said.

"Otherwise, Hugh's honor and Billy's crown would be tainted."

Hereweald glanced sideways at Myrredith, then at Billy, who stood in front of her.

Billy shrugged. "Well, that's what Sir Hugh told me."

"And he was right." Myrredith patted him on the shoulders.

Again, Feolaghe swung his sword. Hugh blocked and stepped back.

Hereweald focused on the combatants. "So, Billy, ... did Hugh share his strategy with you?"

"What do you mean?"

Feolaghe beat on Hugh's shield and continued his advance, increasing his stride and the tempo of his blows. His sword sang out in spirited song of battles won and bravery stirred, and compelled the shield's bass voice to acknowledge it.

The soldiers of Lyonesse cheered.

"Does he intend to let the old man wear himself out before he attacks?"

"No. ... That is, I don't think so."

Hugh spun away from his opponent's next blow and moved past him. He stumbled and revealed that the bottom of his tunic was red with blood.

Myrredith gasped.

"It must be the old wound," Billy said.

"I thought it was healed."

"So did I."

Hereweald frowned. "Good thing we're not fighting to first blood."

Myrredith studied Hereweald out the corner of her eye but never lost sight of Hugh.

Sir Feolaghe took advantage of Hugh's misstep and fell upon him with relentless fervor, chopping again and again like a woodsman. Hugh fell back to one knee. Feolaghe, now frenzied, drew back to smite his opponent with all his might, to end the fight with one deadly blow.

The men of the meadow held their breath as one, each man anticipating the next blow with personal dread or satisfaction. Myrredith's grip tightened on Billy's shoulders.

Without warning, Hugh thrust his sword up through Feolaghe's chest, and all anticipation came crashing to the ground. The meadow was still.

Sir Feolaghe dropped his sword and grabbed Hugh's shoulders as he crumpled to his knees. Hugh caught him under the arms and held him up.

Feolaghe smiled weakly. "Remember your pledge to my family."

"I will guard them as my own."

"Cheer up." Feolaghe gasped for breath. "The better man won. Apologies to your prince."

Ergyfel's champion went limp and fell to Hugh's chest. Hugh lowered him to the matted grass with a prayer and removed the sword from his body. "God help us if Death devised this victory."

The soldiers under Hereweald's command cheered and drummed their shields with their swords.

At that moment, Drif appeared next to Billy and touched his elbow. "Come quickly," she shouted over the ruckus. "It's Shaldra."

Billy turned to face her. "Is he awake?"

"Yes."

Billy and Drif raced past the rows of cheering Gwythian soldiers and entered the tent where Hereweald's physician and Sylvys tended some of the sick and dying of Hereweald's army. Shaldra lay to one side, with Sylvys holding his hand.

"Here's our prince now." Sylvys put Shaldra's hand in Billy's.

Billy searched Sylvys' gloomy eyes as he took the elf's hand. The satyr shook his head. Billy squeezed Shaldra's hand, and the trusty bodyguard's eyes fluttered open.

"Sorry, I got you into this."

Shaldra smiled. "Not me. What an adventure!"

"Adventures are supposed to end happily."

"To whatever end, my prince."

"Your oath to me. I remember. Our days in the forest seem so long ago."

"But never far from my heart."

"I should have left you behind with the others."

"I wouldn't have let you."

"Then, I should have left you to guard Myrredith while we met with Feolaghe."

"And cheat me out of the happiest moment of my life?"

"What?"

"You could not have known, for I have never spoken of the fate I learned so many years ago: to die at the hand of the Ghoul King. I could not outrun my fate, and neither can you, my king."

"Fate." Billy stared at his mother's ring. "Fate is responsible for all the unhappy moments of my life."

"I spent much of my life hoping for a way to put off my fate. Had I known that my death would mean life for my king—my friend—I would have wished it to come on swift wings. I die a happy spirit."

"But you can't die. I still need you."

A tear ran from Billy's eye, as he remembered similar words to John, and his feeble attempt to thwart his death. The tear fell from his cheek and landed in Shaldra's hand. The elf closed his hand around it with a smile.

"I loved your mother, Highness, but she never shed a tear for me. I shall cherish it always. Now ... I'm going ahead to scout ... "

Shaldra closed his eyes and seemed to shrink.

Billy wept. When, at last, he opened his eyes and released Shaldra's hand, the elf appeared smaller than he remembered him, as if he were farther away. Sylvys and Deordrif appeared next to Billy and stated they would prepare his body.

Billy stared at the weave of the tent's fabric. "Thank you. We shall bury him next to my mother, in Orgulous."

"Not Tirn Aill?"

"I ... Maybe, Drif. I cannot speak to that now."

Deordrif looked down and gasped. "Diagor," she whispered. She then rose and left the tent with haste.

Billy's eyes followed her. "What's that all about? What's diagor?"

"Something she fears."

"And that is?"

"More proof of your nobility."

Sylvys respectfully opened Shaldra's hand to reveal a small, smooth, iridescent stone where Billy's tear had landed. It gave off a faint, fading glow.

"This is a diagor. The ring you wear bears one very similar to this."

Billy examined his mother's ring. Its haunting stone stared back at him, its scintillating colors drawing him in.

"It's a frozen tear, Highness."

"A tear?"

"Of our first queen; shed in grief."

Billy exited the tent to a sea of bent knees and bowing heads. Hugh and Myrredith stood next to the tent entrance, smiling at him. Behind them, Billy could see Prince Hereweald sitting outside his tent, with Lady Aderyn tending to his broken arm. The prince nodded and smiled at him.

Myrredith squeezed Billy's shoulder. "These men wish to swear allegiance to you."

Billy stared at the crowd of bowed heads filling the meadow. "How many are they?"

Lord Colomdyn knelt in the front row of men. "Near four-thousand loyal servants of Lyonesse, eager to serve Your Highness. That is, if Your Highness will have us."

Billy leaned towards Hugh. "And the others?"

"Gone or going home."

"Without food?"

"Not all. Most are trading in what weapons they have for food."

"Good." Billy jumped up on a nearby rock and stood straight, looking over the kneeling men. "Men of Lyonesse, if you would join with me to rid our land of the usurper Ergyfel, rise now and feast with me! Tomorrow, we begin our march to Orgulous!"

The men jumped to their feet with a cheer. "Long live Lyonesse! Long live Prince William!"

***

Sir Feolaghe's body arrived at Nyraval on a rainy day, escorted by an honor guard of volunteers. In a just land, he would receive a hero's welcome, with citizens lining the streets in somber colors to pay their respects, and young maidens tossing flowers on the cart that conveyed him. He would be showered with praise in public and toasted in every public house. But the land he had faithfully served was no longer just. The tyrant of Orgulous forbade the people to gather on the street or in the public houses. Moreover, by his royal decree, the honor guard was denied entry to the city. Instead, their charge was slipped away from them and carted off through a narrow gate by laborers from the castle.

And so, the lonely cart that carried his bones was met with no fanfare, no announcement; none of the respect its occupant was due. At first glance, it might have been the butcher's cart delivering its weekly order. However, it did not stop at the kitchen, but clattered its way across the faded, wet cobblestones to the broad steps at the base of the donjon.

Despite its surreptitious entry to the castle, Lady Barane soon heard of the cart parked in the inner ward of Orgulous, and its content. Upon her belief, she rose from her sickbed and walked barefoot to the balcony overlooking the inner ward. Before her daughter could arrive, the Lady of Feolaghe Tor stepped off the edge and ended her life, scant paces from her husband's body.

CHAPTER THIRTY-TWO

The Calm before the Storm

T he air of the king's great hall was thick with a complex mélange of incense smoke, lavender, mint, and decay—the last being the provocation for all the rest. Grey, smoke-laden shafts of light drained into pools on the floor, illuminating the central space between the great oak columns but leaving the outer reaches in stifling darkness.

At each column, facing the center, stood a warrior of bone and steel, armed with shield and spear, and shrouded by a black veil. The dais was dressed in rich black curtains all around and bore a second, smaller throne for Ergyfel's queen. The thrones themselves were draped in black, and the supreme symbol of Lyonesse – a silvered lion crest that hung high on the back wall – was now sable. Beyond these bleak trappings, the chamber appeared much the same as it had when King William unveiled it to his queen; yet those who knew it in its happy glory might think it a different world. The spirit was gone, usurped by a heavy mantle.

To the side of the cavernous hall, near the great doors, a growing constellation of candle flames gradually deposed the darkness from under that corner of the grand gallery. The queen lit the last of five score candles and turned around with tear-streaked cheeks to face the two catafalques, where her mother and father laid in state. The next day, if Hereweald didn't snuff out the light of Orgulous, the citizens would line up to pay their respects. However, now it was Maeven's time.

The queen ambled towards her parents' remains, stopping at the head of their beds to steady herself. She had not slept, nor eaten anything since the day before when she learned of her parents' demise. She couldn't stop crying, no more than she could stop a crushing avalanche.

Maeven looked to either side, still reeling from the sudden turn the world had taken. Her mother and father appeared to be sleeping. For a moment, she was a child looking for Mother and Father to chase away the nightmare that had woken her. She reached out to touch her father's shoulder and found herself pushing up from the floor. Her body was stiff and cold. She sat up with her back to the head of her father's catafalque and noticed that her candles had burned down significantly. What little daylight there had been was fading.

"I'm altogether alone."

A short groan broke her contemplation, and a splinter of light darted across the room as a dark figure entered through a side door and closed it behind him. Maeven grinned, thinking someone had finally remembered where to find her, but there came no voice from the darkness, no calling of her name. Instead, the figure skulked about the doorway.

After scanning the great chamber, the man bolted the door behind him and produced from his cloak a small covered lamp. Its dim light illuminated his plump face.

"Snegaddrick," Maeven whispered.

The portly statesman fixed his eyes on the corner across from him as Maeven ducked behind her father's catafalque. She held her breath, hoping he hadn't seen her.

"Is someone there?"

Maeven held still, only moving to draw in her feet. She heard Snegaddrick take a few steps, then stop.

"Do you need help?" the ambassador called out.

Again, Maeven held her breath, feeling strangely panicked by the presence of this ne'er-do-well creeping around her court. He had always been the enemy in her mind, and now that he was a known traitor, he was twice as dangerous.

Snegaddrick advanced on Maeven's position. Each step he took brought him closer to discovering her. She felt her heart pounding against her chest and heard her blood coursing through her ears. He came closer. Her mind raced to what path she might take if she had to make a dash for the door. Still he came closer. She placed her hand over her mouth to stifle a scream.

Snegaddrick stopped. From the sound of his last steps, Maeven thought he must be standing near her father's feet. The light from his lamp cast sharp, waving shadows on the wall before her.

"You stink as much as your swordplay, old fool!"

Maeven tensed from head to toe to keep from jumping.

Snegaddrick continued. "What were you thinking? Last minute dream of being a hero? Ha! Bit late for that, don't ya think? Did you actually think you could beat him? You were supposed to battle Hereweald's army! You were supposed to delay them for a few days, and while they were licking their wounds, we would all get away. Well, I would. It was so simple!" Snegaddrick kicked the catafalque. "Now ... now I have to move up my every plan, collect my just rewards, and escape this place before Hereweald comes for my head; all because of an ill-timed prick from your timid conscience!"

Snegaddrick turned and started up the center of the great hall to the dais, muttering. "I only hope the battle is distraction enough to cover my escape."

Maeven got to her knees and peered over her father's body at the rogue as he mounted the dais and went to the corner nearest the queen's throne. He reached up and twisted a fluted torch sconce behind the throne while pushing on a panel in the wall. The panel opened, and he stepped through it.

Maeven crept through the hall and snuck across the dais without comprehending why. She peered through the open panel and saw a small room stacked high with bags of coins, finely crafted objects of silver and gold, and a few pieces of armor and weaponry. Snegaddrick squatted to one side, near his little lamp, stuffing bags of coins into some large saddlebags.

Maeven stepped down into the squat room, scuffing the threshold with her heel. Snegaddrick started and bobbled one of the bags, which hit the floor with a splash of gold. Some of the coins rolled across the floor to stop at the queen's feet. Snegaddrick froze.

Maeven now saw the cunning ex-ambassador as a lowly thief, which revived her courage. "What are you doing, Snegaddrick?" The queen crossed her arms.

"Why—I was just collecting the reward your husband the king had promised me, Your Majesty." He gave her a jovial nod.

Maeven scanned the saddlebags brimming with gold. They easily held five thousand coins. "Is that all you are collecting? Nothing *more* than he promised you?"

Snegaddrick's saccharine smile evaporated. He stared at the queen, then picked up another bag of coins and dropped it into his saddlebags. He then stood, heaving the heavy load off the floor as he rose.

Snegaddrick started for the door. As he neared it, Maeven stepped in front of the exit, blocking his way. He stepped into her, pushing up against her body. She turned as he thrust his face at her, grazing her cheek with his nose.

"You better take a look around, missy!"

Maeven returned her eyes to him. His sweaty breath on her ear both angered and frightened her, but he continued. "You think that army camping in the hills is here to give you tribute? Wake up! Your short dance in the sun is over. Time to hide under a rock. Now ... maybe you should be grabbin' some of this and leavin' too."

Snegaddrick shifted his weight back to allow Maeven to get out of his way, but she stayed her ground. The small knot of courage she had left in her stomach was emboldened by her anger. He charged straight ahead as if to frighten her away or go through her, but she did not budge.

"Leave it." She did her best to make it a command.

Snegaddrick turned his face to her again, his heaving chest crushing against her, pressing her shoulder against the wall. A butcher's-knife grin cut across his chubby cheeks, and he laughed.

"Still playing the queen. How comforting that will be for you when Prince Hereweald wraps his fingers around your pretty little neck and attempts to squeeze Gaelyn's life out of you."

Snegaddrick grabbed her by the throat. Maeven gasped.

"Perhaps I should save him the trouble."

The rogue squeezed her throat, and she pushed and beat against him with a flurry of punches. A moment later, he dropped his saddlebags and put a long, thin knife to her cheek. Her courage shrank beneath a cloak of fear. She stopped struggling as her sole focus became the knife. He stopped squeezing her throat.

"I've been playing nice up 'til now, lass. I don't like to use violence against women, especially pretty ones. Don't make me change my mind."

At that moment, the main doors to the great hall opened with a groan. Ergyfel and his guards came in, and he strutted to the dais.

The king snapped his fingers. "Get more light in here."

Snegaddrick thrust his hand over Maeven's mouth and closed the secret entrance to the vault. He snapped his knife back to her cheek and whispered in her ear, "Don't give me a reason to take your life. Be quiet, cooperate, and I'll have no reason to harm you. No reason. Understand?"

Maeven nodded.

Over the next minute, Snegaddrick gagged Maeven and tied her hands and feet. He then laid her on a pile of coin bags on the floor.

"We'll wait a while," he told her as he went to listen at the door.

After many minutes had passed, he crept back to her and whispered. "Hereweald's army has been sighted in the high pass. Your husband has sent away his guards to defend the walls and is alone—working out some kind of magic spell or something. Whatever the case, be of good cheer; it won't be long before he himself is called away to the ramparts. Then I will make my escape and be out of your life forever."

CHAPTER THIRTY-THREE

When the Battle's Lost and Won

"Once we've secured the donjon, we'll raise Malcolm's flag." Billy looked to Orgulous in the valley below and pointed at the tallest spire. "There."

Malcolm brandished a bundle of yellow and red silk, and then slipped it into his tunic.

Hereweald looked up from his pacing. "Six against an entire castle. I don't like it."

"We won't be facing the battlements, Highness, only Ergyfel, and perhaps a few guards."

"Just remember our deal, Hugh." Hereweald pointed a warning finger at them. "I get Ergyfel alive. He will know justice by my hand."

"I will do my best, Your Highness."

Hereweald nodded to Billy. "I know you will. I wish I was going with you on this fool's errand."

Malcolm balanced a long knife on his fingertip. "Who better than a fool?"

Billy snatched the knife from his old juggling master. "Or two."

"Don't forget me," Camion said.

Hugh looked at the giant, then Drif and her bristling arsenal, and then to Sylvys.

"I've felt a fool since leaving Tirn Aill. Why stop now?"

"Fools all, save one brave woman."

"No surprise there." Lady Myrredith appeared behind Hereweald and Aeth. She put her hands on the ex-cutpurse. "Seems all the sensible people are staying behind."

Aeth looked at Billy. "Sure you don't want me along? What if you need to jimmy a lock or trap?"

"You can do that?"

"Well, I ..." Aeth looked up. Lady Myrredith stared down at him with raised eyebrows. "I know someone who ... explained it to me ... once."

"Seven *would* be luckier," Sylvys said.

Myrredith pulled the little thief closer. "You can't have him. He gave you and Hugh back to me, and if I can't hold on to you, I'm holding on to him."

Billy grinned. "Just as well. There aren't any traps or locks the way we're going."

"Speaking of going ..."

"Aye, Malcolm." Hugh bowed to Hereweald. "It's best we were off, Highness."

"Aye. I'm giving you until dawn."

Billy looked very solemn. "If you don't see our flag by then ..."

Hereweald took hold of his arm. "But I will."

"It's time for your medicine, Highness."

The Lady Aderyn approached. She carried a small cake on a pewter plate and a matching cup in the other hand. Billy returned his eyes to Hereweald, but found the prince still watching his new nurse.

*

The incursion team left, riding down the steep hunting trail that led from the high pass to the shore of Loch Nyraval. Hugh stopped his mount and bowed his head to Myrredith and Prince Hereweald. The Lady curtsied and bowed her head prayerfully.

Billy leaned down and whispered to Hereweald, "Take good care of Myrredith."

"I shall."

Hugh and Billy brushed past the others at the mouth of the trail to take the lead. A moment later, they disappeared into the brush.

"Take good care of him!" Myrredith shouted.

The men called back in unison, "We shall!"

***

"Where could they be?" Billy whispered. "Hugh knows these woods and the way to this clearing better than me."

Sylvys shrugged. "Haven't seen them since we started across the loch."

"Blast this fog. We had a good moon to travel by and this wretched fog has to roll in from nowhere."

"It's not from nowhere," Drif muttered.

Billy looked at the elf, who stood near the edge of the tiny clearing. In the glow from the moonlit fog, she was like a black iron sculpture to war. Only the slight movement of her head as she scanned the clearing gave her away. Billy then looked to the satyr sitting on a stump across from him.

"What does she mean?"

"This fog is unnatural."

"What are you saying? It's magical?"

"Aye."

"Summoned ... by *him*."

Sylvys nodded. "Quite."

Billy turned to face the pale walls of Orgulous, which towered over them. Now that he stood so close to his goal, he couldn't remember ever feeling so torn. *I must enter the castle, but all I want is to run away from its walls, away from its master – Ergyfel.*

"I sense his hand, Sylvys, but I don't feel any different. What's it doing to us?"

"To *us*, nothing; but it's obviously having some effect on our friends."

"Are we meant to get lost in it?"

"I don't know. I do not yet fathom the intent of this fog."

"Shhh! I hear something."

Hugh, Malcolm, and Camion stormed into the small clearing, with weapons drawn and bloodlust in their eyes. Camion shouldered Deordrif aside and charged at Sylvys, followed by Hugh, who steered directly for Billy. Deordrif regained her footing and threw up her shield, just in time to block Malcolm's daggers as he cleared the bramble.

Sylvys struck the butt of his spear on the ground. *"Deru!"*

Roots exploded from the earth, and vines and tree limbs from the edge of the dense bramble stretched to bind, gag and entangle the three attackers. Their assault halted when they were lifted off the ground.

Drif drew her sword to strike Malcolm.

"Stop!" Billy struggled to maintain a tight grip on Lura Zahn. "It's the fog!"

The elf glanced back at him, and then to Malcolm, who flailed harmlessly in the thick, creaking web of foliage. She sighed and sheathed her sword.

All three assailants continued to struggle against their restraints, grunting and growling.

"Stand back, Highness." Sylvys stepped forward. *"Dregasteye."* He touched the broad head of his spear. The bronze weapon rang softly with a bell-like voice.

Sylvys raised his spear so that Malcolm's flailing dagger struck it. The two weapons collided with a chime. Sylvys then went to Camion and Hugh and did the same. As soon as their weapons had sounded, each man ceased his frantic thrashing and relaxed. Sylvys snapped his fingers, and the tree limbs, vines, and roots that had trussed them up dropped or sprung away, and the men fell to the ground in a heap.

Billy gave Sylvys a sideways glance. "Never told me you could do that."

Sylvys shrugged.

"Who goes there?"

The whole team froze and looked up to the battlements of Orgulous. Several torchlights could be seen though the thickening fog.

"Who goes there?"

At this, one of the torches flew from the high curtain wall and came plummeting towards them. Billy and his companions scrambled into the thicket. The torch came down with a thump and tumbled across the clearing. It came to rest on the mossy ground near the opposite side, dimly illuminating much of the clearing.

"Get that light out," Billy whispered.

Sylvys stayed him with his hand. "Not yet. Wait. Listen."

A moment later, the satyr jumped up and galloped through the clearing and down the path into the darkness. Billy opened his mouth to call to him but held his tongue and listened instead.

One of the men on the high wall laughed. "Ha! It's only a goat!"

Several other men laughed.

"Wow! You saved us from the dangerous goat!"

After more teasing and laughs, the men dispersed and went back to their posts.

Billy waited and listened. After he was sure the guardsmen had moved on, he said, "We still need that light out."

Deordrif pointed her finger at the torch, and it sputtered and dimmed. A few heartbeats later, it was out.

Billy turned to Hugh. "Why did you attack us?"

"I thought you were Gwythies." Hugh eyed the clearing and the castle.

Sylvys crept back into the clearing along its edge. Then Billy and Hugh crawled from their cover in the thicket. The others followed.

"The Gwythies are on our side right now. Remember?"

"I can't explain it. I just knew the Gwythies had betrayed us and were here to kill or capture you and spoil our mission. You even spoke like them. I—I was compelled to attack."

Malcolm held his hand out to Drif. "And I thought you were MacDowells, an old enemy of my clan. As a boy, the MacDowells frightened me, but that feud's been over for years."

They all stared at Camion. The giant knelt, scratching his head. When he saw that everyone was staring at him, he glanced back and forth at them, then lowered his eyes. He picked up a twig and fiddled with it. "Pirates. I thought you was pirates."

Sylvys drew on the ground with his spear. "It's clear this fog is meant to confuse more than our sense of direction."

Hugh stood and marched in a circle, studying the fog that filled the valley around Orgulous. He sliced through it with his sword as if testing it. He looked at Billy. "Ergyfel?"

Billy nodded. "Aye."

"Then Hereweald and Colomdyn will be riding into a trap."

Malcolm stood up. "We've got to warn them."

Billy stood up. "We've got to stop them."

Hugh glanced at each of his companions. "I will go. I know the way back better than any of you."

Billy cleared his throat. "And yet you got lost."

"He won't get fooled again. Not while my charm protects him." Sylvys put his hand on Hugh's arm. "But you must take me with you. The prince does not fully trust you, but coming from me, he will believe the truth. Besides, I may be able to counter Ergyfel's foul enchantment."

"How?"

"My spear."

"Can it protect the whole army?"

"Perhaps. But we must hurry."

"Agreed."

Malcolm grabbed Hugh's arm as he turned to take Sylvys away. "You'd better let me take him. That wound of yours is still mending. It will only slow you down. I am the fittest."

Hugh looked down at his midsection and nodded. "But do you know the way?"

"I know the way," Sylvys said.

Camion tapped Malcolm and Hugh on the shoulder. "If it's speed with an oar you need, I row better than three."

Malcolm looked at Hugh with a crooked smile. "He *is* a sailor."

"Aye." Hugh returned the smile. "And the loch is the greater part of it …"

"Then, it's settled." Camion held out his hand to Sylvys. "Come, friend. Climb on my back. We'll make better speed."

"Aye." Sylvys eyed the trees. "But mind the low branches."

"You sure you two can find your way back?"

"Your Highness, my way is simple next to yours. Here." Sylvys took the small buckler he wore on his arm and handed it to Billy. "You need protecting more than me."

Billy took the small bronze shield and put it on. "Thank you. Now, go quickly!"

With Sylvys on his back, Camion turned and disappeared into the night.

"Ouch. Mind the branches! This is worse than the boat."

Billy went to the middle of the clearing and found the large stone that covered the secret entrance to Orgulous. Once Malcolm had rolled the stone aside, Billy knelt beside the black hole and sent his faerie light down into the darkness. The dim light revealed a ladder atop a set of steps, just as he remembered.

He leaned forward to position himself to descend the ladder, and paused when he felt a firm hand on his shoulder. Deordrif stood above him.

"I should go first."

When the elf hit the bottom rung, Billy made his descent. Once he reached the small stone landing, he turned and started down the steps, but Deordrif was nowhere in sight, not even her faerie light.

He stared at the dark entrance to the tunnel ahead and whispered as loud as he dared, "Drif! Deordrif!"

Without another word, Billy rushed into the narrow tunnel. He brightened his light and sent it ahead. As he passed through the third or fourth zigzag of the twisting tunnel, an unsettling thought entered his mind.

What if something or someone has nabbed her? One of Ergyfel's pets, or a trap! What if this is a trap? Is Ergyfel waiting for me? What if she is setting a trap?

Billy stopped cold and put his hand on the cool, slimy stones of the tunnel wall. He had told himself that he could trust Drif after all they'd been through together. At that moment, he faced the ugly possibility that he had been lying to himself.

Perhaps Shaldra has kept her at bay all this time. Now that he's gone, and Sylvys is gone, she's free to act—on Malkry's mission!

Billy drew Lura Zahn and looked at the tunnel ahead. He examined the rough, squared-off stones that made up the close, arched passageway. Anything could hide a trap. A knife might be waiting for him around the next corner.

"Billy! Billy!" Hugh and Malcolm cried from behind.

Billy turned sideways in the tunnel and scanned both directions. While both paths yielded to darkness, the way back seemed to promise more light.

Malcolm cursed. "Ouch! Blast, it's dark!"

"Should have grabbed that torch."

Billy backed away from the direction he had been headed. "I'm coming."

"Where are you?"

"I'll be right there, Hugh."

As he turned, the glint of something ahead caught his eye. He brightened his faerie light and sent it further up the passageway. Several yards ahead, the tunnel made an abrupt turn. The arched ceiling there was shorter, and a squat step led up to the next section, so that a taller person would have to duck to pass through. Beyond this portal, a torch rested in a sconce on the wall.

Billy took a step forward but froze when he heard an odd scraping noise. "What was that?"

"What was what?" Hugh replied.

"That scratching, scraping sound."

"Oh." Malcolm chuckled. "That's just me. I'm usin' my flint to light our way 'til we find something to light."

"Stay there. I see a torch ahead. I'll bring it to you."

He stepped forward. As Malcolm scraped his flint, Billy's mind conjured up one of Ergyfel's troghouls dragging its claws across the rough stones of the passageway, but he continued to march forward.

The tunnel was so dark, so cold. He brightened his faerie light, but the brighter it grew, the deeper the shadows beyond it became, and the more worrisome. He pushed forward, forcing back the darkness, forcing down his fear.

At last, Billy reached the portal and peeked around the corner. Another winding corridor led away from him, spawning more shadows at each turn. A tiny rivulet ran over the threshold and disappeared into a crack in the floor. He remembered stepping in water during his escape from Orgulous, but it had been too frantic for him to soak up any more detail.

Billy listened to the tunnel ahead, hoping to hear some rumor of Drif, but only heard the soft, persistent drip of water on stone. He sidestepped into the intersection and put his hand on the torch. The sound of Malcolm's scraping became louder, and he looked to his right to see a dim flicker of light from Hugh and the juggling master just around the bend.

Billy sighed at the sight of the tiny light. "The torch is right here."

He tugged on the torch, but it would not budge. He examined the sconce and found a fine iron catch holding the bottom. As soon as he pulled on the catch, the torch popped out of the sconce. Billy grinned and turned towards his companions, sending his faerie light back to guide them.

A low grinding sound echoed off the walls and the floor shook. Dust fell from the ceiling in stringy plumes. Billy grabbed the wall for support, but it too trembled. Hugh appeared at the end of the tunnel. The grinding sound grew louder.

"Billy! What's happening?"

Billy shouted back. "I don't know!"

Hugh shifted forward as Billy stepped through the portal onto the lower section of floor. The tunnel floor shifted and threw them to one side.

"Let's get out of here." Hugh beckoned to Billy.

Billy stepped forward, and the floor of the tunnel between them fell away. He spun and grabbed the slimy floor behind him as he slipped into the hole.

"Billy!" Hugh cried. Then the stones at his feet crumbled, forcing him back.

The ground still shook and the chasm opened wider. The stones of the tunnel walls and ceiling fell into the abyss along with dirt and boulders. Billy kicked his feet in the empty air under the fragile floor and grabbed at stones only to have them fall away. He stretched to grab the next reach-able stone and began crawling, like a swimmer, across the disintegrating masonry.

Hugh struggled to retreat ahead of the collapsing floor. "Billy, hang on!" At that moment, a fissure appeared in the floor beneath Hugh's feet. He pushed Malcolm back. "Run!"

The grinding became rumbling as boulders and dirt rained down in a curtain from above and blew thick clouds of dust into the tunnel like dragon's breath. The tunnel filled with darkness. The rumbling, grinding, and shaking stopped.

Billy held to a rough ledge with still nothing beneath his feet.

He grumbled and addressed the remnant of floor. "Please, don't break. Please, don't break."

The dust cloud was choking, and the darkness cruel.

Billy tried to pull himself up on the jagged, slippery stones but found he was too weak. He tried again, but each attempt only made him weaker. He hung on, attempting to conserve his strength.

I can't hold on much longer. But I've got to! Tirn Aill is depending on me!

Then, two hands clamped upon his wrists, and he cracked open one eye. In the dim, grimy light, he made out black, clawed hands. He spat the grit from his tongue and shook the dust from his head. He looked again and saw that the black hands were, in fact, gauntlets. Deordrif knelt on the ledge above him. He held onto the masonry that formed the floor of the squat portal.

"One hand at a time, grab my wrists."

Billy did as instructed, and soon he was sitting in the threshold with the elf maiden. Under the illumination of her faerie light, Billy examined the cave beneath them and found that rock and debris nearly filled it. He chortled when he saw that Drif had saved him from a fall of some five feet and a possible twisted ankle. A mountain of rock now stood where the tunnel had once been, blocking their way back—the way to Hugh and Malcolm.

Billy cleared more dust from his throat. "There must be tons of stone between us. And I don't even know if they're alive."

"What shall we do?"

Billy thought for a long while. "There's nothing for it. We have no choice but to go forward."

Drif breathed a heavy sigh and nodded.

"Hey, where were you?"

Deordrif hesitated. "Scouting ahead."

Billy looked into her eyes, wishing he could discern if she were lying. With her expert use of faerie glamour, he couldn't even be certain it was her eyes he was looking at. He wondered if she had caused the cave-in or if it had been the torch he took from the wall.

"Well next time, say something before you run off like that."

"I will."

"What did you find?"

"Some steps at the far end of this tunnel and a stone door."

***

Billy drew Lura Zahn and opened the stone door quietly. The weapon felt comforting in his hand as he peered from behind the tapestry that covered the secret entrance. The lighting in the king's great hall was adequate, except for the area under the grand gallery where he stood. The air was thick with the smell of incense. To his left, a garden of waning candles illuminated two bodies laid upon catafalques, and to his right, the dais with its two thrones. Just beyond the front corner of the dais, between the two rows of majestic wood columns at the center of the hall, he could see a large ring of thick, stubby candles on the floor, connected by an intricate circle drawn in soot and ash. A figure wearing a black, hooded cape knelt in the heart of the circle, facing the grand entrance.

The rich black cape spilled across the floor around the dark figure like roots on an ancient, twisted oak stump. The only movement Billy could discern was a slight heaving as the figure took breath. He listened and discovered that the breathing was tight and pained.

Deordrif slipped out of the secret passage and, together with Billy, crept as silent as dandelion snow towards the kneeling figure. As they approached the central columns, the figure stirred and lifted its head with a loud sniff. They froze, not daring to breathe.

The figure then turned its head to the side and sniffed twice more. "I smell the stench of faeries!" it said in a hoarse voice.

Billy shuddered as he recognized Ergyfel's voice. He'd thought he knew how he would react when he faced the murderer of his mother and father.

He had given it a great deal of thought and even practiced what he would tell the miscreant. But now, his blood ran cold. All his preparation sank beneath a lake of ice.

"Ergyfel."

The usurper chuckled. "So, the wayward son returns."

Billy braved a step forward, and then another until he was standing in the light. Each step, he reminded himself that he must appear confident and bold, or Ergyfel would squash him like a frightened mouse. He glanced at the skeletons adorning the grand columns and tapped one of the bony ornaments with his blade. "Can't say I like what you've done to the place. It's so *you.*"

"Never a guard around when you need one. I must remember to hang someone when I've finished with you."

Without another word, Ergyfel leapt to his feet and spun to face Billy. In his right hand, he held a sword, in his left, a bigger surprise. Ergyfel's thin, well-manicured hand was now fleshy, warty, and sickly-grey. The fingers had grown long, and black, dragon-like claws had replaced the nails.

"So glad you could join me!" Ergyfel hissed from the shadow of his hood. "I was beginning to think you wouldn't come."

Ergyfel waved his hand to his left and whispered. The curtain on the front of the dais flipped up, and the largest troghoul Billy had ever seen loped out and leapt to the top of the dais. It took a stance to pounce into the shadows under the gallery where Deordrif still hid.

"Remember Werian? He's fully mature now."

"I see that."

"Werian, entertain the prince's friend while we complete our transaction."

Billy kept glancing at Ergyfel's grotesque and extraordinary hand. It was familiar and, at the same time, alien.

The king noticed Billy's attention and turned his hand over in the light. "Admiring your handiwork, faerie? It's really quite the trick. How was it that you accomplished it? Oh, yes. You had your mummy's ring. You had better have brought the ring, boy! Or I will slowly peel off every inch of your skin and feed you to—"

Billy held up his hand to show the ring.

"Good." Ergyfel relaxed his stance and stepped back.

Billy's eyes strayed to the troghoul, who fidgeted and kneaded the edge of the dais with its claws. At that moment, he realized Ergyfel's left hand looked like that of a troghoul, and that his mother's ring was the source of the curse.

"You've always wanted this ring, haven't you? You killed my mother for this ring!" Billy took another step forward.

"Actually, your father killed your mother."

"Yes. But it was your sorcery pulling his strings."

Ergyfel tipped his head. "It's amusing how easily some minds are overthrown by magic."

Billy kicked over a candle as he advanced into Ergyfel's magic circle. Ergyfel eyed Billy's gleaming blade and retreated, step for step, to the opposite side.

As Billy reached the center of the hall, Ergyfel spun and struck the shield of the skeleton mounted to the column closest to him. "Now!"

Werian sprung into the shadows. Drif grunted and charged forward to engage him. At that same time, the spear point of the struck skeleton sliced through its veil and came to a stop pointing directly at Billy. He eyed the weapon, wondering if it were some kind of trap. He stepped to the side, but the point followed him.

A crash and a commotion came from the shadows as Drif collided with Werian. Billy spun to face them, and the skeleton wielding a spear jumped down from its column with a crunch. Billy jumped back and faced his new adversary.

Upon straightening, the skeleton warrior glared at Billy with its dark, hollow eyes and circled him. He backed away and countered his ghastly foe's movement. It struck at him with its spear, and he turned it away with

Lura Zahn. It struck again, and he used Sylvys' shield. Billy sensed that Ergyfel was now behind him and leapt aside. Again, the skeleton warrior struck and continued to press its attack, its strikes becoming quicker and more accurate with each attempt. Even with Lura Zahn's help, Billy could only just keep up. He glanced at the shadows, looking for Drif, and the skeleton's spear grazed his cheek.

"Ouch!"

At that moment, Billy's opponent banged his shield with his spear. All the remaining skeletons hopped down from their perches amidst a loud clanking and clattering. With drilled precision, reminiscent of Hereweald's best troops, they struck their shields in unison and dropped into a fighting stance, aiming their weapons at Billy.

He spun around to see a ring of sharpened steel and remorseless bone surrounding him. Laughter sounded and he turned to find Ergyfel leaning against a column with his arms crossed.

"Welcome home, Billy."

The skeletons stepped forward, one half-step at a time, closing the noose around their prey. He leapt forward, swinging wildly at their spears, slapping them aside only to find more waiting. He struck again and again, five, six, seven times, sometimes blocking with the little bronze buckler, sometimes with Lura Zahn. Eight, nine, ten! There were just too many of them.

"Drif, I need you!"

His only answer from the shadows was a grunt and the continued clash of steel and claw.

The skeleton warriors continued to close in.

"Drif!"

The dark elf screamed and her helmet came skittering out of the shadows into the circle. The troghoul let out an unsettling howl, and Billy's heart sank. A loud chomping sound, like a shield rent by a heavy blow, resonated from the darkness, and Werian rolled into the light. The cursed creature came to rest on its feet and stared at Billy through the circle of skeletons. It snarled at him, showing its terrible, jagged teeth, and readied to pounce.

The skeletons advanced another step. They drew back their weapons to impale him.

"Halt," a voice whispered from the shadows. The voice seemed to hang on the air.

The skeletons froze in mid thrust, then shouldered their weapons and turned to face the back of the great hall. Werian nervously scanned the shadows before whining and crawling back to his master's feet.

Billy and Ergyfel turned and watched as the shadow of a large, cloaked man materialized near the bodies of Sir Feolaghe and Lady Barane. The skeletons all bent a knee and bowed their heads. The stranger stepped into the edge of the light, his apparel still the color of shadow. He then raised an arm, stretching out his cloak like a black wing.

"Come."

The skeletons rose at once and shuffled to the back of the hall. One by one they ducked their heads, stepped under the man's raised arm, and vanished into the dark folds of his cloak.

"Who—who are you?" Ergyfel asked.

"Patience, mortal. You will know me, in time."

When the last skeleton had disappeared, the cloaked man reached up and pushed back his hood to reveal his bearded face. He wore a thin gold crown on his head and a trickster's glint in his eye.

"Finvarra," Billy said under his breath. Then an irrepressible smile shattered his grim visage.

King Finvarra, ruler of the grave, returned Billy's smile. "Now, it's a fair fight."

Deordrif appeared from the shadows across from Billy, still breathing hard from her skirmish with Werian. Blood ran from a deep cut on her cheek and ear, and her armor and shield were battered, but otherwise, she seemed well. Billy's smile widened as she leaned against a column and gave Finvarra a nod.

Finvarra scolded Drif with his eyes until she looked away. He then looked at Billy. "It's two against two. We're even."

"Thank you, Your Majesty." Billy gave a curt bow. "My regards to your wife."

Finvarra grunted. He threw the right side of his cloak across his left shoulder with a snap as he turned to walk away. With the ample folds of his cloak still swirling about him, he vanished into the smoky air.

Billy and Deordrif turned to square off against Ergyfel and Werian.

"Time to finish this," Billy said.

"Aye." Drif raised her sword and shield and took a crouched stance. "I'll take the wizard; you get the monster."

Billy stepped forward, but froze and gave her a stunned expression.

"Just kidding." Drif stared straight ahead at Werian. "The troghoul is mine."

Billy smirked and took up a stance similar to his companion. When they left Tirn Aill, he never imagined Drif would be the one beside him at the end. They took a tentative step forward as their opponents swaggered out in front of the dais.

Billy stared over the tiny, bronze buckler on his arm at Ergyfel's long sword. He stole a look at Drif's much larger shield, and then another. "Wanna trade shields?"

Drif chuckled.

"Didn't think so."

A small flicker caught Billy's eye, and he chanced one last glance at Drif's shield. It was then that he noticed her shield hand was free; and in that hand, she clutched a small-but-growing ball of bluish lightning.

Werian, his coarse hair standing on end, shook with pent up energy. He snarled, showing his spiteful teeth, and then sprang. Within two swift gallops, he had crossed the floor of the great hall and leapt through the air at Billy.

The troghoul's sudden turn caught Billy off guard, and he had to hug the floor to avoid its claws. Werian landed in a deep crouch, then spun and pounced at Deordrif.

The elf warrior hunkered down and held up her shield. A pale blue spider web of light danced across it just before Werian hit. There was a crack like a whip and a flash of light. Deordrif rolled her shoulders, and her opponent went sailing over her and back into the shadows under the gallery. The troghoul let out a yowl, and Drif charged after him.

Billy scrambled to his feet. As his eyes found Ergyfel, the sorcerer's hand came out from behind his back. Like Deordrif, he had been gathering energy to cast at his enemy, and the ball of crackling light he now held was as big as a prize pumpkin.

Ergyfel stretched out his hand and flung a bolt of feral lightning. Instinctively, Billy held up his arm in front of his face and ducked. The lightning struck his buckler and bounded for the ceiling. It struck one of the impressive chandeliers, sending huge sparks in every direction and burning through the rope that held it up.

Billy, knocked to the floor by the attack, scooted away as the chandelier came down in front of the dais where Ergyfel stood. Bits of candle, iron, and wood exploded and skittered across the floor. He felt the splash of hot wax on his leg and tried to wipe it off. Then he felt heat on his arm and looked at the buckler, which glowed with a faint red color before returning to its greenish patina. Once again, he righted himself and looked for Ergyfel.

The usurper was getting to his feet on the lower steps of the dais. He gripped his left side and stooped over as if wounded, but already he was conjuring more lightning in his cursed troghoul's hand.

Billy raised Lura Zahn and charged up the great hall. Before he could gain fifteen feet, Ergyfel released his next bolt. The lightning came in low, but bounced off the floor and turned as if seeking Billy.

Once again, he held up his arm, and the bolt struck the buckler. The impact kicked him back, but then the lightning jumped and skipped across the floor in the direction from whence it came.

Ergyfel scurried up the steps of the dais, then dove for the top and rolled away as the lightning smashed into the steps with a boom.

Billy pushed up to his knees and examined the glowing red buckler. It was quick to cool and appeared unharmed, but he wondered how many more lightning bolts it could take.

Drif and Werian broke out of the shadows and landed on the floor in front of the dais, with the troghoul on top. Drif's sword jumped from her hand and slid to a stop out of her reach. The beast grabbed hold of her shoulders with its huge hands and slammed her back and head against the stones. It repeated this battering until she looked like a rag doll.

Ergyfel spun a silver pitcher in the air between his hands at incredible speed. The Magister's sword was stuck in the floor of the dais by his feet. Billy charged the dais, hoping to get past the distracted troghoul and introduce Lura Zahn to his foe. As he reached the half-way mark, a blinding light flashed, and Billy beheld Ergyfel levitating a bright, fiery, roiling glob of molten metal.

The king thrust out his hand, pointing at Billy, and the blazing silver bubble shot across the room. There was no cover, so an instant before the missile hit, Billy raised the buckler and hid his face in his shoulder.

The impact spun him around and sent him sprawling across the floor. Instantly, he felt burning on his left arm and rolled to a sitting position. Most of the molten projectile had stuck to the buckler and turned it into a spurting, fuming bowl of silver and bronze. The liquid metal that splashed on Billy's arm skipped off him, but the heat coming from the buckler was intensifying. The silver was melting its way through.

The entire buckler now felt too hot to touch. Billy reached for the band that held it to his arm and it burned his fingers. If not for his tunic, the heat would blister his flesh. The back of the little shield glowed brighter. Any moment, the molten metal would tunnel its way through the bronze and onto his arm. The band burned through to his skin, and the pain multiplied.

This is the moment of truth. Either I'm a wizard, or I'm not! He focused as best he could against the pain, throwing up every trick his mind could fathom. *It's cold. That's all. It's very cold!* Nothing worked.

Billy closed his eyes and stopped fighting the pain. He allowed himself to feel all the pain had to offer, and then he let it roll over and out of him. He imagined the pain to be smoke carried on a breeze and himself an open window. The pain passed through him but did not affect him. At that moment, he escaped its tyranny.

He flicked the band on his arm with a finger. *"Brehegan!"*

The band holding the buckler to his arm cracked, and it fell to the floor. Billy took a deep breath and placed his hand over the wounded arm. His mother's ring sparkled, and he felt its healing touch.

Werian's claws were now on Deordrif's wrists. He straddled her and threw his weight forward to pin her in place. He lowered his snout to her chest and sniffed and licked and slobbered his way to her face. She opened her eyes, and he bared his teeth in a bizarre and contemptuous smile. He tilted his head and wriggled his crude tongue across her cheek, and she turned away.

Billy turned when he heard the misshapen creature laugh. The sound gripped his heart. He wondered what wickedness could twist such a lovely sound as laughter into such haunting and offensive scrapes.

"Stop playing with your food and come help me!" Ergyfel shouted.

Werian growled at his master, then turned his angry countenance to Deordrif. Bit by bit, he stretched open his jaws to bite her face.

Drif brought her knee up into the troghoul's tender parts. His eyes popped open, and his lips drew together like a drawstring bag. She kneed him again, and a thin whine escaped his shrunken mouth. A moment later, Drif used both legs and launched him over her head.

Before the monster came to grips with where he was, Deordrif spun off the floor, grabbed her sword, and kicked him in the face. Werian's head smacked against the dais and snapped back around. He roared and lunged to bite her leg, but the elf deftly leapt aside and took his head with her sword.

Drif turned to scan around her. The sorcerer-king glared at Billy. He had conjured another handful of lightning and looked ready to unleash it.

She drew her knife and spun it in her palm to hold the thin blade in her fingers, then drew back her arm and targeted Ergyfel's throat. She breathed in to steady her throw and glanced back at Billy. Though he was moving, he was at the mercy of his enemy.

Drif returned her focus to Ergyfel and held her throw. Tiny tendrils of lightning escaped from the dazzling sphere between Ergyfel's hands, striking the dais and his sword. He was losing control, but still he nurtured it. A tendril suddenly arced to his face and shoulder. He cried out and turned his face away, stretching out his hands to release the lightning.

Drif closed her eyes, said, "Curse you, Malkry!" and hurled her knife. The blade sliced through the air and sank into the heart of the king's throne.

Ergyfel released the formidable bolt, and Billy darted for the columns to his left, but the lightning twisted on its course as if drawn to Billy. At that moment, Billy's feet slipped on a patch of candle wax, and he slammed into the floor.

The lightning collided with the column behind him in a deafening crack and split the colossal timber like an axe to firewood. From six feet high to the soaring ceiling, half of the giant oak pillar sheered away and launched a shower of splinters into the air. This massive chunk of lumber then plunged to the floor. Billy covered his head and held his breath. The enormous sliver broke through the stone floor and splintered, pinning Billy to the base of the column.

He pulled a large splinter from his forearm with a yelp, then tried to free himself from the broken column, but he was trapped. When he peeked around the fractured wood, he saw Ergyfel howling and clutching the remnants of the lightning ball. Billy locked eyes with Deordrif, whose back was to their enemy.

"Get out of here, Drif! It's up to you now!

Drif took a step towards Billy. "I'm coming!"

"No! Leave me!"

"I'll get you out!"

"No! You're Tirn Aill's last hope!"

Deordrif's expression became resolute. She turned towards the dais, where Ergyfel had restored his lightning ball to its prior size. Without hesitation, she charged up the steps.

Ergyfel sneered at Billy. "Now, you will die!"

The king thrust out his hands to direct all the lightning he could muster at Billy, but at that moment, Deordrif dove in front of him and stole the lightning from his hands with her armor-encased body. Drif screamed and collapsed to the dais in a heap.

"No!" Billy cried.

Ergyfel fell to his knees, panting, shaking, and clutching his midsection. He rocked back and forth several times before sitting up. He examined the smoking body of the elf warrior lying on the corner of his dais to his right, and then he looked at Billy. He rose to his feet with the help of his sword and kicked the elf, but she did not stir.

Ergyfel pried his sword from the wooden platform. "So.... Once again, it's a fair fight."

Billy placed his hands on the rough oak spar pinning him in place and pushed. He focused on his mother's ring and tried again. The enormous piece of lumber creaked.

Ergyfel observed Billy's efforts. "Oh, please. You're wasting your time and insulting the power of that ring with parlor tricks."

The sorcerer-king rested his sword on his shoulder and descended the steps of the dais. He whistled the first notes of a tune, but stopped when he reached the bottom step. As he sauntered across the floor of the great hall, he spoke to Billy, who was busy trying to push and wriggle his way free.

"You accused me of killing your mother for that ring, but allow me to set the record straight. I killed her because she stood in my way to the throne; the same reason I killed my dear cousins, Kathryn and William. The ring was only ever a bonus, or should have been."

Billy focused on his mother's ring and the pillar trapping him, desperately searching for anything he could use to escape. The wood under his hands felt polished and lifeless.

Ergyfel stopped a few steps from him to lean on his sword. He took a few deep breaths before continuing. "Now, with you. ...When I take your miserable little life, the ring will be a bonus again."

Billy felt a tingle from his mother's ring as it touched something within the broken hunk of column. A tiny spark of life. Dim and dormant. In his mind, Billy saw trees in winter, their limbs stripped bare, and their sap all but stopped. They seemed dead, and yet—come spring—they would be reborn. They would blossom and grow with new life; more life than they had before.

"You need it," Billy said, attempting to stall his nemesis. "You need it if you ever hope to reverse the curse."

"Well, honestly—" Ergyfel stopped to examine his transformed hand. "I will admit, I do need it more than I did before, but I'd still kill you whether you had the ring or not."

Billy remembered the trees he had climbed as a child in the Valley of the Yew, and the trees in Tirn Aill, which had told him of the ancient trees in the lands of men that loved the faeries as their children, and longed for their return.

Ergyfel continued. "You see, I don't like you. Even if I did, you still present a threat to my continued rule. I can't have that."

Billy reached out his mind to contact the spark of life within the wood. It was so tiny, so fragile. He touched it, and the spark transformed, losing some of its intensity, but expanding into an ember. He imagined cupping it in his hands, encouraging it to grow with a gentle breath.

Ergyfel stood over Billy and looked down at him. He eyed Billy's fingers. "I think ... I think I'll just chop it from your hand. Then you can watch as I show you its real power!"

"Help! Somebody help me!" At that moment, Billy felt the life within the shattered column awake.

Ergyfel chuckled and looked around the hall. "It's just you and me. No one is coming to save you this time." He raised his sword to strike.

Billy focused every ounce of energy he could muster on the life within the column, allowing the ring to magnify it. "Remember where you come from."

Ergyfel stopped. "What?"

"Your children have returned."

"You are nothing with that ring, ... but I will be unstoppable."

Ergyfel drew back his sword and took aim.

The stone floor exploded beneath Ergyfel's feet as thick roots shot forth from the broken pillar. This threw him to the side, and his sword struck the living wood. Limbs and all manner of branches sprouted along the length of the column, transforming it into a kind of tree. The branches and roots grew, pushing and pulling the trunk upright enough for Billy to squirm his way out.

Ergyfel's sword was stuck in the side of the new tree. He tugged on it, but it would not budge. Before his eyes, the tree grew bark, which threatened to lock his sword in place forever. He put his foot against the trunk and heaved with all his might. The sword popped loose, but his foot was stuck—surrounded by the quickly hardening bark.

Billy jumped to his feet, saw Ergyfel's predicament, and charged him. He swung Lura Zahn, but Ergyfel blocked the attack with his sword and reposted. Billy ducked and tried again, but the rapidly growing and budding limbs impeded his swings. Ergyfel thrust his sword at Billy's face through the building bramble of branches. Billy's blade blocked this and countered with a quick slash. Lura Zahn sliced through Ergyfel's hood, and it fell back off his head.

Billy froze, shocked by Ergyfel's countenance. The right side of his face appeared the same as it always had. However, the left side was staggering: jagged irregular fangs protruded through coarse, scabby lips in a menacing lopsided grin; the eye, once black as night, was filmy and deep-set, shadowed by a heavy brow and protruding cheekbone; and coarse hair grew in patches from the pink and grey flesh covering his distorted skull.

Ergyfel yanked his foot free of the bark with a grunt and tore his robe further on the rough, clingy branches, which now had leaves. He spun out of his shredded robe and chopped his way through the new growth towards Billy.

The fantastic growth of the tree trapped Billy too. He pushed and ducked his way out of the jumble and into the open hall. Then he was face to face with Ergyfel. He turned to run, and Ergyfel struck with his sword. The blade cut Billy's shoulder, but he managed to roll away.

He rolled to his feet, grabbing his shoulder, then turned around. Ergyfel was almost upon him. Billy struck the floor with the pommel of his sword. *"Deru!"*

Ergyfel's sword arm stopped in mid swing. He tried to complete the swing but found his arm caught in a web of vine-like branches. A moment later, they pulled his arm back and the branches encircled his body and legs. The branches grew thicker, and then whisked Ergyfel off the floor and into the air.

Billy watched in amazement as more and more branches surrounded Ergyfel and bound him in place. At that moment, he realized that some of the branches were not coming from the broken column, but from the adjacent columns. He looked up and saw that both parts of the broken column had transformed into a tree and that the growth was spreading across the ceiling to the other great columns. He returned his eye to Ergyfel, who struggled against his leafy captor, to cast a spell.

Billy said, *"Gweyesan,"* and the limbs, vines, and branches tightened around their prey. *"Gweyesan!"*

Ergyfel let out a gasp. The foliage continued to squeeze him tighter. There was a snap, and he cried out in pain. He tried desperately to free his sword and cut his way from the trees, but they held him fast.

A cracking sounded from above, and large hunks of wood and plaster came crashing to the floor. Billy looked up, and a raindrop struck his face. The growth of the trees had opened a hole in the roof. Lightning flashed in the sky, and Billy jumped back.

Ergyfel pulled the vines from his mouth and shouted, *"Vipera forma!"*

The Magister grew thin, and his skin became dark and scaled. Within a few heartbeats, he and his sword had transformed into a giant black viper with silvery fangs. He slithered down the tree—his wet, slippery body undeterred by the entangling branches. Once on the floor, he raced straight for Billy with startling speed.

Billy retreated, but the snake caught up to him. It rose up in front of his path, hissing and flaring its hood, and forced him back to the center of the hall. He jabbed at the viper with Lura Zahn, but it was far too quick. Before he could react, the snake threw one of its coils behind Billy and tripped him. It raced forward to strike at his face, and he threw up his elbow. The viper struck his arm and retreated into the shadows behind the new trees.

His arm burned hot and cold. His skin felt like flame, his bones ice. He sat up and examined the damage. Two red, swollen punctures marked his forearm. A milky substance dripped from the wound, and around it, his skin grew taut and turned black. Despite his gripping the arm at the elbow, the pain continued to inch towards Billy's shoulder.

A terrible cry rang out. Billy looked up, expecting to face the snake again, and found Ergyfel on his knees. He held his head and side and writhed in agony. His fingers tore at the blistered skin on his torso and neck and revealed that the troghoul curse had claimed these parts of his body. His lower jaw on both sides was now heavier and jutted out beyond his upper lip to give him an exaggerated under bite.

The tremendous pain in Billy's arm brought him back to his own predicament. The bitten arm was now paralyzed, and the burning spread into his chest and neck. He grew weaker, and his legs shook and tingled as they went numb. He fell back onto the cold stone floor. His heart slowed and grew cold. Billy's mind raced. He only had seconds to act. His sight darkened. A spell he had read in the Witan's tree came to his lips. The instant he finished it, the pain retreated. He whispered the spell again, and his heartbeat became normal. One more repetition and he could move his arms and legs.

Billy sighed and opened his eyes. The pain receded, leaving behind tired, sore muscles. He heard muttering and sat up to look for Ergyfel.

The misshapen usurper was standing now and making strange signs with his hands. The same signs over and over. Billy recognized them as a magical gesticulation and got to his feet. Ergyfel raised his voice, and his repetitious muttering became a chant. He looked crazed. At that moment, Billy realized that his enemy was attempting to cast a spell and failing. With each attempt, he grew more turbulent, and then he stopped.

He turned and chopped on the tree closest to him with his sword. After a few frenzied swings, he halted and glared at Billy.

"Curse you, faerie!" he said, with some difficulty.

Billy raised Lura Zahn with a flourish and advanced on his foe. Ergyfel countered his movement by circling towards the dais. As he reached the steps, Billy rushed forward and struck at him. Ergyfel blocked and reposted. Back and forth, the rivals traded strikes and parries as they ascended to the top of the dais. Ergyfel was on the retreat, and still Billy marveled at how well he handled a sword.

Billy was tiring and decided to let Lura Zahn take control of the fight. The sword immediately dished out a flurry of blows that forced Ergyfel to a strictly defensive stance. At last, Ergyfel dodged under an attack and ran behind his throne.

"Who taught you to fight, boy?" His troghoul tongue caused him trouble with speech.

"I might ask you the same." Billy approached the throne. "I didn't think you would dirty your hands with a blade."

"My brother taught me to deal with rodents ... like you."

He struck between the two thrones with his long sword. Billy managed to block, but then circled around the thrones. Ergyfel countered to keep the thrones between them. They circled once and stopped, with Billy once again in front and Ergyfel behind.

Ergyfel moved left and right, first behind the queen's throne, and then behind his own. He did this several times, and then began to taunt Billy.

When Ergyfel stepped behind the queen's throne, Billy put his hands together and threw them apart. "Ah-we!" A blast of wind knocked over the queen's throne and sent it skidding some feet across the dais. Ergyfel jumped behind the king's throne, which was firmly attached to the floor.

With only one throne standing between them, Billy charged around it. Ergyfel took flight across the platform with Billy close on his heels. As he reached the downed throne, Ergyfel kicked it backward at Billy and tripped him.

Ergyfel turned near the front of the dais when he saw Billy was down and lunged for the kill. Billy scrambled to get to his feet and was caught in the legs of the throne. Ergyfel swung, but his blade struck the dais floor, far short of its mark. It was at this point that the combatants realized Deordrif was conscious and holding Ergyfel's foot.

Ergyfel struck at Drif with his sword as Billy stumbled to his feet. Ergyfel's sword clanged against the elf's armor, and he hopped out of her grip, his momentum carrying him back towards his throne.

Billy was about to attack Ergyfel when Drif yelled, "Duck!"

Billy did as instructed and felt something whoosh over his head. Still squatting, he looked over his shoulder. Snegaddrick stood whirling a large saddlebag. The weight of the heavy bag dragged the ambassador around, twisting his feet and throwing off his balance.

Splash! Gold coins exploded into the air as the heavily laden saddlebag walloped Ergyfel's back. Ergyfel dropped his sword with a grunt and sailed face first into his throne while Snegaddrick stumbled towards the front of the dais. Drif caught the stout Gwythian's legs, and he fell off the platform onto his head before Drif finally passed out.

Billy rushed Ergyfel. Before the usurper could push up on the throne arms, Billy booted him in the rear, forcing him back against the seat. Ergyfel spun around on the floor with his back to the chair and made a grab for his sword. Billy kicked him in the face and stepped on his sword hand. He then put his knee into Ergyfel's chest, pinning him to the throne.

Ergyfel took a swipe at Billy with his troghoul claws, and Billy raised Lura Zahn to block. The enchanted blade severed Ergyfel's claws and he yowled in pain. He howled in the manner of troghouls and whined as he cradled his wounded hand.

Billy took Lura Zahn and stabbed the seat cushion next to Ergyfel's neck. Without hesitation, he brought the blade across Ergyfel's throat and applied pressure.

"Don't kill me! Please, don't kill me!"

Billy glared at him. "Don't kill you?" He applied more pressure.

"Please, please!" A tear ran down his cheek. "Please. I beg you."

"Give me one good reason I should spare you."

"Because—because I'm your cousin!"

"That didn't stop *you*." Billy leaned forward to push on his sword.

"Stop, stop, stop! I'm sorry I killed your mother!"

The mention of his mother caught Billy off guard. In the past, when he thought of Ergyfel killing her, all he wanted was revenge. Now that he had revenge in his grasp, it felt insufficient. The emptiness her absence instilled, and the pain since he'd discovered her murder, were together far greater than any single act of violence could undo.

Billy remembered that Hugh had warned him long ago that if Ergyfel ever apologized, it was only because he was up to no good.

"You're lying." Billy pushed a little harder.

"She—she never trusted me. She kept after me, keeping me from the king, relentlessly. I had to do it. But even then, I couldn't do it myself. So I used your father."

Billy recalled the overwhelming heartbreak when he discovered that his mother had died at his father's hands. His hatred thrust up through his chest into his throat. The man responsible for so much agony was at his mercy. He adjusted his grip on Lura Zahn, and blood appeared on the eager blade.

"And—and your father." Ergyfel tried to stall. "I poisoned him, even though he had been kind to me and took me in. I was blinded by ambition. I'm sorry."

"You put your ambition before Lyonesse! Before your king! Before Kathryn and Gaelyn's lives!"

"Yes." Ergyfel attempted to arch away from Billy's blade. "I had them killed, and I framed you. I see now that was a mistake. I'm sorry."

"Sorry?"

"Gaelyn wasn't supposed to die."

"But with every ounce of your black heart, you ordered Kathryn's murder, didn't you?"

"Yes. She had the throne given to her for nothing but her pretty smile. I'm here for years, scraping and bowing, and she walks in, and he hands her the throne? William passed me over without a thought. Made me hate him even more."

"So you drank your hatred for courage and poisoned your own cousin, the king."

Ergyfel nodded.

"And Wyte, and all the other innocents you've trampled into the dust? The people of Lyonesse! How many thousands has your war pushed into the grave so that you could sit on your throne? How many lives destroyed to build your dais?"

"Yes! Yes! I'm sorry for it all! What more do you want of me?"

"Sorry. Sorry just doesn't cut it."

Ergyfel's eyes grew large and stared at the gallery side of the hall. Billy glanced over but saw nothing there save shadows.

"Caenne," Ergyfel whispered.

Billy looked to his right again. After a moment, he turned back to Ergyfel. "You killed Caenne, didn't you? I saw her face in that demon you sent to destroy me."

"No! Unclean spirit. Go away. Please, go away." He closed his eyes and turned away.

Billy watched in amazement as Ergyfel wept.

"I am not your lover. Please ... let me be." He pulled away as if someone was stroking his face in a bothersome manner. "I'm sorry, Caenne. I had to kill you. Dheumon would have taken Maeven. I had no choice."

Ergyfel looked Billy in the eyes. "I had no choice. I had to kill Caenne to save Maeven. Don't you see? I didn't want to kill her. I swear it. But the demon gave me no choice."

A ruckus exploded from the grand gallery above. Billy and Ergyfel turned to see the lords and ladies of the court standing at the railing, pounding it with their fists. Many leaned over it to spit insults and curses at their king, others simply to spit. Some shouted for Ergyfel's death.

"Kill him! Kill him!"

Three armored knights followed by a handful of lords scrambled down the steps from the gallery to the floor. As they approached the dais, the leading knight transformed before their eyes, becoming a coarse, stocky, lopsided fisherman with scraggly wet hair. The air reeked of putrefaction. The lords and ladies in the gallery above gasped and the knights backed away.

The fisherman smiled at Ergyfel with his bulging red eyes and black stained lips.

Ergyfel whispered his name, "Dheumon."

The sinister old fisherman's smile broadened. "A parting gift for Your Majesty," he said with a dramatic bow. Then, without another word, the foul demon collapsed into a dark puddle on the floor and disappeared down a drain, leaving behind only his stench.

The lords and ladies of the court resumed their yelling and cursing and spitting. Billy could barely hear himself think over the hubbub. Their shouts to kill Ergyfel felt like a hammer on his neck and an anvil on his sword hand.

"Quiet!" When at last the hall was still, Billy spoke. "You would have me kill your king? The king you crowned in this very castle!"

"Yes!" they shouted. "Kill him!"

The mob once again erupted in noisy chaos, every soul present clamoring for Ergyfel's death. Billy looked at their distorted faces and recognized many as the same lords and ladies who had demanded his death at his trial before King William. He then looked at Ergyfel, whose grotesque face was as grim as the gallows. All he could feel was pity.

Billy gave a shrill whistle, and the crowd quieted.

"Ergyfel began his reign ... by killing my father, the king." He pressed on Ergyfel's throat with his blade. "It's true, he deserves death."

The crowd interrupted Billy with cheers.

Billy shouted over the mob, "If I am to be your king ... "

The lords and ladies became still, and Billy continued. "If I am to be your king ... my reign will be different, starting right now."

He withdrew his sword, sheathed it, and turned to face the crowd. The lords and ladies stared at him in stunned silence. Whispers grew into mutterings. With each step Billy took away from Ergyfel, the din grew louder. He stopped at the top of the steps to observe their folly. He threw up his hands and started down the steps, shaking his head.

Then gasps and cries reached him from the gallery. Billy looked to his left, and then spun to follow their eyes to the dais behind him. Ergyfel stood above him, raising his sword high over his head. Billy reached for Lura Zahn, and the weapon leapt into his hand. He threw his sword up to block, but in his haste, stabbed the blade into the wooden stage.

Billy glanced down and pulled, but the blade stuck fast. He felt trapped. Ergyfel roared and swung his sword.

A long black blade burst from Ergyfel's chest. His head fell back as he dropped his sword behind him. The weapon clanked onto the wooden deck. Then, with mouth wide open, he fixed his eyes on the blade in his chest. His hands groped the gory blade, and he turned to see his killer.

Ergyfel wavered, and then retreated a step. His heel caught the edge of the dais, and he fell. Billy dodged out of his way, and the usurper landed on his back at the bottom, driving Drif's sword through his body to the hilt.

Billy looked to the top of the steps and found Maeven standing with bloody hands clasped over her mouth, tears streaking her face. He stared at the shaking queen, then back to her husband lying at the base of the steps. A tear bled from the dying king's eye as he gazed upon his wife.

"My love! My love!" Maeven sobbed. "I—I couldn't let you go on ... knowing what you did to Caenne." The queen let out an anguished cry and fell to her knees, pulling the hair at her temples. "Please! Please! Forgive me, my love!"

Maeven held out a pleading hand to her husband. He reached for her with a trembling hand.

"I did it to save you."

Maeven closed her eyes and shook her head. "No. No! No!"

The queen rose up and hurled herself forward onto the blade protruding through Ergyfel's chest.

Billy's breath caught in his lungs. It felt as if all the air in the room had escaped. He closed his eyes. He didn't want to move. He didn't want to breathe. He held his breath until it ached. Then the queen spoke, and he had to look.

"My beloved." Maeven kissed Ergyfel's cheek.

Ergyfel sobbed. "No. Not you. Only one ever loved me. I killed you, too."

"Shhh." Maeven touched a gentle finger to his lips.

Ergyfel gestured to their surroundings. "I thought all this ... would mean something in the end. But it's empty ... except for you."

Ergyfel's face transformed and, in that moment, he was wholly human. Maeven smiled. Ergyfel smiled. They kissed and were still.

The door at the back of the great hall burst open. King Ergyfel's page rushed in.

"Your Majesty! Your Majes-ty!"

The youth stood panting halfway between the door and the dais, staring at Billy and the bodies of his king and queen. His eyes wandered to the wreckage on the floor, and the forest of giant trees that circled the hall and the open roof above. His jaw dropped as he ambled forward.

"What news?" asked one of the knights standing near Billy.

The page shook his head and returned his eyes to his king's body.

The knight demanded, "Lyart! What news?"

Lyart gave his eyes to the knight. "I ..."

"Yes?"

"I come from the wall—" The page's eyes gravitated back to Ergyfel and Maeven lying on the floor. "I have news ..."

"What news, boy?"

"For the king."

The knight shook the royal page by his shoulders. "What news?"

"The battle has begun! The Gwythies are attacking."

Billy looked up at the shattered ceiling and saw blue sky streaked with wisps of cloud. Morning painted golden light on the remaining plaster through the leaves on the column-trees.

The knight nodded to his companion, then turned to Billy. "Forgive me, Highness. We must go. They will have need of us on the walls."

The two knights and a number of lords headed for the exit.

"Wait!"

The men turned to Billy.

"Hang a red and yellow flag from the top of the highest tower of the donjon."

"But Highness, ... those are the enemy's colors."

"It's the signal to call off the attack."

The hall broke into pandemonium, as all present looked about and shouted for a red and yellow flag. Most of the lords and ladies ran from the hall or sent their servants scurrying out the door to search elsewhere.

"And somebody get a doctor for my friend!"

Lyart approached Billy and bowed. "I shall fetch the physician immediately, Your Highness." The page then sped off, dodging rabbit-like between noble and servant alike.

The roar from Hereweald's army and the pounding of their siege weapons filtered through the broken roof. The frantic search continued for several minutes, but they could find no red and yellow flag.

"You." Billy grabbed a passing lord.

The man spun, holding his hands up defensively.

"Take off your hose."

The man was, at first, perplexed, but then dropped his eyes and spied his red and yellow leggings. "Oh!"

Within seconds, the lord's bare feet were standing on the wet stone floor, and his hose were speeding their way to the highest tower in the castle.

CHAPTER THIRTY-FOUR

When the Hurly-burly's Done

Billy sat in the great hall of Orgulous, on the throne of Lyonesse, wearing the crown of his father, King William, which had mysteriously reappeared in its presentation case on the day of Ergyfel's funeral—an event that had a smaller turnout than the local cheese tasting that same day. Billy's coronation occurred a respectable three days later, and so many were in attendance that the ceremony had to relocate outside to accommodate them all. Now, one day after that glorious event, all the inns were still full, and a city of tents covered the hills outside Orgulous and Nyraval for the multitude that wished to meet their new king and swear allegiance.

This being the first day he held court, Billy was nervous, but he soon relaxed when he saw all the smiling faces that crowded the floor and gallery of the hall. All evidence of Ergyfel's reign had been swept away, and the people reveled in the hope and returned glory brought by the heir of their beloved king, William. They also marveled at the colossal trees that now lived in harmony with the great hall, gathering light through an ingenious system of louvers. The initial bramble of branches from these giants had vanished, leaving only smooth, graceful trunks and a lush canopy up top, All else in the hall had been restored to its original grandeur.

Billy took a scroll from a large stack that sat on a table next to his throne. He opened it, scanned it, and then addressed his court.

"First things first. I hereby decree that Lady Myrredith of Cyndyn Hall shall be legally, and in all other considerations, my sister."

The crowd sizzled with whispers, and Billy gave them a moment to quiet before he continued. However, instead of quieting, the crowd passed through muttering and went straight to buzzing. He held up his hand. When that was unsuccessful, he looked to Hugh, who marched to the middle step of the dais and thumped on the steps with his sword. The heavy thudding soon got the court's attention.

Myrredith bowed. "Your Majesty, it is too much!"

"You don't want to be my sister?"

"There are many here who would feel uncomfortable with me as an heir."

"Let them be uncomfortable."

"But—"

"Would you give my father this much trouble if it were his decree?"

Myrredith bowed her head. "I suppose not, Your Majesty. Please, forgive me."

Billy waited until he could see Myrredith's eyes, and then he smiled at her. "Don't worry, sister. Once they have time to chew on it, the people will see the wisdom of my choice."

The new king took another scroll and read it. He then turned his gaze to Hugh. "Are you ready?"

"Yes, Your Majesty."

"Sir Hugh, you are hereby reinstated as a knight of this realm and as King's Champion, with all titles and responsibilities thereof. I also return to you all lands and titles that should be yours by right of inheritance from your mother and father. The word 'traitor' shall be stricken from any record found in the kingdom that identifies Sir Sedgemore as such.

Furthermore, the name of Sir Sedgemore shall hereafter be spoken with the awe and respect befitting a hero of the realm, and I decree that a history and ballad be written to honor his great and chivalrous deeds."

"A song, Your Majesty?" Hugh frowned.

Billy looked up from the scroll. "You're the ones who talked me into accepting this crown. Now that I have, it seems only fair that you listen and accept my gifts and decrees."

"Yes, Your Majesty."

"Of course, Your Majesty."

"I worked really hard on these!"

"Yes, Your Majesty."

Billy handed the scroll to his scribe. "Make it two ballads. Oh, and one for Sir Hugh."

Hugh shot Billy a dismayed look, which the king reposted with a smirk.

Billy picked another scroll from the pile. "Malcolm the Magnificent!"

Malcolm came forward and bowed. "Would you care for some juggling, Your Majesty?"

"Later." Billy gave him a grin. "Malcolm, you have been my teacher, my partner, my rescuer, defender, and stalwart friend. There is much I could reward you with if you would stay here in Orgulous."

"Well, Your Majesty ..."

"But I think you like the road under your feet as much as castle floors, perhaps more."

"His Majesty knows me well," the highlander said.

Billy got up from his throne and descended to the bottom step of the dais. "Since you cannot be persuaded to stay, you must have something to take with you on your journeys. Kneel."

Malcolm looked surprised, but knelt. Billy turned to Hugh and requested his sword with a hand gesture. With sword in hand, he laid the heavy weapon on Malcolm's shoulder. Then, in rapid succession, he touched his shoulder, the opposite shoulder, and back. This went well until the final blow, which grazed Malcolm's ear.

"Ouch!"

"Sorry—sorry!" Billy tried hard not to reach out and touch his old juggling master's ear. He returned Hugh's sword and crossed his arms.

The court snickered, then someone let loose a guffaw, and all pretense of solemnity fell away. After a brief laugh, Billy raised his hand, and the assembly quieted. He watched as the juggling master felt his ear for blood.

"Arise, Sir Malcolm, Knight of Lyonesse."

Malcolm rose to his feet with a grin, his hand still rubbing his sore ear. The court let out a loud cheer. "Sir Malcolm! Sir Malcolm! Hurrah!"

Billy backed up to the top of the platform and raised his hand and his voice. "And I also offer you this gift." He held up three gold balls, each with dozens of star-shaped holes perforating their surfaces. Engraved on each ball were the letters: M.M. "The customary gift for a knight is spurs, but I felt you, and we, would be better served by these. I believe you know how to use them?"

Billy tossed the balls into the air, and bright light shone from the tiny star-shaped holes, splashing dots of light across the entire hall. The crowd gasped, their breath held captive by the dazzling display.

Just before they hit the ground, Malcolm snatched the golden orbs from the air and confined them in his hands like fire stolen from heaven. He then opened his cupped palms to examine his prize. A wide grin spread across his face, as he held the orbs to his chest and bowed to Billy.

As Sir Malcolm strutted back to his place in the crowd, Billy picked up yet another scroll and examined it briefly. "Stitch ... Aeth? Are you here, my friend?"

"Aye," came a voice from the rear.

All eyes turned to watch as Aeth ambled to the front of the great hall with the aid of a cane. His legs were still crooked, but serviceable, and the bandages were all gone. He kept one hand tucked into his new tunic and wore a patch where an eye should have been. Billy smiled when he realized that Aeth's new clothes were in Cyndyn house colors and looked very much like those given to him by Lady Myrredith on the occasion of Kathryn's wedding to Gaelyn. The Lady of Cyndyn stood nearby, nodding to her new friend.

"Your Majesty," Aeth said with a bow.

"I'm sorry we were unable to undo all the wickedness done to you. Perhaps with more time and knowledge, we can one day do better."

"My thanks, Your Majesty. I know ya did your best."

"When last we spoke, you said you weren't sure what name you wanted to be known by. Have you made a decision? I only ask because this is pretty official stuff."

The court giggled.

"Derian, Your Majesty."

"Your father's chosen name?"

"Aye."

"You certain?"

"Yes. I grant ya, the reputation of that name needs mendin', but I'm willin' to put in the effort."

"I see." Billy handed the scroll to his scribe. "With that attitude, I know you're the best man for the job."

"Job, Your Majesty? I wasn't actually looking—"

"I hereby appoint Derian Stitch as Guardian of Dyven. His name shall be added to the charter of noble houses, as a member of my clan, and granted the title of lord." Billy turned to the scribe and said, "Please, read the rest."

The scribe stood and read aloud from the scroll as Billy descended to the floor.

"I further decree that money from the royal treasury be set aside for the building and maintaining of Dyven Home, a home for lost children and orphans, which will be under the supervision of the Guardian of Dyven, as advised by the Lady of Cyndyn Hall, with a royal mandate to help lost children and orphans find their way home."

Billy signaled the scribe to stop and put his hands on Stitch's shoulders. "It goes on a bit more. The point is that you have a new purpose in life, my friend. All the lost children of Dyven—and this war has made plenty—all of them will be your charge. I want you to find them, and then find them all a home—find them a family."

Derian Stitch stood before his friend the king with a tear in his eye. He stood as tall and straight as he could manage. Any semblance to the boy Aeth had all but disappeared. He bowed. "It will be an honor to serve, Your Majesty."

Billy stepped forward, and the friends hugged.

"Derian Stitch, huh?" the ex-pickpocket whispered.

"I thought you'd like that."

"Thank you, Your Majesty."

"You can call me Billy."

"Hey, are you taller?"

Billy pulled back and examined himself and his friend at arm's length. "I suppose I am." The friends parted, and the king ascended his dais.

"Camion!" Billy announced next. When the giant approached, he continued. "Camion, I appoint you to the office of Harbor Master of Dyven."

Camion looked askance at the scroll in Billy's hand.

"What's the matter?"

Camion pursed his lips. "I hoped for a ship job, Your Majesty. I only know ships."

"The Harbor Master of Dyven has his own ship."

"He does?"

"Yes, Camion. A small one."

"Can he sail around Kelmyrr Bay?"

"Anytime he wishes."

Camion's eyes glazed over, and he put on a childlike smile.

"The post also comes with a house."

"I know that house. It's big!"

"Big enough for a man with a family ... ?"

"Yes, Your Majesty. Yes, Your Majesty! Thank you, Your Majesty!"

Camion bowed, spun around, and started for the back of hall.

Billy called after him, "Wait! I have arranged an escort for you and the Guardian of Dyven for your return home."

Camion stopped and turned around. He gave Billy a sheepish grin. "If I must wait, Your Majesty, so be it. But, please, don't make us wait long."

"You may leave tomorrow if you wish, but—*please*—stay for the feast."

"Food? Thank you, Your Majesty."

Billy looked about the great hall. "Wyte! Please, come forward."

A gaunt man, who had been standing alone in the shadows under the grand gallery, stepped forward. His movements were slow but deliberate, and he stooped as if carrying a great pot of lead on his shoulders. A spear served as his walking staff, and his face was as humble and contrite as a priest. His pale skin shone like rough-hewn marble, and he wore his long grey hair pulled back into a ponytail that fell from the back of his broad-brimmed helmet onto a new, blue guard's tabard. Eyes ever down, he approached the dais and bowed.

"How are you, Wyte?"

Wyte blinked and did his best to look the king in the eyes. "Well, thanks to Your Majesty. My mind is finally free of the tyrant."

"Is the light sensitivity any better?"

"Yes, Your Majesty, but the world has left me behind. The friends I had, the family I knew, and the king and queen I served ... they have all gone."

"I am sorry. There are few who have lost as much as you. Because your sacrifice was great, you will be rewarded with much."

Wyte fell to his knees. He removed his helmet and held it in his hands at his chest. "Your Majesty, I failed in my duty to your parents. I do not deserve reward. But I beg you: allow me to remain in your service."

"Nonsense. I saw what happened, Wyte. It's not your fault. You are a victim of the tyrant, just as much as my parents." It felt peculiar to Billy that he should still fear to speak Ergyfel's name aloud, even though he was dead, but he wasn't alone in this.

"I—I should have done more."

Billy stopped and looked around the hall. "Wyte, your accuser is dead. I alone have the authority to judge you, and I say you are innocent. In the oubliette, you put your trust in me."

"And you have delivered me, my king."

"Trust me now when I tell you: any shortcomings of your past are forgotten."

The old guard cried. He held his fist to his head. "I cannot forget, my king."

Billy sighed. "You need to forgive yourself, my friend. If you are to be of service to me, you will need to get past this."

"Yes, Your Majesty. I guess I'm not ready yet."

"Nevertheless, it has come to my attention that you were never officially removed from the rolls of the king's guards, and seeing as you are still wearing the uniform, there is the small matter of back pay."

"Your Majesty?"

"As paying you would likely sap the treasury, I hereby bestow upon you Feolaghe Tor and all lands allotted that fief. May it serve you better than its previous master. Now, as to your service. ...You are also to have the title of lord."

"But I'm a guard, my king, not a noble!"

Billy smiled at his onetime cellmate. "You are now. You want to serve me?"

"Yes, Your Majesty."

"Let me decide how best you can serve."

"As you wish, Your Majesty."

"And don't worry. I will send you plenty of help."

"Thank you, Your Majesty."

As the new Lord of Feolaghe Tor shambled back into the shadows, the king picked through his stack of scrolls. After a moment, he called for Lord Finnalaghe. The elderly gentleman arrived with the aid of his niece.

"Lord Finnalaghe-Finney. I have no gift capable of repairing what harm was done you, nor reward enough to replace your valiant son, Sir Owein, who gave his life to save mine."

"Your Majesty's consideration is reward enough for this old man." Finney bowed. "I'm just happy for a shortage of gallows at the hour of my sentencing, and thankful to be forgotten in the dungeon long enough for the rightful heir to sit on the throne."

"Here, here!" came the cheer from the assembled crowd.

Billy smiled. "As am I."

"As for my son," the elderly lord continued, "I am certain he feels honored to have been of service to King William's heir."

"Nevertheless, I hereby decree that the bridge where your son and his heroic companions lost—no, that's not right—where they *gave* their lives will be rebuilt, with a monument to their courage, and a royal garrison named Owein Tor."

Lord Finnalaghe put his hand over his heart and bowed. As a very proud niece led the old gentleman away, Lyart, the king's herald, approached and bowed.

"What is it, Lyart?"

"Your Majesty, the Prince of Gwythia requests an audience."

Billy nodded to Hugh, who told Lyart, "Bid him enter."

The huge doors of the great hall creaked open, and a voice from beyond them announced in trumpet-like tones, "His Highness, Prince Hereweald of Gwythia!"

Hereweald entered the great hall, accompanied by his officers, his herald, and two of his personal guard. The crowd opened to allow the foreigners to pass through their midst. Fifteen feet from the dais, the men stopped and bowed to Billy in unison. He bowed his head to Hereweald and greeted him with a smile.

"Welcome, Prince Hereweald! And welcome to your men. It is good to see you all again."

Hereweald stepped forward. "The greater pleasure is ours, Your Majesty."

"I trust your stay with us is pleasant."

"Very pleasant, Your Majesty, though I must confess, I miss that curious red and gold banner that flew atop Orgulous on our first day. Odd as it was, it reminded me of home."

Billy smiled. "Well, even as cozy as Orgulous can be, it's still a bit drafty, and Lord Bonting's legs were getting cold!"

The assembly laughed.

"They're still cold!"

Billy tilted his head and stretched up on his throne to look over the crowd. "What's that, Bonting?"

"I said, they're still cold, Your Majesty. Your herald kept my hose. Said he was going to display them with the trophies in the feasting hall!"

The hall exploded in laughter again.

"Apologies, Bonting. That was my idea. I think they'll make for an interesting story on a cold winter's night. Allow me to make it up to you."

Billy turned to his scribe. "Take note to write a decree declaring a feast day to celebrate the 'Savior of Orgulous,' Lord Bonting. And we'll have a song written for Lord Bonting's legs!"

Amid the laughter and cheers, Sir Malcolm shouted, "I don't think Lord Bonting's legs can sing!"

"Why not, Bonting?" Billy asked. "Too cold?"

"Aye, Your Majesty."

Lady Bonting put her arm around her husband. "Don't take it personally, sire, I've been trying for years just to get them to dance!"

After the crowd had its fill of laughter, Billy turned to Hereweald. "Forgive me. I didn't mean to get so distracted."

"It is well, Your Majesty. May every day of your reign have room for laughter."

"Thank you. What can I do for Your Highness today? Do you want to see the prisoner?"

"No, Your Majesty. I do not wish to see Snegaddrick until we leave for home."

"Of course, Prince Hereweald. We will hold him for as long as you like."

"Your Majesty, I will leave soon for Gwythia, but before I do, I wish to offer the use of my engineers and five hundred handpicked men to aid in rebuilding Dyven."

"Handpicked?"

"All of good temperament—some are skilled carpenters."

"How long would they stay?"

"Until Dyven is mended and back on its feet."

"Yes. Perhaps, our people working side by side, mending walls and homes together, can help mend our relations. I welcome your help, Prince Hereweald. Thank you. Speaking of mending: how is the arm?"

Hereweald looked down at the arm he still bore in a sling. "The arm is improving, Your Majesty. However, I have a request."

"Please, tell me."

Hereweald glanced at Lady Myrredith then back to Billy. "Your Majesty, I would like to request the hand in marriage of a lady who has been instrumental in my rehabilitation."

"Marriage? Why are you asking me?"

"Because you are her king, and she is of your family, Majesty." Hereweald's eyes flitted to Lady Myrredith once again when he mentioned the king's family.

"My family?" Billy shot a surprised look at Myrredith.

Myrredith returned his expression with one of panic.

"Yes," Hereweald said.

Billy's eyes danced between Hereweald and Myrredith. "Are you sure you do not wish to discuss the matter in a more private setting?"

"Yes, Your Majesty. I have already spoken to the lady."

Again, Billy and Myrredith exchanged a volley of looks.

"Have you?"

"Yes, Your Majesty."

"And ... what did she say, Highness?"

"Well." Hereweald rubbed his chin. "You are king and the highest ranking member of her clan. She will comply with your wishes."

"Well then, perhaps I should speak privately with the lady myself."

Lady Aderyn of Hillshire slipped through the crowd to stand next to Prince Hereweald. "That won't be necessary, Your Majesty." Myrredith's cousin beamed as she bowed to her king. "Your Majesty, I am in complete accord with Prince Hereweald on the matter."

"You are?" Still confused, Billy glanced at Hereweald, whose usual stony face was grinning as he stared at Aderyn. The lady stared back, her radiant expression a mirror to the prince. Suddenly, Billy's brows lifted. "Oh! You are. ...You are?"

"Oh yes, Your Majesty. Very much in accord."

Billy shared a smile with Myrredith. "Well, in that case, I have no choice but to grant you both my blessing!"

The lady and her prince kissed, and the court applauded. Immediately after, they adjourned to the waiting feast, in the inner ward, where Billy led the court in drinking the first toast to the prince and his fiancée.

The feast was quite sumptuous for a country a few days out of a war. There were also musicians and acrobats for entertainment. However, in years to come, the two most memorable events of the feast would be an impromptu juggling display by the king and Sir Malcolm, which started as an overzealous but friendly exchange of salt and pepper shakers, and the hour or so of enthusiastic dancing after Myrredith placed a lute in the king's hands.

During the feast, Precilla, the Egyptian seer from Dyven, appeared to Sir Hugh from out of the crowd. She bowed to him. "At last, I have found you, my champion."

Hugh stepped back. "I thought you never wanted to see me again."

"My apologies, sir. I was afraid."

Myrredith raised an eyebrow. "Why would you be afraid of Sir Hugh?"

Hugh turned to Myrredith. "Because I was slain by Gwythian soldiers in Dyven and brought back to life through black magic."

"What?" Myrredith exclaimed.

"No, no, no!" Precilla put up her hands. "Yes, there was some black magic, but I was wrong! That is why I followed you here."

Hugh furrowed his brow. "Wrong about what?"

Precilla looked down and took a deep breath before she began to tell her tale.

"I didn't feel right about what happened, so I went to see Adwythane, to get to the bottom of it."

"The wizard?" Myrredith put her hands on her hips. "I thought he was dead."

"Not yet, milady. We have had some minor dealings in the past, so he allowed me to enter when he saw I brought with me a few bottles of wine I had saved from the Gwythies. I got him drunk, and he admitted he had not stolen you from the clutches of Death. I have no doubt you were more in the grave than out, but you were still alive when the boy brought you to him. He made a big show of it and tricked the boy into giving up his eye ... for nothing."

Again, Hugh was perplexed. "Why would he do that?"

"As it turns out, Adwythane held a grudge against the boy's father. Derian stole some locket from him long ago, so he took his cruel revenge on the boy."

"But how did he know Stitch was Derian's son?"

"The wizard saw half the locket around the boy's neck."

"So, everything I've been sensing ... strange shadows in battle ... even the lives I've taken ... they're just coincidence?"

"Much of life appears coincidence until the plan is revealed."

"Whose plan? The Reaper's plan?"

Precilla sighed. "Such things are possible, but now I sense his owl has left you."

"Am I cursed?"

"Show me your hands."

Hugh stuck out his palms, and Precilla examined them. She smiled. "Far from cursed, Sir Hugh. The darkness over you is all but gone. I see before you a great destiny. You will—"

"Stop!" Hugh pulled his hands away. "I don't want to know anything more of my future. My father is restored, my king's heir is restored, the kingdom is restored, and I am restored."

"As I predicted, my champion."

"Look, I want to enjoy discovering the future in the same manner as everyone else."

"'... for I have learned to be content, whatever the circumstances may be,'" Precilla quoted. Then she bowed and backed away.

"Wait! I have a favor to ask."

Precilla smiled. "Don't worry, my handsome champion. I shall never tell the boy—ever." She bowed one last time and disappeared into the crowd.

Myrredith grinned. "That was unusual."

Hugh turned to her. "Promise me you won't tell Stitch."

"About his eye?"

"Yes. He sacrificed his eye for me. I won't take that away from him. In truth, I owe him more than an eye."

Myrredith raised her eyebrows and did her best to copy the Egyptian woman's accent. "I shall never tell the boy—ever."

Billy continued to make announcements and read decrees throughout the celebrations, which included the building of monuments to Lady Enaid and Sir Sedgemore in Nyraval; to Sir Aonghas on the King's Road near Hillshire; to his adopted father John, his wife Moira, and their son William in the Valley of the Yew.

"And now for the architects of this great feast ... Gryff and Dana, please come forward!"

Gryff and Dana looked up from their serving duties in surprise. They stared at their new king and each other, as Billy beckoned them and their children forward. The sometimes-tempestuous couple joined hands and approached the large feasting dais, looking more like devoted newlyweds than the squabbling pair they were prior to Ergyfel's reign.

Billy sat and dangled his feet off the front edge of the dais. "Gryff, Dana. Like a dessert, I have saved your reward for last. It took me some time to come up with a fitting reward for all you did and suffered for my sake. The best news, of course, is that you and your children are back together after your ordeal."

Gryff lifted their youngest in the air as the crowd applauded.

"The second best news is this: I am giving to you and your children my father's inn, The Valley's Finest, in the Valley of the Yew where I grew up. Sadly, it was burned to the ground, but that will only make it easier to rebuild it to its proper grandeur as the kingdom's first Royal Inn."

The crowd cheered, and then Billy continued. "Complete with a royal charter and yearly stipend. The carpenters and masons who are repairing our beloved Orgulous will build it using the finest materials available. The royal architect, with some direction from me, has already begun on the designs and is expecting to meet with you tomorrow morning."

"Thank you, Sire!" Gryff gave a bow. "I always wanted to run my own inn."

Billy winked. "I remember."

Dana bowed and wiped the tears from her red Irish cheeks. "Thank you, sire. I hope the architect won't mind meetin' in the kitchen. We've got a lot to do tomorrow."

Billy laughed. "Dana, you no longer need to worry about our kitchen. Starting now, you are an innkeeper."

"But, who is gonna—?"

290 | K. C. HERBEL

Dilly held up a scolding finger to silence her. "Eh-eh-eh! Innkeeper! The other servants have already voted on your replacements, and I have approved."

"But I—"

"Eh!" Billy pointed to her, and then to himself. "Inn-keeper ... king. Now, I suggest you drop the spoon, take off that apron, and give the old man a spin around the dance floor, because I intend to play my fingers off!"

Billy strummed the first few notes on his lute and nodded to the other musicians to join him in a fast-paced dance tune known as "Cow Kicked the Rooster." The spoon dropped from Dana's hand as she looked at her husband and their children standing behind him. She plucked the tie on her apron, tossed it into the air, and grabbed Gryff by the arm.

***

Camion and Derian Stitch left for Dyven the next day. Wyte left for Feolaghe Tor the day after, and the day after that, it was time for Billy to say goodbye to Finney. So it was that the week following his coronation was a week of farewells for the new King of Lyonesse.

Billy spent much of his time between audiences and sendoffs studying Ergyfel's collection of magical tomes—a collection he hoped would lead him to the discovery of a spellbinder and an end to the perpetual winter plaguing Tirn Aill. Finding the collection had only taken a day, but each day spent delving the dark pages hung on him like a week.

The works in Ergyfel's library were not like those in the Witan's tree, with the exception of the black tome. *That hateful book would have felt at home amongst these.* He found a few scraps of light amongst the darkness, but by the way they were kept, it was obvious Ergyfel had little use or understanding of them.

Billy felt his best hope for success was in these relatively innocuous works, but one by one, they each came up empty. Still, he searched, hoping for a clue or a scrap of a clue that would lead him to his spellbinder.

Can it be here? It must be here! Why else was I drawn to Castle Orgulous, if not to discover these books—if not to discover the secret of the spellbinder in these books?

A knock interrupted him, and the announcement that Prince Hereweald was preparing to leave. He dashed down the donjon in a fashion unbefitting any other king and ran to the outer ward, where the large Gwythian procession waited to start their long journey home.

"Hereweald!"

The prince turned from Sir Hugh and Lady Myrredith with a smile. "King William!"

"I knew that you were leaving today." Billy paused to catch his breath. "But I hoped that it might be another day—that I might have it wrong."

"Alas, no, Your Majesty."

"Remember our deal? You were gonna call me Billy, or William if you must, and I was going to call you Hereweald."

"Forgive me, *William,* but you're the first king I've met that didn't want to be 'Your Majesty' to anything that moved. Even my father requires it of me."

"But you and I are cousins, Hereweald; ever since Gaelyn married Kathryn."

"Yes." Hereweald took his fiancée's hand and brought her to him. "And I plan to make us cousins again very soon when I wed Lady Aderyn."

Billy liked the way Hereweald said Aderyn's name. It was one part longing, one part petition, and two parts hope.

The lady smiled at Hereweald. "Will you always call me *Lady* Aderyn?"

"Forgive me. If nothing else, I am a creature of habit."

"Forgiven!" Lady Aderyn bowed to Billy and Hugh, hugged Myrredith, and climbed aboard the prince's wagon.

"I suppose it is time for us to leave." Hereweald bowed to Billy. "William."

"Hereweald." Billy returned the bow. He then reached out and clasped Hereweald's arm in friendship. "The point I was trying to make, cousin, is this: Whether you get that treaty of ours signed or not, if things go sour for you in Gwythia, you have friends here. You will always be welcomed."

"Thank you, William. I hope that won't be necessary."

Hugh bowed to the prince, and Hereweald clasped his arm as Billy had done to him. "I never thought I would be thanking the Champion of Lyonesse, but thank you."

"It is Your Highness that is owed thanks. We wouldn't be standing here today without you."

"Well, next time you need help taking your own castle, think of me." Hereweald flashed a devilish grin.

"And next time you need a champion ..." Hugh replied with a bow.

Hereweald bowed to Lady Myrredith and looked like he was going to walk away, but then paused. After a moment, he said, "Lady Myrredith, I ..."

"Your Highness. There is no need for tension between us. I am happy for you and my cousin."

"Still, I feel I owe you some ... explanation. If not for you, I don't think I would have seen Lady Aderyn. I mean *truly* seen her."

"She is quite lovely, isn't she?"

"I see *her* when I dream of Cyndyn Hall."

Myrredith looked puzzled.

"I believe, by some mystery, she is the woman I fell in love with there."

Myrredith bowed to Hereweald with a serene smile.

The last thing Billy saw, as the procession rolled out through the Gleaming Gate, was the gloomy face of Snegaddrick as it was swallowed up by the shadows.

***

Billy stood alone by the hearth in the feasting hall, staring into the embers. It was well past midnight and all the usual revelers and servants slept serenely in their beds. The occasional crackle from the fire was his only companion. Billy provoked the coals with a poker and tossed another book from Ergyfel's collection into the fire.

"What are you doing?" Deordrif asked.

Billy glanced up from the colorful flames seeping from the book. "Funny, isn't it? Magic nearly brought this kingdom to dust, but magic is exactly what I need to save Tirn Aill."

"So, why burn those books?"

"I've seen what lurks within these. Only evil can come from them."

Billy and Drif watched as the stained velum pages darkened and curled up. The book's wood spine cracked as the leather cover split open and shrank to the corners with a sizzling whine that sounded like a cry for mercy.

"Nice dress."

Drif blushed. "My clothes are being cleaned, and this … Thank you."

They watched as the last pages turned to flimsy, withered leaves of ash and floated up the chimney.

"Why haven't you come to the great hall when I'm holding court?"

"Why should I? To smell them sweat when I enter their company, to feel their eyes burn into me, to hear more of their conceited whispering at my back?"

"I know you and Sylvys haven't exactly been welcomed here. Ignorance, lies, and time have made them distrustful and afraid."

"Then, why do you want me there?"

"Because I want to reward you in front of everyone. When they see how I value you, they will treat you with respect."

"I do not desire their respect."

"Then, what do you want?"

"I need nothing of man."

"Ask of me what you will and you shall have it."

Drif held her tongue until she had Billy's eyes. "Return to Tirn Aill."

Billy felt shaken. "That's the last thing I ever expected to hear from you."

"You must return. Before it's too late."

"I can't. Not yet."

"Then Tirn Aill is lost."

"I do not know how to cure her."

"Your Majesty, when we started our quest, I didn't trust you. I was set against you. As I'm sure you know, Malkry sent me to make sure you failed ... failed or died. But you proved to be brave, resourceful, resilient, powerful at times, and yet forgiving of heart—all traits Tirn Aill desperately needs in her next king."

"Tirn Aill needs a cure, not a king."

"Maybe they are one in the same."

"Wait a minute. You were gonna kill me or let me die, but now you think I can just show up in Tirn Aill, and everything will work out?"

"That was a long time ago."

"It was a few days ago."

This time, it was Deordrif's turn to look shocked.

"Yeah," Billy said. "I figured out your little secret. I was sitting on the throne in the great hall when it hit me. The only way your knife could have missed Ergyfel and hit the throne at the back of the dais was if you missed intentionally."

Deordrif looked away.

Billy couldn't see what she was thinking and suddenly felt panicky when he realized Lura Zahn was up in his chambers. He cleared his throat and stepped back, placing the poker between them and giving her less of a target. He pretended to tend the fire but kept one eye on the dagger at her hip.

Deordrif put her hands behind her back, and Billy caught a glimpse of the fernlike burn running up her arm—a lasting reminder of Ergyfel's lightning. She had kept the degree of her injuries from him as best she could, but he knew from his physician that they were extensive.

"Malkry was still pulling your strings then, wasn't she? But then you took a lightning bolt for me. What changed your mind?"

"My mind was still against you when that happened."

Billy mulled over her words. "Then, why?"

"I don't know. Perhaps, I ..." Deordrif paused, and her body tightened, from her jaw to her toes. She turned her back to him and crossed her arms. "Oh! Why must you know everything?"

"You tell me you want me for your king, to have dominion over your life, and yet you want to keep something from me?"

The tension drained from Deordrif's frame. "The heart sees what the mind will not."

"I know that," Billy whispered. "Where did you learn that?"

"Gwylid."

Billy nodded. "And what did your heart see?"

"That Tirn Aill needs you." Drif shook her head. "For a long time, my heart kept me from acting overtly on my mission."

"The heart can lead, but the mind must follow ... or else madness."

"And so it has." Drif turned to Billy, an odd, crooked grin on her face. "Maybe I am insane, maybe it's from sleeping, or maybe I've been spending too much time with that crazy satyr, but I believe in you."

Billy gave her an encouraging grin. "How is Sylvys?"

"He's dying."

Without a word, Billy and Deordrif went to Sylvys' room. Drif opened the door and peeked in. Billy peered around her at his friend.

The satyr's hair from horns to hooves was now entirely grey. His pale skin hung on his bony frame like a damp cloth on a grate. His eyes were closed. For a moment, Billy feared the worst, and then Sylvys snored in and whistled out. Billy sighed in relief and watched as his friend took another labored breath.

Deordrif closed the door and faced Billy. The new king rubbed his forehead and stared through the floor. She reached to touch his shoulder, but stopped herself.

"Every day, I hope for improvement," Billy said. "But I'm only deceiving myself. He's going to die soon."

"I know."

They stood in the hallway for a time. Billy made to leave, but Deordrif stopped him with her words.

"I don't understand it. No one I know understands it, but Sylvys is tied to Tirn Aill and she to him, even way out here. If only I had his knowledge of healing magic."

"You think it's flesh and blood we're dealing with here? Or that Tirn Aill is simply rocks and trees? It's not. It is magic ... and spirit. And their reach is far beyond oceans or borders."

"But what's so important about satyrs?" Deordrif sounded annoyed. "They don't seem to do anything but eat and drink and chase after stupid nymphs, who *also* do nothing!"

Billy realized why she was angry and frustrated. Watching Sylvys die by inches was having the same effect on him. "I, too, wish it weren't happening to him."

Deordrif frowned and fought back her tears. She turned away and crushed them into scorn. "Stupid satyr! I wish he had stayed home!"

Billy watched her back as her rigid shoulders fell. She took a deep breath and stared at the wall.

"Maybe if I understood. Maybe if I knew what we are fighting. If I could see my opponent. ... Maybe if I knew what his greater purpose was— how it worked ... Troghoul-snot! Even the satyrs don't know what their greater purpose is."

Billy smiled. "Do you think a bee knows what its greater purpose is?"

Drif thought for a moment. "No."

"And yet that doesn't stop it from going about its business. The bee makes its honey, and we get fruit and bread because of it. It feeds the animals too. Without the bee, we probably wouldn't be here."

Drif faced Billy. "You should have spoken like that when we were in Tirn Aill. Where did you come by this wisdom?"

"I'm not sure. Elzgig said that I would understand the mysteries of Tirn Aill someday. Maybe, now, I do."

Drif scrunched up her eyebrows. "So somehow the satyrs give the plants life and keep winter away from Tirn Aill?"

"Well, not specifically." Billy shrugged. "They are part of each other, like a heart is to the body. Their fate is inseparable. But remember, the life's blood of Tirn Aill is magic. We will never understand all its mysteries. The satyrs' actions have ramifications in other realms. As do yours."

"What? I have no mystical bond to Tirn Aill!"

"But you *do*, and so do I. Your desire for sleep is a manifestation. It's not as strong as the one between Sylvys and Tirn Aill, but it's there. If Sylvys is the heart, then I may be an eye and you a hand."

"So, what I do here has an effect on Tirn Aill?"

"Of course."

"In some unseen way?"

"Yes."

Deordrif grunted. "You're full of answers tonight. So tell me—what's my purpose?"

Billy looked at her. "Right now, your purpose is to ask me to return to Tirn Aill."

"And I suppose yours is to tell me 'no.'"

"For now."

"Wait … when the heart dies, the eye and the hand also die."

Billy's jaw tightened. "That thought has cost me more than a little sleep, but don't worry; it's only a theory."

Deordrif stared at Billy and straightened until she looked like one of Hereweald's soldiers at attention. "Then, we'll just have to find the answer," she said with confidence.

"If there is an answer here, I will find it, but you and Sylvys must go home."

"What?"

"I have thought it over many times; calculated and delayed your going for as long as I can. But time has run out."

"What do you mean? We're still here; we'll find the answer—"

Billy held up his hand, and Drif quieted.

He swallowed hard. "I am no longer certain we will find the cure in time. My dreams of Tirn Aill continue to grow darker." Billy looked to the door of Sylvys' room, and then back to Drif, who dropped her eyes. "He deserves to die at home."

Deordrif nodded.

"I will continue to look for as long as I am able. I will never give up. But I need you to take him home for me. I cannot force you to do this—"

"Then ask me as a friend."

Billy grinned, but cautioned, "It could cost you your life!"

Drif smiled. "A cause worth dying for comes once in a lifetime."

"If the journey doesn't do you in, the weather probably will."

"What, no torture?"

Billy smiled, knowing she was making light of the danger for his sake. She was, after all, the only one who was capable of getting Sylvys home. Billy liked Drif's sense of humor once she dropped her guard. She wasn't as cold as he had once imagined. He remembered his first impression of her: a suit of armor looking for its next victim. Billy bowed to her. "Thank you."

She returned his bow. "Not to be a stickler, but how do we get back?"

"I've already contacted Toady Brimstone—"

"That goblin scum? How can you trust him?"

"I made him believe he couldn't hide from me any longer and that I would be watching. Truth is, it took a lot out of me. I don't know if I could do it again. At any rate, the *Dragonfly* will meet you on the northern coast, near the village of Mershore, on the day of the full moon."

***

Deordrif and Sylvys left Castle Orgulous in the rain, with Shaldra's body and an honor guard in tow. Though the court still bustled with lords and ladies, and Billy had his best supporters around him, he felt profoundly alone. The day passed for him as if watching it through a waterfall.

On the next morning, he held court in the great hall, and for his first order of business, he called Lady Myrredith and Sir Hugh to stand before him. The king's sister and champion took their places before the dais and waited on their liege's pleasure.

Hugh whispered out the side of his mouth, "Any idea what this is about?"

"Not a clue."

A pile of scrolls and books sat on the floor next to the throne, and a stack of papers in Billy's lap, which he was writing with help from his scribe. At last, he looked up from the papers and addressed his dearest friends.

"Lady Myrredith. ... Sister. I am sure you are aware that as your king, I have authority over certain aspects of your life."

Myrredith remained still.

Billy continued. "Likewise, I am certain you are aware that since your father is dead and I, your brother, am the highest ranking member of our clan, I have authority over other areas of your life."

"Have I done something that displeases Your Majesty?"

"Not quite. However, are we in agreement about my authority where you are concerned?"

"You know that I will do anything you ask."

"Good. Then, as is my right as your brother and king, I command you to cease mourning for Sir Aonghas."

Myrredith's expression was one of hurt, but also confusion.

Billy glanced at Hugh, then back to Myrredith. "I know this seems sudden, but I have my reasons. And now that I have officially ended your time of mourning, you have my permission to consider suitors."

A commotion in the crowd ensued, as men of various ages and birth straightened their garb and tried to push their way to the front. There was a loud clank as the king's champion banged on the floor, and the hall grew quiet.

Hugh knelt to his king. "Your Majesty."

"Speak, Sir Hugh. What's on your mind?"

"Your humble servant begs permission to court Lady Myrredith."

"And what are your intentions?"

"Marriage, Your Majesty, if she will have me."

"I see. And have you any references?"

Hugh looked up at Billy in shock. But then he saw the twinkle in his king's eye and the smile splitting his face, and he laughed. The king laughed as well, and the entire court joined in.

After the laughter had dwindled, Hugh raised his voice. "Your Majesty, beyond what you already know of me, I have but the testimony of my heart, which daily yearns for her to make it whole. I would lay down my life for Lady Myrredith."

"What say you, sister?"

Lady Myrredith put her hands on her hips. "Why is it that men rush to say they would die for their love when dying would only break the heart of the recipient of their alleged love? What's more, it's hard to believe they know what love is, as in dying they would—"

"I get it!" Hugh jumped to his feet. "I get it." He turned to Myrredith and took her hand. "Restore my heart, and I will always live my life for you."

Myrredith looked away from Sir Hugh and bowed to the king.

Billy nodded to her. "Well, Sir Hugh. It seems you have our permission."

Hugh grinned at Myrredith. "Thank you, Your Majesty."

"Your Majesty?"

"Yes, Myrredith?"

"I'm not one for long courtships, especially when the outcome is ... predictable. It seems like a waste of time."

A murmur ran through the crowd, but Lady Myrredith ignored it.

"You see, Your Majesty, I have known Hugh, and he has known me for many years. We have, in a way, already had our courtship."

"What are you saying?"

"I married Sir Aonghas whom I knew less than a week. However, I am in favor of a slightly longer engagement, where proper attention can be given to organize ceremonies, dresses, invitations, and celebrations. Not that those are the basis of a successful marriage, but—"

Billy held up his hand. "I think I know where you're going with this, but the *young man* has not asked the question."

"I believe he stated his intentions were for marriage, Your Majesty, if I would have him."

"Yes, but that's hardly a proposal worthy of my sister."

Hugh took a knee. "Agreed." He looked to Billy. "With your permission, Majesty?"

Billy nodded.

Hugh gazed at Myrredith. He took her hand. "Myrredith, I desire with my whole heart to be your husband. Will you be my wife?"

"Hugh, with my whole heart, yes."

CHAPTER THIRTY-FIVE

To Every Thing, There is a Season

Billy spent another sleepless night by the feasting hall hearth. He felt the dawn approaching in his bones as he threw the last of Ergyfel's arcane collection into the fire. In all the books and scrolls he had consumed, there was no sign of the elusive spellbinder. He watched the colorful spurts of flame as the pages crumpled into ash and wished Deordrif were there beside him.

Or Shaldra. ... I hardly think about him anymore. The pain of his death is already gone, and I'm forgetting him. My heart is growing cold. What happens if Tirn Aill freezes completely? What will happen to me? If Tirn Aill dies and I do not, my heart will surely freeze into a lump of ice.

He found himself wandering through the corridors of the donjon, seeking refuge from the bustle that would soon spread through Orgulous, starting in the kitchen and wicking up to the top of the tallest tower. Normally, he enjoyed the bustle of the castle, but eventually it would seep into every corner, leaving him nowhere he could hear his own thoughts.

Where can I go? He looked in all directions. *They all lead to the same place. No matter which way I go, they'll find me and drag me back to their world of demands and polite impersonal conversation. I'm so tired. How did Mother ever cope with this?*

Before he knew it, he was marching down the corridor that led to his mother's haven in Castle Orgulous: the courtyard known as the Queen's Garden.

Billy passed through the portal to the garden, and his tension ebbed away. The reverberation of his footfalls chased him down the corridor and fell to a whisper when his feet touched the walkway of stones and moss. The square of sky above was still navy, but the stars had dimmed. Their reflections stared back at them from the mirror-pond at the center of the garden, which made Billy feel like the garden was floating in the sky.

He walked down the path that led around the pool and passed between the graceful trees surrounding the Queen's Garden. The delicate smell of flowers tickled his nose. At last, he came to the short marble bench at the end of the pool and sat.

A frog jumped into the pond and sent row upon row of black ripples across the smooth surface. The tiny waves distorted, then destroyed the image of the starlit sky.

Funny how such a little thing can change so much. The ripples seem to go on forever.

Without the stars to look at, Billy's mind conjured up his most haunting nightmare: the vision of his mother's murder. He turned his back on the pond and faced the large stone block that marked her grave. The thorn tree, which had once surrounded the dark stone marker, had grown thicker still and swallowed it up entirely.

Billy got up and pushed away the thorny vine-like branches from the front of the stone. They moved away with ease. He pushed against them again with the same result. *Why hasn't someone taken care of this before?* He moved his hands over the surface to sweep the growth away and while the large thorns didn't harm him, they tore his sleeves like lion's claws.

Billy examined his hands and arms and found not a scratch. His sleeves, on the other hand, were shredded.

He seized a handful of the thorny tree branches and put them against his bare arm, then watched in awe as the thorns bent and warped away from his skin, rather than harm him. Billy dropped the branches like hot coals and scrutinized the thorn-covered stone. The area inscribed with his mother's name was the only place free of the spiky branches.

"Eleanor," he read from the stone.

He stared at his mother's name, then grabbed two handfuls of thorns. He concentrated on the thorn tree, focusing his will through his mother's ring in the same way that he had contacted the trees still living in the great hall columns. Instantly, he felt a presence, but fragmented, as if looking at someone through the scattered pieces of a mirror.

He opened his eyes a peek and saw branches of the thorn tree wrapping around his arms and shoulders, like hands. His eyes popped wide open and he gasped, but when he realized that the branches weren't harming him, he relaxed again and focused on making contact.

The image grew more coherent in his mind, but remained disjointed and incomplete. The presence grew weaker and drew away from him.

"Eleanor. Eleanor!"

The pieces of the image came together and grew clear. His mother stood before him, her hands on his shoulders. She looked tired, but happy to see him. Without a word, she held out her hand. Billy reached out, and she put a seed in his palm. Bright light filled his mind, and out of the light came another vision.

Billy saw himself in the royal court of Tirn Aill. Near the throne, he knelt and planted the seed in the ground. A ghostly figure of his mother stood behind him, watching. She leaned close, over his shoulder, and whispered, *"Sakgefan diagor ap ghumilis."* A tear fell from his eye to the ground, and a powerful feeling of serenity overwhelmed him.

Billy opened his eyes and saw that the thorn tree, looking very much like his mother, had produced a large blossom. A berry grew from the middle, bowing the blossom down with its increasing weight. At the same time, the thorn tree blanched and withered. He reached out to support the blossom, and it fell into his hand. That instant, every branch of the tree turned white. When he stepped back, they fell to the ground as ashes.

A disturbance behind Billy made him turn—a half-dozen birds had taken to the air. The leaves and flower petals of the garden fell like snow. The stars faded from the pool and sky as the covetous dawn reclaimed its stage.

Under the youthful light of a new day, Billy examined the blossom in his hand. It was unlike any he had ever seen. He smiled, knowing that at last, he had attained the means to save Tirn Aill. He had found his spellbinder.

***

"I have done all I can for Lyonesse," Billy announced to his assembled court. "There is another kingdom that now requires my help."

The crowd mumbled and grumbled and murmured until Sir Hugh struck the steps of the dais with his sword. The room quieted, and Billy continued. "Please, allow me to finish. I haven't much time."

He looked at all the faces in his court, most of which he considered friends.

"You see, Queen Eleanor was also queen of another kingdom. Now the inhabitants of that kingdom are dying. In fact, I don't know, but many of them may already be dead. They are my friends, just as you are. Just as I would come to your aid in your moment of need, so I must go to them now. At the risk of sounding boastful, I am the only one who can save them from their plight. I alone possess the knowledge and power to fix what has been broken."

The court remained silent. Then Lord Bonting, whose popularity had blossomed since the short-lived siege of Castle Orgulous, stepped forward and bowed.

"Should we raise an army, Your Majesty?"

"No. I must do this alone."

A young lady, whom Billy only knew by sight, stepped forward. She looked near to tears. "When must you go, Your Majesty?" she said as she bowed.

Billy waited until she raised her head and he could look her in the eye. "I am sorry, but I must leave today."

The crowd burst into chattering. Some pleaded with him to stay. Others simply yelled, "No."

He motioned to Hugh, who struck the floor again. He had to bang on the wood steps several times before the mob quieted.

Billy cleared his throat. "While I am away, my sister, Lady Myrredith, and Sir Hugh will rule in my place. I am told they will be married within a month's time. They will be crowned the same day, as prince and princess of the Realm and will be my heirs, possessing the full authority of the crown. Their eldest child upon reaching maturity will be my heir and—"

"Your Majesty?" the young lady said.

"Yes?"

She pursed her lips. "How long will you be gone, Your Majesty? You are coming back, aren't you?"

Billy pondered her words, and in his mind tried to answer. *I don't know when I'll be back. I don't know if I'll be back. I may die in Tirn Aill or on the way there ...*

"I don't know."

Lord Bonting spoke up again. "His Majesty means, he doesn't know *when* he'll return."

The court awaited Billy's affirmation in silence. He looked from face to face again. Then he focused on Myrredith and Hugh. "I promise, I will return, when the time is right."

The crowd erupted as commoner and noble all together raised a ruckus. The noise in the great hall reminded Billy of the furious clamor at his trial when he was dragged from the proceedings by the king's guards.

He stood, removed his crown, and placed it on the throne. Then he looked up at the gouge in the back caused by Drif's knife. *Well, they can't way I didn't leave my mark.* With a heavy heart, he turned and walked away from the throne. Hugh and Myrredith waited for him at the foot of the dais steps.

Billy looked up at the sunlight streaming through the new roof of the hall. "We must hurry," he shouted over the hubbub. "We must leave within the hour to have a chance of catching them."

Sir Malcolm came up behind Hugh and Myrredith. "Don't forget me."

Billy smiled at his juggling master. "Wouldn't dream of it."

The king's guards cleared a path through the crowd to allow him and his companions to exit the great hall unhindered. Once outside, Billy turned to the others.

"Is everything ready?"

"Aye," they answered.

Billy turned to Malcolm. "Are you packed?"

"Always."

Billy smiled. He nodded to his friends. "Good. I need to get my lute. Gather our troupe and meet me in a half-hour at the stables."

***

The next three days proved excruciating for Billy, and yet the best time he'd ever had on the road. Being in the company of his three favorite friends made even the roughest part of the journey—the waiting part—bearable. Fortunately, Hugh had brought his lute, Malcolm his juggling gear, and Billy their audience, in the form of a twenty-man honor guard. Of course, Myrredith was most appreciative of their efforts and twisted Billy's arm for more songs when the others dared not. But, always in the back of Billy's mind lingered Tirn Aill. He had to reach the coast by the full moon, or he would miss the *Dragonfly* altogether, and though he continued to try, he was doubtful he could contact Toady Brimstone again.

Late on the evening of the third day, Billy caught the scent of sea air and hurried his pace. Shortly, he and his companions crossed a ridge and saw the Irish Sea. The sun was but a faint glow in the west, and the moon not yet risen.

Billy urged Briallen into a gallop. "Hurry!"

Sir Hugh touched Splendore Pomponnel's sides with his spurs, and she charged forward next to the king. Myrredith looked at Malcolm with a wry grin.

"After you, milady." Malcolm waved her on. As soon as she was ahead of him, Malcolm slapped his horse on the rump and followed.

The honor guard did its best to give chase, but their weighed-down horses were no match for the mounts of King Billy and his friends. They soon fell far behind and lost sight of them entirely.

Billy reached the beach as the moon crested the horizon. He turned Briallen to the east, with the others just behind him.

"How far to Mershore?" he shouted back to Hugh.

"Less than a mile."

Though already tired, they pushed their mounts up the beach at top speed. Within minutes, they entered the outskirts of the village and saw the horses, wagons, and men of the honor guard Billy had sent with Drif and Sylvys standing in the street in front of a tavern.

Billy stopped and demanded to know, "Where's Deordrif?"

"Your Majesty," their leader said. "We left them just minutes ago on the beach."

Several of the men pointed east, out of town.

"Was there a ship?"

"Yes, Sire. A very peculiar ship."

Billy patted Briallen on her neck. "Come on, girl. One last run."

He and Hugh beat it out of town, with Myrredith and Malcolm a short distance behind. They followed the wagon tracks and came to a well-trampled spot on the beach where Drif, Sylvys, and their honor guard had waited for Toady Brimstone to show up. Billy rode Briallen right into the surf, straining his eyes to see the sails of the *Dragonfly*. He saw nothing but the dark sky over the water.

He tried to reach out with his mind to contact Toady, but it was no use. He was too tired, and the rolling, crashing waves too loud to concentrate against. He threw open his eyes with a gasp. The world spun. The vast sea eroded what was left of his strength.

Billy closed his eyes and sagged in the saddle. The weight of failure threatened to crush him. He would have screamed and cried, but exhaustion deadened him. Sir Hugh rode up beside him and stared out at the sea.

"Too late. I failed you."

"You could never fail me, Your Majesty."

Billy looked at his champion, and tears came to his tired eyes. "I have failed Tirn Aill. They will all die, because of me. Deordrif and Sylvys, too."

Malcolm ambled up on the other side. "It's getting cold out here, Your Majesty. Perhaps we should head back to the village and warm ourselves by the hearth of that tavern."

"Warm ourselves," Billy muttered. He stared straight ahead at the dark sea. "I never told you the fate of Tirn Aill, did I?"

"No." Hugh bowed his head.

"The land is caught in perpetual winter. They're going to freeze to death—the whole kingdom."

At that moment, Lady Myrredith came up beside Hugh, only further out into the surf so she could see Billy. She gasped. All three men looked at her.

Myrredith pointed to the east. "What's that?"

The dejected king leaned forward to see around Malcolm. The moon came out of the sea. With almost half the moon risen, and its reflection beneath, it looked nearly whole. In the center, where the firm heavenly moon merged with the shimmering water moon, Billy could see the tall gossamer sails of the *Dragonfly*, sailing away.

"Wait!" He turned his horse up the shore. He charged up the beach, waving and shouting. His companions stayed right behind him, and they too tried to get the attention of the ship, but it continued on course. It looked like she would slip over the edge of the horizon at any second.

Malcolm called to him. "Billy! Fire might get their attention."

Billy let Briallen's reins go slack so he could concentrate on a spell. She continued to gallop straight up the beach. Malcolm came up beside him and held out the small torch he used to juggle fire in his act. Billy snapped his fingers, and sparks from his fingertips lit the torch.

Malcolm chuckled. "You'll have to teach me that someday."

"Someday." Billy arrested the burning torch from the juggling master's hand.

He held it up as high as he could. *"Stelura!"*

The flame shot off the torch and raced into the sky with a scream and a long tail of smoke. Up and up it went. When it was a puny dot in the sky, it exploded with a boom and expelled a dozen twinkling stars that drifted to earth.

The companions, now tired, and riding tired mounts, slowed. They trained their eyes on the tiny sail as it disappeared behind the waters of the sea. They came to a stop and watched the horizon, holding their breath.

Malcolm sighed. "Well, we gave it our best."

"Aye," Hugh said.

"Wait." Billy looked to Malcolm. "Light another torch."

Myrredith rode up beside him. "I'll wait with you, William."

"Me too," Hugh and Malcolm said in unison.

A long minute crept by. Billy closed his eyes. *Come on, Toady!*

Myrredith reached over and held his hand. When he threw open his eyes, he beheld the highest mast of the *Dragonfly* as it peeked over the horizon. "They're coming!"

Myrredith raised their hands. "They are! Look."

Billy nudged Briallen, and they all trotted up the surf as fast as their mounts would let them. The *Dragonfly* grew larger with each step. Before long, the graceful ship slipped into the breakers within running distance from the shore, Deordrif stood at the side, leaning out over the golden railings while Toady's crew saw to the spider web ropes.

"Hurry!" Toady shouted over the crashing waves. "We gotta get now if we're gonna make it out o' here!"

Billy hopped off Briallen and rushed into the sea. Several steps into the water, he stopped and turned to face Hugh, Myrredith, and Malcolm. His friends dismounted, and he rushed back to them.

He gripped Malcolm's arm. "Thank you for being my teacher."

Malcolm smiled. "'Twas a pleasure. Thank you for being my friend."

Billy then clasped Hugh by the arm. "It feels strange saying goodbye to you again. I remember the day we met like it was yesterday."

"We'll meet again someday, Your Majesty."

Billy contemplated this and touched the dragon scar on his chest. "You may be right."

"You promised … and I'm holding you to it."

Billy smiled. "Someday, I will return."

"Lyonesse will be waiting, Your Majesty."

"Take good care of my sister."

"I will, Your Majesty. You can count on me."

Billy then turned to Myrredith. Tears beat at the doors of his eyes, but he was determined to be strong. He didn't want them to know that he felt he might never return.

He embraced Myrredith. "Sister … " Tears began to flow, and he couldn't stop them. "I can't imagine my life without you."

"I'm so glad we found each other."

"Take good care of Hugh."

"You can count on me."

She released Billy and wiped the tears from her cheeks. "Now hurry, so you can come back to me—and Lyonesse."

"You are Lyonesse to me."

He embraced Myrredith again, then backed away from her and stood for a moment, taking in the three of them.

"I just figured it out. You are my family. I will never forget you."

Myrredith grabbed Hugh's hand for strength. "Nor shall we ever forget you, Your Majesty."

The trio knelt on the sand and bowed their heads to their sovereign.

Billy turned and ran through the surf to the *Dragonfly*. Deordrif lowered a rope ladder and helped Billy climb aboard.

Billy turned to the captain. "Let's away!"

Toady Brimstone smiled. "Welcome aboard, Your Highness." He then called to his crew, "Let's see what she's got, boys!"

The ship surged ahead. Billy went to the railing and waved to his family on the beach as they and Lyonesse receded into the darkness and out of sight.

No sooner had they vanished, than a thick fog descended on the little ship. Their speed increased. The breeze tousled Billy's hair and chilled his cheeks.

Drif gripped the railing. "You better hold on."

Billy grabbed the gold railing, and the gentle wind on his face became a gust. Captain Brimstone let out a howl, and his crew echoed him. The *Dragonfly* rose up and lurched forward, headed straight for the moon.

CHAPTER THIRTY-SIX

And a Time to Every Purpose

The *Dragonfly* sailed through the hazy moonlit fog for what felt like an hour before Billy heard the sound of water under the keel again. The graceful vessel slowed, and the fog lifted. He got up from Sylvys' side and went on deck to examine the sea around them. The moon still dipped in the ocean at their bow, with no sign of land.

"What happened? Is something wrong?"

Toady Brimstone appeared next to Billy and stared up at the stars. "No, laddie. We're almost home."

"How can that be? We've only been traveling for a short time. And isn't Tirn Aill in the other direction?"

Toady smiled and swelled up to where Billy thought he or his warts would pop. "The *Dragonfly*'s no ordinary ship," he bragged. "She don't sail on water or beg speed from the wind like them others, though she can when needed." The captain beckoned to him, and then leaned in close to whisper in his gruff voice. "She can sail on a moonbeam, slip between shadows, glide under the waves, or over the sky." He winked and clicked his teeth. "And the fuller the moon, the faster we travel."

"So how much further is it?" Billy scanned ahead.

The moon's reflection danced in a thousand pieces on the boundless black water of the sea. He could discern only immeasurable ocean and sky. As he watched the moon rise again from its watery berth, Toady studied the stars.

Finally, Brimstone finished his calculations. "Well, we overshot some, so we'll be there in about two, three hours."

"Two or three hours?"

Toady mistook Billy's surprise for anger and tried to apologize. "Sorry, Your Highness. I was havin' a wee bit of fun an' didn't want to stop."

"Oh, um. Carry on, Captain! And tell me when we're close."

"Aye."

Billy returned to tending Sylvys. The air was chill, so he put another cover on him with Drif's help. He then took Sylvys' hand. It felt fish-cold. The satyr lay so still that it was difficult to tell if he still breathed. The bones of his face were prominent—angular.

"He's been like that since Mershore," Deordrif said.

"Hold on, my friend." Billy squeezed his hand. "Just a little longer."

Drif took Sylvys' other hand. "Yes, old friend. Keep fighting."

Some time later, Toady Brimstone approached with a grim face. "You need to see this."

Billy followed the goblin captain to the bow. In front of them, in a jagged profile, the black waters became a vast white field of ice.

"Can we break through?"

"It's too thick, laddie. It'll break her in two. We've got to go around."

Brimstone gave the order, and the *Dragonfly* turned parallel to the ice field. They sailed southeast for an hour, but the ice kept pushing them further and further south. To make matters worse, it started to snow, drastically reducing visibility.

"It's no good. This ice is forcing us away from Tirn Aill."

"I know." Billy pursed his lips. "And if we go north, it will only get worse."

"How do you know that?"

"I've seen it."

"Oh."

"Somehow, we've got to go through. Wait a minute! Didn't you tell me the *Dragonfly* could glide under the waves or over the sky?"

"Aye, but that's ice!"

"Can't we just travel the way we did when we left Lyonesse?"

"Good thought, laddie, but she can't do that until the next moonrise."

Billy looked at the moon peeking through the clouds, and then towards Sylvys. "We haven't got that long. It's got to be tonight."

Billy and Brimstone leaned on the railings of the *Dragonfly* and stared at the impenetrable ice. Both desperately wanted to beat the frozen waste. Billy paced the deck.

"What if—no, that'll never work! Or maybe—"

At that moment, his feet slipped on the snow-covered deck and kicked out from under him. His back hit the deck, and he slid to the railing. He lay there looking up at Toady, who stared at him with his hands on his plump waist.

"I think I have an idea," Billy said.

Half an hour later, with a little magical help from Billy, Toady had the *Dragonfly* up on the ice, skating swiftly for Tirn Aill. The little ship agilely jumped over, skipped across, or sailed around the jagged protrusions and broken ice in her path. Despite the gravity of their mission, Captain Brimstone and his crew were in high spirits, laughing and howling with wild delight at their newfound speed sport.

"Goblins!" Deordrif shook her head and scanned ahead for danger.

Billy grinned. "Well, at least we're making good time."

"Good time?" Toady exclaimed from behind them. "I'll wager no ship ever made this speed on the water!"

At that moment, a wide sheet of ice rose up before the *Dragonfly*. The ship hit the ramp and flew into the air.

"Wahoo!" Brimstone shouted.

"Wahoo!" his crew echoed.

The ship came down with a bump then whooshed across the ice as before. The goblin at the helm giggled.

Deordrif crossed her arms and glared at Toady. "Goblins."

Soon, the *Dragonfly* approached the Isle of Tirn Aill. The lush forests were stripped bare. As there were no evergreens on this side of the island, only twigs and black trunks remained. The tall, gentle hills, now white and grey, slumbered above the black boulders of the silent shore. Far above, where the high hills melted into grey clouds, lightning pulsed in the heavens.

The captain took over the helm and swung his ship around the southern tip of the island to Glitter Gilt Bay and the only dock. As they entered the bay, his crew took in the sails and readied the mooring lines and anchor.

"Wait, Captain! Keep going and take us up the river."

"Aye, Your Highness. But I don't know how far we'll get."

The crew raised every bit of sail as they turned from the dock and let the *Dragonfly* build up speed before taking her straight up the river. Just then, a gust of wind grabbed the ship and accelerated it to an alarming speed. Toady held the first bend without trouble, but on the second, as they passed through the gap in the hills, the ship skidded up the bank and slammed into the side of the steep hill. The *Dragonfly* bounced back onto the frozen river and fishtailed around the next turn.

Captain Brimstone's eyes bulged as the trees ahead closed in.

"Drop the sails! Now!"

The crew hopped to it while their captain maneuvered the ship through the narrowing passage.

With only two bends before they reached the royal court, and far too much speed, Toady shouted for the anchor. A goblin crewmember tossed it over the side and it ricocheted off the ice.

"It bounced off, Captain!"

"Throw your lines, boys!"

The crew threw their mooring lines at the sides of the river, trying to lasso passing rocks or trees—anything that might stop or slow them down. Toady leaned into the rudder with all he had and pushed the ship around the next turn.

The *Dragonfly* swept around the bend, but her stern kept turning. Toady and Billy pulled on the rudder together. A second later, the ship whooshed up the bank backward, snapping off saplings in their path to the royal court. Billy spied over the aft railing and saw the court village racing towards them.

"Hold onto something!"

He grabbed the railing and braced himself. A moment later, one of the crew grabbed hold of his leg. Billy looked down at the small goblin, who shrugged and smiled. Billy put his hand on the goblin's shoulder and noticed Toady still standing at the rudder, facing the rear of the ship with the wind in his face. He seemed determined to steer the ship to the gruesome end. Billy closed his eyes.

The ship came to a complete stop with a loud groan. Everyone aboard got tossed towards the stern. Billy flew over the railing with his new goblin friend and slammed into the rear of the ship, which knocked the wind out of him, and caused him to lose his grip on the railing. They fell to the lumpy white terrain with the crunch of fresh snow.

Billy opened his eyes one at a time. He was sitting at the end of the giant banquet table in the center of the court. He pushed away some snow and found he was sitting on the throne. He squinted up at the stern of the *Dragonfly* and found Toady and Deordrif gawking at him.

"Are you hurt?" the elf asked.

Billy patted himself. "No broken bones. How's Sylvys?"

"Sleeping."

Brimstone laughed. "Did you find your throne all right, Your Highness?"

Billy patted the throne and smiled. "Right where I left it! To what do I owe having a throne and not a pile of splinters?"

Drif looked over her shoulder. "The anchor finally caught on a tree."

Toady brushed off his hands and turned from the railing. "Just like I planned."

"I'll be right down, Your Highness."

"I'm fine, Drif. Stay with Sylvys. Make sure he stays warm. Oh, and have someone lower my pack over the side."

"As you wish."

He stood up as best he could in the knee-deep snow and scanned around him. There was no sign of life. The dark, icy village surrounding the court looked abandoned. At that moment, he heard a muffled cry and looked down beside him. He reached into the snowdrift behind the throne and felt a foot. He pulled on it, and out popped the goblin that had come over the railing with him.

The goblin shivered as Billy helped brush off the snow. He then took off his hat, bowed, and ran to the side of the *Dragonfly* to climb back onboard. Billy smiled at how well his oversized goblin feet kept him atop the snow.

Billy made his way to the closest structure in the village, with the snow crunching under his feet. He tried to open the door, but the snow and ice barred him. He banged on the door. No sounds came from within. He went to the next building but found it in the same condition. Then he spotted someone in a robe, standing before the door of the next hut.

"Hey!" he shouted. When he got no response, he ran. "Must be deaf."

"Hey, I'm back!" He reached to tap the figure on the shoulder and tripped.

He looked up from the snow. A hand had been frozen to the door by a lumpy accumulation of ice. He traced the arm and found the frozen, clenched features of a hobgoblin staring back.

"Ha!" Billy flinched and banged his head on the doorjamb. He rolled away and stepped around the edge of the building, panting and rubbing his head. Still staring at the frozen corpse, he stepped back and bumped into something else. He turned and found someone behind him. "Ha!" he exclaimed with a leap backward. He leaned over with one hand on his knee and tried to catch his breath. "Don't sneak up on me like that."

He stopped when he realized he was talking to another frozen faerie. This one, an elf, held a rope in her hand. Billy followed the ice-cycled rope behind her and found yet another frozen corpse. The rope went into the woods to a dozen frozen faeries, some huddled together, some lying alone on the ground, others frozen in mid-step. Billy fell to his knees and collapsed against a tree at the edge of the woods.

"Too late, too late."

After he threw up and got control of his emotions, he trudged back through the village and around to the side of the ship to retrieve his pack. He opened it on the snow and withdrew a square package wrapped in cloth. The cloth fell away to reveal a wooden box with a stone-lion inlay on its lid. He peeked inside. The thorn blossom was wilting.

It's too late. They're all dead. Nothing I can do. I've got the cure, but it's too late.

Just then, a voice said, "Do what you came to do."

He stepped back and looked up at the *Dragonfly*. Brimstone stood by the railing, giving orders to his crew.

"Captain!" Billy said.

Toady turned to face him.

"Did you just say 'do what you came to do'?"

Brimstone scratched his chin and looked distracted more than thoughtful. "No, but it sounds like good advice. Also sounds like that tempest is moving down towards us. I'd like to be out of here before it does."

Billy looked to the tallest hills. The wild lightning storm swirled around them like a colossal cauldron in the sky. It moved lower, and the thunder grew louder. In the midst of the thunder, he heard the voice again, saying, "Finish the quest. Fulfill your destiny."

Billy reexamined the thorn blossom in the box. While the petals were drooping, the berry still looked full of life.

The thunder growled again, and he knelt. He dug through the snow, but when he reached the ground, he found it frozen solid. "There's nothing for it," he muttered as he drew Lura Zahn and stabbed at the frozen earth. Though it complained, the blade performed well; however, he was still only breaking the crust.

The sound of clattering hooves broke Billy's focus. He looked up and saw Malkry and her warriors crossing the frozen river on horseback. He grabbed the box and got to his feet with the ship at his back. The dark elves ambled up the bank and all but Malkry and her lieutenant dismounted. Her warriors drew their weapons and circled around Billy as Malkry rode up behind them.

"Malkry!" Billy felt behind him for the *Dragonfly's* rope ladder. "Thank goodness you're still alive. And you're just in time to help. We need to dig—"

"I'm not here to help you, you half-breed stench." Malkry glared down at him.

"You're not? ... But I've found it! I found the cure."

Malkry took in the ship at his back, along with its goblin crew. After a moment, she smiled and returned her eyes to Billy.

"And no sign of your bodyguard, Shaldra." She pretended to pout. "I thought Onian's whelps were supposed to be tough."

Billy ground his teeth. *Of all the people to survive.* Lura Zahn rattled at his side, but he restrained the blade and his hand. "What do you want, Malkry? I've no time for games."

She smiled. "Well, I want you dead, but in order to secure my reign, I must, at least, *appear* blameless in your death. So I'm here to watch my friend Gulch do it for me."

Dozens of goblins charged out of the woods and village and scrambled across the slippery river. They ran on all fours and fed in between Malkry's elves, filling every possible gap like potatoes poured into bins. The dark elves sheathed their weapons and stepped back with their arms crossed as the goblins took the front line around Billy.

Then Gulch gave a husky laugh from somewhere behind Malkry. It came closer, and the ranks of elves and goblins moved aside as the chief of the goblins nudged his way through. At last, Gulch swaggered into the center and stood with his fists on his hips, glaring at Billy.

The goblin paced from side to side and drew his curved saw-like sword. "I bet you never expected I would be the end of you. Did ya? Did ya? You gonna tell me to shut up again?"

A clicking sound came from above Billy's head as Toady Brimstone leaned over the side and pointed his crossbow at Gulch. "No, Gulchmelon, but I will."

Gulch stepped back, and his eyes bulged when he saw the *Dragonfly's* captain had him in his sights. "What are you doin', Brimstone?"

"Keepin' an eye on my future king. ... Now, why don't you tell me how you figure to end him when I've gotcha dead to rights?"

Gulch's jaw tightened, and he ground his teeth. Then he growled. "I'll have him skewered on ole Riptooth here before you can shoot."

"That doesn't change the fact that you'll be buried with my bolt between your eyes. An' besides, I'm bettin' Eleanor's son can block ole Riptooth with that dwarf sword on his hip."

Gulch growled some more and wagged his finger at the captain. "I never liked you, Toady Brimstone," he bellowed. "You're a born turncoat!"

"Aye. Me dad would be proud."

Gulch sputtered. "With—with—with seawater in your veins!"

"Oh, to be sure." Toady grinned. "Now, what's in your veins, Gulchmelon?"

"Don't call me that."

"Is it the ink-black warrior blood of our ancestors, Gulchmelon?"

"Stop calling me that!" Gulch threw off his heavy fur cloak and kicked it aside.

"Or is it pale, like milk or lilies?"

Gulch turned his back on Billy with fists clenched at his temples. His whole body quaked, causing jiggling ripples in his corpulent torso. His goblins chanted his name.

"Gulch. Gulch. Gulch! Gulch!"

The goblin chief made a low growl, which crept up in volume and tone until it built to a yowl. Then he threw down his hands and spun around with foam on his lips and blood in his eyes.

Deordrif leapt over the side of the *Dragonfly* with a shriek and landed between the goblin chief and Billy. Gulch drew back his weapon, and Drif brought her sword down on his head.

He collapsed to the snow like a shovel load of dirt, black blood leaking from a deep split in his scalp. The circle fell silent as the goblin pack stared at their fallen leader. All at once, they hooted and screeched. Some of them stabbed the ground with their crude weapons while others bounced from side to side. They became more frenzied with each second and Lura Zahn leapt into Billy's eager grip.

Drif brandished her sword back and forth in front of her and stepped back until she nudged into Billy behind her. There were a few short chirps like crickets from the goblins, first from the left, and then the right. Drif and Billy shifted their stances and prepared for the onslaught of the goblin horde. Then, just like that, the goblins turned and sprinted away even faster than they had come.

Malkry leaned towards her lieutenant. "If you want the job done right ... don't use goblins."

Her warriors drew their weapons and fanned out around Billy and Drif. Malkry inched forward. She peeked over her elves at Gulch's body, and then gave Deordrif an icy stare. Lightning flashed in the sky behind her.

"You wouldn't understand," Drif said.

Malkry turned to Billy. "Obviously, my niece underestimated you, as did her mother. A mistake I shall not repeat."

Billy glanced at Deordrif as the thunder boomed. He remembered the thunder of hooves on the gorge bridge where he came face to face with the Night Queen. Drif's uncanny resemblance to her was more than coincidence, and now he knew the source of it. It also explained why Malkry chose Drif for her agent against him.

"Ready!" Malkry signaled her warriors.

They raised their weapons and took an attack stance.

Deordrif raised her sword. "We are kin, Malkry."

"You are nothing to me, whelp."

Drif appealed to Malkry's lieutenant. "Rafeyn, remind her I am her niece."

"My niece is dead!" When the echo of Malkry's voice receded, she said, "Death to all traitors."

At that, the crew of the *Dragonfly* popped up at the railing with crossbows, gaffs, and ropes. Captain Brimstone chuckled. "Steady, boys."

Malkry assessed her opponents, then gave the command, "Shields!" Her warriors snapped their shields into position to block the crossbows above them. "Ready!"

Without warning, an arrow tapped Malkry on the shoulder, then sunk into the *Dragonfly's* hull with a thud. Malkry's head snapped around as she looked to the woods behind her. Onian crouched on a tree root that protruded from an embankment, with his arms hanging between his knees and his bow clutched in one hand. His eyes were on the ground. His quiver bristled with more arrows like the one that had touched Malkry's shoulder.

The leader of the forest elves raised his painted face to look at Malkry. "Now that I have your attention ... " Onian gave a short whistle, and a score of elves stepped into view from behind trees and atop the court village roofs.

"Don't start without me!" a gravelly voice called from the village.

Billy looked to his left. Thortan came across the snow through an alley, followed by a dozen dwarves. They wore furs over their armor and fuzzy snowshoes like giant rabbit feet, which kept them on top of the deep snow. Frost and gleaming icicles adorned their beards.

Once clear of the buildings, Thortan stopped and pulled out a loaded crossbow from behind him. He pointed it at the dark elves as he panted. The other dwarves did the same as they entered the court. The dark elves shifted their stance and formation.

Still breathing hard, Thortan yelled, "Sorry we're late, Your Majesty. Came as soon as we dug out from an *unexpected* cave-in."

Toady Brimstone cleared his throat. "Well Malkry, looks like you brought a whole lot of swords to a bow fight."

Malkry turned her mount to face the village, and her lieutenant, Rafeyn, moved between her and Onian. She took in the forest elves and the dwarves. "Thortan, Onian, this isn't your fight! That goes for you too, Toady. Go home, and I will put an end to this curse of winter."

Onian stood. "How do you propose to do that, Malkry?"

"I will destroy the cause of this curse."

"Destroy?"

"Kill. ... Then I will use the wild magic to heal the land."

"Heal the land?" Thortan glared at her. "You couldn't heal a hammer blister. Besides, I'm startin' to like this winter."

Malkry ignored Thortan's droll remarks and continued in Onian's direction. "I will spring us out of winter and back into summer where we belong."

"What makes you think you can control the wild magic?"

Malkry ignored the dwarf again and stared at Onian.

The leader of the forest elves stared back. "That's a fair question, Malkry."

She frowned. "I wouldn't expect a dwarf to understand."

"Listen, missy." Thortan squared his shoulders. "Even if I believed you could control the wild magic; given a choice of you and a spring or the boy and winter, I choose the boy and winter!"

"This isn't about holding onto a piece of earth, Thortan."

"You're right." Thortan looked away from Malkry to Billy. "It's about serving your king; holding on to his promise."

Malkry rolled her eyes and addressed Onian. "I told you, he wouldn't understand. Only the elves truly understand the magic. And I am the most skilled of all the elves. The boy knows nothing. He's not even an elf. I alone can control the magic."

"If that were true," Billy said, "you would have done it already."

She turned to him with a snarl. Lightning flashed in the hills behind her.

Billy glanced up at the storm. "You and your elves live in the caves, up in the crags of the high hills, don't you? I'm guessing everything you tried made the storm worse, didn't it?"

"When you're dead, the magic will listen to me."

"To control the wild magic … " Billy held the wooden box over his head. "You must first tame it. And I have gained the secret to tame the magic."

Malkry's hands had been low behind her shield and that of her lieutenant. She shrieked and thrust one hand in the air. It glowed with an eerie blue flame that sent a handful of embers racing into the clouds. Immediately, lightning cascaded across the sky from the storm in the high hills and lit up the clouds above.

Drif stepped in front of Billy. "Don't do it, Malkry! You won't be able to control it!"

Suddenly, the air swarmed with bolts and arrows. Several of Malkry's warriors fell, but her lieutenant's shield intercepted the missiles meant for her. Deordrif swung her sword in an arc, forcing the remaining dark elves to step back. At that moment, Malkry pointed her finger at Billy, and his hair stood on end.

"*Skeldtruma!*" Billy thrust his fist into the air. Sudden, acute pain bit into his forearm.

A broad, crackling bolt of lightning shot from the heavens and blasted the ground between him and Malkry. The blast threw Drif and Billy against the *Dragonfly* and knocked everyone else within ten yards off their feet. A cloud of steam roiled up from the ground. Malkry's elves rolled on the ground, holding their heads.

Billy couldn't see and his ears rang. He could hardly feel the cold snow beneath his cheek. He pushed up and tried to stand, but promptly fell. After taking a deep breath, his vision returned a little. The first thing he saw were two Lura Zahns sticking out of the snow, next to a blurry wooden box with lions on the lid.

As he focused on the box, his mind became clear, and he sat up. Deordrif lay unconscious next to him while the other dark elves lay dead or dying, or crawled on the frozen ground—their weapons and shields scattered about. Rafeyn, though pierced by an arrow in her thigh, fought to remain mounted, but Malkry's mount bucked in the clearing, riderless.

Where is she? My spell should have protected us better than that. And why did it hurt?

Just then, Billy noticed the crater in the ground before him. Not only had the lightning burned away the snow, but it had also burrowed deep into the earth, leaving a hole. He grabbed the wooden box and crawled to the crater. Then he flung open the box, took out the thorn blossom, and placed it in the fresh, warm earth. The petals of the flower were now brittle.

"Please, let this be right." He pushed the dark soil into the hole and formed it into a tiny mound.

With his hands on the earth, Billy did his best to calm his mind and draw together the spell to bind the wild magic. The magic tugged on him. In his mind's eye, he saw the magic encompassing everything, connecting everything. It flowed like water under his knees, floated on the air like smoke, entwined trees like vines, and smoldered in everyone around him. He said the words whispered by his mother in his vision, *"Sakgefan diagor ap ghumilis."*

The magic rose and dipped without warning, curling and churning like the lightning storm descending on the court. At times, it seemed to have purpose, and then it reverted to absolute chaos. No matter how he moved his mind, the magic slipped away like water through his fingers. It seemed as vast and unalterable as the sea.

What am I missing? I have the thorn berry—the last link to my mother. It must be my spellbinder. The magic is all around. It's so ... impossible! I can't do it!

Billy heard his mother's voice. "If you cannot, Tirn Aill is lost."

"Mother?" *It's too big, and I am so small!*

"If you do not solve this riddle, Tirn Aill will be destroyed by the very magic that sustains it."

But I'm not ready. I don't have enough training. I'm alone.

"You are not alone, my son. You have never been alone."

He opened his eyes and saw his mother's ring on his hand. The tiny stone winked at him. He smiled, took a deep breath, and sat up tall. "I am the heir to the kingdom."

At that moment, Malkry stepped out from behind a tree just in front of him. Her eyes swelled with pain and anger when she saw him unharmed and kneeling in the lightning crater. She circled her palms together and chanted.

Though his eyes remained on Malkry, Billy turned his attention to the magic raging around them. He used the ring to focus his mind on feeling the magic's activity. All at once, he could see the magic with his open eyes. Its tumultuous heaving confronted him, but then he saw a ripple in the chaos. The ripple was part of a bigger purpose, and he realized that what he had glimpsed earlier were the actions of an entity or spirit. The wild magic wasn't mindless, nor was it civilized. It was a force with feral instincts and savage passion. Moreover, it was angry.

Billy realized that while the magic had been bound to him, its nature had been tempered by his nature and the power of the ring. At that time, the magic had been a stabilizing force to Tirn Aill, lending power to promote order and protect life. However, when the Witan severed the bond, it was abandoned to its own inclinations. Those inclinations were to altur reality. That was its essence. Thus, it was inevitable that, left unbridled, it would become the agent of chaos and destruction.

Once again, the eerie blue flame encompassed Malkry's hand. She glared at Billy and raised it to the sky. As before, embers shot up into the air, and the clouds flashed and thundered, but this time, Billy could see the wild magic flooding into her. She smiled as if warmed by too much liquor, and her eyes became drowsy.

"Malkry, stop! The wild magic is using you."

Malkry gazed at him and laughed. "You're weak, like your mother."

"It's using you to destroy Tirn Aill—to destroy us all."

"Not all of us." Malkry smiled. "Just you."

Her eyes glanced away from Billy. A crossbow bolt grazed her cheek while another pinned her cloak to the tree behind her. She pointed her finger to Billy's left, and lightning flashed in the village, knocking the dwarf archers off their big rabbit feet.

Billy spoke the words again, *"Sakgefan diagor ap ghumilis."*

He focused with all his strength on the wild magic. It was too big, too powerful, and too rebellious to take it in hand and bind it.

I've got to tame it before I can bind it. He resisted the impulse for self-admonishment. There was no time.

He focused on the magic. "I am Billy, son of Eleanor and William, heir to the crown of Tirn Aill, and I have returned."

The magic's focus drew away from Malkry. It gathered around Billy in twisting, smoky columns. They circled him, sniffing and brushing against him.

Malkry called down a lightning strike on Onian and his elves as they advanced through the trees. It crashed into the woods with a boom, shattering trees and scattering the elves.

Billy continued, "Don't you remember me? You've known me all my life."

The smoky columns drifted away from him, consolidating into a shadowy shape with four legs and a tail.

"Wait!"

The magic beast growled and turned to face him. It had the appearance of a colossal wolf with sparkling eyes and flashing teeth. The hair on its back bristled like quills when it snarled.

Billy flinched. His stomach tightened, and the blood left his face. "I—I—I'm sorry."

The wolf howled, and lightning struck in the forest all around them—past the village and beyond the frozen river. Great trees splintered and burned while boulders burst. Showers of hot rocks clattered through the woods and melted holes in the snow.

"Please, stop."

The wolf paced before him, growling and showing its teeth. Then it barked, and the lightning fell closer. The wolf circled once around him as he spoke.

"I know you are angry. I'm sorry I abandoned you. I have come to change that."

The wolf barked behind Billy's ear, and the lightning struck closer still. It struck the village, and several dwarves cried out.

"I have traveled far, suffered much, and lost dear ones, just to be here with you now."

The wolf came around to snarl and growl in Billy's face. The ring of lightning continued to close in with each strike, this time striking at the dark elves. The ground shook, and Billy could feel Tirn Aill ripping apart. Memory of the death and devastation he saw in Dyven stung him anew. Instantly, he saw the terrifying moment when the life of every precious inhabitant of Tirn Aill would be snuffed out. Crushing despair and loneliness filled the chasm torn from his heart by the vision.

He sank back into his bones and spread his arms wide as he looked up to the heavens. "Take me! Take my life!"

Malkry smiled. "Gladly."

Billy wept and fell with his tear-streaked face to the earth. "Take what you want, only spare Tirn Aill."

Mulkry pointed at Billy, and the lightning plunged from the sky. It clapped and crackled as the brilliant light branched and tumbled to earth. Then the lightning struck.

The thunder roared, then grumbled away. The air stilled.

Billy pushed up and saw Malkry hanging limply by her cloak, still pinned to the tree by the crossbow bolt. The lightning had rent and discolored her breastplate, over her heart. Small ribbons of white smoke wafted from the fissure and lingered in the folds of her clothes.

The storm clouds were motionless overhead. The wind ceased as the last snowflakes drifted to earth.

The wild magic flowed over everything like a fine glaze and hovered lazily in a low mist above the ground. Billy felt the magic curl around him and got the distinct impression of a fluffy tail tickling his nose. He smiled.

"Sakgefan diagor ap ghumilis." He concentrated on the thorn blossom under the earth, using the ring. The ember of life within the berry was fading fast. The tame magic entwined around it and the blossom. The magic formed roots, and the life force brightened. Instantly, the plant grew.

Billy heard his mother's voice. "You have done well, my son." In his mind's eye, he saw her. She drifted away. Her ring felt silent on his hand.

"Mother ... where are you going?"

"Fear not, my son. I promised we would be together one day."

"You did?"

She chuckled. "On the day that I let you go."

Billy opened his eyes, and thorny green sprouts shot out of the earth. They grew at an alarming rate, creating giant, flat leaves and a large, round bulb in the middle. The new plant's expansion forced him back.

Then his eyes caught Rafeyn and the surviving dark elves, who were regrouping on the river. Billy stretched out his hand, and Lura Zahn leapt into it from the snow. He stepped in front of the new plant and readied himself.

"There are only nine of them," he told himself, trying to buoy his bravery. "And they're wounded. And—"

Rafeyn raised her sword. "For Malkry!"

The dark elves started up the riverbank. After only a few steps, they slowed their approach to a wary pace.

Deordrif appeared next to Billy, and he smiled. Next, Onian joined him on his left and Thortan on his right. Billy made a double take of Thortan, for all the hair on his head and in his beard was standing straight out, and he looked like he'd been hanging over a cook fire.

Thortan saw Billy's expression. "What?"

"What happened to you?"

Thortan glanced down at his arms and chest and noticed the sooty color. "Oh, that!" He eyed their adversaries and hefted his hammer. "That lightning packs quite a wallop."

"Lightning?"

"Aye." Thortan nodded. "It's really quite thrilling! Remind me to tell ya about it, after I've rinsed the taste from my mouth with some mead."

Billy glanced at his companions and grinned. "You can tell us all about it. After my coronation."

"It'll be my pleasure, Your Majesty. But first, let's teach these uppity elves a lesson. No offense."

"None taken." Onian drew back on his bow. "They *are* uppity."

Billy, Drif, and Thortan took up fighting stances as Onian took aim. The dark elves raised their weapons and shields. Lura Zahn hummed in Billy's fist and his heart raced. Rafeyn gave a shout, and her warriors charged.

At that moment, bright light flashed from behind Billy and blinded the dark elves. They shielded their eyes and backed down. The light grew brighter still. Billy and his friends turned to see an enormous, translucent flower bud in the center of the thorny plant. Shaped like a candle flame, the bud stood taller than Onian. The light emanated from its center, and as it brightened, the bud became like crystal. It soon glowed too bright for anyone to look at.

All at once, the flower flashed. Billy blinked and his vision cleared. Without looking up, he checked his companions and the dark elves, who were still blind or hiding their eyes. Then Billy heard a sweet voice.

"William."

He looked to where the flower bud had been. His mother stood on the open petals of the flower. She looked just as he had imagined her his whole life: kind eyes, warming smile, long hair, and a flowing dress of pink and white. Around her neck, she wore a faintly glowing diagor on a threadlike silver chain. All he could do was stare.

"Don't be afraid, William."

"I—I'm not." He rubbed his eyes and studied her to confirm what he had seen.

Eleanor held out her arms. "I've waited many winters for this moment. How much longer must I wait?"

Billy ran forward and threw his arms around his mother. Her embrace felt like the comfort from her ring, only multiplied. He had only felt such refuge in the arms of John, his father. He wanted never to let go.

Finally, he drew back to look at her. "How is this possible?"

She looked down at him and smiled. "You made this possible, William. You are the King of Tirn Aill."

"What?" Billy pulled further away. "But you're back, aren't you?"

"Yes."

"You are Queen of Faerie, Queen of Tirn Aill."

Eleanor smiled and shook her head. "No longer, dearest William." She gestured for Billy to turn around.

He released his mother reluctantly and turned to face the river. Onian, Thortan, and their followers knelt on the snow facing him. The dark elves too, save Rafeyn, had taken a knee. Billy grabbed his mother's hand and looked into the forest. All around him, faeries and animals of all descriptions were filtering into the clearing. Whether they tracked across the snow and ice or flew over it, they each found a place and knelt.

Rafeyn growled and gnashed her teeth. Then she shouted at the other dark elves, "Come on! Come on! Let's go!" However, they didn't budge. She pushed several of them over and slogged towards the river. There, she mounted her horse, then wheeled back and forth upon it, glaring at Billy and Eleanor. Finally, she turned and galloped away into the hills.

Eleanor placed a hand on Billy's shoulder. "Don't worry about her."

When the clearing around the court was full, Eleanor turned and faced her son. He held onto her hand, refusing to let go.

"Citizens of Tirn Aill. I give you your king!" With this, Eleanor bowed to Billy, and all present did likewise.

Two small red and blue birds flew into the court and set a fine gold crown on Billy's head. They rested on his shoulders just long enough to bow, and then they flew to Eleanor's hand. They bowed to her and fluffed their fine feathers until they were round, fluffy balls with beaks. Eleanor laughed and held them out to her son.

"I think they have something to say, Your Majesty."

Billy looked at the birds. "What is it?"

"Well, Your Majesty ... " The first bird paused to look at its mate.

The second bird nodded. "We don't mean to complain, Your Majesty."

"But it is quite cold."

Billy looked around him, at the world of snow and ice, of dark clouds and bare trees, of frozen rivers, and shivering faeries, who had never worn so many layers of clothing before. He returned his attention to the birds and chuckled. "Right you are. I'm glad you two didn't fly south."

The tiny birds looked at each other, then shrugged.

He released his mother's hand, closed his eyes, and concentrated on the ground where they stood—on the spot first struck by Malkry's lightning and the dark earth where he'd planted the thorn blossom. He opened his eyes, and golden flames rose up from the ground. Billy's subjects gasped when the flames engulfed their new king and his mother. But he just smiled when the flames tickled him. He took a deep breath then exhaled. The circle of flame expanded in all directions. The inhabitants were first frightened, and then delighted as the harmless flames overtook them.

Gulchmelon the goblin sat up with a start and grabbed the top of his head. He glanced around him, then made eye contact with Billy and sprinted into the woods.

Everywhere the flames touched, snow and ice melted, plants turned green and sprouted leaves and flowers, and faeries became giddy. Even those faeries frozen by the winter thawed and joined the others in song and dance, celebrating their rescue. The fire ring raced away from the clearing to the horizon, and the storm clouds dissolved. As the last cloud vanished, the sun's rays peeked over the horizon and painted a perfect sapphire canopy.

While the faeries were still gazing at the sky in appreciation, Elzgig ran out of the lush forest with his willow twig staff and blue fez in hand. He shouted as he made his way through the crowd around Billy, "Your Majesty, Your Majesty, you have returned!"

"Yes, I know." Billy laughed.

"I came as soon as I—" Elzgig caught sight of Eleanor and froze. After staring at her for several seconds, his bushy white beard and eyebrows twitched, and he blinked. "Oh, my Queen." He bowed low. His voice trembled with tearful joy. "I dared not dream of such a day."

"Dearest Elzgig, the day belongs to our king."

Elzgig turned to Billy and bowed. "Forgive me, Your Majesty. I lost hope. When the ice locked me in my home and I dared not use magic for fear of incinerating myself ... I gave up."

Billy bent down and took Elzgig's tiny hand. "I forgive you, my friend. There were times I, too, lost hope."

"I shall not doubt you again."

Sylvys appeared at the railing of the *Dragonfly*, stretching and yawning as if woken from a long nap. He appeared untouched by sickness or time. All signs of his previous mortal decline had vanished. "Oh good, we're home." He spotted Billy and stopped scratching his backside to bow.

"Deordrif, Sylvys, please, come here. And bring my pack."

"Yes, Your Majesty."

Sylvys hopped from the deck of the *Dragonfly* to the ground. Then he and Deordrif approached their king together. Drif handed Billy his pack, bowed, then stepped back next to Sylvys.

"Thank you." Billy dug into his pack. "Now, I can do what I should have done in Lyonesse."

"What's that, Your Majesty?"

"Why, reward you, of course."

Drif blushed. "You must be tired, Your Majesty. We can do this later."

"You're not getting off that easy." Billy dug some more and came up with a velvet pouch. "Deordrif, please, come forward and kneel."

She did as commanded but wore a worried face.

Billy tried to reassure her with a smile. When this failed, he leaned close to her and whispered, "Don't worry. This is a good thing." He then stood back and addressed the crowd.

"For bravery in the face of terrible odds, for personal sacrifice and placing Tirn Aill above all else, and for rendering invaluable service to her king, I do hereby dub Deordrif, First Knight of Tirn Aill."

Billy took Lura Zahn and very gently tapped Deordrif on each shoulder. "Rise, Lady Deordrif, knight of the realm." At this point, he pulled a set of golden spurs from the velvet bag and handed them to her.

"Thank you, Your Majesty."

"Thank *you*, Deordrif. In truth, I owe you much more than a title and some spurs."

Drif reached down and plucked a small flower from the ground at her feet. She sniffed the flower. "It is enough."

They shared a smile. Billy then looked to his mother, who beamed with pride. He stared at her for a long moment, once again filled with the joy of seeing her. He shook himself from his trance and turned to his right.

"Sylvys ..." Billy looked. The satyr was gone. "Sylvys!" He scanned the crowd. "Now where did he go?"

Just then, a shrill squeal pierced his ears, followed by a chorus of giggles. He looked to the edge of the woods. There, a tribe of nymphs took cover amongst the trees. They pointed into the crowd, where Billy found Sylvys skipping through the mob, showing off his muscles, and posing and strutting like a rooster. Then he ran at the nymphs, who squealed in unison and scampered into the forest like geese from a wolf. Sylvys dashed into the trees behind them and disappeared.

Billy looked at Elzgig. "Well, I guess things are back to normal."

"Indeed, Your Majesty."

Thortan stepped forward. "There's still one thing out of place, Your Majesty."

Billy looked at the beached craft. "The *Dragonfly*?"

"No, Your Majesty. You ought to be on your throne. We can't start the feast until you're seated."

The faerie throng cheered as they swarmed Billy and picked him up on their shoulders. They danced and bounded their way to the end of the immense table and set him on the throne. A chair was set next to him for Eleanor, and fresh bread and pies and flame-licked meats perfumed the air. Moments later, a bevy of faeries burst forth from the village huts, carrying all manner of food and drink to spread upon the table. Once again, the diverse kinship of Faerie zealously feasted and celebrated together. Some blew great horns and made music with flutes, lutes, drums, and tambourines while others danced around the clearing in circles, spinning and hopping as it pleased them. Even the dwarves, though surely the dourest faeries—and single-minded about their drink— stopped imbibing long enough to sing songs, tell tales, and crack jokes. Many were intrigued when Thortan shared his intimate experience with lightning, but Billy gripped them with the recounting of his battle with Ergyfel.

Late afternoon, after the second or third retelling, Billy said, "That's nothing! You should ask Drif about her battle with the troghoul." All eyes turned to the blushing elf maid sitting to the right of their king. "It was the largest and fiercest of its kind I've ever seen."

The faeries pleaded. "Tell us! Yes, tell us, Deordrif!"

The dark elf pursed her lips and looked at her king with displeasure. Billy rested his chin on his hand and stared at her.

She leaned close to him. "My king, I *fight* battles, I do not *talk* about them."

Billy looked from right to left. "I don't see any battles that need fighting right now, do you?"

Drif's eyes shifted back and forth. Her expression was one of pensive confusion.

Billy raised his eyebrows. "Unless you're fighting a battle on the inside."

Deordrif locked eyes with her king, and he smiled.

"My First Knight's tongue must be sharp as her sword."

Billy rose from the table and helped his mother with her chair. Then, hand in hand, they walked away from the table. "And, Deordrif ... leave nothing out. I want to hear a hero's tale upon our return."

***

Billy sat next to his mother on the dock overlooking Glitter Gilt Bay, watching the sun set on his first day as King of Tirn Aill. Fish swam lazily at their feet while the *Dragonfly* raced the wind out near the breakwaters.

He put down his lute. "So the secret component of any spellbinder is sacrifice? Why couldn't the Witan just teach me that?"

"Sacrifice comes from love, not instruction." Eleanor tickled Billy. "And certainly not from cleverness."

He laughed. "All that time, I thought I was seeking something dear to hold on to, not something to sacrifice. Seems like they could have said something."

Eleanor considered his words. "Could they teach you what you learned from witnessing the horrors of war or Shaldra's selfless bravery? Could they have taught you bravery as effectively as confronting Ergyfel, or about responsibility better than enduring the weight of your father's crown? Could they teach you to cherish Tirn Aill more perfectly than through learning to love Shaldra, Sylvys, and Deordrif? Could you have made a worthy sacrifice without first experiencing the woes of your journey? Remember, sacrifice without love has no value. But I think you knew that already."

"I feel the truth of it, but at the time ... it just felt right. I was desperate."

"You're the only ruler of Tirn Aill ever to offer his life to bind the wild magic. Only the Witan could have foreseen that."

He turned to his mother. "What's a paradox?"

"Why?"

"The Witan told me I was a paradox."

Eleanor laughed. "They told me, that because of what you did, your spellbinder could never be broken."

Billy put his hand on hers. "Are you sad, then, that you are no longer queen?"

"No, not at all. This is what I wanted."

"Speaking of the Witan ... do you think they're still angry with me?"

"What makes you think they were angry with you?"

"You know the big black tome?"

"Aye."

"The one in the dark hole, at the back of their home?"

"Yes, I know the one."

"Well, they have now nailed it in place."

Eleanor giggled. "It's always been that way."

"No." Billy shook his head. "It was free when I took it."

"That was a deception—an illusion. I'm sorry I failed to keep you from it. Once you touched the tome, I had a hard time getting through to you."

"I know." He looked away. "I'm sorry I let you and the Witan down."

"It's a lesson we all must learn."

He stared at his mother. "Wait a minute! ... You took the black book?"

Eleanor bit her lip and nodded. "Fortunately, the Witan were right there to save me."

"What would have happened, if it had escaped in Lyonesse?"

"Eventually ... " Eleanor looked thoughtful. " ... Tyranny, lawlessness, anarchy? Who can know where such evil will end?"

After a long silence, Billy spoke. "Should we head back to the feast?"

"All talked out, huh?"

"Well, I ..."

"Don't fret, my darling son. You don't have to ask me everything today. I'm not going anywhere for a while."

"How long can I keep you?"

"Who can say? We are all here for but a moment, then we move on." She paused to smell the sea air and splash the water with her toes. "Still, there's no rush to get back. They'll be at it for days."

"Really?"

"Oh my, yes. Faeries live to spar and celebrate."

The *Dragonfly* drifted by, gliding on the scintillating golden waters. Her captain tipped his hat. "Your majesties."

"Toady."

"Toady."

"Shall I take 'er round again?"

Billy smiled. "Aye, Captain. Once more, at your pleasure."

Brimstone gently turned his beloved ship and sailed her straight into the setting sun.

THE END

* * *

This ends Book Four.
For more adventure,
the story of Myrredith and Hugh begins with
The Sword and The Rose,
a prequel novella of the
Jester King Fantasy Series.

I truly hope you enjoyed reading this book as much as I enjoyed writing it. If you did, I would greatly appreciate a short review on Amazon or your favorite book website. Reviews are crucial for any author, and even just a line or two can make a difference.

Thank you!
KC

ABOUT K. C. HERBEL

I write stories about adventure, magic, intrigue, danger, defeat and triumph. I also write about things that really matter, like: friends, family, love, loyalty, right and wrong, good vs. evil, patriotism, bravery, duty and honor.

†

K. C. grew up in the American Southwest and spent two decades in Southern California. He has traveled much of the U.S. and Europe (both East and West) and has worked in France, Korea, Japan, and China. Now he lives in the woods near Richmond, Virginia with his family, which includes three dogs.

ACKNOWLEDGMENTS

Over the years, I've had a great deal of advice, encouragement, nudging and badgering from my friends, family and fans. I've been cornered at gatherings, cornered in conversations and even cornered in a few uncomfortable alleys. I can finally say to you, thank you for your advice, encouragement and patience. The book is in your hands. Will you lay off now?

Once again, I would like to thank my village; those cunning, wise, foolish and fun around me. You make the work of writing worthwhile.

Thanks to my talented and ever patient editors Harmony Kent, Kerry Hall, and Jack Mercer. I've learned much from you while you patiently smoothed off my rough edges.

Thanks to my mentors Mark, Raymond and Stiles. You helped me to believe in myself. And to John DeChancie, thanks again for your insightful advice and delightful encouragement – especially on this volume.

I also want to give a special thanks to some very special friends: film maker Hiroshi Katagiri, author Leisl Kaberry, and the fine folks at GameFace Publishing. Thank you for your belief in this project and your support. To Leslie Bobb and Carolene Herbel, I could not have published this book without your most generous support and encouragement. It means a lot to me that you believe in me enough to have my back.

Lastly; thank you, Mary Anne. You are a wonder.

K. C. Herbel
Richmond, Virginia
April 2016
God go with you!

The Jester King Fantasy Series

The Innkeeper's Son
The Jester
The Prince
The King

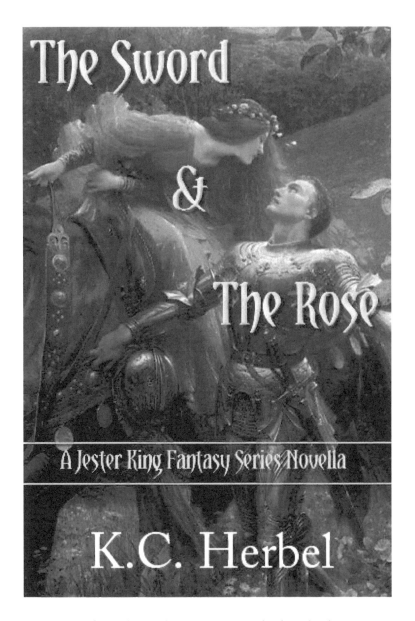

The Sword & The Rose

A Jester King Fantasy Series Novella

K.C. Herbel

Look for details at: www.kcherbel.com

Made in United States
Troutdale, OR
01/08/2024

16786625R00213